FLASHBULB MEMORIES

by

Gail Walsh Chop
and
Margaret Corbett Wiley

lemondrop press

Written in memory
of the victims and families
of the heinous crimes
that terrorized
Manchester, New Hampshire,
in the 1960's
and to the city that survived the terror.

Dedication

To the crew of *Family Ties*, my source of encouragement and support: skippers Walter and Chris Chop, and Shawn Burnell; first mates Jenny Burnell and Sonia Chop; lovable deck hands Hadley and Parker Burnell, Neve and Vincent Chop; and to Alex Chop, our true north, always.

A big shout out to my loves: Chris Wiley, Mike Wiley, Abby Farnham, and Ben Wiley, for cheering me on and throwing questions my way that helped clarify my thinking. And of course, an especially big shout-out to Sam Wiley, who is a source of endless delight to all of us.

1990

"Seat belts fastened, seat backs and tray tables in the upright position…" The announcement jolts my thoughts as the wheels touch down. I am in Boston.

I don't know how Linda talked me into attending my twentieth. I had conveniently been able to dodge all my high school reunions until now. Maybe it was the work I had been doing with Martina that convinced me to attend. I could have come up with a lot of reasons to stay home. I had been accused of being a workaholic many times, so no one who knew me well would be surprised if I declined.

But here I am at the Avis counter ready to sign on the dotted line to rent a car for the weekend. "Do you need a map, Miss?" the attendant asks. Hardly.

My plane arrived two hours late and my Irish-Catholic guilt whispers that I should head straight north to my parents' house. But my desire to avoid 93-North outweighs my guilt. I can't bring myself to drive that route even though Martina told me that it would be a positive step for me in confronting my anxiety. It seems irrational that after all these years, the thought of driving on that road still triggers panic attacks. But Martina explained that my reaction was not irrational. She said that I suffered from flashbulb memories. Memories triggered by images. The teen's body frozen in a snowbank off 93. The front page photo of the girl in her open casket. The balding man in handcuffs smirking at the cameras in the courtroom.

So, I head northeast up Route 1, hugging the coast of Massachusetts into New Hampshire. I stop in Salisbury at the amusement park. I get out of my car and stare. Memories of driving to the park as a kid with my family and then later with friends and boyfriends, came flooding back. Cotton candy, caramel corn, screams of fear and joy as the roller coaster chugged up the first hill. Sipping an illegal beer while listening to Don McLean's "American Pie" or Creedence's "Bad Moon Rising" on an 8-track tape player with the windows wide open as we headed home.

I stop at Seabrook next. The clapboard cottages crowded together along the beach look unchanged. Images of Mom, Dad, Moe, and Joe, and family friends and neighbors; sunburns and poison ivy, sand dunes and popcorn, bring back memories of a more innocent time.

To the north is Hampton Beach, once the grand dame of the New Hampshire coastline. The beach is close to empty except for a few people walking their dogs. Across the street souvenir shops, arcades, and bowling alleys stand elbow-to-elbow, most of them boarded up for the season. Our trips to the beach always included a few rounds of skee-ball and an ice cream cone. Moe, Joey, and I collected as many tickets as we could possibly win and wore them like necklaces for all to admire. But we were sure to cash them in at the end of the day for colorful plastic prizes like whistles, rings, and bracelets.

My anxiety level grows as I turn away from the coast onto 101-West. Martina warned me it might happen. "Open the window and breathe the fresh air. Focus on your breathing. Breathe in, breathe out." I doubt that breathing will help me, but it can't hurt. I breathe my way in and out all the way to the Bridge Street exit.

I scan convenience stores and gas stations as I drive down the hill past Derryfield Park. I spot a payphone at the Texaco on Maple Street. I call my parents and get their answering machine. "Hi Mom. I'm in town, but my flight was delayed. I need to head straight up to Linda's, so we won't be late. Don't wait up for me. See you tomorrow. I love you."

I drop another dime. "Hey Linda, I'm here…"

2

The VA's silver water tower pokes out above the pine trees. Even now it creeps me out. I regret having told Linda that I'd pick her up when I learned that she'd moved to a place near the old Smyth Road extension. I know that I won't like driving this route alone in the dark.

I glance at the index card where I'd scribbled her address. "418- rooster wind vane on garage."

I pass 410, see the rooster, and pull into the driveway. Mrs. Melnechuk opens the front door, holding back a barking little white dog.

"Nora, it's so nice to see you. It's been years." She pulls at the dog's leash. "Mr. Lucky, you sit and behave."

Mr. Lucky appears to have little interest in either sitting or behaving.

Mrs. Melnechuk's voice is stern. "Lucky, go to your place." Mr. Lucky growls but goes to his bed in the kitchen.

She reaches under the sink and pulls out a bottle of Taylor's tawny port.

"I'll be asleep when you girls get back from your party, so I'd like to have a glass of wine with you now." She places three glasses on a little white tray and tucks the port under her arm.

"Lucky, you stay."

Linda comes downstairs looking fabulous. "Oh Ma. Please let's not. We're going to be late."

"Linda, I'd love a quick drink with your mother. And you look gorgeous, by the way." I give her a big hug and feel every Hershey's kiss and potato chip I've eaten since college. "How do you manage to stay so trim?"

"Managing a health club keeps you honest," laughs Linda. "Do you like our little place?' she asks. "Big thanks to my divorce settlement from the a-hole. We sold the family home, and Mom, Lucky, and I moved in together."

"It's perfect for you."

Mrs. Melnechuk kicks off her white wooly slippers and tucks a red pillow behind her back. Mr. Lucky, after growling and giving me several dirty looks, appears to be asleep.

Linda leans back on the recliner and makes a face at her tawny port when her mother looks away. I feel like I'm in high school again. "Great to see you, Nora," she says. "The last time I saw you was pre-divorce when I came down to visit you in DC. That was fun."

"I can't believe that you girls are nearly forty," says her mother. "And neither of you are married." She turns to me. "Linda at least gave it a chance with Tim, the guy with a low sperm count. That's why they never had any children, you know."

I did know about Linda's exhaustive round of in-vitro procedures. I also knew about Tim's cocaine habit but say nothing as I am sure Mrs. Melnechuk is ignorant of all of that. Tim's low sperm count alone was enough to damn him forever in her eyes.

"I never liked Tim. He wouldn't drink any wine I bought and brought fancy French wine to the house because he was so la-di-da."

I make a mental note never to bring French wine to Mrs. Melnechuk. Mr. Lucky opens one eye and growls at me.

"But Nora, you were always so pretty. I thought for sure by now you'd be married and have two or three kids."

Linda laughs. "Ma, if Nora wanted to be married, she would be. She's famous now with two books out and is going to be interviewed on *60 Minutes*. There are lots of guys in DC if she wanted to settle down."

"But if she came back to Manchester, she'd find a nice man. Aren't all the men in DC gay?"

"I haven't met all of them, so I can't comment." I laugh, but I hate being asked about marriage.

"I'm glad that you are doing so well," said Mrs. Melnechuk. "I was surprised when you dropped out of law school. But I guess you're doing okay for yourself writing books and getting TV interviews."

Linda comes to my rescue. "Bottoms up, girlfriend. We need to hit the road, or we'll end up sitting with all the weirdoes."

I down the tawny port in one gulp and stand up. The pantyhose I slipped on in the ladies' room at Reagan are not going to make it through the evening. "Mrs. Melnechuk, great to see you and thanks for the wine."

3

Linda takes one look at the Honda. "Bitchin' car, Nora," she laughs. I ignore her.

We pass Derryfield Park and see Hillside Junior High in the distance. Twilight is approaching, and just above the horizon a couple of planets shine in the dusk. I'd forgotten how pretty Manchester is in the fall. I stop at the red light at Maple and Bridge. The Ash Street School playground is empty.

"How old is Ash Street School, do you think?" I ask.

"I've no idea. But it always gives me the creeps. It seems like the kind of place where the bodies of dead little girls would be found chained to sewing machines in the attic."

The mills are straight ahead. Their white shuttered windows stare at the city with vacant eyes. I'm glad that the traffic going over the bridge is light, but the Wayfarer parking lot is a different story. I drive slowly through the rows of cars looking for a space.

Two Porsches and a Beamer are parked by the "Welcome Saint Agatha Class of 1970" sign.

"We've got some deep pockets here," says Linda. "Maybe you should move your Honda to the far corner of the lot."

"It looks like I've no choice." I pull into a narrow spot next to a white panel truck.

Strains of "Proud Mary" emanate from the restaurant. "Can you believe it?" asks Linda. "Sounds like they're re-playing our prom soundtrack."

"Well, it's better than "Saint Agatha, on the Hilltop High.""

"Dance music makes it seem like we should have dates."

"Well, I haven't had a date in about three years, so I'd be in real trouble. The only guys I ever run into are the ones I see at hearings: wife-beaters and pedophiles. Real assholes."

"Nora, you're too negative. Try making more of an effort. Start dating."

She's right. But I wish she'd shut up.

"You can't let the past kill you. Bad pasts ruin a lot of lives."

I walk a little faster so I won't have to listen to more advice from Linda about how I should improve my life.

4

I push open the door and step into the Wayfarer. Female voices fill the room and thank God someone has turned down the music.

I pull in my abs. I hope that no one notices that I've put on at least twenty pounds since graduation. But of course, they will. A girls' high school reunion is exactly the place where everyone notices everything. I wish I'd bought better pantyhose. I feel them sliding down again.

"Let's get a drink." Linda heads over to a table covered with a bunch of little tea lights and a big bouquet of yellow chrysanthemums.

I follow Linda. She remembers everybody. I'm terrible with names and don't want to get involved chatting up someone who might have sat next to me in classes for four years that I don't recognize.

"Nora Donovan, how are you? It's been ages."

Uh-oh. I turn to the voice, but it's someone I remember. It's my junior year math partner, and she looks terrific: slimmer than she was in high school and wearing a red leather jacket that looks like it's a designer.

"Doris Cote! Good to see you!"

"It's not Cote anymore. I'm Doris Goodwin. I married into the Goodwins who own The Lumber Yard."

I give Doris a big hug. "I probably would have never graduated from high school if you hadn't bailed me out in Algebra II." Good for Doris. Her family didn't have a lot of money, and The Lumber Yard is one of Manchester's most successful restaurants.

"How are you doing, Nora? Married or do you have a bunch of guys that you keep stringing along?"

The topic of marriage makes my teeth ache.

"Oh, I have a bunch of guys that I keep stringing along. I work with childhood trauma victims, and I get to meet sexual predators and abusive fathers all the time. You should see the sixty-seven-year-old guy I saw last week. He's been sodomizing his four-year-old granddaughter. No teeth and BO. A real charm boat."

Doris steps back as if I've slapped her.

"Nora, I'm sure that you're great at your job. I admire you for doing it. I sure couldn't." Doris' voice, gentle and warm, makes me feel ashamed for being so snappish.

She was only trying to be nice. Martina is right. I can't just dump stuff on innocent people.

Someone calls "Doris! Good to see you."

Doris smiles and turns her back. She probably wants to get away from me. I don't blame her. There are days I want to get away from me, too. I head to the bar where Linda is holding court. "Sugar, Sugar" filters through the background noise. Who sang that?

The bartenders, in red vests and black pants, look like they are too young to be pouring drinks.

"A Cabernet, please." I promise myself that my next drink will be a ginger ale. I can't go down Grandfather Donovan's road. I drop some change into the tip jar, wait for the nun-like figure to move away, and join Linda's group.

"Nora Donovan, great to see you!" says a big-haired brunette in a grey sheath. The two other women standing with her give me a hug. Who are they?

Linda comes to my rescue. "Connie LeDoux is now Connie Montcalm. And Patty Carmody is now Patty Lemerises. And Sheila Kinney is still Sheila Kinney."

I raise my glass to the group, whom I now recognize as fellow members of Saint Agatha's High School's yearbook committee. And of course, I've known Patty since first grade.

"Did any of you hear that last week Sister Boniface fell down the church steps and died?" asks Patty. "She had a subdural and never regained consciousness. If anyone deserved a long and slow cancer death, it was Boniface."

"Such a bitch," I said. "I saw her push a boy down the stairs, and he broke his arm." The image of Sister Boniface with her flat gray eyes turns my stomach. It's nice to know that she's dead, but I don't want to think about Bruce Therrian.

I tuck a wisp of hair behind my ear and turn to Cathy.

"Remember our Honors Chemistry class? You were in it, weren't you? We had that dippy Sister Isaac Jogues."

"Oh, yeah," says Cathy. Cathy launches into the story of the shoebox experiment on the school's Beacon Street lawn, and everyone cracks up. Chatty Cathy is still worthy of her high school nickname.

"Remember how Father would hang the painting of the Pope up by the principal's office and hang Saint Agatha just outside the chapel? And then two weeks later we'd see him out with his measuring tape and ladder, hanging Agatha and the Pope side-by-side and hanging Bishop Bradley next to the chapel entrance." Cathy rolls her eyes. Warming up now that she has everyone's attention, Cathy recollects how someone left the Bunsen burner on, and the janitor found fat Sister Isaac passed out in the lab under the poster of the Periodic Table. The scrawny janitor, unable to move Sister

Isaac, had to get our headmaster Father Fitzgerald to help him, and two days later Father had to have an emergency hernia repair.

The ladies appear to have forgotten all about Sister Boniface and are now laughing about Sister Isaac's girth and Father's surgery.

"Lifting all that artwork probably set him up for a rupture," says someone. "Sister Isaac was just the straw that broke the camel's back."

"Or that broke Father's crotch," laughs Linda.

I feel like I can relax a little. I'll make an appointment with Martina when I get back to DC.

At my last appointment, Martina and I discussed my panic attacks and Linda's invitation to our 20th high school reunion. Martina said that lots of people have panic attacks. But I could get over them, with some work. She looked at me through her tortoise-shell glasses, her frizzy gray hair pulled up in a loose bun and pointed out that lots of people never deal with childhood issues. "It would be real progress if you felt that you could return to Manchester and attend the reunion." She felt that it would be a "cathartic" experience for me.

The party of laughing women in front of me fades away. In its place I see the girls' and women's names I wrote down in the little plaid notebook I kept under my mattress. And I hear the comforting thud the deadbolt made when I locked the front door.

I make myself stop. I knew that it was a bad idea to come to this fucking reunion. Why did I take Martina's advice?

5

I edge over to the bar, and a different bar tender refills my wine glass. I take a nice, long swig. I make sure no one is looking, and I give my pantyhose a good yank. They're going to be around my knees before the evening is over. A spotlight goes on and the music stops. A petite woman in a black turtleneck sweater and black slacks appears under the spotlight.

"Who's that?" I whisper.

"I think she's our class president," says Linda.

The president clears her throat. "Welcome to the 20th Reunion of the first and last graduating class of Saint Agatha's High School for Girls."

"Let's get a table," whispers Linda. "I see some of the weirdoes here, and I don't want to be stuck sitting with them." I follow Linda over to the far side of the room. She leans into the ear of a blond woman in a pink jacket seated at the table we are about to invade. "Weren't you in my study hall senior year?"

The woman smiles and moves purses and jackets from a couple of empty chairs to make room for us. "Let's do names after Rita finishes talking." She points to the figure on stage who is still speaking.

"Those of you who gave $20.00 or more to the Mercy Building Fund have been entered into a raffle. Three prizes will be awarded after dinner, so please hang on to your tickets."

Linda looks at me. "You owe me $20.00," she mouths.

I roll my eyes in response.

The president stops speaking, applause fills the room, and the pink-jacketed woman starts introductions.

"I'm Judy Burke, and I don't think I had classes with anyone at this table except for Marilyn." Judy turns to the woman sitting at my right, and I stop myself from gasping. It's Marilyn Marchand, former prom queen and heart throb of every boy who went to Saint Benedict's High School. I would have never recognized her. She's way too skinny, and her hair looks like she'd colored it with henna. Bad henna. It's not a good look. Maybe she'd had chemo. Or was humoring an out-of-control teen-age daughter who talked her into it.

"Good to see everyone." Marilyn looks around the table with that same warm smile.

I feel sorry for her. Marilyn was always a nice girl, and it must be hard to be back at The Wayfarer where once you were beautiful and danced with Prom King Stephen Brady to "Nights in White Satin," and now you look like crap, and every single woman in the Wayfarer ballroom is wondering how you could let yourself go to hell. And maybe you have cancer, to boot. Or a teen-age daughter who pressured you into doing bad henna.

"I'm Judy Burke," says the woman in the pink jacket. "I drove here with Janet Young." She smiles at the woman on her left who is twisting a huge diamond ring. It must be zirconium. No one has a diamond that big.

"I'm Janet Young. I was Janet Loiselle." Janet seems familiar, but I can't place her. Tall, with wide brown eyes and wearing a small gold cross around her neck.

A black-aproned waitress comes by and fills everyone's wine glasses, except for Marilyn's who puts her glass upside-down. A second waitress comes by with salad plates.

Marilyn turns to me. "I was hoping that I'd get a chance to talk to you tonight," she says. She looks away as her eyes fill with tears.

At moments like these I wish that my job was selling car insurance. I glance around the table, but no one notices that Marilyn is upset. I stand up. "Girls, the queen and I are hitting the ladies' room. Linda, here's my raffle ticket. If I win, it's all yours. Maybe it'll be something cool like a painting of Saint Agatha."

Marilyn picks up her black-beaded purse and follows me out of the dining room into a foyer covered in dark blue and bright red paisley carpeting. The line for the bathroom is loud and ridiculously long.

"Catholic girls gone bad," I say over my shoulder to Marilyn, who gives me a slight smile. I see a big wooden door to our left. "Wasn't there some bridge out here with ducks? Let's talk there."

We go outside. I'm glad that we're alone. The view is still beautiful if one turns away from the steady stream of lights heading towards I-93. The air is soft and warm, the ducks quack under the footbridge, (surely, they couldn't be descendants of the ducks we listened to in 1968 could they?), and in the background is the soothing sound of falling water. I flash back to us standing there on prom night, thin girls with big bouffant hairdos and nervous tuxedoed dates, the world all before us, tossing peanuts to the ducks below. Innocent times or so we thought.

Marilyn pulls out a joint and lights it. I try to act nonchalant. I watch the tip glow bright orange and then gradually fade.

"Want a hit?" Marilyn asks, holding out the joint to me.

"I'd better not. I'm driving." I pull my pantyhose up a bit.

"I am, too. But I started smoking when I was doing chemo, and I guess I just built up a tolerance." Marilyn takes another long hit and exhales with pleasure. "Besides, it relaxes me. Are you sure?"

"I'm good."

The smell of pot permeates the air. Marilyn's eyes get watery, and she looks way older than thirty-eight. She dabs at her mouth with a tissue, losing most of her lipstick in the process.

"What's going on, Marilyn?" I ask. I know she's going to tell me that she has a kid with issues. She's probably talked to some priest who's told her to pray.

"It's about my youngest boy Jake. He's a good little guy. Hank and I call him our accident. I got pregnant with him on Easter Sunday, just when I was planning to go back to work. Kate, our youngest, was four and I had her lined up for daycare."

I put on my professional face. It's going to be long if it's starting with Jake's conception.

I'm starving, and I wonder how much of my dinner I'm going to miss. I rarely eat red meat, and I think of the petite filet with potatoes au gratin on the side I'd ordered as a treat. I hate to be unkind, but I hope that Marilyn will cut to the chase about little Jake.

"He's in fifth grade now at All Saints' and all he does is play video games. He used to love swimming, but he refuses to go to the Y anymore. Hank, my husband, thinks it's because he's at that age where he doesn't want to change in the locker room." Marilyn pulls out a new Kleenex and blows her nose. "At first we thought it was my breast cancer that upset him. But my doctor said that they got it all, so you'd think if that were his problem that he'd go back to his old self."

"A parent's cancer can be frightening for kids." My heart softens as I think of the scared little guy. Strict Catholic family and a mother with cancer is a lot of stuff for a kid to carry around.

"I think it's something else." Marilyn looks directly at me. "There's been a lot of coverage of it in the *Union Leader*. Priests are being reported for molesting little boys." She stops, fighting tears. "Jake went on the altar about six months ago, and that's when it started. Father Beaulieu, a new priest from Boston, got transferred to All Saints' last spring. Beaulieu calls Jake a lot and took him to see the Red Sox this summer."

I don't want to hear anymore. My chest is getting so tight it feels like there is some out-of-control creature about to take over my body. I put both hands on the railing and look out at the cars barreling up and down 293, their headlights bright and purposeful. I barely hear Marilyn because I am trying to focus on my breathing.

"I brought it up to Hank. He hit the roof that I'd say something like that about Father Beaulieu. He and Father Beaulieu are both on Parish Council, and Hank thinks Beaulieu walks on water."

"I'm scared. And so beyond pissed," says Marilyn.

I grab Marilyn's joint and take a hit.

The door from the ballroom flies open, and a boozy group of ladies in pink, black, and assorted floral prints tumble out onto the footbridge.

Judy sniffs the air and starts laughing.

"We'll talk later," I whisper to Marilyn.

"Okay, so you girls are out here getting high while the rest of us are stuck inside listening to the history of the Sisters of Mercy." Linda looks at Marilyn and me. "Which one of you has the green stuff?"

"Ta-dah!" Marilyn pulls another joint and a lighter out of her purse and tosses them to Judy.

"God, I haven't smoked pot in years," laughs Judy. She lights up and inhales.

"You guys, I think I'll get my stuff and hit the road," said Janet.

Linda grabs Janet's arm. "Come on, Janet. You deserve to kick up your heels a bit after listening to the tale of Mother Gonzaga's heroic mission to start Catholic education in Manchester."

"Okay," Janet says. "But you'll have to show me how to do it."

"Just inhale a little and hold it for a few seconds. Like this." Marilyn demonstrates, and Janet watches closely.

"OK, my turn. But I swear if Nelson finds out, he'll divorce me."

"None of us know your husband," says Judy.

"I don't know about that," says Linda. "Is he the guy in black leather pants who dances at the Red Onion on Saturday nights?"

Janet coughs, nearly choking. "Oh, God. Nelson is the last man on the planet to wear leather pants. And he's usually asleep wearing his CPAP by 9:00 on Saturday nights." I notice the light hitting the gold cross she wears around her neck.

She takes another toke and breaks into laughter. "Nelson in leather pants! That kills me. He'd have to lose at least fifty pounds to carry that look."

I don't know how much later it is, but the two joints have disappeared. Male voices emerge just as Janet stops singing "Close to You." When the doors open, flashlights blaze, nearly blinding me.

"Party's over, ladies," says a tall skinny guy in a dark green uniform. His partner, in the same uniform and equally skinny but quite short, looks at us like he'll pistol whip us if we give him any shit.

Linda approaches the tall one. "Sir, are you a real police officer or just some flunkey the Wayfarer's hired?"

"Linda, let's go." I tuck her arm under my elbow and head towards the dining room and the exit. The other ladies are laughing and following us, escorted by the two security guards. I hope these guys don't have the authority to arrest us. Linda is still protesting.

"I just want to know if the guy is legit." I keep a firm hold on her elbow.

"Good night, ladies." The tall security guard opens the door. With Linda on one arm and Janet on the other, I leave our 20th high school reunion.

The night is a wonder: chock-full of stars with a crescent moon hanging like a tiny comma in the sky. Except for an occasional car and a light wind rustling through the trees, the highway is quiet.

"Oh, shit, I can't go home high," wails Janet. "Nelson will kill me."

I didn't want to say anything, but I think that she has lost her necklace with the cross. I hope it wasn't a present from Nelson. Seemed like a Nelson sort of gift. If I tell her it's missing, she'll want to go back inside to get it, and I don't think that the security officers are going to want to open the walkway over the duck pond to look for her jewelry. Which now is probably sitting in some duck's gullet. Do ducks like shiny stuff? Or is that sharks? Jesus, I forget. But better she loses that tiny cross than that huge diamond ring.

And right now, I know that I need a cup of coffee before showing up at my parents'. And I hope that I can drive because Linda sure as hell can't.

"What do you say that we go to IHOP on South Elm Street?" I ask.

"Good idea," says Judy.

Linda and I hike to the far end of the parking lot where my rental car sits. I go behind the Honda, pull off my panty hose and toss them in the bushes.

"I like those girls. I wish I'd hung out with more people back in the day," says Linda.

"You've been back in Manchester for a while. You don't see them?"

"Not really."

I turn left on Elm and glance up Lake Avenue. My Nana and her sister lived there in a boarding house when they first came to the United States from Ireland. The old boarding house is now gone, and a Jiffy-Lube stands on the corner.

6

IHOP has not changed a bit. Faux Early American furniture, dim brown low-hanging chandeliers that cast little light, and waitresses in brown dresses with little orange ruffled aprons. But the coffee smells delicious, and I see pie and muffins by the cash register. I wonder who got my petite filet. Judy, Janet, and Marilyn are squished into a booth in the back. Marilyn gives us a big wave.

"Coffee, ladies?" A blonde waitress appears at our table with a carafe in one hand and a bunch of cups dangling from the other.

"I'd like an order of pancakes and a side of sausage." I don't even look at a menu. "I was too busy yakking to finish dinner," I say to the table.

"How about a round of blueberry muffins?" asks Janet. Our waitress disappears and Janet leans forward, giggling.

I pull out a notebook. "Let's share phone numbers and addresses." I don't want to lose Marilyn's contact info because I can put her in touch with resources in New Hampshire.

I don't know if it's the pot, but I suddenly feel fondness for this group. Linda, whom I've known since we were fourteen and now these ladies who before tonight were barely acquaintances.

I think that it would be a hoot to have Janet visit me in DC. But I'll tell her it'll be a girls' weekend. I don't want to wake up to Nelson sleeping on my sofa bed with his CPAP machine hissing in the background.

"Hey, Nora. I forgot to give you this. You won the raffle. Linda pulls the brown wrapping paper off a watercolor of Lake Massabesic and sets it on the table.

"It's beautiful," says Janet. "You should take it to DC as a memory of your hometown."

I look at the watercolor. A lavender sky, reddish-gold trees, and flecks of blue, gold, and purple swirl through the water. It would look nice in my office.

Judy writes out her contact info and passes the sheet to Marilyn. "Does anyone ever think about the Sandra Valade and Pamela Mason murders?"

"We were kids then. And no one really talked to us about it," says Linda.

I'm still horrified by the *Union Leader's* lurid coverage of the torture and murder of two teen-age girls. It often comes up in my sessions with Martina.

"Yeah, we were eight and twelve," says Judy. "And this painting of Massabesic reminded me about the Mason murder. January 18, 1964, was my thirteenth birthday, and the cops still hadn't found her body. My parents arranged a skating party for me at Massabesic. My cousins came. And the police showed up with German Shepherds to search the area around the lake because they got a tip that Mason's body was dumped there."

"Sweet Jesus," says Janet. "Why didn't your parents just take you all home?"

"It was weird. They pretended nothing was going on. We kids knew about it only because other people on the lake were talking about it. One old man scared us, saying that we'd know if the body was found because we'd see a hearse coming down the road."

I decide that I'll give Moe the painting of Massabesic.

"And every year on my birthday, I think of turning thirteen, those horrible murders, and that loser Eddie Coolidge." Judy rolls the paper from her blueberry muffin up in a little ball.

"Coolidge tossed her body in a snowbank," says Marilyn.

But Judy isn't through. "It gets worse. I used to wait tables here at IHOP when I went to Rivier College. And I worked with Pamela Mason's mother for a couple of months."

Our jaws drop.

"What was she like?" asks Janet.

"She was sweet and very pretty. But even though I was only twenty, I could tell that she was a wreck. She'd be late, but no one would say anything because we felt sorry for her." Judy runs her fingertips around the top of her mug.

"My mother told me to be kind to her. And the cops came in a lot late at night. You could tell that they were sort of watching over her."

"God, what a story. And you know that Coolidge has gotten married and is living someplace out-of-state," says Janet. "The US Supreme Court did him a big favor, letting him off on a technicality. I'm sure he killed Sandra Valade and Rena Paquette too. I never understood why they didn't go after him for these other murders."

"You sound like my dad," I say. "He was a police detective and never got over how Coolidge skated through the legal system. And my mother says the fact that Coolidge is getting out has him around the bend."

"That explains a lot," says Judy. "Your dad used to stop by here at IHOP before he retired. Alone. Before the other cops. He'd say hi to me but made sure that he was seated at one of Mrs. Mason's tables, and he tipped her well. He was a kind guy."

"Thanks," I said. I still feel uncomfortable when remembering my dad's visits to pretty Mrs. Mason. I wonder if my mom ever found out.

"Ladies, this has been fun. But I need to be getting home because Jake has piano at 9:00." Marilyn stands up and fumbles in her purse for her keys.

"We should all get going," I say.

"Nora, you'll send everyone the addresses and phone numbers?" asks Marilyn. I hear urgency in her voice.

"First thing when I get home tomorrow night. I promise."

Linda and I get into the Honda and head up Elm. "I barely recognize this as Manchester's main street," I say. "The mall really did a number on it. Remember going to the Puritan on Saturdays and ordering vanilla Cokes and French fries?"

"And their fries were the best."

I turn up Webster Street. I don't know if it was the pot or what, but I barely notice Smyth Road as I drive by. And I had to admit to myself that I had fun at the reunion. Talking about the murders after all these years was unsettling, but I handled it. I recalled Mom telling me years ago that broken things can be mended. Maybe she was right. I'll have to tell Martina.

1960

The sky is gray and the air nose-tight dry. We're in for the blizzard the weatherman talked about this morning. I like middle-of-the-night snowstorms. I like how the flakes fall from the dark sky and shroud the city's grime and mess in silent white.

I pull into the mill yard, park by Laible, and tamp out my cigarette. I load up the dolly, and a guy I don't recognize in a blue toque gives me a big wave as he backs out. I return his wave. Never hurts to have friends in your pocket.

As I bump the dolly into the office, I see her on the phone. Petite, slim, and a head full of brown hair I could lose my fingers in. She hangs up, and I stop by her desk. "You're looking good today."

"Thanks. Sorry I can't talk, Eddie. I need to type these up for a client." She doesn't even look at me.

"A storm's blowing in. Can I give you a ride home?" I ask. "I have a delivery up at the VA and I can do it last. The vets are probably all diabetic and shouldn't be loading up on Coca-Cola anyway." I feel like a fool when I realize how phony my laugh sounds.

"I have a swim class tonight and am catching the bus when it's over." Her voice is cool.

I try to sound nonchalant as I push the bottles into their slots, but my hands have a vice-like grip on them. Who does she think she is? "I could have a beer while you swim and then drive you home. My truck has snow tires that can drive through anything." I know the walk from the bus stop to her home has no streetlights and is dark and lonely. I drove it two nights ago.

She stiffens before replying. "The bus tires can handle the snow. You've offered me rides before, and I always say no. It's still no. Thanks, but no." She tucks a wisp of brown hair behind her ear and starts typing clackety-clack-clack. I'm the kind of guy who can take a hint.

As I drive over the Granite Street Bridge, I entertain myself by thinking about Miss Valade in a swimsuit. "Teen Angel" comes on the radio. I peek up at the sky. The snow has started falling. The plows will be out in just a few hours.

2

I thought I heard the phone ringing in the middle of the night, but I might have been dreaming. I got dressed and as Moe and me walked downstairs, we heard whispering. I knew something must be wrong because the whispers stopped when we walked into the kitchen. Dad was still wearing his uniform, and he hadn't shaved yet. Usually when he looked like that, Mom would say, "Tom, you look like a bum. Go shave." But she didn't complain this morning. She hummed as she carried the steaming hot bowls to the table. Dad said that humming was a nervous habit and listening to Mom hum made me nervous too.

"How did you sleep, kids? Any good dreams to share?" Dad asked. No one answered because we had mouths full of Cream-of-Wheat.

We finished breakfast in silence before we left for school. I heard Dad whisper to Mom as he kissed her good-bye. "The girl was eighteen, Helen. She probably had a fight with her parents and ran away from home. She'll likely be back sometime today. They usually are."

Sandra Valade got off the Webster bus yesterday on Smyth Road near the VA and hadn't been seen since. That scared me because when it was raining and Mom didn't want us walking home from school, she gave us tokens to take the Webster bus. It was always crowded in bad weather, and little kids like me hardly ever got a seat. The bus smelled of wet wool, and I had to hang onto the back of someone's seat so I wouldn't fall as it jerked its way from stop to stop.

Moe was sure that she'd been kidnapped. "Dad doesn't want us to worry but I know that she didn't run away. Who'd run away in the middle of a snowstorm?"

My parents pulled on their boots and buttoned their coats. "We'll be back soon. We're going for a walk to enjoy last night's snowfall," said Mom. Dad tucked the newspaper in the wastebasket. I knew that they were going to talk about the missing girl.

Once they left, I pulled the paper out of the trash. Moe and I read every word. The day Sandra disappeared she'd gone to work at Laible Manufacturing, had supper downtown, went to the Y for her swim class, and got on the Webster bus to go home. But she disappeared somewhere on the dark road between the VA bus stop and her parents' house.

"We shouldn't take the Webster bus home anymore," said Moe. I agreed, my stomach in knots.

"Hunt Missing Girl, Items in Canal Hers," read the next day's headline.

"I'm right! I told you she didn't run away," Moe exclaimed. "Bet you any money that someone she knew did it. I read that murder victims usually know their killers."

I thought about all the men I knew. Our neighbors Mr. Larkin and Mr. Callahan. Our mailman Mr. O'Connell. Uncle Danny. Father Smith. Would any of them want to murder me?

We barely saw Dad for the next few days as he and the rest of Manchester's police searched for Sandra. Everyone talked about the missing girl. Sandra's father was on the channel 9 news. When her high school picture flashed across the screen, his voice cracked as he told listeners that Sandra was popular, fun, and full of pep.

The police got a call from a teenage boy who said he'd seen something sticking out of a snowbank on the Derry Road. It was

Sandra. The *Union Leader* reported that she'd had been tortured, violated, and then murdered. It scared me because we sometimes take the Derry Road when we visit my nun aunt in the Windham Castle. I wasn't sure what violated meant, but I thought it must be something dirty, and I didn't want to get into trouble for asking questions. The article said that Sandra must have been murdered somewhere else because there was little blood left in her body. Where was Sandra's blood, I wondered? My heart stopped when Attorney General Wyman said, "We're searching for a human monster."

Every boy that Sandra went to school with, dated, or worked with was considered a suspect. The list got shorter and shorter because they all had excuses. Dad said that excuses were called "alibis." But he refused to answer any more questions about the missing girl.

"Don't worry your pretty little head. Sandra got murdered while walking alone in the dark. Every night you're at home, safe and sound with your family."

I wasn't planning to go out walking alone at night. But I didn't feel safe at home with my parents and my brother and sister, either. I wondered if the murderer lived near us. Did he take the Webster bus? Did he know where I got off? I wondered if he'd be on the bus the next time I took it. What if he was like a wild animal that could smell my fear? If he was, then he'd know that I'd be an easy girl to kill. Because I'd be too scared to move if he came after me.

I worried. And I worried a lot.

3

Balloons dangled from the ceiling and a big sign saying "Congratulations, Detective Donovan!" hung over the fireplace. The doorbell rang. I could hear the Callahans and the Larkins congratulating my father on his promotion. Moe was busy upstairs, probably fussing with her hair or deciding what to wear. Joey and I grabbed some potato chips and a cup of onion dip and crawled under the dining room table.

I looked at my brother. "Be careful. You're getting dip all over the place." He scooped up a blob from the rug, popped it in his mouth, and licked his fingers. He was so disgusting.

"Nora?" I heard Moe calling me, but I didn't answer. She probably wanted to tell me that I should go around and hand out napkins or Mom wanted me to refill the ice bucket.

People gathered around the buffet table. Especially where Mom had me place the deviled eggs earlier. I saw Mr. Callahan move close to Mrs. Larkin. He slid his hand down and patted her on the bottom.

"No," giggled Mrs. Larkin. But instead of moving away, I saw her green high heels step closer to Mr. Callahan. Holy cow! Joey covered his mouth so our mother wouldn't hear him laughing and make us come out and be polite to our guests. I never liked Mr. Callahan so I wasn't surprised that he patted ladies' bums, but he worked with my dad, so I had to be nice. I didn't think that my mother liked him either, but she liked his wife, Irene.

"What a blessed day this is." Two long black dresses joined Mr. Callahan and Mrs. Larkin. It was Mom's nun aunt Sister Dolores and Father Smith. Auntie might be good at seeing blessings everywhere, but she wasn't good at seeing other things. Like Mr. Callahan patting the president of the Holy Name Society's wife's bottom.

Mrs. Larkin asked Mom if there were any leads in the Valade case. I couldn't hear Mom's answer because of all the noise. I saw some onion dip fall to the floor and elbowed Joey before he reached out to scoop it up.

Dad lifted the tablecloth. "Better join us if you want any dinner, you scallywags."

We crawled out. The buffet was full of Dad's favorite food. Mrs. Callahan's famous yellow Jell-O mold with crushed pineapple and orange pieces. Pigs in blankets, tuna noodle casserole, Swedish meatballs, and green bean salad circled the Jell-O mold. Celery stuffed with cream cheese and raisins and a relish dish with baby pickles and olives were on Mom's fancy platters. A bowl of onion dip and a basket of potato chips sat in the corner.

I handed a paper plate to Joey. "Th-th-thanks," he said. We got in line behind my Uncle Danny who tugged my ponytail and ruffled Joey's hair. Joey hated people ruffling his hair. His stutter got worse when he was mad, so I was glad he kept his mouth shut.

"You kids are hilarious, hiding under the table," laughed Aunt Kathleen. She had a big rhinestone barrette holding back her hair. I loved Aunt Kathleen. "Follow me," she said. She pulled out three plaid notebooks from her purse. "One for each of you," she said. "A salesman at the hospital handed these out free today." I wondered what I'd do with the notebook. It was too small for schoolwork and not private enough to be a diary. I'd stick it in my drawer and decide later.

"Kennedy announced this morning that he's running for president. Can you believe it?" said Dad. "He says that he's the best guy to protect this country from evil."

"If we pray hard enough, we just may put him in the White House. High time we got a Catholic in there." Father Smith brushed some crumbs off his black dress.

Aunt Kathleen leaned down and whispered in my ear. "Never wear black. It shows everything. And wearing a white bib with a black dress is the worst." She winked and pointed to a pineapple chunk on the front of Auntie's dress.

"What's the evil Kennedy's worried about?" I asked.

"There's a Cuban guy named Castro who's friendly with Khrushchev," said Dad. "Cuba is close to Florida, and we can't have Communist neighbors."

"Kennedy doesn't have a snowball's chance in hell of winning, Tom. You know that. An Irish Catholic can't win a national election," said Uncle Danny.

"What's wrong with Catholics?" I asked. "We're Catholic and so is just about everyone we know." I watched Joey pull bits of fruit out of the Jell-O mold and line them up on one side of his plate.

"Some people think that if a Catholic is elected, the Pope will be running the country," said Dad.

"I can't think of anything that would make our Lord happier than having a Catholic in the White House," said Father Smith.

Aunt Kathleen winked at me.

The men filled their plates, took their drinks to the parlor, and turned on the TV. The Celtics were playing the Lakers. Everyone loved the Celtics.

"Best NBA finals every played," Dad said.

"Cousy, Russell, Heinsohn on the same team is just about unbeatable," said Uncle Danny. "And Red Auerbach is the best goddamn coach that ever lived. Hands down."

"Who ever thought they could sweep the Lakers in the finals against a guy like Elgin Baylor?" Dad asked.

Mom dimmed the lights and carried in a vanilla sheet cake with colored sprinkles. "Go Get 'Em Tom," was written on the frosting. Everyone sang.

For he's a jolly good fellow,
for he's a jolly good fellow
for he's a jolly good fellow...
which nobody can deny.

I felt so proud of my dad.

"Speech, speech," someone yelled out.

Dad stood up and cleared his throat. "Well, I'm not one for speeches but I'll tell you one thing for sure. I'm probably not going to be the smartest detective that Manchester has ever seen, and definitely not the most handsome." He paused as everyone laughed. "But I can tell you this. No one will work harder than I will to keep Manchester safe. And that's a promise."

Father Smith got up and stood next to Dad. "I can't think of any detective who will work harder to keep the Queen City safe. I also can't think of a better man to keep America safe than John Fitzgerald Kennedy. Let's bow our heads and ask God to protect and defend these two fine men."

I don't think people knew if Father Smith had given a speech or a blessing. But I was happy that Sandra's killer would be caught now that Dad was a detective, and I wouldn't have to worry about riding the bus anymore.

Later that night when Dad was tucking us into bed, I asked him if he was scared to be a detective. "Don't you worry about me, Nora," he chuckled. "Manchester is a safe place to live, and I'm not in any danger."

I hoped so. I saw Joe Friday get shot on *Dragnet* one night, and he nearly died. I didn't want that to happen to my dad.

4

My teacher was the tallest lady I'd ever seen. If Sister Arnold wore a tall black hat instead of a veil and had a beard instead of a few straggly whiskers on her chin, she would look just like Abraham Lincoln.

Sister used her pointer a lot. When she walked around the classroom, she used it to point out stuff on the chalkboard, to point to the clock when kids were late, and to tap on the floor when she wanted everyone's attention. When she was really mad, she'd whack it across kids' desks to let them know they were in big trouble. When it wasn't in her hands, Sister's pointer hung from a hook next to the Infant of Prague.

The Infant was creepy. He looked like my first baby doll, except he stood up. He wore a long white dress with a big red cape. A gold necklace with a cross hung around his neck. The weirdest part of the costume was his giant red and gold hat with a cross on top.

I jumped when the pointer tapped on my desk. "Are you with us, Nora Donovan? I won't tolerate daydreaming in class," said Sister.

"Yes, Sister," I said.

She walked away from my desk and headed toward the map of the world.

"This week we're going to learn about where we go after death. I'll start with the happiest place first: heaven. Heaven, girls and boys, is where people who are in God's grace go to after they die." She looked around the classroom and smiled. I thought she was looking at me, so I smiled back. But just a little. Sandy Allen was chewing on one of her braids and Donald Morse was picking his nose. No one looked interested in Heaven or dying in the state of grace.

"Can anyone tell us what Heaven is like?" Sister asked.

Colleen Fitzpatrick raised her hand. "I've seen pictures of it on holy cards. It has beautiful flowers and angels playing harp music."

"Thank you, Miss Fitzpatrick. Heaven is indeed beautiful. It's a place where no one's in pain, where you can be with your dearly departed, and you can bask in God's love for all eternity."

I wondered what bask meant. The dismissal bell rang, and we filed out.

The next day Sister taught us about Purgatory. "Purgatory is where dead people go if they are not bad enough to go to hell but not good enough to get into heaven. Purgatory has fires but not as hot as the fires in hell," she said. "You're still in God's favor but have died with impurities. The time we spend burning in purgatory cleanses us so we can enter God's presence. But Sister wasn't finished. "And then there's Limbo. That's where dead babies go if they haven't been baptized before they die. It's the in-between where these unfortunate souls exist for eternity."

Sister told us that only Catholics can go to heaven and so it was tough noogies for the Protestants.

"Hell is the last place we'll talk about, class. Church teachings say that it is a place of fire. A terribly hot fire that never consumes your body but inflicts terrible pain as your skin and eyes keep melting over and over from the heat. Devils dance around you with pitchforks, poking at your burns as you scream in agony. The smell is horrible because flesh has burned there for centuries, and the screams of the damned crying out for water is deafening. But there's no water in hell, just terrible thirst and pain. Once in hell you are there forever."

It seemed to me it might just be better to die as an unbaptized infant and go to Limbo rather than run the risk of joining the damned.

5

"Today is library day, kids." Every Thursday Mom took us to the Carpenter Memorial Library. We could check out as many books as we could carry. She brought a giant canvas bag that she'd fill with her own books. Mom read all the time.

Mom and Joey went to the Children's Room. She thought that reading to Joey would help him with his stuttering problem.

Moe and I headed to the Teen section.

"I think that you belong in the Children's Room, young lady." The librarian with gray frizzy hair and glasses hanging from a chain around her neck looked at me like she thought I belonged in a playpen.

"I've read practically every book in the Children's Room except ones on cowboys and ice-fishing," I said. I wasn't going to let her boot me into the Children's Room.

She didn't make me leave, but she watched me the whole time. I ignored her.

Moe and I took our piles of books to the check-out desk.

"I like being here in the check-out line," said Moe. "I like the sound of the rubber stamper pressing down on the ink pad. Ka-chunk, Ka-chunk."

Moe was so weird. The plaque over the checkout counter said that the library was dedicated to the memory of Eleanora Blood Carpenter. The name "Blood" gave me goosebumps.

"I love the smell of the library," said Moe as we walked out the front door. "It makes my nose prickle in a good way." Mom laughed and said the smell was just the decay of old books. I liked the smell too, but I hated the word decay. It made me think of dead bodies and the smell of burning flesh.

6

"Boys and girls, can anyone explain the meaning of Lent?" Sister asked. She was swinging her pointer, which was always a bad sign.

A few kids raised their hands, but Tommy Hannigan was nearly falling out of his seat. "Sister! Sister!" he begged, waving his arm.

"Very well, Mr. Hannigan. Tell us the meaning of Lent."

"It's when you give up stuff you like."

Thwack! The pointer landed on Tommy's desk. He'd moved his hand just in time to avoid getting slapped.

"You would do well to listen more and talk less, Mr. Hannigan."

Tommy bit his lip and kept his hands folded in his lap.

"Lent reminds Catholics of the forty days Jesus fasted in the desert," said Sister.

I couldn't imagine walking around anywhere for forty days without eating. I looked around the class to see if other kids might be wondering about this. "You'll have the opportunity to be like Jesus, resist temptation, and use this time to become closer to God." I squirmed in my chair a little bit. But just a little. I didn't want the pointer thwacking me.

My parents told us that we were going to do something special for Lent this year. Mom held up a book called *The Lives of the Saints*. "It's time you learned about how saints suffered who followed the Church. We'd like you to study the saints and tell us about a different saint every night before dinner."

Moe rolled her eyes at me from across the room. We took the book upstairs and flipped through the pages. We got excited when we read about Saint Lawrence, Saint Bartholomew, and Saint Margret of Clitherow. They all had the worst torture with the best deaths we could find. My favorite was Saint Lawrence. He was grilled to death over hot red coals. He was brave about it and said to his murderers: "Turn me over, I'm cooked on this side."

Saint Bartholomew was flayed. Moe looked it up in the dictionary and it said flaying was "the removal of skin in strips while still alive."

Joey jumped up and down on the bed. "Th-th-that's a good one."

Saint Margaret of Clitherow was a Saint that even my parents hadn't heard of. She was pressed to death—pressed on her back over a sharp stone with a door on top of her that was topped with an 800-pound weight. It took her fifteen minutes to die.

Saint Agatha had a good story too. The Catholic girl's high school was named after her so we figured we should know something about her. Some guy really wanted her to love him, and she wouldn't because she only wanted to love God, so he had her boobies cut off with iron scissors and burned her to death.

I wondered why all these people who got tortured were made saints. I didn't care enough about being a saint to get tortured. I bet Sandra didn't either.

7

Sister was excited for us to receive the sacraments of Confession and Communion. She pulled down a big chart with the Ten Commandments on it.

"Confession is the sacrament that allows you to receive communion in a state of grace. We will review the Ten Commandments, so you can start thinking about which ones you've broken. The commandments you have broken are the sins you must confess to the priest."

I looked at the commandments as Sister pointed to each one and read it aloud. I didn't think I had any strange gods before me. At least I didn't know any. "Thou shalt not kill, thou shalt honor your mother and father..." so far, so good. I didn't know what coveting my neighbor's wife or my neighbor's goods meant. But I knew "bearing false witness" was lying and not honoring my parents meant disobeying them.

"After you confess your sins to the priest, he'll give you a penance to complete at the altar rail before you can return to your pew. A penance might be as short as two prayers, or it might be as long as a Rosary."

A Rosary. I didn't even know how to say one. But I wondered how many strange gods I'd have to have before me to get a Rosary as penance.

"Catholics go to Confession before they receive the Eucharist so that their souls will be clean on the day that they receive."

Sister Arnold mustn't have a clue that Buddy Lowell would be stealing penny candy from Arti-Lou's Variety as soon as the bell sounded. He always did and was proud of it. Moe said never to take candy from Buddy because his sin would become my sin too. Now that I knew about penance, I knew it was not worth an extra Hail Mary just to get a pack of Smarties.

My first-grade class lined up in alphabetical order in the back of the church.

"Children, there's nothing to be nervous about," Sister whispered.

I caught Missy Callahan's eye. She looked terrified. Tommy Hannigan sat next to me and whispered that his sister told him to lie and tell the priest that "I lied one time," to get the whole thing over with. That sounded easy but it was weird that you had to make stuff up to go to confession.

My knees were shaking when I walked into the small dark box. It looked like a giant wooden phone booth and had purple velvet curtains hanging on the door so nobody could peek in and see you. Behind the curtains were kneelers and a wooden screen that separated the sinner from the priest. You knew it was your turn to speak when he slid open a window and you could sort of see him through the screen. I had butterflies in my stomach because I was having a hard time deciding which sins to confess. I didn't want to copy Tommy, so I said "Bless me father for I have sinned. I disobeyed my parents once and I lied two times."

"You must honor your father and mother," said the voice behind the curtain. "For your penance say three Hail Marys."

The church was cold—it was always cold. Dad said it was expensive to heat a church because the ceilings are so high. I looked up at the light streaming through the saints and angels on the stained-glass windows and knelt to begin my penance.

Hail Mary,
Full of Grace,
The Lord is with thee.
Blessed art thou a monk swimming,
and blessed is the fruit
of thy womb, Jesus.
Holy Mary,
Mother of God, pray for us sinners,
now and at the hour of our death. Amen

I didn't understand about the swimming monk, but I figured Sister would be teaching us about him soon enough.

8

"The sacred host is the body and blood of Jesus." Sister folded her arms across her chest and put her hands in her huge nun sleeves as she spoke. "The host must be treated with respect. When you line up to receive the host, you stick out your tongue and Father will place the host on it. You walk back to your pew, hands folded, and kneel until everyone has returned to their seat. And then you may be seated."

Sister pulled her hands out of her big sleeves and grabbed the pointer. I looked around the room, wondering who was about to get thwacked, but everyone was sitting quietly. "Never touch the host with your fingers and do not chew it. You're to swallow it whole. If the priest drops the host, don't pick it up. Father will get down on his hands and knees and eat it off the floor. You're never to touch the host because that would desecrate it."

I wondered what desecrate meant. Eating anything off dirty All Saints' rug would be disgusting.

I was excited about getting dressed up for my First Communion. The boys had to wear boring white suits, but the girls got to wear white dresses and white veils. Mom said I had to wear Moe's dress and veil, but I could get new shoes because Moe's were too small, and JM Fields was having a spring shoe sale.

First Communion Day finally arrived. Sister lined us up by height in the schoolyard. Girls on the left and boys on the right, we marched up the steps of the church.

"Girls, you look beautiful," said Sister Arnold as we stood waiting to file in. "Young brides of Christ, you are indeed." No one had told us that we were signing on to be brides of Christ.

Moe told me earlier that all the nuns were brides of Christ. "You're lying, Moe. Why would Christ want that many brides?"

"Why do you think all the nuns wear wedding rings, stupid? And they all have Mary as a middle name."

The organ played "Here I Am Lord" as we paraded into the crowded church, our hands folded in prayer. Father Smith and two altar boys walked onto the altar, which was covered with baskets of white lilies.

We lined up to receive Communion. I opened my mouth and felt Father Smith place the host on my tongue. It got stuck on the roof of my mouth, just like Moe said it would. I remembered that we weren't supposed to touch the host with our fingers, so I tried to scrape the Body of Jesus off with my tongue. I snuck a look at Missy Callahan who was a few kids down the kneeler. I saw her reach in her mouth and pull out the host. She put it back in and started chewing. I looked around to see if Father Smith had seen her fishing around with the host. But he was busy putting hosts on tongues. I wondered what kind of penance he'd give her if he knew that she'd desecrated the body of Our Lord Jesus Christ.

9

A strange car sat in the driveway. Dad came out the kitchen door to meet us. "What do you think, girls? We bought the car this morning. She's a beauty, isn't she? Chevy Bel Air. Smooth as a baby's bottom." He ran his hand down the side of the car. It was much bigger and fancier than our other car, and it was painted white and two shades of blue. I don't think I ever saw a car with three different colors. "A new detective can't be driving around the city in an old Ford with rusty sideboards. It wouldn't look right." This car had big, giant fins on the back. Dad smiled and said it reminded him of a rocket ship. I ran back into the house and grabbed Joey because I knew that he'd love it. He was crazy about rockets and space.

"It l-l-looks like a s-spaceship." Joey smiled running his hand along the fins in the back.

"Joey, you should say rocket and not space because Ss are hard if you stutter," I said.

My parents and Moe went inside, but Joe and I stood around the car admiring its fins and whitewall tires. Billy Sweeney came by to get me for a game of Red Rover. He spotted Joey sitting in the driver's seat.

"Hey, we don't have an even number of players. Joey, would you like to try R-r-red R-r-rover?" Billy laughed.

My brother didn't answer, so I answered for him.

"Well, you have an even number of players now because I'm not playing. Get out of our driveway, you loser," I yelled.

10

Dad pulled into a parking place off Elm Street, and we joined the crowd for the Memorial Day Parade. American flags flew from streetlamps and people lined the sidewalks. As sounds of the high school marching bands approached from the distance, I could see Girl Scouts and Boy Scouts, firemen and policemen, marching and waving their flags to the music. Fire trucks with American flags slowly made their way down Elm Street. Army Jeeps carried waving old soldiers in their uniforms decorated with medals.

As the parade faded into the distance, we walked back to the car and headed to the cemetery to visit our dead relatives.

"I feel bad not getting the flowers over earlier," Mom said to Dad. "But with the washing machine dying and Nora making her first Communion on Sunday, driving to the cemetery seemed like too much."

"Helen, I'm sure that the dead will understand," said Dad. He never liked going to the cemetery.

Joey sat on Mom's lap so he could see out the window, and I got to sit on a pillow in the backseat. Moe was tall enough so she could see just fine. The tires made a thun-thunka-thunka-thunking noise as we drove over the Merrimack. I leaned out the window to watch the frothy water crashing below me.

I was surprised that there were so many people at the cemetery. Mom had pots of red geraniums in the trunk, and she gave them to Moe and me to place in front of the family gravestones. She handed Joey some small flags to stick in the ground.

"Thank God the flowers didn't wilt in the trunk." She pulled off a few dead leaves from one plant. I didn't know any of the people whose names were on the gravestones. But I did wonder if my dead family members were in heaven, purgatory, or hell. The only dead relative I remembered is my Grandfather Donovan. And about the only thing I remembered about him was that he yelled a lot. I knew that Mom didn't like him very much, but I hoped he wasn't in hell screaming with the damned.

11

The neighborhood kids were afraid of my dad because he was a policeman, and everyone was afraid of the cops. At least that's what the kids said that their parents said.

"Guilty until proven innocent," said Billy Sweeney. "My old man says the cops that drink down at the Knights of Columbus are worse than most of the criminals in the city."

I didn't know Mr. Sweeney, but I was sure that I wouldn't like him. Dad always came home after work and never went to the Knights of Columbus. And most of the time he was home for supper and bedtime.

I didn't like Billy Sweeney or Jimmy Casey either, but I loved playing Red Rover.

"Jimmy and I will be the captains tonight," Billy announced. No one was brave enough to say we should do eeny-meany-miney-moe to decide. But I didn't mind. All I really cared about was the running because I was good at it. Judy Dolan and Timmy Moore got picked last, just like always. Judy was fat and slow, but she never complained about getting picked last. Timmy had asthma and kids teased him because he could hardly ever run from one side to the other without using his sucker. Mom told Moe and me never to join in if anyone teased Timmy Moore. "Timmy has asthma and if he gets too excited or runs too fast, he gets short of breath and gets wheezy. You kids be nice to him; it's not his fault."

"Red Rover, red rover, let Wheezy come over!" Jimmy yelled.

Wheezy's eyes lit up and he moved his feet back and forth like a charging bull. Halfway to the chain of linked arms, he slowed down, huffed and puffed, and grabbed his sucker. The other kids laughed.

Billy grabbed Timmy's sucker and tossed it to Jimmy. "Let's play Keep Away!" Wheezy looked like he was going to cry. Jimmy tossed Timmy's sucker back to Billy.

Timmy could barely breathe.

"Cut it out," I yelled. "This isn't funny!"

I ran home and got Dad. He marched over, broke up the game, and walked Timmy home to make sure he was okay. After that, Dad went back to the schoolyard and gave those kids a talking-to. I don't know what he said to them, but nobody ever teased Timmy again. At least not in the schoolyard.

I felt sorry for many of the kids I played with. I felt sorry for Wheezy because all the kids laughed at him when he started wheezing. I felt sorry for Judy Smiley who always got picked last because she was fat and slow. I felt bad for Frankie Dolan. He could be a pain in the neck because he talked too much and was hard to understand because he had a lisp. If I had a lisp, I was pretty sure I wouldn't talk as much as Frankie. I even felt bad for Billy Sweeney, who had a big mouth and was mean. His dad was in jail for stealing and I overheard Mom say that his mother drank too much. Billy didn't have much of a chance, I thought. I was glad that my parents didn't drink or steal. And I was glad that my parents didn't let Joey play outside at night in the summer. Billy would be mean to him.

Timmy might like it if Billy had someone else to pick on, but I didn't want Joey to be that kid.

12

"Dad, Dad!" I yelled as I ran in the house, screen door slamming behind me.

Dad sighed and put down the *Union Leader*. "What is it, Nora?"

"Is there such a thing as the boogeyman?" I asked. "Billy Sweeney pinky swore to all of us that he's real. Billy said he comes out at night and peeks in kids' windows and sometimes he snatches them and cuts them into little pieces and feeds them to his pet snake Adolph."

"Nora, that is a wild story. No, there is no such thing as the boogeyman. I've been a policeman for a long time, but I've never heard of a boogeyman," laughed Dad.

"How many times have we told you not to listen to that Sweeney kid?" chimed in Mom. "Why don't you go to your room and read like your sister?"

But I couldn't get what Billy said out of my head.

"Moe," I asked, "is there such a thing as the boogeyman?"

"Of course, there is. I read about them all the time. The boogeyman in *Tom Sawyer* is Injun Joe. He's a bad guy who doesn't like girls and wants to slit their nostrils and notch their ears, so they look like pigs. And Long John Silver is the boogeyman in *Treasure Island*. He's a murderer and a thief and has lots of people killed—he's really a bad guy."

"Yeah, but that's in books—I'm talking about real life."

"Well, I don't know for sure, but I wouldn't worry about it. Nothing bad ever happens in Manchester," said Moe.

I guess Moe had forgotten about Sandra Valade. And how she had no blood left in her body.

After dinner my folks turned on *The Lawrence Welk Show*. I couldn't understand how every Saturday my folks could watch Bobby Burgess in his plaid pants with teeth as big and white as Chicklets, prancing around the stage with Cissy somebody. Or Myron Floran playing the accordion acting like he was having fun. Dad thought he must be Polish because accordions were used mostly to play polka music. "Floran is probably shortened from Florinski or Floranski," he said.

I didn't know much about the Polish. Our milkman Mr. Dobrowski was Polish, but he delivered the milk early, so I never asked him if he played the accordion. The only other Polish people I've heard of in Manchester lived down by the TTK bakery and went to Saint Hedwig's church. They didn't mix in much, so I don't know if any of them played the accordion. Lawrence Welk ended the show with the words, "Good night, sleep tight, and pleasant dreams to you." If I didn't have to worry about Sandra and what Billy Sweeney said about the boogeyman, I might have been able to sleep tight.

13

When I got more practice going to confession, I came up with better sins. "I read my sister's diary once, I lied to my parents twice, and I disobeyed Sister Arnold once."

I got used to the usual three Hail Mary penance, and sometimes the priest gave me an Our Father. The worst part of confession was the Act of Contrition that we had to recite after confessing our sins. The part I really hated was "because I dread the loss of heaven and the pains of hell." I didn't dread the loss of heaven because I didn't know much about it. But the nuns talked about the pains of hell all the time, and I did dread the smell of burning flesh and the cries of the damned. I wonder what Dickie Dumond got for a penance the day he was double dared by his brother Donny to confess the sin of having impure thoughts, whatever that meant.

I decided to try not to sin for two weeks. Every time Moe made me mad by being her bossy self, I just turned the other cheek and walked away. I admitted throwing my dirty clothes on Moe's bed when Mom asked me about it, and I didn't whine about licking stamps and putting them in the Green Stamp Book when she told me to. I looked forward to going to confession to confess my goodness.

"Bless me father for I have sinned. It has been two weeks since my last confession and I have no sins."

I swear that the confessional started to shake. The voice behind the curtain boomed, "Child you have just committed the worst sin of all: the sin of pride. No one is without sin! For your penance you must say a rosary."

I held back tears as I headed to the altar rail. It seemed that the entire flock of mean-looking angels on the stained-glass windows were laughing at poor Nora Donovan who thought she was perfect, and in the end, committed the worse sin of all. And she was too stupid to even know it. I was mad and embarrassed, but I was too afraid to not say my penance. I didn't want to sit in flames and scream with the damned after I died.

A rosary was a lot of prayers. There was the Apostle's Creed and then one Our Father, three Hail Marys, and a Glory Be. Then you had to pray around the loop and say the five mysteries. Each mystery had one Our Father, ten Hail Marys, and a Glory Be. There must be at least fifty prayers in the rosary. I knelt at the rail for a long time, and I knew that everyone watching me must have thought that I killed a nun or robbed the church for getting all that rail time. If only they knew that I hadn't confessed to any real sins.

I left the church angry. I was mad at the mean priest for embarrassing me for trying my best to be good. I vowed that day never to confess to any sin except lying or being disobedient to my parents or the nuns. And to never try to be perfect again.

14

Most of the corned beef and cabbage Mom cooked for our Saint Patrick's Day dinner had disappeared. Dirty plates were piled up next to the kitchen sink. The Callahans were the only guests still in our house.

When *Finnegan's Wake* started skipping on the hi-fi, Mom turned off the music.

Irene Callahan grabbed her husband's arm. "John, we need to head home."

"Thanks to the Donovans for hosting a great Saint Patrick's dinner. See you at the station tomorrow, Tom," said Mr. Callahan. I saw Mrs. Callahan help him after he tripped going down the steps.

"Let's go sit," said Aunt Kathleen as she headed into the living room. "I have an announcement." Her eyes shone and her cheeks were bright pink. "I'm engaged!" She stuck out her hand to show off her diamond ring. "Last weekend at Angelo's Marcel asked me to marry him!" We gave her a round of family hugs. Uncle Danny pecked her on the cheek but said nothing.

"We're so happy for you," said Mom.

Dad flashed a big smile. "When's the big day?"

"Well, if it was up to me, I'd get married tomorrow," she laughed. "But Marcel wants to wait a few years until we both graduate and save enough money for a down payment on a house."

"That's sensible," said Dad.

Kathleen was Dad's only sister. Me and Moe really loved Kathleen. She brought us magazines when she was done with them, and sometimes even bought us little presents like barrettes or matching socks. I heard Dad whisper to Mom once that she was a mistake, whatever that meant.

Kathleen asked me to be a junior bridesmaid and Moe to be a bridesmaid. "You girls will love Marcel's sisters. They're going to be in the wedding too. His brother's a doll, and he and Joey will both be ring bearers."

"What are their names?" I asked.

"Danielle, Doris and Jean," Kathleen replied.

"I thought you said there was a brother." I was confused.

"Yes Nora, Jean is his brother—it's French for John."

"Jesus," muttered Uncle Danny.

"And we're getting married at Sainte Marie's—Marcel's uncle is the pastor there and he'll perform the ceremony." She put on her coat and her fur hat, just like the one Jackie wore on TV the other night. "Got to run, family. I have clinical in the morning. Thanks for dinner." She blew us a kiss and headed out.

"He's a nice enough guy but I don't see him fitting in," said Uncle Danny. My parents ignored him, so he turned to us kids.

"I don't expect you to understand the problem here, but Kathleen wants to marry a Frenchman."

"A F-f-frenchman? S-s-so what?" Joey asked.

"It's a problem because they're not like us; they don't celebrate all the same holidays, they have their own churches, schools, and even language, for God's sake. Maybe the worst of it is that they live across the river on the West Side, and we'll probably never get to see Kathleen if the goddam Frenchie has his way."

"Danny, that's enough!" snapped Dad. "His name is Marcel and it's about time you started calling him that."

My uncle clenched his teeth ---he got mad anytime anyone disagreed with him.

"What your uncle said is partly true," said Dad. "The Merrimack River divides the West Side from the East Side. The French live on the West Side, and the East Side is mostly Irish. And anyone who think they're rich, no matter what nationality they are, live in the North End."

Uncle Danny looked pleased, as though he thought Dad might secretly agree with him. But I knew that Dad was just trying to smooth things over.

"Manchester is a city of neighborhoods," said Mom. "Each neighborhood has its own corner markets and hardware stores. And they all have laundromats and parks."

"And don't forget the churches and schools," said Dad. "In our neighborhood alone we have All Saints', Saint Agatha's, and the Cathedral. And we even have a synagogue for Jewish people."

"Who lives in the south end, Dad?" Moe asked.

"Anyone who hasn't figured out where the hell they fit in," he chuckled.

Mom shook her head. "Tom Donovan's view of the world. Tom, Kathleen probably expects you to give her away. After all, you are the oldest son."

"I know, I know, Helen. It'll be an honor to walk her down the aisle, but it's too bad that my old man can't be there for Kathleen." Dad sighed.

"Well, if he didn't spend so much time with his friend Jack Daniels, maybe he would've lived longer," replied Mom.

Uncle Danny laughed. "Helen, you always have life figured out, don't you?"

Mom just glared at him.

15

"He's the most reliable weatherman in the business." Dad was watching Boston's Don Kent, who said that a monster storm was building off the coast of Africa.

"It'll become a hurricane overnight. Stay tuned for the most up-to-date information right here on WBZ."

"This is going to be a big one, folks." Dad was a weather nut. He chewed our ears off about every storm headed toward Manchester. Kent said that Donna dumped fifteen inches of rain on Puerto Rico, and one hundred seven people drowned. Donna was now officially a Category 4 hurricane. I got excited when Kent warned that the storm was going to hit Florida next and head right up the eastern seaboard to New England.

"Y-y-yippie!" Joey jumped up and down on the hassock. "We n-n-never get good storms here. This will be fun!"

Dad got mad. "You won't think it's much fun when we lose power for days."

"I bet it won't be that bad," I said.

"Hush, Nora," said Mom. "This is a serious storm, and it looks like it may cause a lot of harm. Houses could get damaged by the wind or water or one of the big trees in the backyard could fall on the house and then how would you feel, young lady?" Like a dumb kid, I thought to myself.

Over the next few days, Dad followed Donna as she worked her way up the coastline through Georgia and South Carolina. When she struck North Carolina, Kent said that the eye of the hurricane was unusually large—about 80 miles wide.

"How big is that?" I asked Dad.

"That's about how far it is from our house to Clark's Trading Post up in Lincoln," said Dad. I hoped that the people who worked at Clark's would remember to get the bears out of their rocking chairs and off their platforms before Donna hit Lincoln.

The other weatherman Norm McDonald told us that a Cape Cod man was electrocuted while trying to fix the antenna on his roof. Why would anyone be up on a roof during a hurricane?

Dad explained that hurricanes always get stronger over water and weaker over land. Donna kept switching back and forth between land and water, so she never lost strength. And she did that over and over as she aimed for Manchester with wind speeds of 138 miles per hour.

"That's faster and more powerful than a freight train," said Dad. "And she's headed our way."

Everyone in the neighborhood dragged lawn chairs and bird baths, porch swings, and bicycles out of their yards and into their basements. They filled jugs of water to flush toilets in case the power was knocked out. The Larkins forgot to take down their bird feeder and Dad made Moe go over to remind them about it.

"Do I have to?" whined Moe.

"Offer it up for the souls in purgatory and just go do it!" snapped Dad.

"Tom, you're such a busy body," said Mom.

"Helen, the wind could send that feeder flying through their living room window. Someone could get seriously hurt." Mom said nothing and went back to her book, but I could tell that she was nervous.

Superintendent Keefe ordered all schools to be closed the day Donna was due to hit New Hampshire. Governor Powell told people to stay off the roads and to leave the phone lines open for emergencies.

Norm McDonald reported that one hundred planes had flown from Pease Air Force Base and moved to Iceland to avoid severe damage. I imagined them flying off together like a flock of geese. Boat owners hurried to remove boats from the water at Hampton and Seabrook beaches. "If they don't get all those boats out of the water soon, they'll be nothing but toothpicks by tomorrow," Dad fussed.

The power went out just before we went to bed. The wind roared. The house shook, the windows rattled. I could hear tree limbs cracking and sirens screaming through the streets. It was scary and exciting.

The next morning, we woke up to a new day. The sky was blue, the sun was shining. We looked out the windows. Electric wires and tree branches were strewn everywhere. Leaves clogged storm drains, making huge puddles. We got our power back late that afternoon. Don Kent said that the damage was minor all over the region. No buildings came crashing down, no lives were lost. But it turned out that Donna was a storm for the record books.

The National Weather Service announced that since the storm hit every seaboard state from Florida to Maine with hurricane force winds, the name Donna would be retired forever. "It will never again be used for a hurricane," said Kent.

I wondered why the adults made such a big deal about the storm. In the end Donna only caused headaches for the neighborhood kids who got stuck picking up broken branches and sweeping pine needles off steps and porches.

16

Reporters ignored Kennedy during the hurricane. But once Donna disappeared, all eyes were on the Irish senator. He visited every state, insisting that he was the one who could keep our country safe from evil foreign governments. He was so handsome, and Jackie was so stylish and beautiful that Mom said that she thought there was no way that Kennedy could lose the election.

The day before the election my parents told us to get in the car--- we were going to go see history being made. It was a windy, cold afternoon and already starting to get dark. Thousands of people were heading toward Victory Park to listen to John Kennedy speak. Joey sat on Dad's shoulders and got the best view. "Why on earth isn't Kennedy wearing a hat?" Mom whispered.

As Kennedy came up the steps to the platform the crowd started chanting "JFK...JFK...JFK." It went on for at least ten minutes before he put his hands up to get people to stop.

"Thank you...thank you...thank you." It took several minutes before the crowd quieted down.

Kennedy said that he started his campaign in Manchester last winter, so it was appropriate to end it in our city the night before the election. The crowd went wild. Hooting and hollering and clapping and "JFK...JFK...JFK," all over again.

Kennedy told the crowd the reasons he wanted to do well in New Hampshire. He wanted to see *The Union Leader* have to print the headline that he won. Everyone roared and clapped. Joey fiddled with the feather in Dad's hat as he buried his face in it. He was freezing like the rest of us. Kennedy said that William Loeb had no regard for publishing the truth. Dad looked down and told me that Loeb accused Kennedy of being a Communist. He was outraged that anyone would publish such a lie.

"Finally, tomorrow we have an opportunity to wrap it up and throw it in the lap of William Loeb." When Kennedy finished speaking, the local high school marching bands started playing "Stars and Stripes Forever." The crowd continued cheering and chanting "JFK...JFK...JFK," all over again as they made their way out of Victory Park.

On our way home, Dad started to explain the true meaning of a democracy and the importance of truth. But I couldn't concentrate on what he was saying. I felt proud to be an American and I hoped that the man that Sister Margaret called "The Irish Prince" got elected to be the new president the next day. And he did.

17

Joey opened the window in the Advent calendar. "It's just a stupid donkey lying next to an empty manger." He threw it on the kitchen table and grabbed his coat.

"There's nothing wrong with a good ass," I heard Dad whisper to Mom as he patted her on the bum. Mom blushed.

We hopped in the car and headed down Webster Street. It was a cold but starry night and the light and twinkle in the sky added to the magic. Our excitement grew as we turned left onto Elm. There in the distance was the giant New Hampshire Insurance building. All the lights in the building were turned on and certain windows were darkened to create the image of Christmas trees on all sides. "Oh, Tom," sighed Mom. "I never get tired of seeing this."

"Just be glad we don't have to pay the bill to the Public Service Company," Dad chuckled. We parked the car near the State Theater and started our way down Elm Street. Joey loved the display in Mickey Finn's window. Elves stood near Santa's sleigh holding tackle boxes and fishing poles. Santa stood next to his sleigh showing off his catch for the day.

Pariseau's had a scene of the North Pole with a sign that read "Santa's Workshop." An electric train ran around the sides and through the village that was labeled "The North Pole Express." We crossed the street to listen to the Salvation Army sing Christmas carols in front of Woolworth's. A man ringing a bell next to a red bucket stood nearby. Dad gave Joey a dollar and told him to put it in the bucket and say "Merry Christmas."

At the corner of Hanover and Elm, a short fat policeman stood directing traffic with his white-gloved hand. The best part of the decorations was the star that hung lit in the middle of the intersection between City Hall and the Amoskeag Bank. Colored lights hanging from the star were fastened to telephone poles on all corners, and the display lit up the street for several blocks.

The sidewalks were full of happy people even though it was cold. "Tom, have you noticed that everyone is just strolling, not in a hurry to get anywhere?" She smiled and took Dad's arm.

As we all piled back in the car ready to go home, there was one last place to visit. The big white house on the corner of Bridge and Beech had the best Christmas displays of all. This year there was a sleigh with Santa and his reindeer lit up on one side of the porch, and on the other side was a Nativity scene complete with the shepherds, wisemen, and animals. In the center were Mary and Joseph kneeling beside an empty manger waiting for the Baby Jesus to be born. The star of Bethlehem shone brightly as we slowly drove by. I turned around and looked through the rear-view window until I couldn't see it any longer.

"Get your PJ's on, it's time to call it a day," said Mom as we walked in the kitchen door. I crawled into bed after brushing my teeth and thought about how lucky we were. And then I felt bad because I thought about Sandra Valade. I knew her family wasn't feeling very lucky tonight.

1961

Kennedy had a big smile, and everyone thought that Jackie was beautiful. But he wasn't even President yet, and Sister Margaret made us pray for him anyway. "May our new President protect and defend our country in this time of peril."

Prayers have scary words, like *peril* and *evil*. The Act of Contrition had *detest*: "detest my sins."

"Why are we in *peril*?" I asked. Mom stopped putting pot roast on our plates and looked at me.

"What kind of peril are you talking about, Nora?"

"Sister makes us pray that Kennedy will save us from *peril*," I said.

"Nora, I think Sister is talking about the Communist threat," said Mom as she took off her apron.

"But it'll be okay. Don't worry. Kennedy was a war hero and he'll make short work of the Russians." Dad took a sip of water and smiled at my mother. "Great pot roast, hon."

"Same old, same old," Mom said. She turned to Joey. "Joseph, don't play with your food."

Joey frowned and rubbed his eyes.

"Eat up, young man. We have brownies for dessert: your favorite."

"B-b-b-brownies!" Joey began shoveling food into his mouth.

"Joey, what's the difference between a mortal sin and a venial sin?" asked Moe. Joey's mouth was full.

I glared at Moe. She knew Joey didn't know, and she was just being mean.

"Moe, leave him alone. It's suppertime. And Joey, don't eat like a wild animal," said Mom.

"He's making his First Communion this year, and he doesn't even know half the stuff he's supposed to know," huffed Moe.

"I am sure he'll have it all learned by the he receives the Sacrament." Mom smiled at Joey. "Joey, can you tell everyone about your speech therapy?"

Joey squirmed in his chair and looked around the table. "I h-h-have a stutter," he said.

I had to keep myself from laughing. We all knew Joey stuttered. He didn't have to tell us. I didn't dare look at Moe.

We waited, but Joey said nothing. Mom decided to explain more.

"Your dad, Joey, and I met with Mrs. Moore. She's trained in speech therapy and is sure that if Joey practices the exercises she gives him, he'll be speaking like President Kennedy in no time."

I wasn't sure about Joey talking with a Boston accent.

"Good for you, Joey. I'll help you if Mrs. Moore gives you homework," said Moe.

"I'm sure we'd all be delighted to help you, Joey," said Mom. She turned to Moe. "Right now, you and Nora have to do the dishes. And Joey has to take out the trash."

My parents invited Father Smith for coffee and apple pie the night before Kennedy's Inauguration. I thought that Father Smith was creepy. He had one real eye and one glass eye. It was hard to figure out if he was speaking to you or not because one eye went one way and the other eye went the other. Moe and I had just finished drying the dishes when Father Smith rang the doorbell.

"How old are you, young man?" he asked Joey. "Twelve, thirteen?" Father winked at me from what I thought was his glass eye. But I wasn't sure if it was the glass one because if he looked straight ahead, both eyes looked the same. "Old enough to be an altar boy?"

Joey knew that Father Smith was teasing him, but he liked the idea of someone thinking that he was twelve or thirteen, even if the person was kidding. Father brought a box of Van Otis chocolates but told my mother not to bother opening them now.

"Let's have your delicious apple pie now, Helen. Enjoy the chocolates tomorrow after you hear New Hampshire's famous poet read at the inauguration."

"I'm not sure that the kids know about Robert Frost, Father," said Dad.

When Father Smith realized that we didn't know who Robert Frost was, he stood up and recited a poem from memory about a horse in the woods at night.

"Did you like that?" he asked.

"That was good," I said, though I thought if the horse was galloping instead of just standing doing nothing in the middle of the night that it would have been more interesting.

"Well, tomorrow's the country's big day, children. You'll get to hear Robert Frost from New Hampshire read a poem on TV," said Father Smith.

I hoped that it wouldn't be the horse one but didn't say anything.

Father Smith stood up. "I should go before the storm gets bad." One eye looked at me, but the other stared at the door.

"Father, would you bless the house before you leave?" asked Mom.

"Heavenly Father, bless the Donovans. Watch over their steps as they seek to do Your will. And keep them from peril."

Peril again. Father raised his right hand as he said, "In the name of the Father, the Son, and the Holy Ghost."

"Thank you, Father," said Mom.

Dad walked Father to the front door. We felt a blast of wind as he stepped out.

"Wasn't that lovely," said Mom. "And nice of Father Smith to come out when a storm is predicted."

The wind howled all night, and when we got up in the morning, our driveway was filled with snow. And school was canceled.

"Good thing no one has to go in at 7:00." Dad looked out the window. "I hope this weather doesn't interfere with Kennedy's Inauguration." He brought his coffee into the living room and turned on the news.

"Give them credit, they've done a good job with the plowing." Dad looked at the TV. "They must have called in the military, because they don't know how to handle snow in DC the way we do in New Hampshire."

"Kids, you need to come in and watch this," said Mom. "It'll be a long time before you see another Irish Catholic getting sworn in as President."

We went into the living room. Joey sat between Mom and Dad on the couch, and Moe and I sat on the floor in front of them. Joey kept swinging one of his legs, and he kicked me in the shoulder.

"Joey, stop kicking me,"

"Children, don't squabble." My mother grabbed Joey's leg and put it on the couch.

Joey farted, and I started laughing.

"Stop it right now! This is important, and you'll be telling your children about this in another twenty years." Dad was mad. "You're going to sit here like good Catholics and good Americans and watch Kennedy getting sworn in or I'll know the reason why."

Even Joey knew enough to stop. We sat there trying to be good Catholics and good Americans. A bunch of people said prayers, and a big negro lady sang the National Anthem.

"What a beautiful voice on that Marian Anderson," exclaimed my mother.

I liked Jackie's hat. But it was so windy that it blew our old New Hampshire poet's hair all over the place and sent his poem flying into the crowd. So instead of reciting the poem he had written in honor of Kennedy, he stood and recited a poem that he already knew by heart. I could barely hear him, but I don't think that it was the horse one.

Kennedy gave a speech warning us about our enemies. This must be the *peril* Sister Margaret wanted God to protect us from. But I felt proud when I heard him say, "ask not what your country can do for you, ask what you can do for your country."

"Well, that was fun," said Moe. She flounced up the stairs to our bedroom carrying a pile of magazines.

"Dad, what's Kennedy so worried about?"

"Nora, we talked about this the other night. The Russian leader Khrushchev is a bully. He has people in Cuba, and Kennedy has to get them to leave."

Joey crawled into Dad's lap. I knew that this Russian talk was scaring him.

"The Russians have been working on their space program, ever since Sputnik. Remember when we all went outside at night to see it over our house?" asked Dad.

I nodded. I remembered that Joey was asleep, so we left him inside, but the rest of us stepped out into the darkness to watch for it. It was pitch black, and all our neighbors were out, faces upturned to see what Russia had done. I got cold, so Dad picked me up, and then I saw it. A little blinking light moving slowly across the night sky.

"Americans don't want the Russians staying ahead of us. That's why Kennedy wants us to be the first country to put a man on the moon."

I was proud that our county elected Kennedy. And if we were the first nation to put a man on the moon, it would be way better than that little Sputnik thing the Russians sent up a few years ago.

2

Joey was nervous about speech therapy. When we walked to school the next day, he said that Mrs. Moore seemed nice, but he was scared that he wouldn't get rid of his stutter.

"Joey, the lady's going to give you some exercises to do. If you do them, you will be talking just fine. Altar-boy promise," I said.

"Y-y-you can't do an altar boy promise. You're a girl," he laughed.

"You'd better watch it, Joe," said Moe. "Vatican II is changing all kinds of stuff. And who knows? Maybe the Pope will let girls be altar boys. What if Nora and I were in your altar boy training class?"

"I w-would hate that," he said.

Moe and I were drafted into helping Joe with his speech exercises because our parents were going to Montreal the week that he started therapy.

During the week before they left, Dad kept checking the weather map in the paper and giving Mom the latest forecast.

I couldn't wait for my parents to leave for Canada. My mother had her two best dresses dry-cleaned and had even bought a Jackie Kennedy pillbox hat to wear to Mass.

"We'll go to Mass on Sunday at Notre Dame, and I don't know what kind of hats are in style in Montreal. But Jackie Kennedy speaks French, so I'll bet that some women will be wearing pill boxes."

"Helen, you'll look beautiful no matter what you wear." Dad stood by their bed, looking at his watch and then looking at the little piles of clothing she'd laid out. He'd packed the night before.

Mom finally snapped the suitcase shut, Dad picked it up, and I followed them downstairs to the kitchen where Joey was drawing a picture.

"M-m-me in a space suit," he said proudly. He held up the picture of a huge guy in a blue suit with a big helmet and black gloves. Next to him stood a yellow rocket with orange flames shooting out from below.

"Great job, Joey," said Mom.

Dad tucked Joey's picture under an Old Man of The Mountain magnet on the refrigerator. Joey's smile spread across his face. Dad put their suitcases in the car. Mom waved at us as the car backed out of the driveway.

We had a three-day weekend because the nuns were attending a retreat in Windham, and Aunt Kathleen was babysitting us. Joey dumped his tinker toys on the living room rug and was busy building a spaceship. I followed Moe upstairs and into the bathroom.

She pulled some small packages out of a little pink pencil case. She leaned over the sink and started dabbing around her right eye and then her left.

She turned around so that I could see. She looked more like fifteen than twelve.

"How do you know how to do this?" I asked.

"I've been practicing when no one's around. I bought some make-up at Mammoth Mills with my babysitting money."

"Mom will kill you if she finds out." I'd heard her tell Moe several times that she wasn't to wear make-up until she was fifteen. She didn't want Moe to be like Linda, the oldest Benson girl who started wearing make-up in eighth grade and now has two kids, is married to a dope, and lives in the project.

I stretched out on my bed and looked out the window. A gray day. I picked up *The Diary of a Young Girl* and tried to imagine how the Donovans would do cooped up in a small hiding place for months with another family.

"Do you like my hair like this?" Moe stood in the doorway. She'd teased her hair into a big puff.

"It's okay," I said, going back to my book. I thought that she looked like Linda, the oldest Benson girl, but I didn't tell her that. Moe was so crabby all the time that I didn't want to argue with her about anything. Ever since she started wearing a bra, she thought that she knew everything. I decided that I'd help Joey with his catechism so she wouldn't be able to bug him about it anymore. And I bet she couldn't even remember what the difference was between a venial and a mortal sin. Once Joey had it memorized, he could ask her about it at dinner. Miss Smarty-Pants. And I was sure I that when Aunt Kathleen arrived, she'd tell Moe to fix her hair and wash her face.

Moe looked at her watch. "Do you want to come down and watch *American Bandstand*?"

"No, thanks," I said.

Two seconds later Moe had Chubby Checker blasting on *American Bandstand*. Anne Frank was writing about how having her period was her own sweet secret. I didn't even need a bra and didn't like reading about Anne Frank's stupid period. I could tell that Moe had started getting periods because I'd see bunches of toilet paper all wadded up in our bathroom wastebasket.

The doorbell rang.

Moe got to the door first. Aunt Kathleen was still wearing her blue and white striped student nurse uniform. Her hair was pulled back in a bun, and she had tiny pearl earrings in her ears.

"I didn't know that you could leave the Sacred Heart wearing your uniform," said Moe.

"I'm not supposed to. But I hustled to catch the Webster bus before Sister Augustine saw me. I couldn't wait to see my favorite kids."

I hated Kathleen riding the Webster bus.

"You know what I did today? I spent most of the day giving shots to kids in the Pediatric Clinic." She turned to my brother. "I stuck big needles into little kids just about your age, Joey." She gave his bottom a pinch, and he shrieked.

"Mom said to tell you that she put clean sheets on their bed for you," said Moe, leading the way up the stairs and acting all-important.

I wished Kathleen hadn't taken the Webster bus. If Sandra Valade's murderer was on it, he might have gotten off to follow Aunt Kathleen because she was so pretty. And he'd have followed her right to our house.

I stopped at the front door and peeked out the window. All I saw was the Callahan's holly hedge and some litter blowing around in the gutter. I slid the dead bolt into place.

3

Kathleen and Moe came downstairs. Kathleen had changed into a red plaid skirt and a black sweater. Moe still had a little bit of eye stuff on and was wearing bright pink lipstick. But her hair was now back up in its ponytail.

"Doesn't Moe look pretty?" asked Kathleen. "I loaned her my lipstick, and we wiped off some of her eyeliner. We don't want every boy in town following her around."

Moe blushed. Aunt Kathleen made everyone feel good.

"Joey, I hear that you are turning into quite the reader," said Aunt Kathleen. "And you and your buddy Paul are going to start training to be altar boys."

Then she turned to me. "And has my brilliant niece Nora decided to be a lawyer or a brain surgeon?"

I was pleased that Aunt Kathleen thought that I was smart.

"I'm good, thanks, Aunt Kathleen. But I don't really know what I want to do." I didn't want Moe making fun of me for thinking that I might be a brain surgeon or a lawyer. Her with her stupid eye make-up.

"Guess what, guys? "

"What?' Moe asked.

"We're having a party tonight."

"Oh, boy!" said Joey.

"Yup. Marcel's coming over for dinner. Oh, and I invited Uncle Danny, too."

"Uncle D-Danny scares me," said Joey.

Uncle Danny kind of scared me too, but Joey could get away with saying this because he was little. And Uncle Danny never brought us presents or had surprises for us like Aunt Kathleen did.

Aunt Kathleen raised her eyebrows at Joey. "It's because Uncle Danny is the youngest brother, just like you. And youngest brothers are always scary!!!" She started tickling Joey until he yelled, "S-s-s-s-stop!"

There was a knock at the door. A tall guy in a navy-blue jacket stood there, holding a bunch of pink carnations.

"Are these for me, Marcel? Thank you." Aunt Kathleen took the flowers and kissed him on the cheek.

Marcel was so handsome that I felt a little nervous. He had brown eyes and dark brown hair and smiled like someone on a toothpaste commercial. I hoped that he was nice. I'd feel terrible if Aunt Kathleen married someone mean. Like Mr. Callahan. Or Uncle Danny.

Marcel looked at me and Moe. "Wow, Kathleen. You're right. You have the most beautiful nieces in the world." He saw Joey's drawing on the refrigerator. "Did you draw this?" he asked.

Joey nodded and looked at the floor.

"Well, guess what? We're going to get along just fine because I work at a place called Sanders. It's in Nashua, and I work on equipment for the space program."

Joey's eyes went wide. "Do you know President Kennedy?"

"Well not yet," laughed Marcel.

"Joey, Marcel will probably be getting phone calls night and day once Kennedy finds out how smart he is. But right now, he works only part-time because he's in school." Kathleen planted a big kiss on Marcel's lips.

We stared at them, caught in their magic. They were like the Kennedys.

A car pulled into the driveway, its radio blaring.

"It's Danny," said Kathleen.

"I figured as much," laughed Marcel.

"Hey, sis," said Danny, as he opened the door. "Oh, I didn't know that Joe College was going to be here, too. I thought it was just going to be family." His voice was kind of slurred.

"In 1963, Marcel will be family," said Kathleen.

"Yeah, but it's only 1961 now. Kind of pushing things, I'd say."

Aunt Kathleen acted like she didn't hear. "Kids, would you please set the table?"

"I bought beer, if anyone wants one."

"Water is good for me," said Kathleen. "Dan, are you sure you don't want water?"

"I'll have a beer." Uncle Dan shot my aunt a dirty look.

"I'll have one too, Dan. Thanks," said Marcel.

Aunt Kathleen said nothing as she doled out the spaghetti.

Danny slid a beer over to Marcel. He looked closely at Moe. "Well, well, Miss Moe. Is that eye make-up you're wearing? You must've known I was coming over tonight." Dan leaned back in his chair and turned to Marcel. "I have that effect on the ladies. They like to look good around me."

Moe blushed and looked like she was going to cry. I didn't blame her. Uncle Danny was so embarrassing.

"Dan, stop that now," said Kathleen. "Right now."

"Oh heck, I forgot the French bread," said Marcel.

Danny laughed. "Marcel, if anyone at this table could remember French bread, it should've been you." Little bits of sauce sprayed out of his mouth as he spoke.

The rest of us stopped eating, not knowing what to say. Marcel acted as if nothing had happened.

"Okay, okay. No hard feelings, man," said Danny. "It's just sort of a Manchester joke that the Irish and the French don't marry."

"Marcel and I are breaking that trend, aren't we, sweetie?" Kathleen smiled at Marcel.

Marcel had no chance to answer because Uncle Danny started talking again. "Well, the Irish and the French, it's not like it is with the niggers and whites, oh pardon me, nee-grows and whites. Do you know that I've been reading in the *Union Leader* that some nee-grow preacher is trying to force white colleges to take in nee-grow students?"

"His name is Martin Luther King," said Aunt Kathleen. "He's a good man."

"Well, I just want to say that we're lucky that Marcel is working at a place that makes weapons because there'll be trouble here if Martin what's his name decides to let nee-grow kids into our schools. We'll need weapons because that ain't going to happen."

Marcel wiped his mouth with his napkin. "Dan, we already have a few negro students at Saint Anselm's. One of them is a friend of mine. Nice guy."

Dan chugged down his beer, pushed his chair back, and stood up. "Kathleen, thanks for dinner." I looked at his plate. He'd eaten only one-and-one-half meatballs and hadn't touched his spaghetti. "Marcel, I'm sure you're a good guy even though you're a Frenchie and you hang out with nee-grows." He turned to Kathleen. "I want you to note that I used the right word: I said nee-grows. But I just don't know what this family is coming to, what with you liking Martin what's-his-name and marrying folks from the West Side."

Kathleen stood up. "I'll tell you what's happening. Our family is getting bigger and better. It's 1961, dear brother, and the times are changing. So, if you're through, feel free to leave." She walked him to the door. "You'd better drive carefully, because if you get stopped, you'll be in trouble."

She came back to the kitchen table and leaned against Marcel. "I'm sorry," she said.

He put an arm around her waist. "Danny will come around. But the best thing about Danny leaving is, more ice cream for us! Joe, help me clear the plates. We'll give the girls a rest."

"Goody!" yelled Joey. He grabbed my plate, dropping my fork on the floor.

"If only he didn't drink," I heard Aunt Kathleen murmur to Marcel. "When he's sober, you couldn't meet a better guy."

I remembered hearing those words a few times before. They were what Dad said to Mom any time she got mad at Uncle Danny.

When my parents returned on Sunday, Moe's face was scrubbed clean of make-up, and we'd agreed not tell them that Uncle Danny was out of sorts when he came for dinner. "We all have bad days sometimes, and we don't like people talking about us," Aunt Kathleen said.

"Nice to go away, but it's even nicer to come home," said Mom as she kissed each one of us. "And Dad and I bought presents for you kids."

I couldn't wait. It would be the first time that I'd gotten a present from a foreign country.

Mom handed Joey his gift first. It was the biggest and its brown paper bag was taped closed. Joey ripped the bag open and pulled out a Sergeant Preston hat. He put it on. It was a little big, but Joey didn't care.

"Do you remember the show, Joey?" asked Dad.

"It was my favorite," said Joey.

"Joey, Dad is sort of like Sergeant Preston. They say that 'the Mounties always get their man.' Well, Detective Tom Donovan of the Manchester Police Department is just like a Mountie. He'll always get his man." Mom threw Dad a big smile.

I wasn't so sure. Sandra Valade's killer could still be taking the Webster bus and have his eye on Moe or me. But I didn't say anything.

Mom handed Moe and me each a small box. I opened mine and saw a black lacy thing. I couldn't figure it out. Moe grabbed hers and ran to the mirror over the mantel. "A mantilla," she exclaimed. "Just like Jackie Kennedy."

"Let me help you with it," said Aunt Kathleen. "You need a bobby pin." She pulled one from her hair and fastened Moe's mantilla.

"Nora, let me help you." She pushed me over to the mirror, put the veil on my head, and bobby-pinned it. "Beautiful!' she exclaimed.

And for that moment, I felt like I was. Beautiful.

4

Sister Margaret told me to stop daydreaming.

"Miss Donovan, if your arithmetic problems are done, please take this note down to Sister Lucinda's office." She handed me a piece of pink notepaper that she stapled closed. As if I'd peek at whatever message she wanted me to give Sister Lucinda.

After I delivered the note, I heard noise coming from upstairs.

Sister Boniface, the scariest teacher at All Saints', stood at the top of the stairs. She'd grabbed a fourth-grade boy named Bruce Therrian by the collar and gave him a push. Our eyes met as he tumbled down the stairs. He screamed when he hit the floor, grabbing his crooked arm. Sister flew down the stairs, her veil streaming out behind her. She ran right past Bruce. She came over to me and leaned down until her face was a few inches from mine. Little white hairs sprouted on her chin.

"If you tell anyone about this, Miss Donovan, you'll rue the day you were born," she whispered. Her face was white and pinched, and her eyes were like flat gray stones.

It scared me that she knew my name. She marched over to Bruce. "Stop crying, Mr. Therrian. It serves you right that you fell down the stairs. You were fooling around when you should've been listening."

She turned to me. "Miss Donovan, go to the principal's office and have Sister Lucinda call Bruce's mother. Tell her that Bruce was playing on the stairs and fell down."

Detest. Peril. Rue. I hated those words. And I hated that I was going to lie for Sister Boniface.

Bruce looked up as I went to tell Sister Lucinda that he fell while playing on the stairs and to please call his mother.

I never liked Bruce very much, but I felt ashamed when he showed up at school two days later wearing a cast. I was glad that he wasn't in my grade, so I didn't have to face him.

But I started including Bruce as well as President Kennedy in my morning prayers about *peril*. "Dear God, please help Dad catch Sandra's murderer. Dear God, please make Bruce's arm heal quickly. Dear God, please keep the Russians away from us." I threw the Russians in to be safe, but I wasn't as worried about them as much as I was worried about Dad catching Sandra's killer. That is, until they sent a man into space.

Joey was thrilled by the Russian space flight, but it was only because he didn't know the difference between good astronauts and bad astronauts. And he didn't understand about *peril*.

Dad stayed low key about it, showing Joey pictures of the rocket in the *Union Leader*. "The Russian scientists figured out a way to shoot the rocket up and allow it to break off pieces it didn't need so it wouldn't be carrying around a lot of extra weight when it landed," he explained.

I didn't understand, and I am sure that Joey didn't either. I just knew that our Irish Catholic President with his beautiful wife had let us down. Americans, not the Russians, were supposed to be leading the frontier into space.

Then Kennedy let us down again. He helped Cuban rebels who wanted to get rid of Castro invade part of Cuba. But Castro stopped them. I began to worry that our Catholic president was not all he was cracked up to be.

"Is Russia going to attack us?" I asked Dad after checking to make sure Joey wasn't around. Dad looked at me over the paper.

"I really doubt it, hon," he said. But he didn't say he was sure that they wouldn't.

"I think that they figure that we're weak because we snuck up on them and they beat us."

"Don't borrow trouble, Nora. The people that got defeated were Cubans who came here to get away from Castro. We sent in some men and supplied them, but we didn't attack them with the full force of the US military."

I was still worried. That night on the news, President Kennedy said that he was responsible for the defeat in the Bay of Pigs.

The reporters shouted questions at Kennedy. They sounded mad.

"Is this a *peril*?" I asked. "Dad said Loeb thinks the president is a Communist."

"Good word, Nora," said Mom. "It could be perilous, but I'm not going to worry, no matter what Mr. Loeb says. Our president is no Communist, and I trust that he will do the right thing."

Mom could trust all she wanted to, but I worried. Big missiles with nuclear warheads were just a few miles from Florida. Politicians and priests were telling us to build bomb shelters. My parents started a pantry in the cellar with canned food, bottled water, and blankets.

"It's always a good idea to have extra supplies," Mom said. "And we save money by buying cases of food instead of just buying a few things at a time."

She made Joey write the dates that we bought food on little pieces of scrap paper and then tape them on all the cans. I knew that her talk about saving money was not the real reason she and Dad and other neighborhood parents were hoarding food in their cellars. They were planning on using their cellars as bomb shelters in case the Russians attacked us. The adults were afraid of Russia, and we kids weren't supposed to know.

5

In May, Kennedy began to look better. Alan Shepherd, in Freedom 7, became the first American in space. The country went wild.

"No longer will we be trailing the Russkies," Dad crowed. "America is going to be leading the world in space exploration."

"I can't wait to talk to Marcel about this and see what he thinks," said Mom. "Imagine, the first American in space is from Derry, New Hampshire, right down the road from us." She turned to Joey, "And your soon-to-be Uncle Marcel may have worked on Freedom 7. This is amazing for New Hampshire and amazing for the world!"

"Will Marcel come to my First Communion?" Joey asked.

"Oh honey, we can invite only our immediate family. The church isn't big enough to hold everyone's relatives."

Joey's face fell. "F-Father Smith told me that Sister Edwina said that I knew my catechism better than anyone in the class."

"Joey, that's wonderful. I'll be sure to tell Marcel. He'll be proud of you." Mom shot a glance at me and Moe. "I don't recall hearing that either of your sisters were the best in their catechism class."

Moe was reading a magazine and didn't hear. I rolled my eyes at Mom.

I was glad that Joey was doing so well in his First Communion class, but I knew he wouldn't be if I hadn't forced him to memorize the answers to the questions the nuns fired at us from the *Baltimore Catechism*. Why did God make you? God made me to know, love, and serve him in this world. What was Lucifer's sin? Lucifer's sin was the sin of pride. Pride was the sin I'd committed in second grade and got yelled at by the priest and ended having to say a rosary as penance. I thought God seemed a bit mean, punishing people forever in Hell. And sticking unbaptized babies in Limbo made no sense to me.

6

It was sunny and warm the morning of Joey's First Communion. Except for Joey, the Donovan family looked like the Kennedys. In the front seat Dad was hatless, and Mom wore her white pillbox. In the back, Moe and I wore our mantillas fastened with bobby pins as instructed by Aunt Kathleen. WKBR was on, and they played their little Sunday jingle urging Manchester to go to church.

We got there early so we could get a good seat. I put my white gloves under the little clasps meant for them and got on my knees. The plastic under my knees was all cracked and felt scratchy, and I knew that Mom would be mad if she ruined another pair of nylon stockings on All Saints' ratty kneelers.

The organ sounded and the little kids, led by Sister Edwina, paraded down the aisle. The congregation craned their necks, and bulbs flashed from big cameras. The parish priests filled the row behind the little kids. Then came the sisters, their veils forming big squares on top of their heads. It took them a few minutes to get into their pews, so there was a line of nuns waiting to be seated. Then I saw the flat gray eyes.

It was Sister Boniface. I thought that my heart was going to stop. She gave me a thin, mean smile. When I dared to look up again, she had disappeared into the sea of black veils.

7

Dad worked a lot of evenings. He'd hunch over the phone, pulling its curly long cord as far away from us as possible so we couldn't hear what he was saying. I knew that he was talking about Sandra Valade's killer. They still hadn't found the guy.

That summer Mom started back at work part-time in Labor and Delivery at Sacred Heart Hospital. "Tom, I'm so happy working with the young mothers. And it's magical to watch a child being born."

Mom going back to work gave us so much freedom. She gave us permission to bike up to Livingston Pool if Moe and I kept an eye on Joey, and we agreed to lock our bikes. We'd swim all afternoon and if we had any money, stop off at the take-out window of the Puritan at 4:00 o'clock when afternoon swim ended. There'd be a bunch of kids in wet bathing suits, towels wrapped around their waists, waiting in the take-out line for ice cream cones or curly French fries. We'd hang out in the hot parking lot licking our cones or chowing down on fries, laughing with our friends and careful to move away from boys like Billy Sweeney who liked to snap his wet towel at girls' legs.

School started the day after Labor Day. I was in fourth grade with Sister Callista. She let us go down to the washrooms in the basement once in the morning and once in the afternoon. If we thought we might wet our pants, she'd let us go down with a partner but made it clear that we were not to be getting up and leaving the classroom willy-nilly. "Well-regulated bladders make for well-regulated souls," she told us. The girls' bathroom was dark and disgusting, and I would have rather wet my pants than go down there alone. As our class hurried up the stairs one morning after our bathroom break, a priest who looked like Father Smith passed me going down the stairs. A short boy from the eighth grade was with him. I wondered why he was going down to the yucky kids' bathrooms instead of using the nice bathroom the nuns had on the first floor.

8

Joey was excited about altar boy training. He and his buddy Paul had joined Youth Fellowship, some sort of boys' club held at the rectory. Between going to the rectory and practicing his breathing exercises, he stayed busy.

"Okay, Moe. Do you know how altar boys use their right and left hands on the altar?"

Moe looked up, bored. Mom turned to Joe. "Honey, I have been going to Mass my whole life and I never once noticed how altar boys moved their hands."

"When we hand stuff to the priest, we use our right hand. When we take stuff from the priest, we use our left hand."

"We'll have to tell Auntie about all the things you're learning when we bring our Christmas gift to her down at Windham Castle," said Mom.

"W-why do they call it a Castle?" asked Joey. "It d-doesn't look like one to me."

"Joey, please talk more slowly. Try again, with no stuttering," said Mom.

I saw Joey's tummy pouch out a little as he took a deep breath. Then he laughed.

"What's so funny?" I asked.

"I forgot what my question was!"

"You wanted to know why Windham Castle is called Windham Castle," said Mom. "You should ask Auntie when we visit."

"I'll bet she won't know. She doesn't even know how to pronounce Windham. She calls it Win-ham," said Moe.

"Maureen, Auntie is over seventy and does very well for a woman her age." Mom got annoyed if we said anything bad about Auntie. I didn't know why. We all knew that she got on Mom's nerves.

When we drove into the parking lot, I could see how someone would call Windham a castle.

"They've renovated it and taken down some of the stuff that made it look like a castle," said Dad. He pointed to the back of the building. "You can see there used to be an old turret over there."

Auntie was waiting for us in the foyer. "Helen, I'm so happy you brought the family to visit."

"Auntie, it's good to see you." Mom kissed Auntie on the cheek.

"Merry Christmas from our family" said Moe handing Auntie a gift-wrapped package.

"Thank you. Should I open it now?"

"Why don't you save it for Christmas," suggested Mom.

"I'll do that. Sister Stephen's family always puts up a beautiful Christmas tree in her room that she shares with all of us. I'll put my gift under her tree." Auntie turned to Moe. "Sister Stephen and I were novices together decades ago and we've been friends ever since. Maureen, do you ever think that you might have a vocation?"

Dad turned his head to the side so Auntie wouldn't notice him laughing.

Moe took a deep breath. "Auntie, I've never thought that."

"Well, you never know, my dear. Many are called but few are chosen."

Auntie led us into a parlor. A novice came in and offered us cookies and cocoa. Mom told Auntie that Joey wanted to know why her building was called a castle.

Auntie perked right up. "Joseph, a rich English gentlemen built this castle at the turn of the century. It's an exact replica of a castle in Oxford, England." She sipped her cocoa. "But the family couldn't afford to keep it up. So, the sisters bought it about twenty years ago. Part of the original building had to be torn down because it was dangerous."

"Wow," said Joey. "That's cool."

It was dark by the time we piled into the car. "Dad, was the guy who built Windham Castle a Catholic?" asked Moe.

"I don't think New Hampshire had Catholics rich enough to be building castles at the turn of the century." Dad smiled and looked at Moe in the rear-view mirror. "I think that the only thing a Catholic would be doing in an English castle at the turn of the century would be sitting in a dungeon or scrubbing pots and pans." We all laughed.

"Tom, on the way home let's drive up Elm Street," said Mom. "The Christmas lights are up, and it'll be fun to see them for the first time this year."

"But we'll still get to do the Christmas walk, won't we?" asked Joey.

"Of course," Mom replied. "I can't imagine Christmas without the Christmas walk."

The lights grew brighter as we approached Elm Street's shopping area. Every store window was decorated for Christmas. We drove by angels, Santa Clauses, choirboys, nutcrackers, and Christmas trees.

"Elm and Hanover is coming up," called Dad.

We craned our necks to see what special light display would overhang this major intersection. A huge star in white lights dangled in the night sky above our heads. It was beautiful.

"Manchester has outdone itself this year," exclaimed Mom.

"Helen, you say that every year," laughed Dad. He leaned over and kissed her on the cheek.

1962

"…Five…Four…Three…Two…One… BLASTOFF!" Joey jumped off the couch, his toy rocket orbiting above his head. He was super annoying sometimes. I knew that he loved space, but it would be nice if he had other interests. He didn't play with other kids very often, and I knew it worried Mom and Dad. He told me that when he stuttered, kids made fun of him.

Joey didn't stutter as often since he started speech therapy. Except when he was nervous or excited, and then his stuttering got much worse.

"J-J-John Glenn is the greatest astronaut EVER," shouted Joey.

"Didn't you say that about Alan Shepard last year?" I asked.

My father picked Joey up and spun him around. "Joseph Donovan, did the good sisters let you watch the launch in school today?"

"Yes. It was amazing! Glenn went around the earth three times and was in space for five hours."

"I hate to burst your bubble, but the Russians are way ahead of us with their space program."

I watched Joey's face fall.

"Don't get me wrong, young man. What Glenn did today was a great accomplishment," said Dad. "I just meant that he wasn't the first to do it—that's all."

My brother looked like he lost his best friend, which would be really bad. He only had one friend. Paul.

"Glenn is a genius. His automatic control system failed, and he managed to steer his capsule safely into the Atlantic while traveling hundreds of miles an hour. That's more than the Russians have done."

Joey looked at me. "Did you know that astronaut means 's-s-star sailors'? And cosmonaut means 'sailors of the universe'? And s-s-someday I'm going to be the best star sailor in the world."

I didn't know any of that. "You'll be a great astronaut, Joey," I said.

"America has a lot of heroes out there, kids. Not just astronauts, but priests who sacrifice their lives in places like the Belgian Congo. And doctors and nurses like your Mom." He gave her a wink. "Then there are professional athletes who break records and are good role models for kids. They're all heroes in their own way."

Dad was a big sports fan. Baseball, football, basketball, he loved them all. "Hey, kids! They said it could never be done. Wilt-the-Stilt Chamberlain scored over 100 points last night. The Warriors killed the Knicks." He laughed. "That's what being seven feet tall will do for you."

Joey didn't like sports and neither did Moe. She used to, but now she was too busy looking at herself in the mirror and flipping through magazines. I liked sports a lot. And Dad liked that I liked sports.

The Celtics were his favorite team, but if they weren't playing, he pretty much watched any team and any sport. Bill Russell was his favorite Celtic. "He's not just a star basketball player, Nora, he's a gentleman. The guy has it all."

Baseball came a close second to basketball, but the Red Sox always seemed to break Dad's heart. One night Uncle Danny came over to watch the Red Sox play the Orioles. We waited for the national anthem and the first pitch. "The Red Sox haven't won the World's Series since 1918 when they beat the Cubs in six games," said Dad.

A bunch of Brockton high school kids sang the national anthem. "The problem is the pitching." Uncle Danny paused and spread some Cheese Whiz on a cracker. "Three of the starters have an ERA of over 5.00. It's impossible to win games with lousy pitching."

"I have a good feeling about this year, Dan. With Yastrzemski in left and Malzone on third, it'll be hard for hitters to go long on that side of the field."

"You're crazy to start talking about the World Series this early in the season," said Uncle Danny. "The Sox always fall apart after the All-Star break, you know that."

"Did I tell you how mad Callahan got last week?" asked Dad. "When the Sox couldn't even squeak out one run in the rubber match against the Yankees, he put his foot through the TV screen and blew the picture tube!" said Dad.

Uncle Danny laughed, nearly choking. "Yeah, but at least they have a strong closer this year. Tough to hit Radatz when he's on the mound." Danny pulled another Ballantine out of his bag.

The game went into extra innings, before the Orioles won. But only by one run. I knew I'd be tired the next day but staying up late and sitting with Dad on the couch made me feel special, so it was worth it.

2

Friday was fish day. Sometimes Dad treated us to fried haddock and French fries from Frye's Fish Market. Catholics weren't supposed to eat meat on Fridays. They didn't have to eat fish. They just couldn't eat meat.

"Jesus sacrificed his flesh for us on Good Friday, boys and girls. To honor His sacrifice, we deny ourselves the pleasure of eating meat on Fridays," said Sister Callista.

"Dad, why can't we eat meatloaf and pork chops on Friday, but it's okay to eat fish? Don't fish have flesh?" I watched Mom dump a can of salmon and a can of peas into a pot for supper. Then she added a can of Campbell's Cream of Mushroom soup. I looked away because I thought I was going to throw up.

"You're too smart for your own britches, Nora." Dad opened the kitchen window. I guessed that he didn't like the smell of the salmon either. "Fish do have flesh, but they are cold-blooded, and cows and pigs are warm blooded. Jesus was also warm blooded, so that's why we don't eat any warm-blooded flesh on Fridays."

Joey wandered into the kitchen looking for a snack. He stopped and pitched his nose. "Ewwww…What's that smell?" Nobody answered.

"Well, reptiles are cold-blooded. Could we eat alligators and snapping turtles on Friday?" asked Moe.

Dad sighed. "Now you're being ridiculous. Just accept the fact that on Fridays the Donovan household sticks to eating fish, for heaven's sake. Abstinence from eating meat is supposed to be a form of penance, and a little penance won't kill any of us."

"But how can it be penance if you like eating fish? I thought penance was supposed to be punishment," I asked.

Dad groaned and put his face in his hands. "Helen, what do you say we save your delicious salmon and peas for another night and treat ourselves to Frye's tonight?"

"That's fine, Tom. But we can't waste food. We'll have to eat it over the weekend. Think of the poor children starving in China. They'd be happy to eat my salmon and peas." Mom covered the pot and put it in the refrigerator.

I went with Dad to Frye's. The line was long. Every Catholic family in Manchester must have decided to get fish and chips. My stomach growled when I smelled the grease. The teenage boy at the window loaded up our cardboard boats with fish and fries and handed Dad a big paper bag. By the time we got home our car smelled like the restaurant.

We set the table with ketchup and malt vinegar. Dad said he'd learned about putting vinegar on his fries when he was in the Air Force in England. The rest of us liked ketchup and poured pools of it into the middle of our plates so it was easier to dip our fish and fries. I gave my tartar sauce to Dad because I didn't like mayonnaise.

I wondered why Dad didn't answer my question earlier. How could eating Frye's delicious fish be penance? Now eating Mom's canned salmon and peas, that would be in the penance department for sure.

3

The phone rang. It was Dad. Mom answered and began to whisper. And when she whispered, I always knew something was wrong. "Oh Tom, no. Really? That's terrible," was all that I could hear.

"Dad won't be home for supper tonight, kids. How about grilled cheese and tomato soup?"

"Mom, what's up with Dad?" I asked.

"Something's come up at the station."

"What?"

"All I can tell you is that he's meeting with a detective from Boston. Now finish up and help me with the dishes. Then you can watch *Rawhide* before bed." I had a nervous feeling in my stomach when we went to bed at 9:30 and Dad still wasn't home.

I heard coffee percolating in the pot when I opened my eyes the next morning. I knew Dad was home because Mom just drank tea. She said coffee stains your teeth.

"Dad, why were you late last night?" I asked as he leaned over to give me a hug.

"I had some business to discuss with a detective from the Boston PD."

"Boston?" I asked.

"Yes. A woman was strangled there, and they asked me to look at the crime scene photos.

I must have looked worried because he hugged me again. "Don't you worry. The police will find the killer and put him behind bars." I wasn't so sure I could believe him since Sandra's murderer still hadn't been caught.

"Was she on the side of the road like a rag doll?" I asked. I thought about the *Union Leader's* pictures of Sandra.

"No, she was at home." He stared out the window sipping his coffee. Dad told us we'd always be safe at home. But that woman in Boston sure wasn't.

I was terrified listening to the news that night. Reporter John Henning said that Anna Slesers was a mother. She was supposed to be at a church memorial service. "But Anna Slesers became a victim," said Henning.

I got really scared when he said that her blue bathrobe was ripped open, and she was strangled with its belt—he left it tied around her neck in a bow. What kind of sick person would do such a thing?

Her son was interviewed. "My mother didn't have any enemies." Just like Sandra, I thought.

A few days later at recess, Missy, Patty and I got together. "Have your dads said anything about the murder in Boston?" I asked.

"My father told me that it was probably just a random killing. He said that there's no evidence that it has anything to do with the Valade murder," said Patty.

"My dad said pretty much the same thing. I heard him telling my mom that Detective Donovan is the only one that thinks that the murders could be related," added Missy.

My dad was way smarter than Missy's and Patty's dads and if he thought the killer was the same guy, I knew that he was probably right.

By the end of June, three more Boston women were found strangled in their homes. They were all much older than Sandra. By the end of summer, there were two more to add to the list.

After Sandra's body was found, Dad said that she'd put herself in danger walking alone at night on a dark road. He said that I was safe because I was at home every night. But these Boston women got murdered in their own homes. Why was I safe when they were not?

I forgot all about Aunt Kathleen's plaid notebook until I felt it in the back of my underwear drawer. I pulled it out and decided to use it to keep track of the murdered women and the dates and cities where they were murdered. I began with Sandra Valade in 1960. I remembered that she was murdered during the winter, but I wasn't sure of the month. But I knew the place. Manchester, New Hampshire. I wrote down Anna Sleser's name, date, and place that she was killed. But I didn't know the names of the other Boston women who were murdered, so I left a big space so I could fill it in later. I thought that I could help Dad if I found a pattern. I tucked the notebook under my mattress so nobody would find it.

The Boston Police were certain that the Massachusetts murders were committed by the same person. "The victims were all single, all killed in their homes, all strangled by pieces of their own clothing." The killer became known as "The Boston Strangler." As near as I could tell, the Boston killings had nothing in common with Sandra's murder. Did Dad still think that they were related? I hoped not. And if he was wrong about this, he could be wrong about a lot of things. Moe and I might not be safe after all.

I felt sorry for the murdered women. And for their families. But all the attention on Boston didn't do anything to help Sandra.

4

Dad turned on the news. Hundreds of soldiers, negroes, and white people were fighting in front of a big brick building. The headline at the top of the screen said "Riots Break Out at Ole Miss."

"What's going on?" I asked.

"We'll talk about it when the news is over," sighed Dad. I watched in silence as police attacked the crowd with clubs.

He turned off the TV. "Nora, this is about a young man named James Meredith who wants to go to the University of Mississippi.

He's been rejected twice because he's a negro. They only admit white people."

"That's not fair, Dad." I thought about how the Irish were treated when they came to America and how Uncle Danny and Aunt Kathleen talked about "nee-grows" and Martin Luther King Jr. at supper when our parents were in Montreal.

"And it's not legal either. James Meredith's case went all the way up to the US Supreme Court, and they said it was illegal to keep him out." Dad stretched his arms over his head. "Kennedy sent in thousands of soldiers to protect Meredith when he enrolled. Imagine, the first negro ever to attend Ole Miss." He looked back at the television. "And we haven't seen the end of this sort of thing. It's about time negroes get treated equally and the violence stops."

Moe had just finished *To Kill a Mockingbird* when I crawled into bed. "What's it about?" I asked.

"A white lawyer and his kids live in the south. Their mom died and they got a negro housekeeper." She yawned. "Atticus is the father, and he defends a negro named Tom Robinson who is accused of abusing a young white girl." It gave me chills.

"Atticus gave the court lots of reasons why Tom could not have been responsible for abusing the girl. He thought that the girl's own father was guilty, but Atticus lost the trial. Tom got killed and then the girl's father got killed."

"Why read it if it's so unhappy?" I asked.

"Because there are a lot of good lessons to learn. When you're old enough, you should read it too."

I was sick of learning lessons after people died. Why couldn't we just learn stuff without people getting killed?

5

I kept thinking about the blue bow the Strangler put around that woman's neck. It scared me that he wanted to dress her up like a clown. I wondered what her bedroom looked like. Did she have a mannequin that she used when she sewed ladies' dresses?

"Nora Donovan, stop your day-dreaming right now." Sister's voice cut the air.

"Yes, Sister."

When she looked away, I glanced at the clock just as the dismissal bell rang.

I met Moe and Joey on the front steps of All Saints'. It was pelting rain and the wind was whipping. "Let's head down to Moreau's and catch the bus," she said. I hadn't taken the bus since Valade's murder, telling Moe every time it rained that I liked walking home and jumping over puddles. But it was so windy I was afraid that I'd get knocked over, so I pulled up my jacket collar and ran after her and Joe.

We could barely squeeze onto the bus. Moe and Joe got the last two seats near the front, and I got pushed to the back and stood in the aisle hanging on to the back of someone's seat trying not to fall as it jerked its way up Maple Street. I looked around. A nasty-looking man with a gray beard smiled at me, but I pretended I didn't see him. Big boys crowded in the aisle, and I was afraid that I'd miss my stop and end up getting kicked off the bus at the VA because I didn't have money to return downtown. In the seat next to where I was standing, a man my dad's age with a plaid hat was reading a folded-up newspaper.

"Nora! It's our stop!" I heard Moe calling me. She must have known I wouldn't know where to get off if I didn't have a window seat. "OK," I yelled. I just wanted her to shut up.

The man in the plaid hat looked up at me. "So this is your stop, Nora," he smiled.

I didn't smile back. The bus pulled to the curb. I pushed my way through the big boys and jumped out. Moe and Joey were running through the rain ahead of me.

I didn't like how the guy was so friendly to me. And it scared me that he knew my name and where my stop was.

6

Sister Magnus was nice, but some kids made fun of her. Behind her back, Donny Crotty called her Sister Maytag because she was chubby like a washing machine. From her armpits to her knees, her body went straight down. And to make matters worse, she was short so she kind of did look like a washing machine.

Sister Maytag reminded me of *Queen for a Day*, a show where the Queen would win a Magtag appliance. Each show started with Jack Bailey introducing four women and asking, "Would YOU like to be Queen for the Day?" The ladies took turns telling sad stories. The lady with the saddest story was crowned *Queen for the Day*. The queen received a crown, a cape, and a wand. And a really big prize.

One lady told the story of her house burning down, trapping her husband and her cat. When the fire department arrived, the house collapsed, killing them both. "That poor woman certainly deserves to win," said Mom. Jack Bailey ran down the aisle and put a jeweled crown on her head, a velvet cape around her shoulders, and led her to a fancy throne. She sobbed when she was told that she won a new Maytag washer and dryer. But I wondered where she was going to put them.

Sister Magnus was so wide that the boys took bets on how many giant beaded rosaries had to be hooked together to make it around her waist. The only way to figure it out was to count the beads and so a bunch of kids made a bet.

"Mister Demos," Sister's voice boomed. "What are you staring at? Everyone knew that he was counting the beads on the front of Sister's waist.

"Nothing, Sister," said Teddy. "I was just thinking."

"Thinking would be a first for you, wouldn't it Mr. Demos?" Sister asked.

At recess, we all giggled about what kind of sin we would have to confess to have the priest say, "For your penance, say two rosaries—Sister Magnus' rosaries." We laughed at the thought of spending the whole day praying our way around the beads on Sister Magnus' rosary belt. Marilyn Marchand said she peed her pants she was laughing so hard.

"You'd probably have to murder someone to get stuck with a Magnus rosary penance," Jane Longley said. I thought of the time I had to say a rosary for committing the sin of pride a when I was little. It took forever just to say one rosary. To get stuck with two Magnus rosaries, you'd have to be at the altar rail most of the day. It might be better just to go to hell.

7

"Kids, get down here now," Mom yelled. We raced into the living room in time to hear the guy on the news say, "We continue this news hour and will pre-empt regular television programming with an important message from the President of the United States."

President Kennedy sat in the Oval Office at his Resolute desk. He took a slow, deep breath before he told us that there was "unmistakable evidence that a series of offensive missile sites is now in preparation on that imprisoned island."

"Cuba," Dad mouthed.

The President talked about the missile sites, but all I heard was nuclear strike…western hemisphere…one-thousand-mile range…Washington DC… He didn't use the word *peril* or *evil*, but I was old enough to know that was what he was talking about.

"Girls, why don't you take your brother out to the kitchen for some ice cream," said Mom as her head nodded toward Joey. His eyes were as big as nickels.

"Wait, Mom. We want to know what's going on!" Moe sounded upset.

Dad cleared his throat. "Okay, kids. Castro is in Cuba. Everyone knows he's in cahoots with Russia. They are trying to spread Communism all over the world and they think the United States is a threat to them."

"Think?" My mother's voice was soft.

"They set up missiles in Cuba that can hit American cities. That's what the President is so concerned about," Dad continued.

"Why do they care if we are Communists or not?" I asked. "Can't they be Communists and just mind their own beeswax?"

"That's the point, Nora. They don't want to mind their own beeswax. They want to control everyone just like they do in Russia." Dad paused.

Mom sighed and shook her head. "They don't reward people for hard work. Everyone gets the same."

"Kids, how would you like it if we were playing a family game of Monopoly and all the money, houses, and hotels were divided equally among the players?" Dad asked.

"That wouldn't be fair," said Moe. "Everyone knows that the blue properties like Boardwalk and Park Place are worth more than the yellow and green ones. And nobody wants to give up the money they earn."

"Exactly my point, Moe," said Dad. "But with Communism that's what would happen. Don't you worry." Dad stood up and tousled Joey's hair. "No matter what, we'll keep you guys safe. That's why I built the shelter in the basement last year. I pray to God that we never have to use it."

Dad was always telling us not to worry. But whoever killed Sandra was still on the loose. And if Dad is praying that we don't have to use our bomb shelter, maybe he's worried we'll have to.

At All Saints', Sister Lucinda got on the PA and called everyone into the gym. "On your knees, faculty, boys and girls." Here we go again, I thought to myself. "Let us pray to our Lord, Jesus Christ," she began. "Mighty God, please deliver us from the Cuban peril and grant us the blessings of a safe new day. We are eternally grateful for Your great love and protection. Amen."

Everyone started to rise but quickly fell back on their knees when Sister continued, "Boys and girls, please offer a silent prayer to our Lord that he guides President Kennedy." I looked around and most of the other kids were fidgeting, probably trying to come up with something to say to the Lord that we hadn't already said.

The next day Kennedy sent American war ships to surround Cuba so Russian delivery ships couldn't get through. Khrushchev offered Kennedy a deal that if he removed the missiles, Kennedy would have to swear never to invade Cuba. By Sunday, our prayers were answered. The missiles were gone and the Donovans didn't have to sleep in our bomb shelter.

8

My parents called a family meeting. Nothing good ever came out of family meetings. They usually ended up with jobs for the kids.

"Kids, we want to do something different for Christmas this year. We had a speaker at the Holy Name Society who asked us all to adopt an under-privileged family for Christmas," said Dad. "The speaker was from Catholic Charities, an organization that has been helping the needy for many years."

"Are they coming to live with us?" asked Moe.

I sure hoped not.

"Oh, no. The family that got assigned to us lives in Kentucky in a coal mining town." Dad opened an envelope and took out photos of the family. Two parents and three kids sat on the steps of a one-room shack that looked close to falling down. Another photo was taken on the inside where there was a dirt floor with just a ratty old rug on it. "Meet the Bailey family. Perley and Ruthie are the parents. The kid's names are James, Paul, and Maggie." We all stared at their faces without saying a word. Their eyes were dull. And they had really crummy teeth.

"They look like the Beverly Hillbillies," said Joe. Except no black oil, Texas tea for the Baileys I thought.

"What we'd like to do is ask Santa to skip the Donovan house this year. We can all go down to Zyla's Auction House and buy gifts for the Bailey family. Chances are, there won't be much of a Christmas for them otherwise." Joey was in the third grade, and he still believed in Santa Claus. Billy Sweeney ruined it for me in the second grade when he announced that there was no such thing as Santa Claus. I didn't mind knowing the truth. I could never understand why Santa had his favorites, and rich kids got mountains of gifts while poor kids like Donald Morse were lucky if they got new socks and maybe a winter hat and mittens.

We were all okay with giving up Christmas and looked forward to shopping for the Baileys.

Going to Zyla's Auction House was always a treat. Ceiling to floor, the shelves were filled with games and toys. It was hard walking up and down the aisles looking for the perfect gift for someone you'd never met. I was told to buy gifts for Maggie who had just turned eleven. I chose Parcheesi and Chinese Checkers. And a hairbrush with a matching mirror.

We put our gifts in the trunk of the Bel Air and headed home to wrap them in time to be shipped to Hazard, Kentucky. I wondered why anyone would want to live in a place called Hazard; it would seem like you were asking for trouble. Dad assured me that Perley Bailey's black lung disease that put them in the poorhouse had nothing to do with living in Hazard. He got it from working in the coal mine and now he could hardly breath and couldn't work anymore.

On Christmas Eve we got a letter from the Baileys thanking us for our generous gifts. I guess the Baileys didn't know when Santa was supposed to come. And there were some photos of the kids playing Parcheesi. Maggie's hair looked shinier, and I was pretty sure she must be using the hairbrush I picked out for her.

Christmas morning surprised us because a few gifts sat under the tree. "Santa came anyway!" exclaimed Joey. There was one gift for each of us. Joey opened a game called *Mousetrap*. I got the game of *Life*. Moe ripped the paper off her gift. She'd gotten a *Ouija* board. I was jealous and couldn't wait to ask it questions.

Dad and Mom went into the kitchen to start breakfast. "Helen, what were you thinking buying Moe a *Ouija* board? Father Smith talked about this at Holy Name last month and he thinks it's a tool of the devil. Moe better not go around broadcasting it. I don't want her getting in any trouble at school over this."

"Oh, Tom it's harmless. Lots of nurses at the hospital play with their boards on break, and it's a lot of fun. Don't read too much into it."

That afternoon Moe and I went upstairs and pulled out the board. The directions were simple. Put your fingers on the triangular pointer called the planchette. The word YES was written on the board in the upper left corner; NO was written on the right top corner. There were two rows of letters written in the middle of the board. A row of numbers was under the letters, and above the word GOODBYE.

"I'll go first," said Moe. We put our fingers on the planchette. "Will I ever get married?" The pointer started moving around the board slowly and stopped at the word YES. "Wow, Nora this is cool. Your turn."

"Okay. Will Joey ever get rid of his stutter?" The pointer went to individual letters and spelled out M-A-Y-B-E. "What's that supposed to mean?" I asked.

"Will my husband be handsome?" YES. Moe swooned.

"I'm going to read for a while," I said. I didn't want to listen to any more of Moe's dumb questions about her future husband.

After supper when everyone was plopped in the living room watching *Gunsmoke*, I went upstairs and pulled out the *Ouija* board. Would it agree with Dad that the Boston Strangler killed Sandra Valade? I took a deep breath, put my fingertips on the pointer and asked, "Did the Boston Strangler kill Sandra Valade?" The pointer started moving slowly and stopped when it reached the word NO.

The *Ouija* board confirmed what I already knew. Dad was wrong about the Strangler.

1963

"Segregation now, segregation tomorrow, and segregation forever," he proclaimed. Deep dark eyes, black hair, and bushy eyebrows stared at me through the TV screen.

Some of the crowd cheered and clapped. Others booed and waved signs. Two men holding signs reading "End Segregation Now" and "Negro Rights are Human Rights" got knocked to the ground by police.

"Who is that guy?" I asked.

"George Wallace, the new governor of Alabama. And he's a horse's ass." Dad sighed.

"Wallace wants to keep negro and white people separated in Alabama. And the fact that the President is calling to end segregation all over the country makes him furious," said Mom.

Brinkley, the news guy, leaned into his mic. He said that Wallace denounced Kennedy for depriving the people of Alabama of their rights.

Dad shut off the television. "I can't listen to any more of that nonsense. The guy is dangerous."

I thought about negro rights.

"Why don't we have any negroes in Manchester?" I asked.

"Most of the people living in this city were born here, and negroes just didn't settle in the north back when Manchester was growing. Can you blame them, Nora? Winters in New Hampshire can be pretty cold."

"If we're not racists in the north why does Arti-Lou's sell Nigger Babies?" I asked.

Mom and Dad looked at each other in surprise.

"Nothing gets by you, does it, Nora? It's just chocolate candy," said Mom. "But the name is no longer appropriate. It's just one of those sayings from the past that nobody bothered to question. Until you did, Miss Smarty Pants."

"Eenie, Meenie, Miney, Mo, catch a nigger by the toe," laughed Moe.

"That is another unfortunate carry over from the past," Dad said. "No need for any of us to say that anymore. You can catch anything by the toe. How about catch a Joey by the toe?" He grabbed my brother and tickled him.

"There are quite a few negroes stationed at the Pease Air Force base in Portsmouth, come to think of it," said Dad. "I served in the war with a fair number, and I never had a problem with any of them. The guys that I knew were hard-working, decent people."

I knew Dad was a good judge of character because he was a cop. If he believed that negroes were hard-working, decent people he was right, no matter what that crazy Alabama governor thought.

2

Dad didn't talk too much about the war, but I'm pretty sure he was a big hero. I know because of the stuff that I found in his bureau. My parents would be mad if they knew I snooped through their top drawers. Junk drawers, they called them. I found medals in velvet boxes in Dad's top drawer when I was poking around. One was a heart-shaped medal with a purple ribbon that had a side view of George Washington. Another was a gold star with a red, white, and blue ribbon. When I asked about them, he said was that they were from his time in the Air Force. And that's all he said.

Dad had a giant scar on the left side of his chest just above his heart. I figured the medals must have had something to do with that scar. I only saw it when he took his shirt off at the beach. I pretty much forgot about it the rest of the year.

I found a big jar of loose change in Dad's drawer. I had no idea why he would keep change in a bureau drawer. When you need change, it should probably be in your pocket. Maybe the best of all the stuff in Dad's top drawer was a big, ugly bullet, ragged around the edges, surrounded by plastic that had a small plaque on the front that said: *Sgt. Thomas Donovan, 8th Air Force, Dresden, 1945.* I'll bet it was the bullet that left the big scar.

After Dad got out of the war, his mom was sick and went to the Sacred Heart Hospital. On 3-East, he met a pretty nurse named Helen and they got married. "I lost my dear mother, God rest her soul, but at least I got a beautiful wife." Mom would blush each time he told the story.

After they got married, he went to Saint Anselm's. He got to go for free because he was a soldier. Along the way they had us three kids, and he joined the Manchester Police Department. I'm pretty sure a lot of soldiers became policemen after the war. I guess if you could be taught to kill people, arresting them would be easy.

Mom's junk drawer was different. Hers had a box of buttons. All sizes and colors. Some were plastic, some were wooden, some were metal. Mom said she never threw away anything that might have another use. She learned that as a child from her mother who lived during the Depression. "You never know when you're going to need a spare button." I heard that more than once.

Next to the button jar she had a box full of cards. Old birthday cards, Christmas cards, you name it. And holy cards. A picture of the dead person with a poem on one side and a picture of the sky with light streaming down through the clouds, or a picture of Jesus with praying hands on the other side. "*May the road rise up to meet you…and until we meet again, may God hold you in the palm of his hand.*" That was written on a lot of the holy cards. Dad said it was an Irish Blessing to help the dead get to heaven before the devil knew they were dead.

With all the rules about getting into heaven and avoiding hell, being held in God's hand seemed like the simplest way to get there.

3

Sister Clare, our music teacher, met with parents and faculty to organize the Annual All Saint's Saint Patrick's Day Musical Review. After planning the show, the rehearsals began.

Everybody knew who the favorite kids were. The ones that sang well, the ones who could dance. "That little Cissy Larkin sounds just like Shirley Temple," I heard one mother say. "And those curls are just precious. She'll go far."

The Donovan kids had no such talents and were always in the chorus. That was fine with me.

"Let's begin by remembering the reason we celebrate Saint Patrick's Day," said Sister Clare. "Can anyone tell me why we honor him?"

"Jimmy Dolan, stop biting your nails and tell me why Saint Patrick is so important."

"He got rid of the snakes in Ireland, Sister."

"Mr. Dolan, that's nothing but a myth." Sister glared at Jimmy. "No, we honor Saint Patrick because he converted the pagans to Catholicism. But we also celebrate the day to honor Irish success after centuries of prosecution. Under English rule, the Irish couldn't vote, and their land was confiscated. When the potato famine arrived, thousands of starving Irish fled to the US where they again faced discrimination. On Saint Patrick's Day we honor our great saint to celebrate how far we've come, because no people on earth have suffered as much as the Irish."

I wondered if Sister Clare knew about the suffering of the slaves or the negroes in the south today. It seemed like there was plenty of suffering to go around. And I wasn't sure that the Irish suffered more than anyone else.

Sister looked at her watch before continuing. "Many people felt threatened by the Irish because they were a beautiful people with many, many talents.

I didn't believe that for a second because there was no talent in my Irish family and there were plenty of homely kids at All Saints' School. "Beauty is in the eye of the beholder," Mom said to Moe one day when Moe was upset because she thought her nose was too big for her face. Sister Clare might believe everyone was beautiful, but she had Coke bottle glasses and probably couldn't see ugly little details.

"Boys and girls, did you know that March 17 is President Kennedy's favorite holiday?" Sister pulled a piece of paper from her pocket and read a quote from the president.

"It is that quality of the Irish—that remarkable combination of hope, confidence and imagination—that is needed more than ever today."

She broke out into a big smile. "So I want all of you, whether you are singing in the chorus or performing a solo, to put your heart and soul into making our 1963 Saint Patrick's Musical Review the best one ever."

The whole parish turned out for the show. Nuns and priests from different parishes filed in and it was rumored that even the Bishop might show up. Aunt Kathleen, Marcel, and Uncle Danny came, but Danny sat in the back row laughing loudly with some of his friends until Sister Lucinda turned around and hissed at them to be quiet.

"Molly Malone" was the first number. Marty Doyle sang about a girl who was a fishmonger. Molly Malone walked slowly across the stage pushing her wheelbarrow, pretending she was selling fish. The chorus sang *"Alive, alive, oh...alive, alive, oh crying cockles and mussels, alive, alive, oh."* Molly slowly dropped to her knees and played dead at the end of the song.

Next the third graders took the stage for "McNamara's Band". A little boy with orange hair and a fake bushy red beard, dressed like a leprechaun marched back and forth across the stage with a baton. *"Me name is McNamara, I'm the leader of the band, although we're few in numbers we're the finest in the land."* The audience laughed when the chorus pulled out our plastic trumpets and pretended to play along with the music.

Mikey O'Neil was next, wearing a green sequined top hat and a green cummerbund around his waist. He tap-danced to "It's a Long way to Tipperary". As the pace of the music picked up, so did the speed of Mikey's feet. I couldn't believe how fast he moved them.

Sister Clare always picked the eighth-grade boy with the best voice to sing her personal favorite "Danny Boy". *"Oh, Danny boy, the pipes, the pipes are calling, from glen to glen and down the mountainside...."* Danny Foley used to sound like a boy from right out of the Vienna Boys' Choir, but now his voice cracked all the time, especially when he went for the high notes. When he reached the part where he had to sing *"Oh, come ye back...,"* he started out okay but when he got to the word *back*, he got into trouble. The note started out high, fell low, and then slowly scratched its way up high again. I was glad for him that it was a short word, or he really would have been in a predicament.

Parents held their hands to their faces, others looked at each other with mouths open in disbelief. Poor Danny Foley. He will always be remembered as the kid who slaughtered *Danny Boy* in the Annual All Saints' Saint Patrick's Musical Review.

The show ended and we crowded into the church hall for cupcakes and green punch. Everyone agreed that it was the best Musical Review ever. I overheard Uncle Danny ask Dad, "whatever happened to "Whiskey in the Jar?" Dad just frowned at him and walked away.

We were tired on the ride home, so the car was unusually quiet. I thought about what Sister Clare said about no one suffering more that the Irish. But tonight, no one suffered more than Danny Foley who butchered the daylights out of "Danny Boy."

4

Aunt Kathleen's wedding day sparkled. Mom wore a green print dress and had her hair done in a French twist. My aunt ordered a yellow corsage for her so she wouldn't be the only one in our family without flowers. The morning was sunny and blue. Just the kind of day we all hoped for.

I stood in the back of Sainte Marie's Church next to Doris, holding my bouquet of blue and white flowers. Doris seemed nice enough. She didn't talk much, but she told me that she liked her dress. Moe and Danielle stood and talked with the two other bridesmaids who worked with Aunt Kathleen at the Sacred Heart. Moe pretended she didn't even know me. I peeked in at the church. It was beautiful; the altar was filled with blue and white flowers, and big white ribbons hung from each pew. A white paper carpet lined the middle aisle, and I could see Marcel in his tuxedo, laughing in the front with his best man. Mom was already seated in the second pew on the left next to Uncle Danny. I knew Uncle Danny was the last person in the world Mom wanted next to her, but she didn't have much of a choice.

The bridal limousine pulled up. Kathleen told us that Marcel had gotten a deal because he rented it from the Connor Funeral Parlor. I'd never seen Dad in a tuxedo before, and he looked like a movie star. He turned to help Aunt Kathleen out. She had to duck her head down so she wouldn't knock off her veil. When she stood up, the bridal party gasped. She looked like a Disney Princess. She wore a pillbox hat with a veil that hung down over her face and poufed out in the back. It looked like something Jackie Kennedy would wear. Her white dress had a high waist and a big flouncy skirt, followed by a long train that swept the ground as she walked. She held a huge bouquet of white and red roses with green ivy trailing down. She and Dad walked up the church steps while Doris and I straightened her train.

"Don't anyone kiss her!" hissed Moe to the bridal party. "You'll smudge her make-up!"

Aunt Kathleen laughed out loud. "Moe is right. Stay away from me, everybody! Kisses later."

When the organ began to play, Marcel's Uncle Roger, the Monsignor at Sainte Marie's, walked slowly down the center aisle holding a large gold cross on a pole. He met Moe, the first bridesmaid to walk down the aisle, then he turned and led the procession toward the altar.

Doris and I walked down the center aisle side by side. I was nervous at first because everyone was staring at us, but they were mostly smiling. A lot of them held hankies. I wasn't sure if that was a French thing, or if they had hankies because they thought they might cry.

I couldn't figure out why Uncle Danny said that he didn't like French churches. This one looked a lot like All Saints' except it was bigger and fancier; there was more gold everywhere. With the sunlight streaming through the stained-glass windows, swatches of blue, purple, and green sparkled over the congregation. Mom smiled as I approached the altar. Marcel winked at me, and I felt special. The organ started playing the bridal march. Everyone stood and craned their necks to see my beautiful Aunt Kathleen walk down the aisle with my dad. When they reached the altar, Dad kissed Kathleen on the cheek and then patted Marcel on the back. Marcel took Kathleen's hand and together they walked up onto the altar.

The Monsignor seemed nice and everything seemed pretty normal. I wasn't sure I would know if anything French was going on anyway. He cleared his throat and then said something in what I am pretty sure was French. I heard a groan from my Uncle Danny. And then "Good morning, and welcome to Sainte Marie Church for this special occasion." I overheard Uncle Danny whisper to my mom that it was going to take all day if everything was going to be said in both French and English. Mom ignored him.

After a long Latin mass, the time came for the wedding vows. Joey and Jean brought the pillows to the Monsignor so he could take the rings.

The Monsignor asked Aunt Kathleen in French and then in English if she took Marcel to be her lawful wedded husband. She replied in French and then said, "I do," in English. Behind me, Uncle Danny sighed as Marcel spoke his vows. The Monsignor said something in French and then said, "I now pronounce you man and wife. You may kiss the bride."

The congregation clapped as Marcel lifted Kathleen's veil and gave her a big kiss. I heard sniffles behind me. Good thing those ladies brought their hankies.

The organ music started up. "Ode to Joy" is one of my favorites," whispered Mom. Mr. and Mrs. Marcel Boucher walked down the white carpet and started the procession out of the church and onto the sidewalk of Notre Dame Avenue.

As we stood talking to guests, I tried to figure out what was so French about Sainte Marie's. Whatever it was, I liked it.

5

Moe and me were in our bedroom when Joey came bursting in. He was dressed in that dumb mouse outfit with a big red towel, a yellow tee shirt, yellow tights that he stole from my room, red gym shorts and red socks. "Here I come to save the day…. that means that Mighty Mouse is ON HIS WAY," he sang.

When Joey sang, he never stuttered. Mom said that King George the Sixth, Queen Elizabeth's father, stuttered all the time until he got a speech teacher that taught him to slow down and sing-song his speeches. After he started doing that, he didn't stutter much either. Joey's stuttering had gotten a lot better since he'd started working with Mrs. Moore. Between that and being an altar boy, maybe he just had more confidence in himself.

"Kids get down here now," yelled Dad. "History is being made."

Moe rolled her eyes. "Here as we go again."

"It's estimated that there are 250,000 people here at the National Mall," said the reporter. People were stretched out from the Washington Monument to the Lincoln Memorial. White people and negroes stood side by side, some singing, others hugging. Famous people like Charlton Heston who was Moses in the *Ten Commandments*. Marlon Brando, Harry Bellefonte, and Burt Lancaster locked arms in support. A folk singer named Joan Baez sang *"We shall overcome, we shall overcome, we shall overcome someday."*

Martin Luther King Jr. walked onto the stage to a roaring crowd that quieted when he began to speak. "I have a dream that my four little children will one day live in a nation where they will not be judged by the color of their skin but by the content of their character." He took a breath. "I have a dream that one day right there in Alabama, little black boys and black girls will be able to join hands with little white boys and white girls as brothers and sisters." The crowd went wild.

"This is terrible," said Dad. "If you lived in Alabama, negro kids couldn't use the same bathrooms or water fountains that you use. Think about that." He paused. "And if you took the bus downtown, negroes could only sit in the back of the bus. The front's reserved for whites."

King's speech made me think how horrible it must be to be treated differently because of your skin color. And then I thought about that awful Governor of Alabama George Wallace who said that he wanted "segregation forever." If I were black and living in Alabama, I would buy a one-way bus ticket to New Hampshire even if I had to sit in the back. I know that people like me would welcome them. But then I thought about my Uncle Danny and his friends. They were a different story.

6

School started. Moe wasn't around this year because she started at Saint Agatha's High School for Girls. Joey was in the fourth grade, and he got stuck with Sister Callista just like I did. I was a sixth grader now. I got lucky and got assigned to Sister Xavier's class. She was way younger than any of the other nuns I'd had before, and she had a pretty smile. She was excited about Martin Luther King's speech. "Even though he is not a Catholic priest, he is a man of God and I believe his words will change the hearts and minds of our nation."

But when the evening news came on, I learned that Sister Xavier was wrong. Not everyone's hearts and minds were changed. John Chancellor shocked the nation with a story about a bombing at the 16th St. Baptist Church in Birmingham, Alabama. "Four little black girls were killed in the basement while putting on their choir robes." Who would do such a terrible thing to little kids? "The Ku Klux Klan is thought to be responsible..." My mother made the sign of the cross.

"Dear God in heaven, what kind of nation have we become?" Dad muttered.

A few days later Martin Luther King Jr. spoke at the little girls' funeral. He told people not to despair despite the darkness of the hour. He said that black people should not be bitter or retaliate with violence. He paused and looked like he was about to cry. "We must not lose faith in our white brothers."

"What a man," Dad said. "Negro people are suffering from violent acts every time we turn on the news, and this black man is telling his own people to be peaceful and not lose faith in white people. The guy is a saint."

Why do the men in our country keep murdering women and being mean to negroes? Negroes getting beaten up by the police. Little girls getting murdered in church. I thought about all the women killed by the Strangler. He murdered eight last year and three more this year. I thought about Sandra Valade. They still hadn't found her killer. I pulled my plaid notebook out from under my mattress and studied it for a few minutes. I felt like I had to remember these murdered girls. It scared me to see the victims' names because their killers were still on the loose.

7

"I'll be right back, class. Work on the practice problems at the end of chapter eight." Sister left the classroom after a knock on the door.

When she returned, she had red circles around her eyes. "Girls and boys, President Kennedy was shot in Dallas, Texas a few hours ago. He's been pronounced dead." The room was silent. "Let us pray for the soul of President Kennedy." We knelt next to our desks and bowed our heads. "May the Father, the Son and the Holy Ghost receive the soul of our President and welcome him in through the gates of heaven. Eternal rest grant unto him, O Lord, and let perpetual light shine upon him. May his soul, through the mercy of God rest in peace. Amen."

We stayed on our knees. No one knew what to say or what to do. Sister Xavier dabbed her eyes with a hankie. "Class, we're having an early dismissal. Walkers, please leave the school quietly and find your patrol leader. Go be with your families as our nation grieves the loss of this wonderful man."

I burst through the kitchen door and saw Mom and Dad watching the news. The motorcade, the hospital, pretty Mrs. Kennedy with blood all over her pink suit standing behind Vice President Johnson while he was sworn in as the new president. The casket loaded onto Air Force One. It seemed so unreal.

The TV was on in the Donovan house day and night over the next few days. A newscaster said that a quarter of a million people were waiting in line at the Capitol to pay their respects. Some people had waited for up to ten hours in a line that was forty blocks long.

Two days later, the police in Dallas arrested Kennedy's killer, Lee Harvey Oswald. The reporter said that Oswald was a former marine who defected to the Soviet Union after getting discharged from the Marines.

"What does defected mean?" I asked Dad.

"It means to abandon your own country," he replied. I wondered if Oswald worked with Khrushchev or the guy in Cuba who hated the President.

The day before Kennedy's funeral, the news showed Oswald being led by through the basement of the Dallas Police Department. A man jumped in front of the TV cameras. He shot and killed Lee Harvey Oswald right on the spot.

Jack Ruby committed the murder on live TV in front of every family in America. Mom flew off the couch when she saw it happen. "I can't believe my eyes," she said. It didn't take me long to figure it was probably a good thing, because Oswald was a bad guy. He was likely on the stairway to hell before his body even hit the ground. *Peril. Evil.*

Monday was the day of the funeral and a National Day of Mourning. School was called off. We sat silently in the living room and watched the funeral. The Marine Band headed the procession. A soldier led a riderless black stallion that Dad said symbolized our fallen leader. Kennedy's casket was loaded onto a caisson for transport from the Capitol back to the White House and on to Saint Matthew's Roman Catholic Cathedral.

When the congregation left the church, the funeral procession headed to the Arlington National Cemetery. Walter Cronkite told the nation that as a tribute to Kennedy's Irish ancestry, thirty cadets from the Irish Defense Forces of County Kildare would perform the Queen Anne graveside drill that Kennedy admired when he visited Ireland. After the drill, they placed an eternal flame at the burial site that was then lit by Mrs. Kennedy. I was sure our President would be pleased to know that an Irish delegation was asked to honor him.

I went to my room that night and pulled my plaid notebook out from under my mattress. I flipped through the pages to where I'd listed Martin Luther King and added John Fitzgerald Kenndy. I shoved the notebook under my mattress. A murdered girl in Manchester, eleven strangled women in Boston, four murdered little black girls in Birmingham, and now a murdered president. Who would be next?

I got into bed and opened *Travels with Charlie*. Moe came in, her hair in rollers. She opened *TEEN* magazine and flipped through the pages. I couldn't focus on my book.

"Moe, let's ask the *Ouija* board some questions."

"Okay." She pulled the board out from underneath her bed. I put my book down, sat across from Moe, and put my fingers on the planchette.

"You go first," Moe said.

"Did the Russians kill Kennedy?"

The planchette shook a little bit and slowly moved up the board to YES.

Moe looked at me. "Are you surprised?"

"No," I said. "I think Russia and Cuba worked together to kill him. But dead is dead."

"My turn," said Moe. We put our fingers on the planchette. "Will more girls get murdered in Manchester?"

The planchette moved to YES. Moe looked at me wide-eyed.

"Are Nora and I in danger?" The planchette again moved to YES.

"I don't want to do this anymore," Moe said.

"One more question. Please," I said.

Moe took a deep breath.

"Will Dad find the man who murdered Sandra?"

It seemed that the planchette could not make up its mind. Maybe it didn't want us to know about the future. It slowly made its way over to over to the letters and spelled out M-A-Y-B-E.

"Thanks, Moe," I said. I put the board back in its box and shoved it under her bed. Maybe we were safe. But then again maybe we were not.

8

The girls giggle and line up around the coke machine waiting for their turn to drop in their coins or to beg me to make change for them. A skinny nun standing in the back of the cafeteria grading papers gives me the stink-eye. She reminds me of the nasty nun at OLPH who made Donny Guilfoyle eat a rotten banana. But I'm more interested in checking out the girls crowding around me than trying to remember if I know the old lady. I've got to be careful: I know she'll come right over if I talk to any of them.

A fat blonde with gobs of blue eye shadow pulls a Coke out of the machine. Why don't these lard-ass girls drink Tab, I wonder. She holds a chocolate bar in one hand, her Coke in the other. I turn away. "Moe, let me help you," I thought I heard Lard-Ass say. But I wasn't sure if I heard correctly over the clinking change falling into my bag.

I turn. Just three feet away from me stapling a poster to the bulletin board is a gorgeous girl who looks about fifteen. Slim with long, brown curly hair. She has a bunch of posters tucked under one arm. The poster reads, "Moe Donovan for Student Council: Go for Moe!"

Well, well, well, I thought. I could certainly go for Moe.

Sister Mary Somebody heads in my direction. I flash her a smile, push the dolly down the corridor and out to my waiting truck. Moe Donovan. I wasn't going to forget that name. As I jump into my truck, I look up at the sky where snow is gently falling.

9

I hated babysitting. It wasn't fair that when I finally got to be eleven and could stay up later, neighbors started wanting me to babysit.

"Nora don't be that way," sighed Mom. "You should be flattered that so many people think you are trustworthy and responsible. And it doesn't hurt to earn a little spending money."

"Nora, Mrs. Wyman is on the phone." Mom smiled as she handed me the receiver.

"Hi Mrs. Wyman," I said with my fingers crossed.

"Hello, Nora. How is school going this year?" she asked.

"It's going fine. I like it better than fifth grade," I replied.

"Wonderful. Well, it helps that you are a good student." Here it comes, I just knew it. "Mr. Wyman and I have plans to go to the New Year's Eve Ball at the Carousel and if you're free, we'd love to have you babysit."

"Sure Mrs. Wyman. What time?" I had nothing else to do.

I hated babysitting. Especially for the Wyman kids. It wasn't that they were so bad, they were just a lot of work. Stevie Wyman always had a runny nose and watery eyes. Mom said that he had lots of allergies and couldn't help it. And even if his allergies weren't making him cough and sneeze, he still had watery eyes. Moe said that most people with carrot red hair and skin so pale you could just about see through it had watery eyes. She said it was a fact and I guess she should know because she used to babysit the Wyman kids all the time.

Stevie's older sister Susie Wyman talked too much. Mostly about nothing, but she always seemed to think she was interesting. Once she talked about how dumb it was for Hansel and Gretel to use breadcrumbs to track their steps when they were old enough to know that something would come along and eat them.

I got to the Wyman house at 6:00. "You don't mind feeding the kids, do you, Nora?" asked Mrs. Wyman as she smeared on red lipstick and bit down on a tissue. "We don't want to be late."

"It's fine." Kraft Mac and Cheese were on the counter waiting for someone to get to work.

The Wymans were always out late on special occasions. It's not that I minded staying up late. But it got boring after midnight when television went off the air, and all you could see and hear was static. I had to keep myself busy doing something else. So I decided to check out the closet in the Wyman den. Under a bunch of boxes of board games, I found two piles of magazines in the back corner. I pulled out a few copies and couldn't believe my eyes. *Playboy* and *Penthouse*. I heard about them from boys in the schoolyard, but never actually saw one. Dad never had magazines like that. That had brown paper over the covers at the newsstands. I was shocked. I tried to put everything back the way I found it so Mr. Wyman wouldn't know that I knew his secret.

When the Wymans got home that night, they were giggly and Mr. Wyman smelled like cheap whiskey. One of my few memories of my grandfather Donovan was going to the Knights of Columbus with him one day. I asked him what the smell in the room was. He said it was the cheap whiskey that had been spilled on the floor the night before. And that is what Mr. Wyman smelled like.

"Mr. Wyman will walk you home, Nora." Mrs. Wyman kicked off her high heels. I hated this part. I never knew what to talk about. As we walked past the Larkins', Mr. Wyman grabbed my hand. I was horrified. As soon as I saw my house around the corner, I ran the rest of the way and yelled "thank you" over my shoulder. What a creep. Of course, I would never tell my parents because somehow, I thought it might be my fault because I found his stash of girlie magazines.

When I got home, Moe was still awake. "Mom and Dad went to bed after the ball dropped and I told them I would wait up for you." I was glad to have someone to talk to. I didn't tell her about

Mr. Wyman, but I wondered if he had ever tried to hold her hand when he walked her home.

Moe was listening to her newest 45 record and dancing along. Watching *American Bandstand* every day after school paid off. She was a good dancer. "I like side B even more than A…listen to this, Nora."

The song was about a seventeen-year-old girl who the singer saw just standing there. Wherever "there" was. And apparently, he thought she was way beyond compare. But I was only half listening. My mind was still on Mr. Wyman.

"I bought this record down at Manchester Music this afternoon. My very first Beatle record," she said as she swayed with her eyes closed. I couldn't remember when Moe started acting so girlie but going to Saint Agatha's with all those other girls seemed to make it worse.

"Listen to side B before we turn off the light…please?"

I couldn't believe my ears. The Beatles were singing about wanting to hold someone's hand. And they couldn't hide the feeling they got when they held her hand. Just like Mr. Wyman.

When the music stopped Moe finally turned off the light and crawled into bed. "It's been a long day and I'm really tired," I said. Lying in the dark Moe said "Just one more thing, Nora. The Beatles are going to be on Ed Sullivan on February 9. I can't wait!"

"Me too," was all I could manage to say.

1964

Sister Xavier had us scraping tape off the back of cardboard angels and stars. They'd been hanging up since November when they replaced stern Pilgrims eating turkey with smiling Indians.

Someone knocked at the door, and in stepped Father Smith with another priest.

"Good afternoon, boys and girls," said Father Smith.

"Good afternoon, Father Smith," we sing-songed back.

"I want to introduce our new priest Father Murphy, who comes to us from Nashua."

Father Murphy had a haircut like JFK and was younger than Father Smith. He was tall and wore glasses with black plastic frames.

"I'm delighted to be serving with Father Smith at All Saints' and look forward to getting to know all of you." He turned to the picture of JFK hanging in our classroom. "As we grieve the loss of our president, let's not forget that Catholics have a lot of work ahead of us." He looked around the room. "I ask you to please pray that President Johnson will be successful in helping America's poor."

I wasn't sure how I felt about Johnson. He had a terrible accent like the people on *The Andy Griffith Show*. And the name Lyndon was awful. His wife looked like somebody's Nana, and the name Lady Bird was even worse than Lyndon.

"I know that the Johnsons might not seem as glamorous as the Kennedys, but Johnson's dedication to helping the poor is a cause dear to the heart of our Savior."

Eyes lowered, I looked around. One of Father Smith's eyes looked at the class, but the other looked out the window.

As the priests left, I watched Father Smith lean over and whisper something into Donald Morse's ear. Donald slouched down in his seat. He had a mark on his face, and I couldn't tell if it was dirt or a black-and-blue.

2

Mom smiled. "I think that between the speech therapist and Father Smith, Joe's stuttering has improved."

I hadn't noticed. But I had noticed that Joe was at the rectory a lot.

"Why give Father Smith credit? He's kind of crabby," said Moe. She'd gotten an attitude ever since she'd gotten elected to Student Council.

"Moe, the priests serve God. Father was kind to you when you were little. He might not know how to act around you now that you're a young lady."

I knew Mom meant that now that Moe had gotten boobs that neither of Smith's eyes knew where to look.

"His eye is creepy," I said.

"Do you know the story about his eye?" Mom asked.

I wasn't interested, but Mom continued.

"Father was a chaplain in World War II. He got shot and ended up losing his eye. He promised God that if he lived, he'd devote himself to doing good deeds."

"But if he's a priest, shouldn't he be doing good deeds anyway?" I asked.

"Maybe he does extra good deeds." Mom said.

I wondered what extra good deeds Father Smith did. Volunteering to set the table so his housekeeper didn't have to? Taking out the trash at the rectory? I bet he didn't do any extra good deeds.

3

Dad was working the graveyard shift and already out of bed when we got home. "Serious weather's coming our way," he read aloud from the newspaper.

"Great," said Joe. "More shoveling." He picked up a cold pancake left over from breakfast.

"Did you kids have a good day?" asked Dad.

"It was okay," I said.

Moe and I went skating at Dorrs Pond, and Joe went over to Paul's. Skating wasn't much fun. High school boys were playing hockey, and lots of pucks came zinging our way. We got cold so went into the hut to warm up by the fire. Then we took off our skates, laced up our boots, and headed home in the thin winter light.

Our parents were in the kitchen talking.

"And now this one's close to Kathleen's age," I heard Dad say.

I looked at Moe. She hadn't heard them.

"Take off your boots before walking on my clean floor," called Mom when I opened the door. The floor didn't look that clean to me. I knew that she just wanted Dad to stop talking. She folded up the newspaper and put it in the trash.

4

After dinner, I pulled the newspaper out of the trash and shoved it under my sweater.

"I'm going upstairs to read," I said.

I popped into bed and flipped through the paper. And then I saw it. A 19-year-old girl had been sexually assaulted and strangled in her Boston apartment. My heart stopped. She was close to Sandra's age.

Joey and I tried to be quiet when we came home from school, but Dad was already up. "More snow coming our way."

I was sick of Dad talking about the weather. In the winter they predicted snow all the time, and we lived in New Hampshire, so what was the big fuss?

Moe came home, and Dad gave her a look.

"What?" She stood on the rug, shaking snow out of her hair.

"I've noticed that you're coming home earlier," said Dad.

"I decided to walk faster," she answered. "If I'm covering the same distance, why not just speed up? It burns more calories."

"Will we have a snow day tomorrow?" asked Joe.

"I don't know," said Dad. "But if we get what they're predicting, Moe will be able to burn off calories shoveling."

Moe stuck out her tongue. "Ha-ha. I'm going to dry my hair."

I went upstairs, sticking Joe with Dad and the weather. Moe's hair dryer whined in the bathroom. I pulled up my comforter and opened *To Kill a Mockingbird*. Boo Radley gave me the creeps.

Moe came out of the bathroom with little red bows in her hair.

"Moe," I paused. "Do you know if Dad still thinks that the Strangler murdered Valade?"

"I doubt it. The Boston women get strangled in their homes. Valade was kidnapped on a dirt road and then shot."

"Are you worried that Valade's killer is still on the loose?" I asked.

"Not really. It's been a long time since anyone's been murdered in New Hampshire, and Valade was murdered years ago. Let Dad sort it out."

He'd had four years to sort out Valade's murder, I thought, and the killer was still walking the streets.

5

"I've got something to tell you," said Moe.

"What?"

"I have a boyfriend."

I couldn't believe it.

"When did you meet him?" I asked.

"A couple of months ago when a bunch of us went to the Puritan after school." Moe looked in the mirror over our bureau.

"Is he nice?" I asked.

"He's sooo nice," beamed Moe. "His name's Gene Tardiff. He's got a car, and he's been giving me a ride home from school."

"You mean he's at least two years older than you? Dad's going to hit the roof."

"He's not two years older. He's just sixteen. And I'll be fifteen in May."

She had a point. "How did he get a car?"

"His grandfather owns Tardiff Chevrolet on the DW Highway. So that's why I've been getting home early some days. Gene drops me off on Brook Street. That way, if Dad's up he won't see us."

"When are you going to tell Mom and Dad?" I asked.

"Pretty soon. I'm waiting for the right moment." She looked at herself again in the mirror.

"Moe!" Mom called. "Time to set the table."

"Moe, I said. "Have you kissed him yet?"

"Yes. But I haven't let him French kiss me."

French kissing? I wondered what that was. Probably some weird thing people did on the West Side.

6

"A metaphor is a term used to link two unlike objects without using the words like or as," Sister said. She gave us an example. "The snowstorm vented its anger, killing both women and children."

I wondered why Sister said that angry storms kill women and children. Didn't they kill men and boys, too?

"We all know that people die in snowstorms," Sister said. "And sometimes we say storms are angry. But entities that get angry in real life are human beings. The two unlike items that are being compared here are storms and humans." Our homework assignment was to write ten sentences each containing a metaphor, and we were to list the two unlike objects being compared. I loved thinking about metaphors and by dinner had written ten sentences.

On Sunday, Dad announced that we were in for a blizzard.

"No school!" yelled Joe.

"Don't count your chickens, Joe," said Mom. "Tom, please swing by the A & P after Mass and pick up a few things in case we're snowed in. I'll make you a list." She grabbed a piece of scrap paper and began writing. "I know we'll need bologna and a few cans of ravioli for the kids."

"We have ravioli in the stockpile," said Dad.

I was annoyed that Dad called our bomb shelter food "the stockpile." He said last year that it was a bomb shelter in case Russia attacked us, but now he and Mom were calling it a stockpile like we'd forgotten that at any minute Russia could blow us to smithereens.

We ate our Frosted Flakes and listened to WKBR for school closings. The reporter tortured us by going through the names of closed schools in neighboring towns. Then came the announcement: "Manchester School Superintendent says that all Manchester schools, both public and parochial, will be open today. Repeat. Manchester School Superintendent says that all Manchester schools, both public and parochial, will be open today."

"Oh, no," groaned Moe.

"It's not fair," whined Joe.

I knew they hadn't done their homework. Moe was on the phone for hours last night, and Joe was glued to the TV most of the evening.

We got dressed and headed off to school. It wasn't very cold, but my nostrils tightened up with each breath. Snow was coming.

After morning prayer, Sister Xavier called on a few kids to share their sentences, but most hadn't done their homework.

"Okay, who has done their homework and can bring it up to my desk now?"

Only me, Anne Leavitt, and Patty Carmody brought papers to her desk.

"Boys and girls, these are the kinds of students who will be successful in life. Mark my words."

She told the three of us that we could pick a book to read out of her "library" in the back of the classroom, and everyone else could work on composing metaphors.

Sister had the worst library. I grabbed a ripped-apart *National Geographic* with pictures of the pyramids on the cover and went back to my seat.

My desk was by the window. I took breaks from reading about the Pharaohs to see if the snow had started. But it wasn't until after the dismissal bell rang and I met Joey by the playground fence that the first fat snowflakes started falling. Joey and Paul ran ahead of me up Union Street, their stocking hats swinging behind them. Joey waited for me on Paul's front porch. Paul wasn't allowed to have kids in the house to play because his mother had a nervous condition. I'd asked my mother about Mrs. Connors. Mom said that the woman wasn't quite right ever since she'd had a hysterectomy at the Infant Asylum, and something went wrong with the anesthesia.

I hated the Asylum. It had bars on the windows, and Mom always pointed it out when we drove past it. "There it is, Nora. That's the Infant Asylum where you were born." The word asylum made me think of a place where they'd put mental patients in straitjackets. No wonder Paul's mother had a nervous condition. I got nervous just looking at it.

Joe and I had cocoa and I was rinsing our mugs when Moe came in the door.

"It's really picked up," she said.

I looked out the window. Moe was right. The snow was getting heavy, and the wind was whipping it into furious funnels. The Bel-Air's ghostly headlights were barely visible when Mom turned into our driveway.

She came in, shaking snow off her coat. "You kids will be happy," she said. "I can't imagine you'll have school tomorrow. "But I feel bad for your father. Work will be terrible for him tonight."

"Did someone take my name in vain?" Dad appeared, showered, and dressed.

"Tom, don't tell me that you're planning on going in now?"

"Moi? I got dressed in case I get called in early." He looked out the window. "How's the driving?"

"It's gotten slippery in the past hour," replied Mom.

"Joe, you may get your wish. I doubt you'll have school tomorrow," said Dad.

"I hope that we don't lose power," I said.

"School or no school, tomorrow morning you kids need to shovel out the driveway so Mom can get to the Sacred Heart by 6:45."

We groaned.

Mom shooed us off to bed because we had to get up early. I didn't know why the Larkins and the Callahans could afford snow blowers, but the Donovan kids had to go out in the dark and shovel.

7

I watched Moe pull out her bin of rollers.

"What do you do on Student Council?" I asked.

"We talk about whatever Sister Annunciata wants us to talk about. Usually, it's about girls who roll up their uniform skirts too short and how we'll decorate the bulletin board by the main entrance." She clipped the sides of her hair up and started rolling the top.

"And what stuff gets put up on bulletin boards?"

"We pick a saint whose feast day falls that month. February 5th is Saint Agatha's Feast Day, but Sister said that she gets enough attention because the school is named after her."

"So, who are you doing?"

"Saint Valentine," she answered.

"Moe, even Protestants know about Valentine. Who knows anything about Agatha?" I asked.

"I spent one study hall last week in the library reading *The Lives of The Saints*, and I learned a lot about her," said Moe.

I couldn't figure Moe out. She sneaks off on car dates with her boyfriend, but in study hall she reads *The Lives of The Saints*.

She tied a big white scarf over her rollers and climbed into bed. "Really bad things happened to her. She was born in Italy hundreds of years ago and was beautiful. Some Roman guy tried to marry her when she was nineteen, but she wanted to be a nun. He had her stretched on a rack and ordered that her breasts be cut off."

"No!".

"And then he set her on fire and rolled her on pieces of glass."

I couldn't believe this.

"Anyway, she's the patron saint of women and girls who suffer sexual attacks, breast-feeding mothers, and bell founders."

"What's a bell founder?" I asked.

"People who make iron bells for big cathedrals."

"What do bell founders have to do with sex-attack victims and breast-feeding mothers?" I asked.

"I don't know. But when do you think I should introduce Gene to our parents?"

"Dad's going to find out, so you should tell him before he does," I went back to my book.

Moe turned her radio on low.

"Hey! Listen to this." She cranked the volume up a bit. "It's Dylan. Gene loves him."

The song was about changing times and how we all might drown if we don't pay attention.

I thought the guy's voice was terrible but didn't want to hurt Moe's feelings.

"I'll have to listen to it again to get it," I said. "Do you like it?"

"I don't know. I don't want to drown, but I don't want things to change either. Change scares me," said Moe.

I plumped up my pillow and turned on my side. "I'm more afraid of Russians and getting murdered than I'm afraid of change. We're good people, and if we changed, it would be for the better, I think."

"You're probably right," said Moe. "Sometimes I think that you're smarter than I am."

Of course I was.

8

Mom shook us awake. "Get a move on, ladies. Joe's already dressed."

It was pitch black when we went out except for where the porch light cast a ghostly white circle. There was a lot of snow, but it was fluffy and dry. Easy to scrape and toss as we worked our way out to the street. Mom came out on the porch to check our progress. "Oh, that's wide enough, kids." Dad can finish it up when he comes home from work this morning."

The kitchen smelled delicious. French toast and sausages were warming in the oven. She pulled on her coat. "Keep the radio on to see if you have school. Be good, sweeties."

We piled our plates with food.

"Joe don't take all the maple syrup, "I said. "You're going to be diabetic."

"What's diabetic?" he asked.

"It's when you get fat and they cut off your toes. Be quiet and let's listen."

WKBR announced that Manchester's School Superintendent said that Manchester schools, both public and parochial, would be open today.

Moe got up and scraped her sausage into the trash.

Outside, it was bright and sunny. Mr. Larkin waved and yelled something to us, but we couldn't hear what he said over the whirring of his snowblower. The street plow had pushed a pile of icy snow into our driveway that Dad would have to clean out when he came home.

Paul was waiting for us outside his house. His mother was shoveling their driveway. I hadn't seen Mrs. Connors before, except once when she peeked out at us from behind her kitchen curtains. I thought she looked pretty normal for a woman who had nervous troubles, whatever they were.

I was surprised when I got home that the icy mess left by the plow was still blocking our driveway. Maybe Dad was working late.

"Joe let's shovel this up so Mom can get into the garage," I said.

We'd just finished when Moe showed up.

"Is Dad home?" Her voice was tense.

"No."

"There's a girl missing from Manchester. Pamela Something. I'll bet he's on the case."

My heart flipped.

"How do you know?" I asked.

Joe grabbed a bag of potato chips and stood by the kitchen counter eating them.

"Pamela's from the West Side. Cops came in and pulled kids from her neighborhood out of class to see if they knew anything."

"What did they say about her?"

"Not much. She was nice and an Honor Student. They think she either ran away or was murdered by the guy she babysits for."

I thought of Mr. Wyman's sweaty hand.

Mom opened the kitchen door. "The story about the missing girl has been on the news all day. Her family must be frantic." She glanced at the kitchen clock. "Kids, Dad won't be home until late, so let's pick up grinders from Perillo's." Mom was clearly trying to distract us.

"Yes!" exclaimed Joe.

Mom asked me to go with her to pick up the food. On the way home, the smell of roast beef made me feel sick. I didn't say anything because I didn't want her asking me if I was having my period.

By the time we got home, Moe had already set the table. I took a bite of my sandwich. Drips from the roast beef made a bloody little pool on my plate that ran into my potato chips.

"Nora, you're barely eating anything," said Moe.

"I'll eat what Nora doesn't want," said Joe.

Moe frowned at me as I passed my plate over to Joe.

"Why don't you kids do your homework. I'll load the dishwasher, and then we can watch TV."

Joey charged into the living room when a man's booming voice told us to listen to a story about a man named Jed. *The Beverly Hillbillies* was his favorite show. We just heard the part about Texas tea when the phone rang. Moe and I followed Mom into the kitchen.

"Yes, they are."

She twisted the cord around her fingers.

"I'll tell them."

She turned to us.

"Dad wants you to know that they think Pam's a runaway. He doesn't want you to worry."

"Girls who are Honor Students don't run away," said Moe.

"Don't jump to conclusions, Moe."

The roast beef I'd managed to choke down was grinding around in my stomach. We went to bed after the *Beverly Hillbillies*.

"What do you think happened to Pam?" I bunched my pillow under my head.

"I don't know. But she didn't run away, I'm positive of that."

As I tried to sleep, I remembered that the *Ouija* board said that more girls would get killed in Manchester. Now I wondered just how many.

9

Pamela Mason was all we talked about at recess.

"Did your father say anything?" I asked Missy.

"Not really. He had yesterday off but is going in tonight. And he was on the phone all day yesterday."

Probably talking to my father, I thought.

Patty Carmody said that Pam put a sign on a laundromat's bulletin board looking for babysitting jobs.

My father wouldn't talk to us about Pam, but the *Union Leader* covered her non-stop. Reporters interviewed her parents who sat on her bed next to one of her dolls. I liked Pam's floral print wallpaper and the way her ceiling slanted down. Her mother was pretty and seemed nice, and Pam had a younger brother just about Joe's age. In one article her mother showed the police the Christmas present Pam gave her: a statue of praying hands. When I read this, I knew that Moe was right. No one who gave their mother a statue of praying hands would run away from home.

Sister Xavier worried about Pam. During morning prayers she'd ask God to safely return all who were lost to their families. By not mentioning Pam's name, Sister made whatever had happened to Pam grow bigger and scarier.

Moe told me girls in school said that police had come to their homes and questioned them.

I knew that Dad was questioning people because I heard him tell Mom that the last person to see Pam alive was her little next-door neighbor. He was out shoveling when Pam jumped into a car that pulled up in front of her house. Dad and Mr. Callahan interviewed him. "I felt sorry for him, Helen. He's just Joe's age and sat with eyes like saucers when we questioned him. I had to stop Callahan from pushing the boy too hard. The kid just didn't see much."

That night in bed I wondered what it would be like to be this boy who was the last person to see Pam alive except, of course, for the murderer. I wanted to ask Dad a bunch of stuff about Pam, but I knew he'd just get mad. We were only supposed to know what he told us.

10

"I'm telling Mom and Dad about Gene," Moe said.

"Who's Gene?" asked Joe.

"My boyfriend," said Moe.

"When?" I asked. I wanted to be there.

"I'm doing it today if they're both home."

"I don't know. Dad's been so crabby with the Pam investigation," I began.

"Well, what if they never find her? I've got to tell them sometime."

Mom was making spaghetti sauce, and Dad was reading the paper when we came home from school. He said hi without looking up, but Mom asked about our day.

"I want to tell you something," said Moe.

"Sure, honey." Mom turned down the heat on the spaghetti sauce.

"I have a boyfriend."

Dad looked up for a second and then returned to the sports page.

"Tell us about him," said Mom.

"He's nice and super-smart, and he's a year ahead of me at Saint Benedict's. His name's Gene Tardiff." Moe turned to Dad. "He's a point guard for the basketball team."

Dad didn't even look up.

"That's wonderful," said Mom.

"His father's a lawyer. And he's got a younger brother and sister, just like me."

"When can we meet Gene?" asked Mom.

"He can come over after school any day this week."

"I'm home early enough every day," said Mom. "Tom, what about you?"

"Not sure when I'll be free."

Mom turned to Moe. "Why don't you bring Gene over tomorrow? I'll put some brownies in the oven tonight."

The next afternoon as I read "Solid Leads Lacking in Pamela Mystery," Moe dragged a tall, skinny guy into the kitchen.

"Mom, Nora, and Joe, this is Gene."

"So nice to meet you," said Mom.

Gene had brown hair, brown eyes and his face wasn't too pimply. Moe couldn't stop smiling at him.

"Moe says you play basketball," said Mom.

"Yes. I'm on the Saint Benedict's team." He reached for a brownie.

Joey had moved to the other end of the kitchen table and carefully arranged his model plane kit on a dishtowel.

"Delicious brownies, Mrs. Donovan."

What a suck-up, I thought.

Gene looked at Joe's model.

"Wow! You've got a P-51 Mustang," he said. "That's one of the most important planes in World War II."

"You know about the P-51?" asked Joe.

"Buddy, everyone knows about the P-51."

"I like it because it could gain altitude and still be able to fire at the enemy." Joe grinned.

Those were a lot of words for him to get out when meeting someone new. And for Mom, the way Joe talked around people was a test about how good they were. He spoke perfectly in front of Gene, so Gene now walked on water.

That Saturday, I heard my parents bickering.

"Helen, can you pick up my shirts at the dry cleaner's?" Dad's voice was sharp. "How do you expect me to go to work wearing the same shirt for three days?"

I couldn't hear Mom's reply. I knew that Dad hadn't had a day off since Pam went missing. But I didn't care. He shouldn't be biting off everyone's head.

11

I was the first to see the newspaper that January afternoon.

There were two photos, each of a dead girl. One was Sandra Valade. The other was Pamela Mason. Both bodies were on the side of a road and covered with a coat.

"HUNT KILLER OF PAM: 14-Year–Old-Girl Sex Fiend Victim" read one headline. "Stress Striking Similarities in Mason, Valade Slayings." And "Veteran Probers Claim Killings Could be Work of One Human Monster," read another.

The police said that Pam, like Sandra, had been murdered elsewhere because there was little blood found beneath her body. I was terrified. When Moe came home, I showed her the paper.

"I'm scared." Moe began to cry.

Mom came home, raced through the door, and hugged us. "I know. I saw the headline at work. But I didn't have a second to read the paper. That poor child." Her voice cracked.

Mom kept shaking her head as she read. She put her arms around Moe and me. "I'd die if anyone hurt you," she said. "And Joe, too. Your father's been worried about this very thing for weeks."

The phone rang. "I'll bet it's him."

"Hi Hon. Yes, they saw it."

Mom listened for a bit, curling the telephone cord in her fingers. "I know. Yes, of course I'll tell them."

She hung up.

"Dad wanted to tell you himself that Pam's body has been found. But he's been so busy at the crime scene that he didn't have time to call."

Joey came tromping into the kitchen. Mom put the paper in the trash. "How was Fellowship?"

"Good," said Joe. "Is there anything to eat?"

"Have a banana, but don't load up. We'll be eating in an hour," said Mom.

She gestured to Moe and me to come upstairs. She pulled off her uniform and tossed it in the hamper. "Don't say anything to Joe about this. The *Union Leader's* coverage is irresponsible."

"Why is it irresponsible?" I asked.

"The public doesn't need to know that a fourteen-year-old girl was sexually tortured." She was fuming. "How are her family and friends going to feel reading this stuff?"

I began to cry.

Mom stroked my hair. "You and Moe can do things right now to protect yourself. We've locked our doors since the Valade murder. And for now, don't ever be alone unless you're in a public place. I looked at her. How could I never be alone again? "It's okay for you to walk home from school. But never walk alone after dark. Is that clear?" She pulled on her blue housecoat.

We nodded. Moe gave me a look when Mom mentioned walking home from school, but I knew that with the Mason killer on the loose, neither Mom nor Dad would care about Moe being in a car with Gene. Maybe Moe could talk Gene into picking up Joe and me.

"And we don't want you reading the paper. Dad will tell you what you need to know about this case. Is that clear?"

We said "yes," but I had no intention of not reading the paper. Dad wouldn't tell us a thing that would make us worry, and I knew that we had plenty to worry about.

We went to bed before he came home that night. But he was in the kitchen the next morning. He looked like he hadn't slept or showered in days. Joe was in the living room watching cartoons, something never allowed on a school morning.

"I told Mom to get me up before she left for work because I wanted to talk to you." Dad pulled pancakes out of the oven and sat down. I couldn't stand to look at them, but I took one.

He cleared his throat. "This is hard. Very hard. There's a maniac out there killing girls. I want you to know that the guys at the station will work non-stop until we arrest him. And I want you to know that you're safe."

I poked at my pancake. Moe was silent. We knew we weren't safe.

12

It seems that I'm the guy the cops call every time a girl disappears. They hadn't been able to pin Valade's murder on me and I was goddamned if they were going to get me for Mason's. Wasn't my fault the stupid girl put a sign up in a laundromat. I looked at my watch: 1:45 am. Jesus. We'd had pizza hours ago. My stomach is growling. Were they planning on giving me breakfast, too?

"Guys, can we take a break and meet later for a few beers?" My lip is twitching. It's a thing I do when I'm nervous. I cough into my fist to hide it.

Detective Donovan is a big guy with glassy blue eyes. I think that I know him from someplace. He offers me a cigarette and taps one out for himself. Every time I answer a question Officer Coakley, who sits at the end of the table, takes down what I say. Then I remember.

"Aren't you Dan Donovan's brother?" I asked. I can tell I've struck a nerve because Donovan's head snaps up like a fish on a line.

He leans forward. "Listen Eddie. Get this straight. I'm the one who's asking the questions and you're the one answering them. Is that clear?"

"Yes, sir." My answer is sarcastic. I feel bad for Dan having such a turd for a brother.

"Eddie, folks at the laundromat have told us that you spent several minutes in front of their bulletin board."

"Big deal. So, I look at bulletin boards. Since when is that a crime?"

My lip is twitching again, and Donovan gives me a long stare. I feel my neck getting tight, and my ass is killing me from sitting in the metal chair. I'd like to pick it up and smash Detective Donovan's brains out with it and then do that skinny little Coakley jerk too. "Someone in the laundromat who saw you looking at the board told us that you read Pamela's ad out loud."

My chest tightens. It had to be that cleaning lady bitch. Always sneaking around in her red-checked apron and pretending to be so friendly. I wonder if she was peering out her window and saw me drive by a few nights later. If she did, I am in deep shit. I smile, forcing myself to keep my voice even. "Look, Detective. I live in East Manchester. Why would I be looking for a babysitter way the hell over on the West Side?"

"That's what I'm wondering, Eddie. That's exactly what I'm wondering." Donovan taps out his cigarette.

We sit in silence. I'll be damned if I'm opening my mouth. I yawn and look at my watch.

"Okay, Eddie. You're free to go for now. But don't leave Manchester." Donovan gets up and nods to the guy taking notes.

Before I can even think of leaving Manchester, I have some business that I need to take care of. I get into my car and slam my hand again and again against the steering wheel. Damn that woman. She and I are going to have a little chat.

13

The police suspected that both Sandra and Pamela were murdered by the same psycho. Coroner Lavoie would determine if

Pam had been sexually molested before or after death. Lavoie said that Pam couldn't have been murdered in a car, because what had been done to her required a lot of room. My heart stopped when I read this.

Dad wasn't home for dinner that night. Mom wanted to talk about our school day but didn't mention Pam's murder. She went downstairs to our bomb shelter, brought up a bottle of wine, and poured herself a glass.

Sister Xavier was as upset as we were about Pamela. She had us pray for Pam's family, for the policemen who spent hours looking for her, and that God grant eternal rest to Pam. She looked at me and Missy when she mentioned the policemen.

Life got scarier as the police searched for Pam's killer. Manchester residents kept their doors locked.

And yet, in spite of locked doors, another Manchester female was found dead. Wife and mother Rena Paquette had gone to the Police Department offering information about Pam's killer. Days later, Rena's son and brother-in-law found her burned to death in a pigpen on her farm. Although it was February, she was wearing only her slippers, nightgown, and bathrobe. The Attorney General concluded Paquette's death was a suicide. He noted that she'd made wild accusations about who she suspected was the killer.

Although never friends, Missy and I became partners of sorts because our fathers were detectives.

"I don't know why she'd go out to a pigpen without a jacket and boots in the middle of winter," said Colleen. "It makes no sense."

"I thought the same thing," It killed me to agree with Colleen. "And the newspaper makes it sound like Mrs. Paquette was mental."

"My father's sure she was murdered," said Missy.

We stared at her.

"He saw her body. He said that three big logs were placed against the pigpen's door. Mrs. Paquette couldn't have put them there if she was inside setting herself on fire."

Why would anyone set themselves on fire? I thought of Joan of Arc, who burned to death, but it wasn't a suicide. She was tied to a stake.

"Remember what the newspaper said about Pam's murder?" asked Colleen. "She couldn't have been murdered in a car because the killer needed more room to torture her. I'll bet he murdered Pam in Mrs. Paquette's pigpen. And then pigs lapped up the blood. Maybe Mrs. Paquette knew about it and the killer murdered her to shut her up."

The recess bell rang, and we went inside for geography. Sister Xavier handed out maps of Europe with its major rivers. We had to write in the rivers' names in blue pencil and the names of the European capital cities in red.

I wondered if Mrs. Paquette really knew who murdered Pamela and if Colleen was right about the pigpen. Maybe Sandra got murdered there, too.

14

It was Saint Agatha's feast day. I asked Moe if the school was doing anything to celebrate, and she said no. I told her that they should rename the school. Saint Agatha's story was terrifying because her murder was too much like Sandra Valade's and Pamela Mason's. Maybe stories like Saint Agatha's encouraged psychos to torture teen-age girls.

"You can do it when you're on Student Council," she said.

I couldn't stay away from the newspaper. Mom told me not to read it, but I hurried from school so I'd get a chance to skim it, wrap it up, and leave it on the kitchen counter before she came home. On days Mom was off, I'd fish the paper out of the garbage after she went to bed. I knew that she suspected me, because she began using the newspaper to absorb bacon grease and wrap up vegetable peels.

I learned a lot reading the grease-stained news. Barry Goldwater was the Republican favorite for president. William Loeb wrote that New York politicians were trying to help negroes only so that they could get their votes, even though helping negroes was not in the best interest of white people. I didn't understand why white people had different interests from negroes. I read that a sixteen-year-old girl was beaten, raped, and strangled in Lawrence, her dead body found in a ditch near the Merrimack River. I'd gotten used to girls getting raped and strangled. Maybe it had always been going on, but no one mentioned it. Manchester was celebrating the start of the 1964 Winter Carnival. Senator Margaret Chase Smith of Maine was running for president, but New Hampshire Republicans, both men and women, agreed that the country wasn't ready for a woman president. Someone said that teenagers should be enlisted to find Pam's killer because they drove their jalopies all over Manchester and might know something about Pam's disappearance. I wondered if Gene knew anything. A man chased a girl on Hayward Street, but she got away by running into Our Lady of Perpetual Help Church. I wouldn't run into a dark church if I was being chased. Running into the road made more sense. Eighty-four whites and negroes were arrested in an Atlanta civil rights demonstration. Lee Harvey Oswald's wife told government officials that Oswald was a Russian agent and guilty of JFK's murder. New Hampshire Attorney General Maynard said the probe for Pam's murderer will not end. And teens all over the US were planning on watching the Beatles on Ed Sullivan on February 9.

Dad got that weekend off so Mom could go with her friend Shirley to a Catholic Nurses' Retreat. When she came home, she said that even the priests leading the retreat were going to watch the Beatles.

We sat in front of the TV along with the rest of America. The audience went wild when the four Beatles wandered onstage and wouldn't stop screaming until Ed Sullivan threatened to send for a barber.

They sang "All My Loving" followed by "Til there Was You". Moe sat starry-eyed.

The camera did a close-up of John Lennon with a caption, "Sorry girls, he's married."

"Look at their hair," Mom giggled.

"They look foolish," said Dad. Moe looked at me. Crabby Dad was back.

15

"Let's talk about what we're giving up for Lent," said Sister Xavier. I didn't see how giving up anything helped the world or my soul. The day before, the *Union Leader* reported that our Attorney General said folks in Manchester should give up gossip for Lent. Maynard said folks had to accept facts: Rena Paquette committed suicide by setting fire to herself in her pigpen. I was sure that he was wrong. Someone had murdered Rena Paquette. Forget telling Manchester to give up gossip. Maybe someone in the AG's office should give up lying.

"Nora?" Sister Xavier sounded impatient. "Please tell us what you plan to give up."

I jumped.

"Candy," I said.

It would have been saintly of me to give up reading newspapers, because reading the newspaper was my favorite thing to do. The only articles I read were about Pam, but I scanned all the headlines.

The FBI agents helping the police on Pam's case were working hard but had no leads. Eighteen-year-old Malden girl Georgia Ellis escaped attack by would-be strangler. I wished that the article told us how she got away. Terrorists killed US soldiers in Saigon. I wondered where Saigon was and what we were doing there. LBJ signed historic Civil Rights Bill. I was glad about this, but I wondered how guys like my Uncle Danny felt.

On Good Friday, we sat reading or praying silently at our desks from noon until three, marking the three hours Jesus hung on the cross before dying. It would be terrible to be crucified. I'd always thought that Jesus died from blood loss, but Moe said no. Her religion teacher said that Jesus was asphyxiated because He got so weak that He couldn't hold up His head to breathe.

After spending three hours at school meditating on Jesus' torture and crucifixion, I came home to the news that the police had arrested Pam's killer. The man who tortured, raped, and murdered her. The man the police suspected tortured, sexually assaulted, and shot Sandra Valade. The man who probably murdered Rena Paquette. The man who terrorized Manchester for years.

I examined his picture. He looked like a guy who could be your mailman. Like a guy who would ask you to babysit his kids. Eddie Coolidge terrified me because he looked so normal. The paper said that Coolidge was being held at the Valley Street Jail until his trial early next year. Coolidge in jail lightened my life.

I heard Dad come home in the middle of the night, but he was at work when I got up. Mom was in the kitchen with her back to me, so she didn't know that I was there.

"Shirley, we did what we could. That ass of a doctor didn't take any action."

I didn't know what Shirley said, but my mother started up again.

"Yes, I knew it was him when Tom said that the Mason girl had human bite marks all over her torso. Just like we saw on his wife when she was in having her baby."

Shirley said something.

"We did what we could," said Mom. "How could we possibly know? Tom said they're going to nail him. I've got to run, Shirley. The kids will be up any minute."

I stepped into the kitchen. "How's Shirley?" I asked.

"Her back is bothering her, but otherwise she's good. Do you want some cocoa? It's chilly."

"Cocoa would be great," I answered. Mom didn't know I'd overheard her conversation. And I'd heard quite enough about bite marks.

16

Gene was working as a counselor at his uncle's camp on Winnepesaukee. So Moe and I spent a lot of time together, swimming at Livingston and belting out our favorite tunes on the radio.

Joe was proud he got picked to be Lead Altar Boy, working with the younger kids who'd just started altar boy training.

"I hope Father knows that our family is going to Hampton Beach for a week in July," said Mom.

"Oh, we had to give him our schedules the last week of school," said Joe. "And guess what? Father's taking us to see the Red Sox play in August. Then he's taking us out for Chinese. We're staying overnight at a hotel in Boston."

Mom raised her eyebrows. "I don't know why he can't buy you kids hot dogs and come home after the game. Hotels are expensive."

"He's just being nice, Mom."

"Let's talk to your dad about it," she said.

I had a family party for my twelfth birthday. Joe and Moe gave me a charm bracelet and my parents bought me a navy-blue Pandora sweater.

"President Johnson has given you a birthday gift," said Mom. "He's signed the Civil Rights Act into law. I hope that this will put an end to racial hatred in this country."

I wondered how Governor Wallace and his followers would feel about this. And people like Uncle Danny.

Joe went with Father Murphy, Paul, and some other kids to see the Red Sox play the Yankees in late August. When he came home, he was quiet. I told him if the priests had another Boston expedition that he should request to be dropped off at the Museum of Science. He scowled.

17

I trudged up the stairs to Sister Imelda's room. I wanted to get the new lay eighth-grade teacher, but no luck.

Sister took attendance. She made Missy and Donald go around the class passing out our textbooks. Missy gave me a fake smile and put a beat-up pile of books on my desk. Donald showed up a second later.

"Here, let's swap, Nora." His voice surprised me. He sounded like a man. He put a new set of books on my desk and put the crappy pile Missy gave me on his desk. I blushed and looked down so no one would notice

Sister Imelda told us how she planned to run the class.

"I have a strict attendance policy. See this?" She held out a skinny arm and dangled a key in front of us. "I expect you in your seats at 8:00 AM sharp. After that, the door will be locked."

Bobby Langdon raised his hand. "What do we do if we get locked out, Sister?"

"That's up to you, Mr. Langdon. You can wander the streets of Manchester, go shoplifting at Leavitt's, or sit in the Carpenter Memorial Library all day for all I care." She fluttered her fingers in the air as if she couldn't be bothered with such worries.

Missy raised her hand.

"Yes, Miss Callahan?"

"The city has a truant officer. Would you get arrested if one of us got picked up as a truant?"

"Don't threaten me with police tactics, Miss Callahan. If you get arrested for shoplifting at Leavitt's, that would be one story. If the truant officer arrested you in the library reference section, that would be quite another. Any other questions, class?"

It was going to be a long year.

That fall, Albert de Salvo admitted to being the Boston Strangler. The court found him guilty, and he was sent to Bridgewater State Prison for a psychiatric evaluation. Seemed to me that trying to figure out if he was crazy or not was a waste of time. If he was guilty, he was guilty and should just be locked up.

18

Moe took a sudden interest in cooking. When we'd go to the library on Thursday evenings, she'd spend her time copying dessert recipes from ladies' magazines.

"What's going on with her?" I whispered to my mother as we stood in the checkout line.

"Gene's going to join us for dessert on Thanksgiving." Mom laughed quietly. "Next thing they'll be planning a wedding."

I didn't think it was funny. I wondered why Mom wasn't warning Moe about the oldest Benson girl who got married young to some dope, had two kids, and lived in the project.

Moe decided that she'd make a lemon meringue pie, Gene's favorite.

"What the hell kind of guy likes lemon meringue pie?" I heard Dad ask. "I hope you'll make a pecan and an apple pie for the rest of us."

"Kathleen is bringing an apple pie, and of course I'll do a pecan. I hope your brother doesn't make an ass out of himself," she added.

"I promise you that Kathleen and I will keep him in line."

Our Thanksgiving table looked beautiful. Mom bought a new white tablecloth and Marcel sent a centerpiece from Chalifour's. The doorbell rang. It was Marcel and Aunt Kathleen. She wore a green dress and her hair was up in a bun. When she kissed me, I smelled Chanel. She handed Mom an apple pie.

"It looks beautiful, Kathleen. Thank you."

Aunt Kathleen pulled us aside. "Tell me about school," she said. "Joe first."

"I'm in fifth grade, and I have Sister Ernestine."

"Sister Ernestine?" Aunt Kathleen widened her eyes. "Oh, I always wanted to have her. Girls, you didn't have her either, did you?"

Moe and I shook our heads no.

"And Joe, Marcel and I love seeing you on the altar when we attend Mass at All Saints'."

"What about you, Nora?"

"Oh, I got stuck with Sister Imelda," I said.

"Not Imelda!" Aunt Kathleen lowered her voice. "She's nuts. Has she locked you out yet?"

"No, but she's locked out a couple of kids. Donald Morse gets locked out a lot because he's always late. But Sister Lucinda walks him back to the class, and Sister Imelda agrees to negotiate."

"Get locked out at least once. It would be good training in case you decide to go to law school," she said.

"Now Moe, are you still seeing that handsome guy?"

Moe blushed. "Yes, and he's coming for dessert."

The front door opened, and Uncle Danny walked in with a pretty brunette. He hadn't even knocked.

"Moe, go set another place," whispered my mother.

"Folks, I'd like you to meet Rosemarie."

Rosemarie handed my mother a Whitman's Sampler. "You have a beautiful house, Helen. And thanks for inviting me."

Dan laughed. "Rosemarie, you weren't invited. But I knew that I could bring you along because you eat like a bird, and there's always plenty of food at my brother Tom's place."

Rosemarie's face turned red. Uncle Danny was such a jerk.

Aunt Kathleen took Rosemarie by the elbow. "We're happy that you're here. I'm Dan's sister and used to his baloney. I just ignore it."

Rosemarie turned to Dad. "Tom, it's so nice to be here. Dan talks about your wonderful family all the time."

"Thanks, Rosemarie." Dad looked surprised. So was I. I couldn't imagine Uncle Danny saying anything wonderful about any of us.

"Marcel, Dan has told me about your work at Sanders on the space stuff. That's exciting."

Marcel smiled. "The truth is, I was in the right place at the right time."

"I don't know, brother-in-law," said Dan. "I don't seem to be ever in the right place at the right time. Now being at the wrong place, I'm good at that."

Rosemarie smiled. "Danny, let's sit down. Helen's put out cheese and crackers."

"Can I get you a drink? Tom has scotch, beer, Coke, and Blue Nun," asked Marcel. I was wondering who would offer my uncle a drink. I knew that my mother would rather die, and my father would pour him the smallest drink possible.

"I'll take a beer," said Uncle Dan.

"Blue Nun is my favorite," said Rosemarie.

We sat in the living room as the turkey cooled on the kitchen counter. Mom cracked the living room window when it began getting hot.

The ladies gossiped about the Sacred Heart. Aunt Kathleen wanted to hear about Shirley's baby—not a great sleeper but fine—and Mom wanted to hear about the latest doings in the ICU. Dan, Dad, and Marcel talked about football. Marcel tried roping Joe into the conversation, but Joe said little. Uncle Danny got up and got himself another beer. Rosemarie covered her glass when he offered her a refill.

"Tom, please put the turkey on the table," asked Mom. "Moe, please fill the water glasses and pour milk for you kids."

"Let me help," said Rosemarie.

"Thanks," said Mom. "I'll get you an apron and you can start putting the vegetables in the serving dishes. Joe, I left matches by the candles. Please light them. And be careful."

"This altar boy lights candles more than anyone else in the room," said Joe.

"What are Danny and me?" called Marcel. "Chopped liver?"

"I'll enlist you for cleanup," said Mom.

Danny turned to Marcel. "Look at Joe. The kid's got it made in the shade. All he's got to do is light a few candles, and he's done. But Helen would have me slaving in the kitchen for hours washing pots and never bat an eyelash."

Mom turned to Rosemarie. "I've never done that."

"Oh, I'm sure you haven't," laughed Rosemarie.

We took our seats. Dad said grace.

"Nice job on the candles, Joe," said Uncle Danny.

Joey gave him a thumbs-up.

As Dad carved, Mom cleared her throat. "Let's go around the table and say what we're thankful for."

Moe sighed.

"I'll start," said Uncle Danny. "I'm grateful that I found Rosemarie, and I'm grateful to live in the USA."

Marcel went next. "I'm grateful that Kathleen agreed to marry me, and I'm grateful to our country."

Dad followed. "I'm grateful that Helen hasn't booted me out. I'm grateful for my kids, and I'm grateful to my country."

"I'm thankful to be part of this wonderful family," said Aunt Kathleen.

How did adults come up with stuff so fast? I was grateful that Eddie Coolidge was in the Valley Street jail and hadn't ravished and murdered me, but I knew that I shouldn't say that. So I said that I was grateful that the Civil Rights Act had passed.

Everyone stared at me.

"That's so sweet that you mentioned the Civil Rights Act," said Rosemarie. "My brother-in-law is a negro, and he's had a terrible time in the military," she said.

Uncle Danny was aghast. "Corinne married a n-n-negro?" he asked. "Why didn't you mention this?"

Rosemarie took a sip from her water and ignored Uncle Danny.

"Tom, why don't you plate the turkey, and we'll pass the side dishes around?" asked Mom. "And I want to say what I'm grateful for. This has been a tough year for Tom with the terrible Mason murder, but he's never wavered. I'm grateful that I found such a good man. I'm blessed with a lovely family, and like all of you, I am happy to live in the USA."

Joey said that he was grateful for his family and that he lived in a country with such a cool space program. Moe said she was grateful for her family and her nice boyfriend.

I think I was the only one who noticed that Rosemarie didn't say what she was grateful for. I wanted to ask her so that she wouldn't feel left out, but the men started talking about sports and the women talked about the turkey and the sweet potatoes.

The conversation moved to Vietnam and how LBJ was going to launch a full-out attack to prevent Communism from spreading in Southeast Asia.

"Kennedy decided that he was going to fight Communism in Vietnam," said Marcel. "So Johnson's plan is no surprise."

"But Cuba is next to Florida and they're Communist. So why do we care if some far-away country becomes Communist?" I asked.

"A little Communist pinko here," laughed Uncle Danny. "Don't let Loeb find out or he'll write an editorial about her."

I was embarrassed and a little mad. I didn't know what I'd said that was wrong.

"Nora, you're right about Cuba being Communist. And Cuba's not bothering us. People get all worked up about Communism being a threat. You know what I read?" asked Aunt Kathleen. "I read that Jesus was actually the first true Communist."

136

"Oh, Lordy," groaned Uncle Dan.

My father stared at Aunt Kathleen like she'd grown another head.

"Think about it," said Aunt Kathleen. "Jesus was the one who said if you had two cloaks, give one away to a poor person. Jesus was all about sharing things." She turned to my father. "Sharing everything."

"That makes sense," said Moe.

"I think that Jesus might have been speaking metaphorically," said Marcel.

"What's metaphorical about two coats, Marcel?" asked Aunt Kathleen. "Seems pretty straightforward to me."

"Yeah, I think the idea that Jesus was a Communist makes sense," said Moe. "He didn't like the rich."

"But remember that thousands of people have died because of Communism," said Marcel.

"Did Jesus die because he was a Communist?" asked Joe. I thought that was a good question. But no one answered.

"Interesting idea that Jesus was the first true Communist," said Mom. "When I was at my retreat last spring, Father O'Donnell said that if Jesus came back, he'd come back as a black man."

My father almost fell out of his chair.

"That priest was absolutely right," said Rosemarie. "Negroes are treated horribly in this country. I know because Cliff, my brother-in-law…"

Danny got up and threw his napkin on the floor. "You and your sister. What is it with you two nigger lovers? I'm leaving right now. If you want a ride home, you'd better come with me."

"We're happy to give you a ride, Rosemarie," said Marcel.

Rosemarie dabbed at her mouth with her napkin. "I think I'll stay for dessert, Dan. But you leave now if you want to."

Mom and Dad looked at each other across the table as Uncle Danny stormed out.

Gene knocked at the door, and Moe ran to let him in.

"Who's that guy who just left?" I heard Gene ask Moe. "As I was coming up the walk, I asked him if there was any lemon meringue pie left, and he shouted, "Only assholes eat lemon meringue pie!"

"That's just Uncle Danny," Moe said. "Don't mind him."

Gene came in and met the family. Moe's lemon meringue pie—actually all the pies—were delicious. No one said another word about Jesus being a black Communist, and Rosemarie went home with Aunt Kathleen and Uncle Marcel.

And I went to sleep that night thankful that Eddie Coolidge was behind bars.

1965

I opened my eyes when I heard the car back out of the driveway, wheels spinning on a frozen crust of ice. The house was quiet except for the radiator hissing next to my bed. Mom was working at 7:00 because she'd had Thanksgiving and Christmas off. Dad was heading to the station to meet with other detectives and the state prosecutor to work on the case against Coolidge. "It must be airtight. We need all the prep time we can get."

Moe and other student council members were delivering flowers and candy to local nursing homes. Gene was picking her up at Saint Agatha's at noon and they were heading to Hampton Beach.

Even Joe had plans for New Year's Day. Father Murphy was hosting a breakfast for the altar boys after Mass. After breakfast, he was taking them sledding at the Derryfield Country Club.

I wandered down to the kitchen. It was a mess.

Nora, take the ham out of the fridge at 2:00 and stick in 1/3 cup cloves. Drizzle the glaze over the top and pop it in the oven—350 at 3:00.

Mom XO

At least Mom didn't write the "nice ham." She hardly ever used the word ham without the word nice. I wondered if other people did the same. I never heard Mom say, a "nice chicken" or a "nice meatloaf."

So much for a quiet and restful day. And then I saw another note.

Nora, please run the vacuum. The house is full of dead needles.
And pick up the kitchen? Hope to be home for kickoff. Dad

My day was going to stink. Running the Hoover on New Year's
Day was vacuuming at its worst. It took forever to suck up all the
dry needles and stray pieces of tinsel that got stuck in the carpet and
clung to the legs of the furniture. No matter how hard I tried, we'd
be finding needles until Easter. And having needles in the cracks of
the floor always drove Dad nuts. It took me until noon to finish my
cleaning chores. I barely had time to shower before fussing with the
nice ham.

Jabbing cloves into the ham was a waste of time. Dad told me
once that if you ate too many cloves, they could send you into liver
failure. As far as I could tell, the only reason for using cloves was to
make the kitchen smell good.

Mom said that a ham looked particularly nice if you created a
diamond pattern with the cloves and hung pineapple slices from
them.

Dad walked in the door just as I finished forcing the liver
hazards into the nice ham. "Did you have a nice morning, sweetie?"

"Yes. I had a nice morning fiddling with the nice ham. How
did it go with the Coolidge stuff?"

"We're going through every piece of information we have to
build the strongest case possible. It seems like a slam-dunk, but we
don't want to take any chances." I saw his eyes scanning the floor
for stray needles, but he must have been satisfied. "Looks like the
trial will start sometime at the end of May."

Fingers crossed that they have enough evidence to nail the
psycho, I thought.

Dad plopped himself in his Barcalounger and turned on the
Rose Bowl Parade. Pasadena's sun made Manchester's skies seem
even more gray.

We watched marching bands and baton-twirling majorettes
from all over the country. Sun-tanned people who looked like TV

models rode floats decorated with roses. My favorite was the Sees' Candy float, which had the Chipmunks dancing in circles and singing Beatles' songs. Dad was happy that Arnold Palmer was the Grand Marshall of the parade. "I'm not a fan of golf, but I like Arnold Palmer," he said. "Behind the scenes, he does a lot for the less fortunate."

The parade ended with the Rose Bowl Queen sitting on a throne wearing a tiara and a long white dress covered with sequins that sparkled in the sun. A bouquet of red roses rested on her lap, and she waved her hand side- to-side like the Queen of England.

"We've got the Michigan Wolverines against the Oregon State Beavers. Who are you rooting for?" Dad chowed down on a bowl of mixed nuts.

"I don't know much about either team, but it seems to me a Wolverine is stronger than a Beaver. I'll cheer for Michigan."

"Good logic, young lady. I'll root for Oregon. I like to see the underdog win."

Mom walked in as the parade wrapped up. "The ham smells divine, Nora. I need to run upstairs and take a quick shower. Then I'll be down to start the carrots."

Father Murphy dropped Joe off just as the game started. He was smiling and his cheeks were bright red. "How was sledding?" I asked.

"It was fun. And Father Murphy brought a t-t-t…"

"TOBOGGAN!" snapped Dad.

Joey looked down.

"Were you warm enough?" I asked. I didn't know why Dad was acting like such a jerk.

"I was fine, and Father took us to the Puritan for hot chocolate before he brought us home."

"Well, he better not have ruined your appetite, young man." Mom pulled her apron off its hook and tied it around her waist.

Gene's car pulled up in front of the house, and Moe jumped out. She walked in the door just as the referee did the coin toss. "How was your day?" asked Mom.

"Nursing homes are depressing, but the people were happy to see us."

I doubt she would have been any happier staying home vacuuming or doing battle with the cloves and the nice ham, but I kept my mouth shut.

Kickoff was at 4:00. The Beavers scored first even though the Wolverines were favored by eleven points. At halftime, Michigan had a slight lead at twelve to seven. "Dinner's served," called Mom.

"It's your favorite, Tom. A nice ham with brown sugar, pineapple, carrots, and potatoes. And lots of gravy."

"Nora, the ham is divine," gushed Mom.

"Thanks Mom." I hoped no one had to go to the hospital because I overdid it with the cloves. I added more than I should've because the pineapple rings kept sliding off into the pan.

We chowed down quickly.

The second half was all Michigan and they ended up winning the game thirty-four to seven. The Beavers never even scored in the second half. "Congratulations, Nora," said Dad.

Later that night Dad snapped at Joe because he couldn't spit out the beginning of a sentence. "For Christ's sake, Joseph. Stop your stuttering and start over." I felt sorry for my brother. He started to cry and went upstairs. Mom didn't say anything.

"Why are you so grumpy all the time?" I asked.

"Nora, work gets to me. I think that if we had been able to find Sandra Valade's killer, Pamela Mason would be alive today." He and I sat in front of the TV for the rest of the evening and watched *The FBI*. We barely said a word. I couldn't help but think that Lewis Erskine from the FBI would have been able to find Sandra's killer. I wondered if Dad wondered the same.

2

"Welcome back, class," said Sister Imelda. "I hope you are well rested after all the joyous activities celebrating the birth of our Lord." I looked around the room. Nobody looked either rested or joyous.

"As you know, our President makes a State of the Union address every January to talk about goals for the upcoming year. This evening, the speech is going to be televised for the first time in history. For homework, you're to watch President Johnson and be prepared to discuss his priorities during *Current Events* class tomorrow."

That night we watched Johnson speak about his vision of a Great Society. He wanted to end racism once and for all, attack disease, fight poverty, give free health insurance to the elderly and the poor, reduce crime, and improve the environment. That seemed like a lot of work for one year. "Not a bad speech," Dad said after it was over. "But he's no JFK."

"Tom, he didn't even mention his goals for Vietnam. It's like the war doesn't exist."

"Let's give him the benefit of the doubt, Helen. Maybe he was just focused on his domestic goals."

When Sister Imelda asked for my thoughts on the speech the next day, I said that I was most excited about reducing crime and ending racism once and for all. "He's no Kennedy," I quoted my dad. "But it sounds like he wants to make our country a better and safer place to live."

"There'll never be another JFK," Sister said. "Now on to our next writing assignment." I hated the way Sister Imelda used the word "our" when she really meant "your." It wasn't like she had to bust her butt writing over the weekend. "You're to write a five-page paper on a Catholic leader whom you admire and who has influenced you. Who and why: that is our assignment. Due Monday."

I guessed that half the class would write about Pope John XXIII or JFK. I didn't want to write about those two men, and I wanted to stretch beyond the usual stuff in *The Lives of the Saints.*

I got Moe to meet me at the library after school. I went straight to the biography section. After searching the stacks, I found a book called *Hero of Molokai: Father Damien, Apostle of the Lepers.* Here was someone worth writing about.

"Moe, look at these pictures," I said as I flipped through the pages on our walk home.

"That's disgusting!" She was right. The pictures of the lepers zoomed in on their open, oozing sores. Fingers and toes falling off and the horrible facial deformities were sickening. That afternoon I read about Damien. He went to the Hawaiian Islands from Belgium and became a priest. "Moe, listen to this. 'When Damien found out that the Hawaiian government was deporting lepers to a settlement on the island of Molokai, he volunteered to go there and run the settlement to improve the treatment of the lepers. He taught them, dressed their seeping wounds, helped build houses and dug graves'."

"He must have been nuts!" exclaimed Moe.

"He probably knew he'd die there because there was no cure for leprosy; no one who went to Molokai ever returned. He got the disease himself and died there when he was forty-nine!" I said.

I wrote my report over the next two days. I began by saying that Father Damien would influence me for the rest of my life for the sacrifices he made knowing that his own life would likely be cut short. I was proud of the way I ended it. "Most people were tortured, killed, and made saints because of what they wouldn't do. Father Damien should be made a saint because of what he did do."

Just as I thought, most of the class wrote about John XXIII and JFK except for Donald Morse. He wrote about Father Smith and said he admired him "because it's hard to find men to look up to."

After I read my report to the class, Sister stared at me with her beady little eyes. "Nora Donovan, since when have you become qualified to judge who should become a saint? Next confession, be sure to tell the priest that you have committed the sin of pride."

I fell for that "sin of pride" baloney once when I was a little kid. I wasn't going to do that again. Sister was wrong. This had nothing to do with me and everything to do with Father Damien. He was a good man, and I knew that someday he'd become a saint. And when Mom dragged us to confession on Friday, I'd say that I'd disobeyed my parents and lied twice.

3

"Nora, Joe, come look at this," yelled Dad. We went downstairs. "Did you ever think you'd see the day that baseball was played indoors?"

John Chancellor was showing highlights of the eighth wonder of the world—the new Houston Astrodome. "Mickey Mantle hit a homerun this afternoon. He'll go down in the record books as the man who hit the first indoor homerun." Chancellor showed the crowd cheering as Mickey rounded the bases. He was met at home plate by his teammates who cleared the dugout, arms wide open.

I went back upstairs to tackle my math homework and heard my father grump "Damn Yankees."

Every time it snowed that winter, I had a sick feeling in my stomach. Was another girl was going to turn up dead? Dad tried to make me feel better. "Nora, we've got our man and he's sitting in the Valley Street jail waiting to go to trial. Mark my words, we have the right guy."

I wanted to believe him, but he was wrong before when he wondered about the Boston Strangler being Valade's killer. I was anxious for the trial to start in May. I wanted Coolidge to go to prison for the rest of his life so we could all get back to normal. Whatever that was. Maybe it'd be better if New Hampshire had the death penalty like Texas, and then we could execute the jerk and be done with him.

4

"Let's go to the Castle on Palm Sunday and take Auntie out to lunch," said Mom. Dad sighed and mentioned an unfinished report due at the station. Mom gave him The Look but didn't insist he join us. "Gene and I...," began Moe. She also got The Look, but Mom ignored her. Mom, Joe, Moe, and I piled in the car after Mass at All Saints' and headed down 93-South. I closed my eyes when I saw the sign for Derry. I knew we were near the spot where Pamela's body was found.

We picked Auntie up in front of the Castle and drove to a small restaurant down the road.

"Helen, everything on the menu looks yummy. I just can't make up my mind. Would it be alright if I ordered two lunches and brought one home for supper?" Moe kicked me under the table, and Joe covered his mouth to stifle a laugh.

"Of course, Auntie. Order whatever you want," said Mom. I knew that it probably wasn't okay with Mom since she always reminded us that money doesn't grow on trees.

Back at Windham Castle, Auntie asked me to hold her food while she grabbed her cane and hobbled into the second-floor kitchen to stick her supper in the refrigerator.

"Is anyone coming?" she whispered. I said there was no one around. "That's good. If Agnes saw us, she'd be down here in a flash to see what I was tucking away. She's always snooping in the refrigerator," Auntie grumped. "I don't trust her as far as I can throw her. Food goes missing around here all the time."

When we got back to Auntie's room, she told us that Sister Stephen's room across the hall was decorated for Easter. "Her family decorates for every holiday. Just last week they took down the shamrocks and leprechauns from Saint Patrick's Day, and two hours later her room was set for Easter."

I looked around Sister Stephen's room and saw a hodge-podge of stuff ranging from a picture of Jesus Christ rising from the dead to bunnies and colorful eggs. Pastel colored streamers hung from the tops of the window and door. On her windowsill stood a resurrection display with Jesus standing on a rock with his hands outstretched. A crowd stood around, gazing adoringly.

I'm pretty sure Auntie was hinting that her family should decorate her room for every holiday.

"But Auntie, aren't these decorations a fire hazard?" asked Mom. There was no response from Auntie who plainly hadn't considered the safety issues associated with over-decorating.

Auntie gave us a building tour. We started at the cafeteria where she usually sat at mealtime. "I sit here because the waitress at this table is Roseanna, and she doesn't care that I'm diabetic. She gives me whatever I want to eat." After the cafeteria, we made our way to the multipurpose room. "We have exercise classes here during the day and wakes at night." Maybe the Connor Funeral Home should start holding exercise classes during the day. Or maybe run bingo at night to make ends meet during their dry spells.

The visit ended in the refectory where a young nun, probably drafted to play cards or do jigsaw puzzles with the old ones, served peanut butter cookies and milk to the visitors. We said our good-byes and drove home. "Mom, that was torture." Moe was grumpy about missing an afternoon of who-knows-what with Gene.

"Maureen, just offer it up for the souls in purgatory," scolded Mom. I couldn't imagine that those poor souls would find any redemption in Moe giving up an afternoon with Gene.

5

The bell rang, and recess was over. I saw a little girl trip over a baseball bat that someone had left on the playground.

Her knees were bleeding, and she had sand in the cuts on her hands. She was crying hysterically. I walked with her into the nurse's office and distracted her while the nurse cleaned up her cuts and covered them with Snoopy Band-Aids.

As I headed back toward my classroom, I stopped. I turned left and marched straight into the principal's office. I wasn't going to give Imelda the satisfaction of locking me out. I'd talk to Sister Lucinda who was much more reasonable. Lucinda was understanding and thanked me for staying with the little girl in the nurse's office. "Nora, I'll walk you back to your classroom and explain the circumstances to Sister Imelda."

She knocked on the classroom door. Sister Imelda greeted us. "May we come in?" asked Sister Lucinda. Without waiting for a reply, she brushed past Sister Imelda and stood with me in front of the classroom. "Sister Imelda, Nora is late for class because she tended to the wounds of a frightened little girl who had an accident on the playground. Boys and girls, let's strive to be like Nora Donovan who followed the lessons taught by our Lord Jesus Christ and demonstrated 'do unto others as others would do unto you.' Well done, young lady." Sister Lucinda winked at me as she turned and left the classroom.

I smiled at Sister Imelda. Her beady eyes followed me all the way back to my seat. I couldn't wait to tell Aunt Kathleen.

6

My head feels like it's going to explode. The girl I almost picked up that night instead of Pam—Barbara somebody—and Mrs. Mason are driving me crazy, waving prayer books and crying. I look at the judge. Why doesn't he tell them to shut up? Mrs. Mason must have been a looker; she's still hot for a woman in her thirties. Pam wouldn't talk about her mother, even though I pushed her. She only cried, which really pissed me off. The guy who stopped to help me after I made the drop-off takes the stand. I remember the snow blinding me as I told him I was fine. My lip starts trembling, and I cough to cover it up. Remembering the snowstorm brings it all back. My wet pant legs. The screams. The smell of blood. Hot blood making pink smoke as it hits the snow. The smell is intoxicating, but

I have to make it go away. I take some slow, deep breaths. My lip stops its craziness, and I reach for my water glass. The judge calls for a recess. I'm dripping with sweat. My lawyer looks at me. "You okay?" he whispers.

"Yeah, fine. Just fine."

7

The trial started on May 17. I stopped at Arti-Lou's on my way home from school and glanced at the headline. "Coolidge on Trial Today for Murder of Manchester Girl." They moved the trial from Manchester to Nashua because Coolidge's defense team said legal proceedings wouldn't be fair in Manchester where both Pamela and Sandra lived. And so it began.

As usual, there was no chit-chat at home about what was going on in the courtroom. I had to get all the unpublished details by sucking up to Missy Callahan and Patty Carmody, whose father was a State Trooper. Kids on the playground talked non-stop about the trial. It didn't seem like their parents cared what they knew about the case. Every day, Missy, Patty, and me got together at recess to piece together what was going on in Nashua. Neither reporters nor the public were allowed in the courtroom, Missy said, because the judge didn't want to turn the trial into a circus.

"My father thinks that it's pretty much an open and shut case," said Missy. It made me feel better that our dads agreed. Coolidge would rot in prison for the rest of his life.

Mrs. Mason said Pam was a smart and lovely young woman. A Rainbow Girl. A popular babysitter. An honor student. A notice in the laundromat. Police said she was kidnapped. Shot twice in the head. Stabbed four times. Throat slashed. Sexually molested. No blood. Must have been killed somewhere else. School books found scattered near the body. Navy pea coat. Blouse, ecru color found frozen to the ground. Olive green ski pants. Loops under the arches. Side zipper. Crotch cut out. White fabric athletic socks. Cuts on body. No blood on clothes. Stabbed naked. Clothing removed for killing and then put back on. No undergarments. Undigested fried egg sandwich in stomach. Killed between 7:00 and 10:00 PM.

The playground conversations echoed in my head night after night as I lay in bed. Images of Pam's murder made it impossible to fall asleep. It didn't seem to bother Moe. Even with bristly curlers in her hair, she managed to knock off as soon as her head hit the pillow.

"What's that red mark on your neck, Moe?" I asked as she changed into her nightgown. Her face got just about as red as the mark on her neck.

"What red mark?"

"The red mark of the right side of your neck that's the size of Massabesic Lake," I teased.

"Oh, it's nothing," she said.

"What do you mean it's nothing? It's a big, giant red mark on your neck," I pressed.

"Okay, but if you tell Mom and Dad, I'll kill you, I swear. Gene kissed me on my neck and sucked my skin so hard that it left this mark. It's kind of like a bruise. It's called a hickey. A love bite. And lots of guys give them to their girlfriends."

I burst out laughing and bounced on my bed and sang "Gene, Gene, the kissing machine…" as she put her curlers in her hair. Finally, Moe started laughing too.

But when she dropped off to sleep, I thought about the coroner saying that Pam had bite marks all over her breasts and abdomen. And Mom saying that Coolidge's wife had them too. I tossed and turned, trying to get comfortable in bed. When do love bites turn into hate bites?

8

Coolidge took the stand. He said that he went to his social club the night Pam was murdered and then drove to Haverhill, Massachusetts to buy his wife an anniversary present. All the stores were closed. When asked if he had killed Pamela Mason, he replied "No sir, I did not."

"How could anyone believe a bullshit story like that? Of course the stores were closed," Missy said. "There was a raging snowstorm! How could he think the jury would believe his story?" Missy's dad told her that the strongest evidence against Coolidge was Pam's hair and clothing fibers found in his car. And a gun the police grabbed from his house matched the bullets found in Pam's head.

Dad came home and burst though the kitchen door. Finally, he had something to say. "It's over, folks! Coolidge has been convicted of the Mason murder and will spend the rest of his God-forsaken life behind bars." I couldn't believe how relieved I felt. I didn't have to worry about being murdered, Dad could put the case behind him, and we could all get back to normal.

"What about the Valade murder. Did they get him for that too?" I asked. "And what about Rena Paquette?"

"No, Maynard said they had so much evidence against him in the Mason murder that it made little sense trying to nail him on any others. He's locked up for life and that is what's most important."

"So, you're telling me that he'll never get out of prison?" I asked.

"Well one can never say for sure. He's entitled to appeal the verdict and he likely will. That's the right of every American citizen."

"But an appeal can't change the facts or the evidence, right?" I asked nervously.

"That's right, sweetie. The hair and clothing fibers found in Coolidge's car tie him to the Mason murder. It'll take some time for them to re-try this case, so let's just be glad he's locked up in the maximum-security prison in Concord."

I hoped that things would return to normal now that Coolidge was in prison. Although I had kind of forgotten what normal was.

9

I said goodbye to seventh grade and good riddance to crazy Sister Imelda. Mom said that she heard through the grapevine that they were encouraging Sister to retire to the Castle in Windham. They must think she's crazy too, I thought. I wondered if she would lock the other sisters out of rooms in the Castle. Or hold visitors hostage in the refectory and lose the key. Or maybe put a lock on the refrigerator to avoid midnight thievery. Windham would be a good place for Imelda, I thought. Dad said that it was the perfect place for all those old ladies who had passed their expiration date.

I plopped down with my parents to watch the news. Walter Cronkite said President Johnson planned to increase the number of troops in Vietnam. And he planned to do it by doubling the draft calls to 35,000.

My friend Donald Morse's brother Richard was drafted earlier this year. Donald said it was probably a good thing because his brother smoked and drank too much, and always got into trouble. Last spring, Richard got arrested for drag-racing on the Daniel Webster Highway between the Puritan and the Hooksett line.

Johnson said that he didn't find it easy to send the flower of our youth, who are our finest young men, into battle. I never thought of Richard as being "the flower of our youth." And I didn't understand what the heck we were fighting about in Vietnam. All I knew was that the North Vietnamese were trying to spread communism into South Vietnam. And we were helping the South Vietnamese fight against the North Vietnamese. It sounded like what happened with our country and Cuba not long ago. I wished our leaders understood that war never solves anything.

10

A young negro named Marquette Frye was arrested for drunk driving. Angry witnesses shouted because they thought the police used excessive force. A large crowd gathered, and then, as Dad liked to say, "all hell broke loose." People started throwing bottles, looting stores, destroying cars, and setting businesses on fire.

"This isn't just about some guy getting arrested. It's the straw that broke the camel's back. This is about negroes feeling like they are not treated equally," said Dad.

How many times will treatment of negroes keep popping up, I wondered. "But the Civil Rights Act was signed last year," I said.

"You're right," said Dad. "But actions speak louder than words, and it'll take a hell of a long time to change people's attitudes."

People rioted in Watts for five nights. Cronkite reported that thirty-four people died, over a thousand were hurt, six hundred buildings were burned to the ground, and there was forty million dollars in property damage.

I didn't understand why negroes didn't leave places like Watts and move somewhere safe. Like New Hampshire.

11

Mom took me and Joey shopping at JM Field's for back-to-school clothes. Moe wore a uniform, so she didn't get to go.

I wore my new gray tweed skirt, white blouse, and my gray cable knit sweater for the first day of school. I put dimes instead of pennies in the slots of my new loafers. Dimes were more practical than pennies anyway. I could always make a call from a pay phone with a dime.

I got assigned to Sister Francis's class. I didn't know what to think because she was new at our school.

If the first school day was to tell the story of the rest of the year, it was going to be a long one. Sister had schoolbooks piled along the side wall of the classroom according to subject. She had each row of kids line up and take one book out of each pile. When we were all seated with our pile of books, she gave us each three paper bags.

"These bags, students, were donated by the A&P on Maple Street. Please ask your parents to shop there to show our appreciation." No way, I thought. My parents go for the green stamps at the Grand Union. My mother had her eye on a toaster oven that she saw in the S&H Green Stamp catalogue. And she only needed another book and a half. "I am going to demonstrate how you're to cover your books. For homework tonight, take your books home and cover them as I am about to demonstrate."

Sister showed us how to cut the bags so we had one flat sheet of paper and fold it to fit the dimensions of the book. Most important to her was that all the margins be trimmed to two inches. "And don't take any shortcuts. I'll be around with my ruler tomorrow. And one more thing." She paused and looked around the room. "The subject of the book must be printed in block letters in the middle. Your name belongs in the upper right-hand corner. Our classroom, number 201, should be in the lower right-hand corner. And NO doodling on your book cover. Ever. Any questions?"

From bad to worse, I thought as I lugged my books home for an evening of measuring, cutting, and taping.

Joey started sixth grade and came home excited. "N-N-Nora, there's a new kid in my class, and he rode to school today on a thing called a skateboard.

"Slow down, Joe" I said. "Take your time." I could tell that he was excited.

"He l-l-let me try it, and I could do it! He brought it from California."

"What does a skateboard look like, Joe? I never heard of it," I said.

"It's l-like a little surfboard on four wheels, and it's a whole lot of fun."

"Well, your birthday is coming up in a few weeks. You should ask Mom and Dad for one." My guess was that they'd buy him anything that got him out of the house for a little exercise.

When I got up for school, Mom and Dad were sitting at the kitchen table drinking coffee and chatting with Joe about the skateboard. "Joseph, we'll consider it depending on how much it costs," said Mom. "Money doesn't grow on trees." Mom's comment didn't sound promising for Joe. I hoped he wasn't counting on it.

12

The phone rang in the middle of the night. I heard Dad shuffle to the phone in the hallway and say "Hello. Detective Donovan." Whenever we got a call in the middle of the night, it was always police business, so that's how he answered the phone. "I'll be right down."

I heard muffled conversation between my parents but couldn't make out what they were saying. Then when I peeked under the blinds, I saw headlights backing out of the driveway.

"Dad, where did you go last night?" I asked at breakfast.

"Police business," he snapped. He got up from the table. "I'm running late."

Moe came down the stairs. "I was looking out the window and just saw Dad yell at the Larkins' dog. What's going on?"

Mom rolled her eyes. "Your father's upset. He got called down to the station late last night because your Uncle Danny got arrested. The officer on duty called Dad and asked him to post bail."

"Why did he get arrested?" I asked.

"He started a fight in a bar about the race riots in Los Angeles. He punched a guy who's now at the Sacred Heart for observation." No one had much to say. "Don't talk about it outside this house. It's an embarrassment to your father and to our family."

And nobody did talk about it. Not even inside the house. That is, until the following Saturday night when the doorbell rang during *Gilligan's Island*. Dad stepped out onto the porch, leaving the door ajar. I crept over by the door so I could hear their conversation. "You've a hell of a nerve showing up here after the disgrace you've brought upon this family, Dan. When are you going to act like a man and accept some responsibility?"

I think Uncle Danny was crying. "I'm sorry Tom. I've always looked up to you, but I'll never be the man you are."

"Well, you can start by keeping your goddam racist opinions to yourself."

"Tom, I came here to tell you that I've been thinking about stuff for the last couple of days. I know I can be a real asshole, and there's nothing I want more than to make you proud of me. I went down to the recruiting office this morning and joined the army."

I couldn't hear Dad's response.

"I'll hear back in a few days when I need to report to basic training at Fort Benning, Georgia. I'll be there for eight weeks, and probably get shipped off to Nam by the first of the year."

More muffled comments continued for a few minutes longer. Dad came in the house and said, "Helen, kids, I'm heading to bed. It's been a long week."

The next morning Dad was in good spirits. "Helen, we have cause to celebrate. Let's give Dan a going-away party. He joined the Army and will be shipping out soon. What do you say?"

I figured my mother would do just about anything to get Uncle Danny out of our hair for a while. "Great idea, Tom. We better do it soon if he's leaving in a few weeks."

Mom called Kathleen and Marcel. And Rosemarie. They called Uncle Danny's friends. Before the afternoon was over, the date was set, the guest list confirmed, and the potluck menu decided and delegated.

The following Saturday, Moe, Joey, and I decorated the house. We got dizzy from blowing up the balloons that we tied on the mailbox, porch railings, and the lamp post. Mom made a giant sheet cake and added some of Joey's miniature Army men and a few tiny tents for decorations. She plopped a jeep in the corner and wrote, "Bon Voyage, Private Donovan," with her blue Wilton icing tube.

People started arriving around 5:00 with trays of food. Jell-O molds, Swedish meatballs, mini hot dogs floating in barbecue sauce. Cole slaw, chicken fingers, and potato chips with onion dip.

Just after 6:00, Dad walked into the house with Uncle Danny. Everyone clapped and cheered. When it came time to make the toast, Dad stood with his arm around Uncle Danny, looking proud. Mom snuck around the kitchen passing out glasses of pink champagne while Aunt Kathleen snapped photos with her Polaroid.

Dad whistled and waited until everyone was quiet. "First of all, thank you all for coming to honor my baby brother Danny, who will soon be inducted into the United States Army. Please raise your glasses…"

"Wait," interrupted Danny. "I want you to pick up a glass and toast me too, Tom." I was nervous to see what Dad would do because I'd never seen him drink alcohol. He said it was because his father drank too much, and he never wanted to be like him.

"Okay, Dan. For you," he said as he picked up a glass. "Please raise your glasses to Private Daniel Donovan. Dan, come back to us safe and sound. We'll keep you in our hearts and prayers." I noticed that Rosemarie hugged and kissed Uncle Dan as the crowd drank their champagne and sang, *"For he's a jolly good fellow, for he's a jolly good fellow, for he's a jolly good fellow…which nobody can deny."* I watched Dad raise his glass, but he didn't take a sip. Uncle Danny was too busy smooching with Rosemarie to notice.

My family met Aunt Kathleen, Marcel, and Rosemarie at the Carpenter Hotel on a crisp September morning. Danny was taking the 7:00 bus to Boston to catch a plane to Fort Benning. Just before the bus arrived, a taxi pulled up and out popped Danny with a giant duffle bag on his shoulder. He broke out in a big smile when he saw us all waiting. "Surprise," we shouted. The goodbyes were quick. He barely had time to hug us all and get on the bus before it headed south to Boston.

Nobody said a word as the bus pulled away, and we all waved and got our last glimpse of Uncle Danny as he faded into the distance. "Let's head up to the Red Arrow. I'll treat you all to breakfast," said Dad.

Rosemarie had tears in her eyes. I didn't know what she saw in Uncle Danny but seeing her sad made me feel sad too.

13

Mom picked up a large package addressed to Joe. It had been mailed by Uncle Dan a few days before he left for Fort Benning.

"Uncle Danny never remembers our birthdays and never buys us presents," said Moe. Joe pulled off the paper and opened a box. Inside was a skateboard. And a note from Uncle Dan. "You'll be the most popular kid in your neighborhood. Happy birthday! Love, Uncle Danny."

"Oh, w-wow! I can't believe he got me this."

"Neither can I," growled Dad. My parents had decided that Joe shouldn't have a skateboard until he was a little older. He wasn't the most coordinated kid, but no one wanted to tell him that.

"C-c-come outside with me, and I'll show you how to ride it," said Joe. We trooped out to the driveway to watch him demonstrate.

"Maybe you should start on the flat part instead of the downhill," warned Mom.

Joe ignored her. He barely had time to stick his arms out to the side before the front wheels hit a crack in the pavement and he flew off the board. He grabbed his left foot and shrieked.

"Dammit!" hissed Dad. "You okay, Joe?" he asked.

Joey whimpered but said he'd be fine.

"Take my arm," said Dad. He and Mom helped Joe limp up the steps and into the kitchen.

"Thank the Lord you didn't whack your head," said Mom. She got ice from the freezer, wrapped it up in a dishtowel, and put it on Joe's ankle.

"Leave it to my brother. He's out of the state and still managed to break my kid's ankle."

"Tom, please. We have no idea if it's broken or not. Dan meant well."

"Yeah, he always does, doesn't he?"

Mom lifted the dishtowel. Joe's ankle was swelling up and turning red. "Tom, we'll have to take him to the ER for x-rays."

Moe and I had ravioli from the stockpile for dinner. My parents walked in the door around 8:00 with Joe who had a cast on his leg and was walking on crutches. "He's a little groggy from the medication girls, so give him some space," warned Mom.

"He's going to be fine, but he'll be on crutches for the next few months," added Dad. "Big thanks to my brother for sending Joe this thoughtful gift." He rolled his eyes at my mother.

It seemed like the only luck Uncle Dan and Joey ever had was bad luck.

14

"Boys and girls, last night Bishop Primeau informed us that our Holy Father Pope Paul VI has planned a trip to New York City at the end of the month. This will be the first time a Pope has left Italy since 1809 and the first time a pontiff has ever visited the United States. It's a momentous occasion." Sister Francis was more perky than usual, on account of the Pope's visit.

Walter Cronkite covered the event on the evening news. It turned out that the Pope only stayed for fourteen hours. In that short time, he got a lot done. He gave the apostolic blessing to Cardinal Spellman at Saint Patrick's Cathedral, spoke in front of the United Nations General Assembly, and met with LBJ at some fancy hotel called the Waldorf Astoria. Before flying home to Italy, the pope said Mass at Yankee Stadium. "Why did it have to be Yankee Stadium?" growled Dad.

The next day, Sister Francis wanted us to discuss the Pope's visit. "Let me read you our Holy Father's message when he arrived in America. *'Greetings to you, Americans. The first pope to set foot on your land blesses you with all his heart. He renews, as it were, the gesture of your discoverer, Christopher Columbus, when he planted the Cross of Christ on this blessed soil'."*

"What do those words mean to you as young soldiers of Christ?" asked Sister. Donald Morse raised his hand and Sister said "Yes, Donald," with a surprised look on her face. Donald never raised his hand or asked questions about anything.

"Why does he talk about himself in the third person?"

"Because he is talking about the pope."

"But he IS the Pope," said Donald.

"But he's talking about the human being that sits in the apostolic chair of the Supreme Pontiff," said Sister with annoyance in her voice. "The being that is closest on earth to Our Lord Jesus Christ." Everyone in the class perked up, enjoying the banter.

"But he IS the Supreme Pontiff...I just don't get why he referred to himself as 'he' instead of 'I'," Donald responded.

"It's a gesture of humility to keep the man who is serving as pope separated from the figure of the pope. And this humility reminds us that he's a mortal human being who has the privilege of serving Our Lord in the role of Pope." Sister's voice was getting louder as it always did when she was angry. "And it wouldn't hurt you, Mr. Morse, to show a little humility and stop talking when you clearly know so little about what you are talking about!"

Sister's face was beet red.

But Donald did know what he was talking about. And I was proud of him. He was right and he spoke up. Sister couldn't even give him an intelligent argument. She was so flustered by the conversation that she forgot about making us discuss what the Pope's visit meant to us as young soldiers of Christ. "Take out your arithmetic books," she said as she adjusted her wimple and fingered her rosary beads. I caught Donald's eye and flashed him a smile.

15

Dad attended the 9:30 Mass because it was the first Sunday of the month and that's when the Holy Name Society had their meetings.

"What's Holy Name anyway?" I asked Dad.

"A group of Catholic men that meet once a month after Mass. We dedicate ourselves to serving the underprivileged in our community. All the parishes have these societies."

"Oh Tom, tell it like it is. You sit around and have breakfast served to you, maybe have a guest speaker, and then talk about the Celtics or the Red Sox or God knows what else," said Mom.

Dad laughed. "Mom's right. But nothing wrong with that, honey."

After the meeting, Dad came home and said that the guest speaker from the bishop's office gave a sneak preview of some of the changes that were going to be announced since the Vatican II Ecumenical Council had just ended.

"What did he say, Dad?" I asked.

"Well, I guess there's no harm in telling you. But don't go blabbing to your friends. I'm sure the sisters would like to be the ones to share the news."

None of us had heard of the Catholic Church making any changes, so we listened eagerly to Dad. "Well, the first one is going to affect Joe more than any of us. The Mass will no longer be said in Latin. Instead, it will be said in the native language of each country. And the altar's going to be turned around, so the priest and the altar boys face the congregation."

"I d-don't want to face the people," Joey said. "I'll be too nervous."

"Don't worry about it, Joe. I'm sure the priests will help you all adjust. And girls, no head coverings will be required from now on. Too many forget their hats and pinning a Kleenex to the top of their heads is nothing short of foolish."

Maybe the most shocking change was that the nuns would be allowed to shed their heavy veils and habits and wear more modern clothes. The thought of seeing legs that hadn't seen the light of day in a long time was frightening. And we had no idea if the nuns even had hair. Maybe they were all bald and that's why they signed up to join the convent in the first place. It made sense that they would want an excuse to cover their heads and hide behind a veil.

1966

Patty Carmody and I walked to our classroom wondering what Francis's new outfit would look like.

It turned out that Sister had hair after all. She wore a short black veil and a black dress with silver buttons that came just below her knees.

"I like your dress, Sister," said Colleen.

Colleen drove me crazy. Like she'd be caught dead wearing Sister's dress.

"Thank you, Miss Fitzpatrick." Sister took attendance and made us pray for our soldiers, for our President, and for all the faithful departed. I said an extra silent prayer that Uncle Danny would be okay. The nightly news showed flag-draped coffins arriving back from Vietnam, and I worried he might come home in one.

Joey had Youth Fellowship that afternoon and said he'd get a ride home with one of the priests. It was sleeting, so I walked down Bridge Street to catch the Webster bus. I remembered how scared I used to be riding it, afraid that Sandra's murderer might be sitting in the back and decide to get off at my stop. I got the last empty seat next to an old lady with a big black purse. She frowned, pulling her wet coat away from me so my wet coat wouldn't drip on her wet coat.

The tire chains thwacka-thwacka-thwacked against the pavement as the bus moved up Maple Street. I wondered if the bus I was on might be the same one Valade took the night that she was murdered. I looked around, wondering where she sat six years ago.

Did she know Coolidge? She must have, or how else would he know that she'd be walking alone on Smyth Road that night?

Coolidge probably sat in his car in the dark and watched her get off at the VA. When the bus disappeared, he followed her down the dark road leading into the woods. *The woods are lovely, dark, and deep.* He pulled up and offered her a ride. Did she take it, even though she was scared? Or did he pull out a gun and force her into his car?

The old lady next to me pulled the cord, and I stood, letting her get out of her seat, this time careful not to drip on her.

Where did he murder her, I wondered. Missy Callahan said that her dad thought that Coolidge murdered both girls in the Paquette's pigpen. Coolidge knew the Paquettes, and the pen was far enough away from the house so that no one could hear the girls scream. Missy's father thought it was suspicious that Mrs. Paquette was found dead only hours after the police questioned Coolidge. When I asked Missy why Coolidge was questioned, she said she didn't know.

Maybe Dad knew. But I was afraid to ask him. He was mad that Coolidge was getting a fancy legal team to re-try his case because that's what people who got life sentences did. Rich law firms could afford to let lawyers work free, and it was good publicity for them. Pro-bono it was called. Wait until Dad finds out that one of the lawyers is from Gene's father's firm, I thought.

I pulled the cord as we approached my stop. I thanked the driver, and jumped off, just missing a big puddle. I raced home, chin tucked in so that water wouldn't run down my neck, my books against my chest to keep them dry.

I grabbed the paper, unlocked the door, and started my homework. On top of writing book reports, Francis was making us do an art project for each book we read. Our January assigned reading was *The Old Man and the Sea*.

I was barely into chapter one when I heard Moe at the back door pulling off her boots.

"How was your day?" she asked. "And why are you reading that book? I hated it."

"I've got to write a book report and do an art project on it."

"Nora, you aren't exactly artistic, are you?"

"I suppose that you think you are?" I asked.

"I always got As in art. Remember when I was in eighth grade that I was picked to crown the Blessed Virgin at All Saint's?" Moe had the know-it-all-look that I couldn't stand.

"Hey, does Dad know that Gene's father's firm is working on Coolidge's appeal?" I asked.

"I think so," she said, plopping down near me. She sounded sad. "This morning Dad said that too many lawyers were scallywags who worked against the police."

"But could the lawyers win? The whole city hates Coolidge. Everyone knows that he murdered Sandra Valade and probably Rena Paquette. Dad told Mom that the police think he probably murdered other girls."

"I didn't know that." Moe's eyes were wide. "Gene says that the lawyers are only working the Mason case. He could still be tried for the Valade and Paquette murders."

"What about Sandra's rights? And Rena Paquette's rights? What about the rights of everyone in Manchester who was scared to death for years because of that jerk?"

"I know," sighed Moe. "But Gene says his dad won't talk about the case. Just like Dad won't talk about it. Besides, someone in Gene's dad's firm is handling the case. Not Mr. Tardiff." Moe ran upstairs.

I was glad Mr. Tardiff wasn't trying to help Coolidge.

2

"Hi, Nora," said Joe.

"How was Fellowship?" I asked.

"Good. Father Murphy gave me and Paul an extra Devil Dog because we stayed late to help him move furniture in the rectory. They're having the carpets cleaned."

I knew that Mom was on Joey's case about eating desserts because he was getting kind of fat. But I didn't want to talk to him about his weight.

"How many boys are in Fellowship?"

"About five."

"Five out of all the fourth-graders and up? Seems like a small group," I said.

"It's fourth-graders and up who are altar boys, not just all fourth-graders and up."

It still seemed like a small group to me.

It was Moe's night to set the table. She was listening to Boston's WRKO, a station the coolest kids listened to, or at least according to her. Simon and Garfunkel were singing about darkness and silence. The words scared me. The song was about a young woman getting stabbed in New York City. She screamed for help, but none of her neighbors opened their doors. I wondered if folks in Manchester would have rushed to help Sandra Valade and Pamela Mason as they bled to death. I would have answered yes a year ago. But now with Gene's father's law firm helping to free Coolidge, I wasn't so sure.

I settled on doing an undersea scene for my art project. I painted most of a poster light blue for the ocean and painted a little red boat on top. I used a black yarn as the old man's fishing line, glued it to the poster, and drew a big marlin on the line, one that I copied from a *Visit Florida!* brochure at the library. I spray-painted dried noodles around the marlin to make starfish and squid. Crumbled-up graham crackers glued to the bottom of my poster made a good seabed. Even Moe liked it.

Sister said she thought that it would take her a week to grade our projects.

The morning we were supposed to get our art projects back, Sister Francis frowned in my direction.

"Nora Donovan, please see me after school." Her voice sounded mean.

I couldn't imagine what the problem was.

"The winner of the art project this month is Colleen Fitzpatrick." Sister stood in front of the class and gave Colleen a big smile. "Colleen, please come up to the front of the class and tell us what you learned about benteak?"

Sister placed Colleen's project on the chalkboard tray. Colleen pasted a boat made of popsicle sticks painted brown on top of a dark blue sea. Silver stars were pasted against a navy sky. In the center she'd colored in a tree with pink flowers on a little island.

Colleen stood next to her poster. "I never knew how interesting the Bahamas were until I began researching my project. I was so excited about what I learned that I stayed after school one day to talk to Sister about it."

"That she did," chuckled Sister.

I couldn't believe how low Colleen would go.

"Well, what I learned was that the old man's boat was probably made of benteak."

I looked around. No one seemed interested. But Colleen plowed ahead.

"Benteak is a dark wood used for centuries to make ships in the Bahamas. It's durable and related to the crape myrtle, which I've painted in over in this corner. I colored popsicle sticks with brown shoe polish to make the old man's boat," she giggled.

"Does anyone have any questions?" asked Sister.

No one did.

"Thank you, Miss Fitzpatrick. Now let's have a round of applause for Colleen's useful information on benteak!"

We clapped per Sister's request, and Colleen smiled as she took her seat. Sister distributed the projects. Everyone around me got an A or a B except for Donald Morse, who just drew some sea horses in the water with no boat, no old man. I saw a red D before he had time to hide it.

Sister Francis called me up to her desk when school ended.

"I left the art projects in the convent's receiving room. As you know, the convent is an old building, not in the best part of town."

I didn't understand what that had to do with me.

"We leave the receiving room closed during the week to save money on heating. When we opened the room on Saturday morning, mice were jumping all around. They came into the convent to eat whatever sugary cookies you used in your project." She paused. "What do you say, young lady?"

I didn't know what to say. Yet Sister wasn't through.

"Do you know that we'd invited the Bishop over for coffee on Saturday morning? Imagine how we felt, opening the French doors and having mice jumping everywhere."

"I'm sorry, Sister."

"You may go now. And you've failed this assignment."

I was still mad when I got home. Mom felt bad for me. "Honestly, it's not your fault that they have mice. Sounds like they had a lot of them. Your graham crackers wouldn't bring that many mice into the building."

Dad was in hysterics. "Nora, I'd kill to have seen the Bishop's face when the nuns opened the doors and mice were jumping all around!"

Fine for Dad to think it was funny. I wished one of the mice had bitten Sister Francis and given her rabies. "Honey, it wasn't your fault. The convent must be loaded with mice. They could have chewed out the wiring, caused a fire, and the nuns would have burned to death in their beds."

"Really?" I asked.

"Absolutely. You probably saved their lives." Much as I wasn't nuts about Sister Francis, I was glad that I prevented a fire. I wouldn't want her to be burned to death like Joan of Arc or Saint Agatha.

That evening I launched Operation Crown the May Queen. I told no one about it, but I was determined that next Mother's Day, the congregation at All Saint's would turn adoring eyes my way as I crowned the Virgin Mary. I remember that everyone said how beautiful Moe looked crowning the Virgin three years ago.

But I had to win over Sister Francis, who held my future in her bony little hand.

3

Mom said that next weekend we should attend the nuns' Saint Patrick's Day Social with Auntie.

My father groaned. "Helen, the best basketball games of the season are on that weekend."

"I don't like the Social," grumbled Moe.

"What if we take Auntie out for breakfast, and we can be home in time for the game?" asked Mom.

"I'll do that," said Dad.

"Good. I'll call Auntie." said Mom.

It was gray and foggy when we pulled into the parking lot at Windham Castle.

Auntie hustled down the hall, cane tapping and her veil flying behind her. I gave Joe a little kick when he went, "whoa."

None of us had seen Auntie in her new outfit. She wore a black mid-calf dress and a little headband with a short black gauzy veil. She looked like someone's mémère who had dressed up to give out candy for Halloween. "Auntie, I haven't seen you in your new outfit," said Mom.

She slowly turned around "Do you like it?"

"You look amazing!" exclaimed Moe. I had to give her credit. She picked exactly the right word.

Auntie looked at Joe.

"Young man, do you like my dress?"

Joe just stood there, not knowing what to say.

Auntie turned to my mother. "What's this boy's name?"

"Auntie, he's Joe. My son Joe." Joe looked at me. I looked at Moe. Moe looked at Mom.

"Joe and Moe! Helen, what were you thinking? They sound like a circus act."

"Auntie, the brunette here is Nora," said Dad. "She has little athletic talent. It's all she can do to walk upright. Moe and Joe will be on trapezes someplace, and Nora here will be at some fancy college."

Moe made a face at Dad.

Auntie turned back to Mom. "Helen, nice of you to bring the athletes and that other girl with you. But I wonder if you'd mind if I don't go out for breakfast? We'll be eating lots of cake and ice cream this afternoon, and I'd be happier just having a cup of tea."

Dad smiled. Even Mom looked relieved.

"But let me show you Sister Stephen's room. As you know, her family decorates for the holidays," said Auntie. A skinny nun answered the door. "Sister Stephen, you remember my niece Helen and her family," said Auntie. "Could they see your Saint Patrick's Day decorations?"

"Of course," said Sister Stephen.

She stood back so that we could admire her room. Four enormous green shamrocks were on the wall above her desk, and a life-size, lighted-up statue of Saint Patrick, his right hand extended in benediction, revolved slowly on its base. A tenor sang *Danny Boy* in the background.

"Danny Boy always gets me going." Sister Stephen dabbed at her eyes. "It also plays "The Minstrel Boy," and "Christmas in Killarney." So, I get two holidays out of the good Patrick." Sister Stephen turned to us. "Isn't one of you in school with my grandniece Colleen Fitzpatrick who does my holiday decorating?"

"I am, Sister." I couldn't believe that Colleen did this insane decorating for Sister Stephen.

"Well, I can tell by the looks of you that the two of you are fast friends."

I saw Moe laughing.

"Well thank you, Sister Stephen," said Auntie. "I'll walk my family to the door and be right back."

Auntie forgot our names and she forgot our tea, but that was fine with me. We waved to her as Dad pulled out of the parking lot.

4

"I hope that Veterok and Ugolyok make it back to earth," worried Joe.

"Gene said that the Russians have sent animals into space, and most of them died," Moe whispered to me. "Let's keep our fingers crossed that Vet and Whoever return alive."

The next morning, Sister was in a tizzy, not about Russian dogs but about John Lennon. Lennon had said that the Beatles were more famous than Jesus.

"How did that young Englishman with the crazy hair decide that he and his friends were more famous than our Lord and Savior?" asked Sister Francis.

No one said a word. I didn't think the Beatles were more famous than Jesus, but I knew that they were a lot more fun. There was really nothing fun about Jesus. Christmas was fun, but the rest of the stuff about Him was awful. His crucifixion was terrible. And when Jesus rose from the dead, He asked Doubting Thomas to stick his hands into the hole in Jesus' side so Thomas would know that He was truly Jesus. Jesus or not, I never would've stuck my hand into His bloody side.

Sister said that John Lennon was a disciple in Satan's army. She had us pray that teenagers would ignore Lennon's foolishness. She didn't tell us to pray that our President would win the war on poverty, nor did she mention the Russian menace. Evidently, John

Lennon was a bigger threat to our well-being than poverty or nuclear war.

5

George Orwell's *Animal Farm* was our next reading assignment. I was impressed that Sister picked such a radical book. But it bothered me that the novel dealt with pigs. Anytime we drove down Brown Ave, I'd look down the Paquette's driveway. It sat on a spit of land between the road and the Merrimack River that fanned out to a wider, wooded area that must have held the pigpen. But there was no way that I would try to connect Coolidge to *Animal Farm,* even though the *Union Leader* told us for weeks that whoever tortured and murdered Pam was "an animal."

Joe was thrilled when the two Russian dogs landed safely on earth. The feel-good story about the dogs was followed by footage from a Viet Cong prison. American POW Jeremiah Denton was led out by his captors and pushed before a TV camera. Denton kept blinking like he wasn't used to bright light. Dad leaned forward, watching Denton.

Walter Cronkite said Denton was brilliant, blinking to send out the message "T-O-R-T-U-R-E."

"I knew he was signaling," exclaimed Dad. "But I forgot Morse Code. What a brave American!"

Denton's story was followed by coverage of anti-war protests all over the country. Hippies in Berkeley threw flowers at each other and at the police. Braless girls and guys with ponytails and bushy beards held peace signs and chanted as they marched. Somebody in Central Park started a fire in a garbage can, and a fight broke out when the cops arrested the protestors. I was shocked to see a priest get handcuffed.

"Our country is in a mess," exclaimed Mom. "It's hard to know what's the best thing to do."

"Fighting with police who are trying to keep people safe is definitely not the best thing, Helen." Dad's voice was sharp.

"I'm not saying that fighting with the police is the best idea. But Johnson's drafting more kids this year than he did last year. I don't see an end in sight," said Mom.

"I worry about Uncle Danny," said Moe.

Moe surprised me. I'd no idea that she worried about anything, much less Uncle Danny.

"I do, too," said Mom. "Rosemarie says that he's keeping his spirits up, but we'll all feel better when he's home."

"What's the big deal if South Vietnam becomes Communist?" I asked. I remembered Aunt Kathleen saying how Jesus was the first true Communist. Why should Denton be tortured over this? And why might Uncle Danny die just because South Vietnam became Communist?

"It's because of something our leaders call the domino effect. It's a metaphor. Do you know what a metaphor is?" Dad asked.

"Yes," I bristled.

"Well, why don't you give us the definition?" Dad thought that I didn't know what I was talking about.

"It's a figure of speech that implies comparison between two unlike entities without using the words like or as," I said.

"I'll be writing a check to Harvard in another few years," Dad laughed.

"Oh puh-leeze," groaned Moe.

I didn't tell Dad what I really knew about metaphors. Metaphors are words used by dangerous people to cover up their lies.

6

I couldn't have even found it on a map, but Vietnam was always in the news. We watched Americans fighting in the jungle and flag-draped coffins coming home from Vietnam. "The Ballad of the Green Berets" was on the radio every five minutes. I didn't know why Barry Sadler thought that if he died fighting in Vietnam, his widow should encourage their son to join the Green Berets. I would tell the kid to do something safe, like being a violinist or an electrician.

Mom and I were folding laundry when the phone rang. I raced into the kitchen to answer it. Rosemarie was on the other end.

"Can I speak to Tom?"

"He's at work, but Mom's home." Mom flapped her hand at me to go away. I stepped into the dining room and listened.

"Oh, no," she said. There was a pause. Mom said that she was sorry.

Had Uncle Danny been killed?

"Well, that's good news," said Mom. "Thanks for calling. I'll tell Tom and the kids. And we'll pray that Dan has a speedy recovery."

Rosemarie said something else.

"You, too. Bye, Rosemarie."

I tiptoed back into the living room. Minutes passed before Mom joined me.

"Is Uncle Dan okay?" I asked.

"Yes. He got a mild concussion when the Viet Cong surrounded his unit and killed a lot of guys. Dan's lucky."

I was shocked that Uncle Danny came so close to dying. "Will he be okay?" I asked.

"I'm sure that he'll recover just fine. He's young and strong," said Mom. "But your uncle has a hard time handling his feelings. I don't know how many of his buddies died in that battle."

Mom pulled towels out of the laundry basket and piled them next to her.

"Joe, come down and give me a hand with sorting the laundry," she called up the stairs.

I heard Joe clomping across his room.

"Will they send him home?" I asked.

"I'd be amazed. His injuries aren't serious."

"Who was on the phone?" asked Joe.

"Rosemarie, Uncle Danny's girlfriend," said Mom. "Uncle Danny's had a minor injury, but he'll be okay."

Joe's eyes filled with tears.

"Get going on these towels, buddy. Donovan men are tough, and your uncle's no exception," said Mom.

A minute later Joe was prattling on about how annoyed the priests were at All Saints' by the Vatican II changes.

Mom winked at me. "Imagine what the priests would do if they had to cook dinner and do laundry? They wouldn't have time to worry about Vatican II."

Mom's comments were lost on Joe, who was busy telling us that he'd fold towels and his and Dad's underwear, but no way was he touching girls' bras and panties.

That night I assembled my art project for *Animal Farm*. In an almost Colleen Fitzpatrick move, I decided to compare the Seven Pig Commandments with the Ten Commandments God gave Moses on Mount Sinai. I divided my poster in half, colored in a blue sky, filled the sky with stick-on stars, and penciled in two tablets. The tablet on the left held the words to the greedy pigs' Seven Commandments; the tablet on the right had Yahweh's righteous Ten Commandments. It took me about a half hour.

"Francis will love it," Moe said.

The following week, Sister placed my project on the chalkboard and asked me to discuss it. I explained how the pigs became selfish and power-hungry and put together evil laws. God however, being all-good and worthy of all our love (I still remembered that line from coaching Joe on his catechism), put together a perfect set of laws. Sister thought it was wonderful.

"Class, let's give Nora a round of applause for her thoughtful discussion of God's laws."

I got an A+. Donald Morse was in the back of the class laughing at me, and I crossed my eyes at him as I walked by his desk.

The morning arrived that Sister Francis planned to announce what eighth grade girl would crown the Virgin Mary. I was sure I had it knocked. Colleen had been being extra-nice to me all week. She probably smelled defeat.

Sister walked to the front of the room. "Many of the girls in this class embody the qualities of the Blessed Virgin, and two have high grade point averages: Colleen Fitzpatrick and Nora Donovan. Nora's grades are higher than Colleen's, but..."

My heart stopped. Was I about to get robbed? Colleen sat up a little straighter in her seat, button nose in the air as if sensing a change in the wind direction.

"But this year Colleen Fitzpatrick has been selected to crown the Virgin," announced Sister.

Some kids clapped; others looked at me in surprise.

"The reason that Colleen slightly edged out Nora is because Colleen has a great aunt at Windham Castle, our beloved Sister Stephen," said Sister.

I slumped down in my seat.

"Art impacts all of Colleen's existence, according to Colleen's mother. Colleen decorates Sister Stephen's room at the Castle for every holiday. Every holiday!" Sister was over the moon. "Colleen's mother told me it was as if the Holy Ghost Himself had lit tongues of fire in Colleen's brain."

I think even Colleen was surprised by the idea that she'd had a visitation from the Holy Ghost.

"Colleen, please take the guide outlining your duties as Bestower of the Crown."

Colleen's cheeks were flushed with excitement. I wondered if her mother called Sister Francis to push Colleen to victory. Nothing would surprise me about those Fitzpatricks.

7

We went to the China Dragon to celebrate Moe's birthday, and my parents invited Gene to join us. I loved the carpeting with fire-breathing dragons, the little footbridge leading into the restaurant with red and gold koi swimming underneath, and the paper screens separating groups of tables, so you felt as though you were really in China.

"Dad, why don't you guys go to our table? I'll stay here with Joe so he can throw pennies in the wish pond."

I knew all Joe wanted to do was to hit a couple of fish. But he had no luck. I couldn't figure out if the fish saw the shadow of his arm in the water or what, but they darted away in a blur of gray, gold, and red.

The hostess saw us and smiled. "Follow me, please. Your father asked me to show you to his table."

I got stuck sitting next to Gene.

"Gene, will you play basketball at Saint Anselm's next year?" asked Dad.

"I'd love to, but I want to concentrate on academics."

Suck-up, I thought.

"What are you looking at, Joe?" Dad put on his glasses to read the menu.

"I am h-h-having Butterflied Shrimp," announced Joe. "I love them."

"Where did you develop a love of Butterflied Shrimp?" asked Mom.

"F-father Murphy took me and Paul here once last year, and he said that we'd like them."

I wondered why Joe was stuttering so much.

My mother poured us tea and announced she was having cashew chicken.

8

Every day the *Union Leader* carried stories about negroes rioting down south and our soldiers fighting Communism in Vietnam's jungles. Race riots and Vietnam seemed distant to me, even though I admired Martin Luther King's nonviolent movement and worried about Uncle Danny. But I got nervous when I read about the Supreme Court Miranda decision.

An eighteen-year-old girl was leaving her job at a Phoenix movie theater when Juan Miranda kidnapped and raped her. He even admitted it. But when the police arrested him, they didn't tell him that he had a right to remain silent, to have a lawyer, and that anything he said could be held against him. So he got another trial.

Why was everyone helping rapists and murderers, I wondered. It seemed that Americans could be sent a letter once a year reminding them of their rights. And if someone like this moron Miranda guy couldn't remember his rights when he was arrested, tough noogies for him. I hoped that the policemen who arrested Coolidge read him his rights, or he might be soon walking the streets of Manchester hunting for another girl to kill.

I asked Dad about the Miranda decision. He shook his head, saying it was a Supreme Court trick to keep lawyers in business. "Taxpayers will now be paying for every dead-beat with an axe to grind. It's a crazy world out there."

The week before my graduation, eight student nurses were raped and killed in Chicago. One survived by hiding under a bed, and she identified twenty-five-year-old Richard Speck as the killer. Speck had a history of petty crime, and the police noted that wherever Speck lived, bodies of dead women turned up. I pulled out my plaid notebook and wrote down the date. I copied down the victims' names from the newspaper and stuffed the notebook back under my mattress. For the next few days, the murdered nursing students were all we talked about during recess.

"I hope that Speck was read his rights so he couldn't get another trial like Miranda did," I said.

"Who's Miranda?" asked someone.

"A rapist in Arizona who got another trial because of a technicality," I said.

"Like Coolidge might," said Missy.

"The courts won't let Coolidge out, will they?" asked Patty.

The bell rang, calling us back to class.

I sat as Sister went over our math homework. I wondered if Speck hated nurses. I didn't want anyone hurting my mother or Aunt Kathleen. Especially now that Aunt Kathleen was expecting a baby. The paper said that Speck wouldn't get the death penalty because it's illegal in Illinois. Just like it was in New Hampshire when Coolidge murdered Sandra Valade and Pamela Mason and probably Rena Paquette. I wished again that we had laws like Texas, and killers like Coolidge and Speck got electrocuted.

9

We marched into the church to "Pomp and Circumstance" on graduation day, the girls in white robes, the boys in black. I had to sit in the front row with some of the priests and nuns because I was valedictorian. I hated my speech, which took me forever to write. I wanted to say that women should not live in fear, that white people should stop treating negroes so horribly, and that we should bring our soldiers home from Vietnam and stop worrying about dominoes.

"Hon, I agree with your ideas," said Mom. She sat at the kitchen table, a pencil tucked behind her ear, looking over my rough draft. "But take out the bit about Jesus being a Communist."

"That's my favorite line," I said.

"Well, you can say the same thing without directly saying that He was a Communist," said Moe. "You can say that He wanted us to help the poor, not be selfish, and do unto others."

Mom scribbled something in the margin.

"You're re-doing my whole speech," I protested. "I should be able to say what I want."

"If you say what you want, Father Smith or the Bishop will pull you off the altar so fast you won't know what hit you. William Loeb will write an editorial about your anti-American speech at a Catholic grade school graduation," Mom laughed.

I grudgingly agreed. So I gave a sappy speech about kindness and world peace. But at the end, I took a deep breath. I said that my Uncle Dan was fighting in Vietnam, and I knew that many families in our parish had loved ones in Vietnam. I asked for a moment of silence so we could say a private prayer for our soldiers.

When I looked up, Dad was smiling so hard I thought his face would break.

The parish ladies served the Graduation Buffet in the church hall. Pancakes, sausages, bacon, piles of muffins, coffee, orange juice: it smelled like heaven. I was starving because I'd been too nervous to eat breakfast. I tried to make my way to the buffet line, but I could barely move because so many people were crowding me.

"Nora, I'm so glad that you had us pray for our soldiers. I have a son over there who I haven't heard from in weeks," said one lady in a gray dress who I didn't know. Her eyes were teary.

"You were wonderful, Nora!" Aunt Kathleen hugged me, and I felt a tap on my shoulder. It was Mr. Jameson, our school custodian.

"Great speech, young lady. I lost my son Mark in Nam six weeks ago. Thanks for having us pray for our soldiers."

"I'm sorry about your son." I was sorry, but my stomach was rumbling. I hoped that there'd still be some food left by the time I got to the buffet table.

Sisters Francis and Imelda appeared at my elbow. I felt bad for Imelda. Mom told Dad that the nuns sent her to Concord for treatment. When she locked the elderly Father Cote up in the multipurpose room, insisting that he tried to assault her, her psychiatrist recommended electroshock therapy.

"Your speech was excellent, young lady," said Sister Francis.

"Nora, you were punctual when I had you last year. You're a girl who's going places," said Sister Imelda. Both sisters' plates were piled with food.

I stared at the muffins on Sister Imelda's plate. Marcel saw me, laughed, and disappeared into the crowd. He soon re-appeared with orange juice and a plate of pancakes.

"I'm always doing food runs for Kathleen," he laughed. "I'm well-trained."

It all seemed so safe here in the All Saints' church hall. The war seemed far away, but perhaps not for poor Mr. Jameson and the nice lady in the gray dress.

10

I stood in a circle around the flagpole with the new freshman class at Saint Agatha's. Sister Annunciata led us in a prayer for world peace and for a successful school year.

The Glee Club marched out, Sister sounded her pitch pipe, and they sang our school song. When they finished singing, Sister Annunciata asked us to give the talented songbirds a round of applause and then, with a flourish, told us it was her great joy to introduce our headmaster Father Fitzgerald.

Sister stood back and Father took her place. He was short and bald with horn-rimmed glasses. He looked at the ground as he asked us to prepare for his blessing. As we knelt on the damp grass, he gave what must have been the shortest blessing in Catholic history. He pushed his glasses back up on his nose and disappeared into Saint Agatha's. What an odd duck, I thought. I noticed a girl on the other side of the circle laughing her head off.

We marched to homeroom where we heard Sister Annunciata's voice over the intercom. She told us to sit quietly and listen to the first in a weekly radio series called *Religion in The News*. The announcer read off a list of countries with new converts to

Catholicism, the numbers of babies baptized, and the number of people who signed up to be priests and nuns. What did anyone care about how many babies were baptized in Uganda? I snuck a peek around the room to see if anyone else had my reaction. We learned that Catholics were making advances in countries all over the world. Except, alas! in France, where vocations were down--no surprise. If I lived in France, I could find more fun things to do than to join a convent.

It took me about a week to get into the swing of things. In English, our first unit was on Edgar Allen Poe.

"The death of a beautiful woman is the most poetical topic in the world," said Sister Sebastian. "This is what Edgar Allen Poe wrote in his famous *Philosophy of Composition*. What do you think of this idea?'

I used to like Poe, but now I wasn't so sure.

Jeanette Donnelly raised her hand. "Poe might be right. I'm not in favor of having women die, but lots of popular songs are about dying women, like 'Teen Angel' and 'Last Kiss.'"

Well, Jeanette was a little chunky with beady eyes and an overbite, so if men wanted to kill only beautiful women, she'd be safe.

The girl I saw laughing at our opening ceremony raised her hand.

"Miss Melnechuk, what are you thinking?"

"Wasn't Poe crazy?"

"Being crazy doesn't mean that you can't write well. Lots of writers suffer from mental illness. Doctors today would say that Poe suffered from depression," said Sister.

"Yes, but he could have crazy ideas. Look at the horrible murders that have taken place in Manchester. Eddie Coolidge isn't writing any great books."

The class laughed nervously.

"Good point, Linda," said Sister. "Something to keep in mind is that many of Poe's female family members died young, including his teen-age wife."

"Maybe he killed them," suggested Linda.

"Very amusing, Linda, but not correct. They died of natural causes." Sister flipped through the Poe anthology and directed us to read "The Raven" quietly to ourselves before we discussed it.

I wondered how accurate autopsies were over a hundred years ago. Poe could've killed his teen-age wife, especially if he thought that the death of a beautiful woman was the best poetical topic.

At lunch period, I made it a point to sit at Linda Melnechuk's table. Patty Carmody and some girls I didn't know joined us.

"Wasn't that weird about Poe liking dead women?" Patty opened her lunch bag. "Who likes dead women?"

"Psychos, I guess," said one girl.

"Let's do names," said Linda. "I'm Linda Melnechuk."

"Catherine Hogg," said the next girl.

"Sandra Wilson," said the next.

"Debby Dumais,"

"Marie Chalifour."

"Nora Donovan," I said.

"Patty Carmody."

"Well, I can tell you when Sister said that thing about Poe, all I could think of was Pamela Mason," said Catherine. "My older cousin Suzanne used to live behind Coolidge, and anytime we were out in the back yard, he'd come out and stare at us. It was creepy. My aunt told us to ignore him."

I took a few bites of my ham sandwich.

"Teen-age girls who babysat for him said that he'd removed the door handles on the passenger side," said Catherine. She took a swig from her Fanta. "At least that's what Suzanne told me. Maybe Pamela knew that she was in trouble when she noticed the door handle missing."

That was a question that I wondered about. When did Pam know that she was in trouble? Did Coolidge make up some bullshit story about the passenger door handle not working so she didn't know what was going on until he started driving into the woods off Brown Ave? *The woods are lovely, dark, and deep...* I was sure that Coolidge had flat, gray eyes, like Sister Boniface. Maybe it was when Pam saw his eyes that she knew he'd kill her.

11

Aunt Kathleen had been cramping, her back was bothering her, and Mom said that she could deliver any day now.

"Wouldn't it be fun if she had her baby tomorrow on Joe's birthday?" she asked.

"Joe would like that," I said. "But maybe the day after would be better, so the baby doesn't steal any of Joe's thunder."

"Joe's twelve now, Nora. I think his birthday glory days are behind him."

"What are you getting him?"

"A subscription to *The Smithsonian*," replied Mom.

"Why?" I asked.

"Your dad's hoping that we can take him to the Air and Space Museum in DC next spring.

"Joe would love that," I said. I hoped that the "we" meant Moe and me.

"Where is he, by the way?"

"He and Paul are at the rectory helping Father Murphy with the new altar boys."

The phone rang, and I picked it up. It was Marcel.

"Nora, you've got a new cousin. Colleen Donovan Boucher."

"Wow! Aunt Kathleen had a baby girl," I called to my mother who joined me by the phone.

"Everybody's good. Colleen showed up today at 2:15 PM. She weighs seven pounds." Marcel couldn't have sounded happier.

"Congratulations, Marcel. Tell Kathleen I'll see her early tomorrow morning. And I'll let you go so you can make your phone calls. Love to you both," said Mom, hanging up the phone. "Colleen is a beautiful Irish name, and her last name is French, so she's truly a Manchester girl."

Why did Aunt Kathleen have to name her baby Colleen? If she wanted something Irish, she could have picked Deirdre. Or Erin.

Mom was right about Joe not fussing about his birthday. All he wanted for his birthday dinner was a cheeseburger and a chocolate cake with vanilla frosting. He came home from Youth Fellowship with a birthday present.

"Wasn't that thoughtful," said Mom. "What did they get you, Joe?"

Joe pulled out his gift. *Twister.*

Mom was speechless.

"Sex in a box," squealed Moe. "I saw Johnny Carson play Twister with Zsa Zsa Gabor on *The Tonight Show.*"

"I can't believe the priests bought you that," said Dad.

"It was the Youth Fellowship who bought it," murmured Joe.

"Can I borrow it and take it over to Gene's?" asked Moe.

"No, you may not," thundered my father. He took the box and shoved it in the garbage.

Joe's face turned red, but he didn't say a word.

"Joe, do you want to see what Moe and I got you?" I wanted to switch the topic from *Twister.* "I hope you like it." At least I knew that my father wouldn't throw our gift in the garbage.

"Wow! Model kits of Freedom 7 and Friendship 7!"

"Your mom and I got you something that we think you'll enjoy." Dad handed Joey an envelope. "And it's a bit related to your sisters' gift."

Joe read the gift card. "It's a gift subscription to *The Smithsonian.* And wow! Dad and Mom are taking me to Washington over April vacation to go to the Air and Space Museum. Thank you!"

"Girls, we're hoping that the whole family can do this DC trip. I just have to figure out the finances," said Dad.

I was excited. I'd never been to DC. And I'd never been on a plane.

I was happy for Joe. This was a way safer gift for him than the skateboard he got from Uncle Danny last year. But altar boys pitching in to buy him "sex in a box" was just plain weird.

12

We went to see baby Colleen at Aunt Kathleen's. She let us take turns holding her and said that if Colleen was as pretty as her Donovan cousins, she would be a lucky girl. Colleen was red and sort of fussy; I thought she'd be cuter but didn't want to hurt Aunt Kathleen's feelings.

"Hey, does anyone have Father Murphy in their parish?" asked Sandra the next day at the lunch table.

"He's at my parish. All Saints'."

"He was at our parish in Nashua but got moved because parents complained about him." Sandra took a bite from her apple. "He had a breakdown or something."

It didn't surprise me that priests had breakdowns. I couldn't imagine being a priest, listening to confessions all the time and giving funeral sermons and house blessings. I found a quarter and headed towards the ice cream machine.

When I returned to the table, the girls were watching Father Fitzgerald move the picture of Saint Agatha to where Pope Paul had been hanging and moving Pope Paul to where Saint Agatha had been hanging.

"Why is he doing that?" asked Linda.

"My sister Moe is a senior, and she says he's in here with a ladder all the time, moving pictures around."

"Talk about a breakdown," muttered Catherine.

A few days later, Joe announced that he and Paul were asked to stay on as Senior Altar Boys. "F-father picks just a few kids each year to be Senior Altar Boys." Joey's cheeks were pink with excitement.

"Does that mean you will get stuck serving at more Masses?" asked Moe.

"Wow, congratulations, Joe," I said. "That's quite an honor."

"Joseph, I am really proud of you," said Dad. Joe's smile lit up the room.

13

"Won't that be too much for you with the baby?" asked Mom. She was talking to Aunt Kathleen on the phone. Mom hung up and turned to us.

"Kathleen wants to host the Christmas buffet this year. She'd like you girls to go over early to give her a hand."

We were thrilled to help out. Aunt Kathleen told Moe that Gene was welcome to join everyone for dessert if his family would part with him on Christmas.

"Thanks, but I don't think he'll be able to," said Moe. "I'm going to Tardiff's on Christmas Eve, and Gene is going to his grandmother's in Boston on Christmas Day."

Rosemarie's family lived in Chicago, so she was joining us at Aunt Kathleen's for Christmas. "Chicago's the kind of place you visit in April or September," Rosemarie told my aunt. Rosemarie was saving up her vacation time so that she could take time off when Danny came home.

"Danny is lucky to have her," Mom said.

On Christmas morning a couple of gifts for Joey sat under the tree, but Moe and I only got cards from our parents. I was disappointed. Moe and I had bought my parents nice gifts at Jordan Marsh. We got Mom a Lenox cake platter and Dad two Hathaway shirts. I had a sinking feeling that our cards would hold checks that we had to deposit in our college funds. Moe opened hers first.

"Wow!" she yelled. "Nora, we're going to Washington!"

I was psyched.

Joey opened his gifts, but he wasn't all that excited about a new pair of chinos and a plaid bathrobe. I didn't feel one bit bad for him. We were going to Washington!

Moe handed Joey the present she and I got him.

He began ripping off the paper.

"Easy, Joe. If you don't rip the paper to shreds, we'll smooth it out and use it again," said Mom.

"Wow! *Risk!* We play this all the time at Youth Fellowship." He took off the cover and opened the board on the living room floor so we could see the map of the world.

"I w-wanted this game so m-much, Thanks!" he said.

"Okay, Moe and Nora. It's time for you two to shower. Dad's going to bring you over to Aunt Kathleen's to give her a hand, and I'm going to organize the sweet potatoes." Mom turned and looked at Dad. "Tom, you and Joe are in charge of the cheese tray."

I ran the vacuum at Aunt Kathleen's. Marcel and Moe put the leaf in the table, and then Moe and I set up the buffet. Aunt Kathleen played Bing Crosby's *Christmas Album* quietly because Colleen was napping. The Boucher clan arrived first with bottles of champagne, apple juice for the kids, and two big pie plates wrapped in aluminum foil. Something smelled wonderful.

"Tourtière. My mother makes it every year," said Marcel.

I hadn't seen Marcel's family since the wedding. Jean came up, looking for Joe. "He'll be here any minute," I said.

Doris and Danielle were wearing green mini-skirts with matching Christmas tree sweaters. Each tree was decorated with little silver jingle bells. "I know. They're horrible," whispered Danielle. "But my mom got them for us to wear today. What did you guys get?"

I felt bad when I told her we got airplane tickets to Washington DC.

"No way," said Doris.

"No way what?" asked Marcel's uncle, Monsignor Boucher.

"Merry Christmas, Monsignor," said Moe.

"Hey, I'm family now," he laughed. "You girls should just call me Uncle Roger."

The Donovan family arrived, and Colleen started crying.

"Kathleen, I'll give her a bottle. You visit with your family for a bit before dinner." Marcel turned up the music and left the room. Joe and Jean were off in a corner laughing about something. I noticed that Jean had gotten a Christmas sweater too. His had a reindeer on it. Joe Donovan should thank his lucky stars for his plaid bathrobe.

Uncle Roger was taking drink orders.

"Just water for me, thanks" I heard Dad say. Mom agreed to a glass of white wine.

The doorbell rang and in stepped Rosemarie with a box of Van Otis chocolates. She'd cut her brown hair quite short and was wearing a green miniskirt with a black turtleneck and black boots.

"Merry Christmas," she said.

"Merry Christmas!" said Aunt Kathleen, taking her coat and handing me the chocolates.

The phone rang. Kathleen picked it up. She frowned for a few seconds like she couldn't hear the person on the other end.

"Oh, holy mother, it's Danny! From Vietnam!"

Everyone crowded around the phone. "Be quick," ordered Aunt Kathleen. "And let Rosemarie go last. After we each wish Dan a Merry Christmas, let's head into the living room and give Rosemarie some privacy."

Aunt Kathleen pushed the phone into my hand.

"Merry Christmas, Uncle Danny." I was surprised because I thought that I was going to cry.

"Merry Christmas, Nora." His voice had a tinny sort of echo, and I could barely hear him. I had never been on a long- distance call before.

"Uncle Dan, we pray for you every day at school, and I mentioned you in my graduation speech."

"Rosemarie told me. That was great. Thank you."

"Bye Uncle Danny." I handed Dad the phone.

The living room was so crowded that the kids had to sit on the floor. Marcel spread a blanket on the rug and set Colleen down. She was wearing a red dress, tights, and lacy white pants over her diaper. She looked like a Christmas ornament.

Uncle Roger got down on his hands and knees, making faces and cooing like a crazy pigeon. She laughed big belly laughs.

Rosemarie joined us about ten minutes later. Her eyes sparkled. She looked beautiful. "Hearing from Dan was the best Christmas gift ever."

"I'll bet that talking to you was Dan's best Christmas gift, too," said Dad.

I looked at the twinkly Christmas tree, at the old priest playing on the floor with Colleen, at Rosemarie's happy face, at Joey laughing with Jean, and I thought that my heart would burst with love.

1967

The sun peeked between the slats in my window shades, practically blinding me. Moe's bed was carelessly made. She knew she'd get in trouble if she didn't make it. "It doesn't make sense to make your bed when you get back into it the same day," was her never-ending argument with Mom. Moe always fought those losing battles.

Moe and Gene had a day-long date, beginning with Mass at the Cathedral, followed by a matinee of *A Man for All Seasons* at the State.

"What's it about?" I asked.

"I don't know, but Gene said it's about Saint Thomas More." It didn't sound like Moe's cup of tea, but Moe always did what Gene wanted to do.

After the movie, they were meeting the Tardiff family for a New Year's buffet at the Derryfield Country Club.

I had nothing going on except the 11:00 Mass with Mom and Dad. Joey was on the altar. I watched him ring the little bells and hold the water and wine for Father Murphy. I paid attention to what hand he used when giving and receiving items from the priest. I wanted to make sure he hadn't been making stuff up about the hand rules. We got lucky because the sermon was short, and Dad took us to lunch at the Red Arrow. Nothing fancy like what Moe was being treated to at the Derryfield Country Club. I thought about her sitting in a ritzy dining room eating shrimp with a tiny fork, pinky in the air, and drinking out of a glass with a stem.

"Tomorrow's the Rose Bowl, Nora," said Dad.

"Why aren't they playing it on New Year's Day like other years?"

"Because today is Sunday, and it's never played on Sunday. It's something to do with people riding horses to church. Organizers were afraid that the loud parade would spook the horses and disturb the church services along the parade route," said Dad. "Just one of those carryovers from the past, I guess."

"But people don't take horses to church anymore. Kind of crazy if you ask me." I watched Joey lick the whipped cream off his hot chocolate.

"Well, in two weeks, there's going to be another football game that I think you might be interested in. It's called the Super Bowl and this game WILL be played on a Sunday. It's to decide the football championship for the first time ever. It's sort of like the World Series of football."

"Is Boston playing, dear?" Mom never had any idea of what goes on in the world of sports.

"God no, Helen, the Boston Patriots finished last in the AFL— only won three games and lost ten," laughed Dad.

"Who's playing?" asked Joe. I was surprised because he was never interested in football.

"Two mid-western teams. The Green Bay Packers and the Kansas City Chiefs are going to face each other in Los Angeles."

Dad wiped his mouth. "I'm rooting for Green Bay. That coach Vince Lombardi is a classy guy. Joey, I read that in his younger days, he was an altar boy too. You have a lot in common."

Joey looked at me and rolled his eyes.

"Why are they calling it the Super Bowl?" I asked.

"I heard on the radio that the organizers were having a hard time agreeing on a name. And one day, one of them was bouncing their son's Super Ball and said, 'I've got it—let's call it the Super Bowl'."

I had nothing to do so I agreed to play *Risk* with Joey. I didn't know anything about the game, but I thought if a bunch of altar boys could learn how to play, it couldn't be too hard.

"The goal is to conquer the world, Nora." Joey explained that each player had to build up their armies, attack adjacent countries, occupy entire continents, and then march on to conquer the world."

Joey won Kamchatka and sat back, a big smile on his face. "Who cares about Kamchatka?" I asked.

"See that dotted line from Kamchatka to Alaska? That means that I can sweep down through Alaska into North America, and you won't be able to stop me. You may as well concede now," gloated Joe.

I smiled. It was great that Joey could say the word Kamchatka when a few years ago he could barely say his name without stuttering. And now he'd taken over the world. Where else could he feel so powerful? Never at the school playground where he'd been bullied for being a loser. I promised myself that I'd play *Risk* with him more often.

2

"Nora and Moe, ever since you were little girls, I've been looking forward to having you both at Saint Agatha's so that I could take you to the Father-Daughter Dance."

"What's it like, Moe?" I asked when we climbed into bed.

"Well, it would be super embarrassing except that all the girls are in the same boat. Everyone stands around talking and sipping the awful Ladies Guild punch. And when the music starts, people dance."

"Do they have slow dances, Moe?" I worried that they would play "Strangers in the Night," which made me nervous ever since Eddie Coolidge came into our lives. It reminded me of Manchester's murdered girls.

"Yeah, they have some but sort of fast-slow songs like 'The Girl from Ipanema.' But not super-slow songs. Slow dancing with Dad would be weird." We lay in the dark for a while without speaking. "The worst thing about Dad is that he tries to put everyone to shame. He whirls around the dance floor like he's the Tasmanian Devil. Last year, we spun around the whole gym three times during 'Roll Out the Barrel,' and before I got to catch my breath, Dad dragged me back out for 'Doghouse Polka.'"

I was grateful that there were two of us and only one of him. I felt bad for the kids in school who didn't have fathers. I overheard Mom saying Connie Ledoux was born out of wedlock. That meant she never knew her father. The nuns said that if you didn't have a father, you could bring your grandfather or uncle. I thought that if you went with your grandfather or uncle everyone would assume that you were born out of wedlock. Why put yourself through the embarrassment? Better just to stay home and watch *Saturday Night at the Movies*.

Moe and I got dressed up for the dance. Mom smeared a little pink lipstick on me so I wouldn't look washed out. That surprised me since we've all been warned about the Benson girl and her makeup.

When we came downstairs, Dad was in a suit and tie and holding two corsages.

"Oh, Tom, you need to pin them on the girls," said Helen, queen of all things proper. Dad tried to jab the pins through our dresses without either touching our skin or stabbing us by mistake.

"Photo time." Mom pulled out the Polaroid. "Say cheese on the count of three, everyone."

When we walked into Saint Agatha's, Sister Annunciata greeted us. Moe forgot to warn me that there would be nuns at the dance. "Good evening, Detective Donovan," she said. "Girls, be sure to introduce your father to the other Sisters. And have a wonderful time." She flitted on to the next awkward couple coming through the door.

The gym was decorated in red and white streamers with pink Valentines. Women from the Ladies Guild stood at the back of the gym ladling out punch.

"Big Girls Don't Cry" by The Four Seasons was blasting over the loudspeakers.

Dad saw Detective Callahan across the gym and headed over to talk to him. I was afraid of getting stuck with Missy all night and watched as Moe stepped back, put her finger to her lips and snuck away to talk to her friends.

"Okay, dads and gals," said the DJ. "Everyone out on the dance floor and get yourselves warmed up with the "Hully Gully."

Mom and Dad loved the "Hully Gully." They danced to it on Saturday nights when they went to the Carousel.

"It's called line dancing, girls." Mom demonstrated the steps while she hummed the tune one Sunday morning. "You don't even need a partner to dance."

The DJ called out the "Hully Gully" steps slowly at first. The lines moved to the left, then to the right. Forward. Backward. Hands clapped to the rhythm as we kept up with the quickening speed of the music. When the music stopped, everyone scattered breathless to the edges of the gym.

Moe came back just in time for "The Doghouse Polka." Dad turned to me. "Nora, I'll start with Moe but don't move. Halfway through, I'll drop her off and take you for a spin."

Our flowers began drooping. More punch got spilled at the back of the gym. We practically had to rip our shoes off the sticky floor just to move. People started edging their way toward the back door while quietly making their exit.

"Girls, do you want to go home and see what's up with Mom and Joey?"

Do we ever, I thought. I followed Moe and Dad past Saint Agatha's portrait. She looked down at me with a sympathetic smile. I knew that she'd had a miserable life and death, but at least she was spared the torture of the Father-Daughter Dance.

On the ride home I thought more about Saint Agatha. What was the difference between Agatha and the girls Coolidge murdered? Agatha was considered a saint. Yet the two Manchester teens were considered victims.

3

Moe had been begging us to go to one of Gene's basketball games. But Dad worked a lot of evenings, and it never seemed to work out. "C'mon guys. It's Gene's senior year, and only two home games are left in the season."

"Okay, Moe," said Dad. "I'm off on Tuesday. Let's go then."

We piled into the Bel Air and drove to the high school to see Saint Benedict's face Memorial. Moe said this game was a big deal for both teams. They were tied with the same number of wins and losses. Gene was the point guard. "Tom, what do point guards do?" asked Mom.

"Helen, all players need to be able to pass and dribble and shoot, but to be a point guard you must be a leader, a person of character," Dad explained.

"Well, I think we can all vouch for Gene's character," said Mom. Moe blushed and giggled. I could tell that she was happy as we entered the gym.

The whistle blew. The game started. Saint Benedict's won the tip-off. Back and forth, back and forth, went both the ball and the score. Toward the end of the first quarter, Gene dribbled the ball down the center of the court looking for an open player to pass to. Suddenly, a Memorial player crashed into him and sent him sprawling head-first down the court. The referee blew his whistle and called a foul on the Memorial player. "Poor Gene," said Joe.

Moe looked worried. "I hope he's okay."

Gene got up slowly. But instead of going to the foul line for two free throws, he charged the Memorial player and sucker-punched him in the jaw. That cleared the benches on both sides.

Chaos exploded on the court. Shocked spectators stood in the bleachers in disbelief. Memorial's coach ran to help his player whose mouth was gushing blood. The referees restored order quickly, but not before the head referee gave the old heave-ho sign and threw Gene out of the game for unsportsmanlike conduct.

We quietly left the game at half-time. There was no more Gene to watch.

Halfway home Dad cleared his throat, which he usually meant that he was about to say something uncomfortable. "There is no excuse for the behavior we all witnessed tonight."

"But Dad..." Moe interrupted.

"But nothing, Maureen," he snapped. "And if you ever see it again, I hope to God you'll have the sense to call it off with him or I'll know the reason why. Believe me, girls should steer clear of men with bad tempers."

I wondered if Dad ever recognized his own bad temper. Probably not.

4

My excitement grew as the Greyhound bus pulled up in front of the *Eastern* terminal at Logan. Joey was thrilled about going to the Air and Space Museum, and I was excited to see the Capitol where the congressmen hung out, the White House lawn where the Kennedy kids played with their pony Macaroni, and the Lincoln Memorial where Martin Luther King gave his famous "*I have a dream...*" speech.

When we boarded a plane, the stewardess smiled at Joey. "How old are you, young man?"

"I'm twelve and we're going to the Air and Space Museum for my last year's birthday present," beamed Joey. Moe looked at me and rolled her eyes. Joey could be so embarrassing sometimes.

A minute later the stewardess showed up at our seats with a pin for Joey: a gold set of wings that said *Eastern*. "A special gift for first time flyers." She winked at Moe and me. Joey pinned it to his shirt and broke out in a big smile.

I couldn't believe how pretty the stewardesses were. They wore their hair in beehive hairdos without a single strand out of place. And boy, they were skinny like Twiggy, the model who was on *Cosmopolitan's* cover last month. "That looks like such a glamorous job. Maybe I'll be a stewardess someday," sighed Moe.

"Well, you're probably skinny enough but you have to be pretty," I teased. Moe jabbed me with her elbow and giggled as the plane picked up speed on the runway.

The Holiday Inn seemed fancy to me. We hadn't stayed in many hotels. "I'm glad you like it," said Dad. "At this location, we're close to everything." We walked back to our hotel from the corner diner after a supper of fish and chips.

"Kids we've got a full day tomorrow, so lights out by 9:30," Mom decreed. With two double beds and a roll-away in our room, there wasn't much space to move around. We had to step on the end of Joe's cot to go to the bathroom, but we were so excited to be there, it didn't matter.

On Saturday morning we got to the Air and Space Museum just as it opened. The Wright Brother's plane was hanging from the ceiling in the lobby.

"Kids," said Dad. "They built this in 1903. That's sixty-four years ago. Can you believe it?"

"Check out the *Spirit of St. Louis,*" said Mom as she walked across the lobby. "It says here that Charles Lindbergh piloted this plane for thirty-three and a half hours on his voyage from New York to Paris. Can you imagine staying awake that long? Look, he didn't even have a windshield because they had to save weight for fuel storage. That's amazing!"

I could tell that Joe was getting impatient because he really wanted to see the space stuff. As we turned the corner, there it was— the Mercury *Friendship 7.* "Guys, this is the spaceship that John Glenn piloted when he orbited the Earth three times in under five hours. I can't believe we're seeing it!" For the next three hours we looked at every display in the space galleries and listened to Joey read every sign aloud.

On our walk back to the hotel, we heard a lot of commotion across from the White House. As we got closer, I realized that it was an actual protest—an in-person protest like the ones we see on the news. A guy with long hair and glasses who looked like John Lennon held a sign in one hand and a megaphone in the other. The sign read, "Hell no, we won't go. Burn your draft card now." A bunch of guys were passing a lighter around. They set their draft cards on fire and cheered as they burned. I even saw a couple of priests standing with the protestors.

"Cross the street kids. I don't want you seeing this kind of nonsense," said Dad.

I let my family get ahead of me, pulled out my camera, and took a picture. They didn't even notice. I shoved the camera back in my bag and ran to catch up with them. Funny how Dad could find no fault with priests when it suited him— just not when they were protesting.

The guy with the megaphone started playing "The Eve of Destruction." As we walked away, I heard words about being old enough to kill but not to vote.

"Your Uncle Danny is fighting so that we can be free and safe, and these jokers are protesting? They should be ashamed of themselves." No one dared say a word.

We checked off the boxes of everything we wanted to do in DC. The Lincoln Memorial and Washington Monument. The Capitol with Lady Freedom perched on the dome, the tidal basin surrounded by the last of the cherry blossoms. We took a bus out to Arlington National Cemetery to see the grave of John F. Kennedy. The eternal flame that Jackie lit was still flickering. Mom cried. Dad held his hat over his heart. We took the bus back to Logan Circle in silence.

Our weekend in Washington was cut short by an early bedtime. "We need to be up by 5:30 tomorrow, gang," Mom said. "We have a 7:30 flight back to Manchester."

When we got back to New Hampshire, I was amazed by how far behind our Spring was. The trees and flowers were in full bloom in Washington, but in Manchester the leaves were still tightly furled as though they feared Spring would never come.

I couldn't wait to pick up my pictures at Woodman's Photo Hut. But no way would I let Dad see the shot I took of the demonstration.

5

Mom signed Moe and me up for sewing lessons at Mrs. Minnie Robichaud's. She was supposedly Manchester's best sewing teacher. Moe liked the idea because she worked at Martin's and was a know-it-all about fine fabric, but I had no interest in either sewing or fine fabric.

Mrs. Robichaud had a room set up in her house with twelve sewing machines. Mom told us she sewed all her own clothes. She probably had a hard time finding clothes that fit her in department stores, because she had the biggest breasts of any women I'd ever seen. So enormous that she had to sew double sets of darts in her dresses to accommodate her giant bosom. One set of darts pointed up. The other set pointed down. Her boobs looked like a pair of over-inflated balloons.

The cats were the worst part of going to Mrs. Robichaud's. There were eight or ten of them, but it was tough to know because they were never in the same room at the same time. Malcolm was the one I hated most. He'd leave paw prints and claw pulls on our fabric. We'd have to be careful about shooing him away because he was Mrs. Robichaud's favorite, and she'd yell at us for being mean to him. When she scolded us, he'd leap on one of her hair-covered living room chairs with his back to us and clean his fur with long, slow licks of his tongue.

And if you were on the lookout for a sneaky cat when you were sewing a seam and your seam was a little crooked, Mrs. Robichaud made you rip it out and start all over again. It seemed like I was always ripping out stitches. The apron and skirt that I sewed were either bunched-up or had little holes from where I had pulled out and re-sewed seams that Mrs. Robichaud insisted were crooked. But Moe managed to turn out store-quality productions: a cute little apron with grosgrain trim and a hip-hugger skirt.

"Nora, you don't pay attention to detail," she said. But what she didn't realize was that I kept Mrs. Robichaud's cats away from our worktables while she concentrated on her perfect seams.

Joe and Dad were watching the Channel 9 news when we got home from sewing class. "Girls, please set the table. Dinner will be ready in five."

Mom doled out beef stew and dumplings and we all sat down.

"Mom, when can we go shopping for my prom dress? Donna thinks that the dresses will be all picked over if we don't go soon."

"Maureen, what makes you think that I plan to buy you a prom dress?" asked Mom.

"Because you bought my dress for last year's prom, and I just assumed—"

"I think you should sew your gown," Mom interrupted. "You've become a good little seamstress since I spent a small fortune sending you to Mrs. Robichaud's." Moe stared at her, unable to come up with a quick response. Joe and I just looked down at our plates.

"But Mom, NOBODY sews their own prom dress. I'll be the laughing-stock of Saint Agatha's." I thought Moe was going to cry.

"Moe, you work at Martin's and get an employee discount so think of how much money you'll save by sewing your own dress. I'll buy the fabric and pay for an updo at Houle's. You won't be a laughing-stock. You'll be a trendsetter."

A few days later Moe started sewing. She wouldn't let anyone see what she was working on. "I want it to be a surprise."

Priscilla Presley had just married Elvis, and I figured Moe's dress would look something like hers. "Her dress was gorgeous," swooned Moe. "Simple but really classy."

"Do you know that Elvis put wire in his hair to shape the perfect pompadour for his wedding?" I asked.

"What's that got to do with Priscilla's dress, Nora?"

"Nothing. I just thought it was interesting."

Moe got back from Houle's just before 5:00. Just as expected, her hair was teased and wrapped into a perfect beehive. She looked really pretty, but I didn't tell her that. She raced upstairs to get ready for the prom.

The doorbell rang at 6:00. "Come in, Gene," said Dad. "You sure do clean up well," That was the friendliest I'd seen Dad with Gene since the night of the infamous basketball game.

Moe came down the stairs. We were stunned. The dress she'd secretly been working on looked nothing like what I'd imagined. Judging from the looks on my parents' faces, they felt the same. There was nothing prissy, frilly, or lacy about Moe's dress. It was a simple but elegant full length, pale pink satin dress with no shoulders and no sleeves. Just a V-shaped loop that went around her neck to keep the dress from falling down.

"Maureen, may I see you in the kitchen?" Mom marched out of the living room. I followed her because I knew that an argument was about to take place and I didn't want to miss it. "What kind of dress do you call that, young lady?"

"It's a halter dress, Mom. If you followed the fashion magazines, you'd know that this look is the rage in London right now. Twiggy wore one on the cover of *Vogue*." There was defiance in Moe's voice as she twirled around. "You said I should be a trendsetter."

"You're not wearing a bra, young lady. What is Gene going to think?"

I wondered if Gene would be thrilled or scared out of his mind.

"Mom, get real. I'm wearing pasties on my nipples."

"Pasties? I thought only strippers and exotic dancers wore pasties. They may cover your nipples, but they give you no support."

"Mom, look at me--I don't need support. Why do you think that wearing a bra that makes your boobs stick out like cones is the right thing to do?" Anyway, you can't wear a bra with a halter top, so pasties it is." Moe headed back to the living room, her chin high.

I had to hand it to Moe. She'd been told her to sew her own dress and that's what she did. She looked fabulous as she and Gene walked out the door. Thank God he bought her a wrist corsage because there wasn't enough dress to pin one on.

6

"Frost led a tragic life," said Sister. "Depression ran in his family, and they didn't have treatment for people with mental illness like they do now."

I wasn't so sure that people who were mental today were getting good treatment. I thought of Mrs. Connor, Paul's mother, who hadn't been right since her hysterectomy at the Infant Asylum. And I thought about Sister Imelda, who still locked doors because she thought people were trying to hurt her.

"Stopping by The Woods on a Snowy Evening" is one of Frost's most famous poems, and I'm sure most of you read it in grammar school," said Sister.

Heads nodded.

"It's fascinating to think about how artists' lives impact their art. It was written in 1923, just after Frost had his sister committed to a mental institution. Many scholars believe that it's a suicide poem: the dark and lovely woods signify death, and they do not frighten the speaker. The poet is tempted to embrace death, yet he has promises to keep." She looked around the classroom. "What kind of promises might the speaker feel he has to keep?"

"He might have a family to support," suggested Colleen.

She turned and wrote 'Support Family' on the blackboard. "Good. Anyone else?"

"Maybe he's a doctor or a priest or someone who has the skills to help others," said Marie.

"Excellent." Sister wrote "Doctor or Priest" on the board. "Other thoughts?"

Sister paused for a minute and scanned the classroom for questions. "How might this poem impact Catholics?"

I raised my hand. "I didn't know that Frost was Catholic."

"He wasn't. But he might have imbibed Catholic teachings from his Catholic friends," Sister responded. "Are any of you familiar with the sin of pride?"

I sunk down in my seat.

"Proud as a peacock?" offered a girl in the back of the room.

"Yes, but that's not what I had in mind in relation to our faith. I am sure that you've heard of the Seven Deadly Sins. Pride is considered the worst of these sins." Sister wrote "pride" on the blackboard. "Pride was Lucifer's sin, and suicide is a manifestation of pride. Suicide is a mortal sin, and anyone who commits suicide is damned to hell forever. Suicide suggests that one's ability to sin exceeds God's willingness to forgive. Those who fall into despair are denying God's willingness to love and forgive them."

That sounded like a stretch to me. Miles existed between a little kid telling the priest that she has no sins to confess and an adult committing suicide and pissing off God, who in my mind seemed to get pissed off altogether too often. Robert Frost may have felt depressed, but Sister's linking his poem to the Church must have New Hampshire's poet spinning in his grave.

7

I squirmed uncomfortably in my pew and stared at the first Station of the Cross: Jesus Condemned to Death. I felt condemned stuck in the Cathedral at Moe's graduation. I thought it would never end. "In closing, may the blessed among you find religious vocations where you will serve God first." Sister stepped down from the podium to a rousing round of applause.

Moe wanted a quiet family party because she had a date with Gene. My parents gushed over Moe and her Ladies Guild Scholarship to the Sacred Heart School of Nursing. "I'm so proud that you are following in my footsteps, Maureen. You will be a wonderful nurse!"

8

My first official job was at the Sacred Heart Hospital in the Housekeeping Department. Training started with a tour of the hospital, followed by a few hours of job shadowing with an experienced housekeeper, and then a couple of basic tips from Flo, the head housekeeper.

Flo was a woman who looked a whole lot older than she probably was. She had bleached blonde hair and black roots sprang from her scalp. Her red lipstick was crooked, and she had a big space between her front teeth. "Never clean a toilet with your mouth open," she warned as she snapped her gum on that first morning. "If you are a nail biter, don't do it on the job—too many germs in the hospital." And "don't let yourself get behind by chit-chatting with patients. They need their rest."

"Pay close attention to detail if you want to keep your job." Flo flicked her gum into the trash and lit a cigarette. It was useful for her to have a space between her teeth because she could hold held the cigarette there while she continued talking. Flo told us about the star housekeeper who got fired a few weeks ago for mixing up the denture cups on the patients' nightstands. "Can you imagine having someone else's teeth in your mouth?" asked Flo. "Damn disgusting if you ask me." I couldn't imagine having any false teeth in my mouth, never mind someone else's.

The housekeepers were assigned to different floors of the hospital. We were expected to clean all surfaces in the patient rooms, empty the trash, and keep the staff lounges neat and tidy.

At 7:00 am we gathered in the basement to get our assignments.

"How many bags do you want?" asked Flo, as she held an unlit cigarette in the space between her teeth. She was referring to bags for all the dirty linen that we collected when patients were discharged. How the heck was I supposed to know how many bags I'd need when I had no clue how many patients were going to die or get discharged today?

I was paid $1.28 per hour, and I earned every penny of it. After I paid my parents back the money they'd loaned me to buy my blue polyester uniform, I didn't have much left over. But I went to Manchester Music with Linda and bought myself the new Beatle's *Sgt. Pepper's Lonely Heart Club Band* album. The cover had a picture of the Beatles standing in front of a collage of famous people. I couldn't make sense of the psychedelic artwork, but maybe people doing drugs understood it.

My favorite song on the album was "Lucy in the Sky With Diamonds." Its language was magical. Marmalade skies. Newspaper taxis. Tangerine trees. Although I had no clue what plasticine porters were, I told myself to look it up in the dictionary. Dad said that he wished that I'd never wasted my money on such garbage. "A guy at the station said that song is all about drugs. LSD, Nora. Take the first letter out of Lucy, Sky, Diamonds. LSD. That's what you get."

"I don't think so, Dad. I read that John Lennon's son Julian did a drawing in nursery school that inspired all those images. Why do you get so hung up on stuff like that? Your generation just can't relate to all the changes going on." I headed up the stairs to my room.

9

Walter Cronkite warned viewers that hippies were going to invade San Francisco.

"What's this world coming to?" Mom sighed. News coverage showed thousands of kids with headbands and long hair, peace signs and bellbottoms, hanging out for the summer in San Francisco. Signs with *Flower Power* and *Give Peace a Chance* were everywhere. Newscasters called it the Summer of Love.

Young people from all over the United States flooded to Haight-Ashbury, following Timothy Leary's advice to "turn on, tune in, and drop out."

"Goddam hippies," my father fumed. "What kind of parents would let their kids travel to California to do nothing but take drugs and fornicate?" They should be working and saving money for their futures. Goddam trust fund kids are probably what they are."

Reporters said that a counterculture was brewing in California. I'm not sure what that meant, except teenagers were rebelling from their ordinary lives. I was sick of crazy nuns and cleaning dirty toilets at the Sacred Heart. Girls getting murdered, negroes getting attacked, and flag-draped coffins getting unloaded from military planes. Escaping this stuff appealed to me. If I had money, Haight-Ashbury would tempt me too.

Dad turned off the news in disgust after watching a clip of a mock hippie funeral.

"Don't get any crazy ideas, kids," said Dad. "Manchester won't tolerate a revolution."

10

I loved the movie *Cool Hand Luke*. Paul Newman played Luke, a guy who was arrested for sawing the heads off parking meters when he was drunk. He got sentenced to two years on a chain gang in a Florida prison. The prisoners respected him because he questioned authority. That's why I liked him, too.

The captain told Luke that he would eventually get used to wearing chains. "Don't you never stop listenin' to them clinking…" he warned.

Luke looked back at the captain and said with a big twinkle in his eye. "I wish you'd stop being so good to me, Cap'n."

The captain turned to the chain gang. "What we've got here is a failure to communicate. Some men you just can't reach."

Luke refused to let the captain break his spirit.

I thought of Luke when I read about Richard and Mildred's Loving's inter-racial marriage in Virginia. Inter-racial marriage was illegal in that state, even though the Lovings got married legally in Washington. Instead of confronting them during the day, Virginia police burst into their bedroom in the middle of the night and arrested them. But like Luke, their spirits weren't broken.

Their lawyer sued the state of Virginia stating that their 14th Amendment rights had been violated.

"What does the 14th Amendment say?" I asked Dad.

"It says that states can't take away the privileges granted by the Constitution." I liked that the US Supreme Court ruled that banning inter-racial marriage was unconstitutional. The verdict made it extra sweet since their name was "Loving."

It seemed that the Supreme Court was hearing more cases about negroes. Boxer Mohammed Ali got drafted by the Army but refused to go for religious reasons. He was stripped of his boxing titles, convicted of draft evasion, and sentenced to five years in jail. But like Luke and the Lovings, Ali's spirit wasn't broken. The Supreme Court threw out his conviction, and Ali never had to go to jail.

"Thank goodness for the Supreme Court," said Mom. "Without it, the civil rights struggle wouldn't have gotten off the ground."

I didn't like every Supreme Court decision. I thought of Miranda who confessed to kidnapping and rape but was let off the hook by the Court because the police hadn't read him his rights. The Miranda decision scared me because I was afraid that Coolidge might get out on some technicality. I didn't want any more Manchester girls to be raped and tortured by the guy. I wanted Coolidge broken.

11

Baseball was on everyone's minds by the end of the summer. But people didn't dare talk about winning out loud because of the curse. One night at supper, Dad explained the curse to us.

"The Red Sox were one of the most successful teams in baseball after winning the first World Series ever played. They went on to win a total of five out of the first fifteen World Series titles." He paused and studied our faces for a reaction and then continued. "But ever since they sold Babe Ruth to the Yankees after the 1919 season, they haven't won another one. Some think the Bambino put a curse on the Red Sox for trading him."

Dad told us about the curse because he didn't want us to jinx Boston by talking about the Sox winning the series. "Baseball fans are superstitious," he said. "And there's a four-way tie going down the home stretch right now."

Once September arrived, fans crowded around their television sets whenever the Red Sox played. It was anyone's guess which team would win the American League pennant. It came down to the last game of the season on October 1. The Red Sox pulled out a win against the Minnesota Twins. But that wasn't enough to win the pennant. We had to wait for the second game of the double-header, the Tigers against the Angels. If the Tigers beat the Angels, there would be a tie for the pennant, and the Red Sox would have to play the Tigers the next day.

"This could be it," said Dad as the Tiger's star Dick McAuliffe stepped up to the plate. "He's already driven in three runs; let's hope his luck has run out." We sat quietly in front of the television, fingers crossed.

"IT'S A DOUBLE PLAY!!!" shrieked Ken Coleman. "The Tiger's season is over. THE RED SOX WIN, THE RED SOX WIN!".

Dad jumped out of his Barcalounger. "I wish Danny was here to see this!"

The cafeteria was abuzz the next day. The ladies making BLT's and ladling out soup were talking non-stop about the game. Marie Chalifour and Patty Romero were laughing as I joined them. "You wouldn't believe how many times my father swore during the game," said Marie.

"My mother was so mad at him."

"That's nothing," said Patty. "My dad is so superstitious that he wore the same tee shirt every game the Sox played in September. He never washed it." We all laughed. "Yesterday my mom walked into the living room and asked, 'what stinks in here'?" She sprayed air freshener around the room. " 'I think it's my shirt, Mary. And I'm not going to wash it until this season is over,' he said."

Patty laughed. "And now that the Sox won the pennant, he's going to wear his stinky shirt until the end of the World Series."

Newspapers dubbed the 1967 Red Sox "The Impossible Dream Team." In the same breath that our teachers told us to pray for our soldiers in Vietnam and those starving in Biafra, they told us to pray that Boston would win the Series.

The World Series started on the following Wednesday. The Red Sox faced the Saint Louis Cardinals. Game One went to Saint Louis. Boston took Game Two but lost the next two games. Dad made us say a rosary before Game Five. "We need all the help we can get," he said. With a 3-1 advantage for Saint Louis, the Sox needed a few more miracles. They got what they needed and pulled off wins in Games Five and Six.

By the time Game Seven rolled around, Dad was pacing back and forth across the living room. Moe sat in the corner with a stack of magazines on her lap. Even Joe joined us, biting his nails, for once interested in baseball. Mom looked up from her knitting more often than she usually did. "This is it, gang. It ends here tonight," said Dad, his voice shaking.

Jim Lonborg was on the mound for the Sox with only two day's rest. Bob Gibson had an extra day to recover his pitching arm. Lonborg struggled from the beginning. Three hits and a wild pitch put the Sox behind 2-0 in the third. Gibson himself hit a home run in the fifth and two more runs scored. The Red Sox dream quickly unraveled in the sixth inning on a three-run homer by Julian Javier off our arm-weary Jim Lonborg. With the 7-2 defeat, the Red Sox's Impossible Dream ended one win short.

We sat in silence as the Cardinals stormed the field amidst deafening cheers from the stands.

"It was a great season, kids. Boston has nothing to be ashamed of." Dad turned off the TV.

The next day the mood in the Saint Agatha's cafeteria was subdued. It occurred to me that in spite of the disappointment of losing the World Series, something good came out of it. Baseball brought everyone together. For a short period of time, we didn't have to think about the protests, the coffins, and the racism tearing our country apart.

12

Joey walked in door waving a large manila envelope. Mom was breading veal cutlets while I mashed potatoes. "Guess what, everybody?!"

"Joseph, look at the snow you just dragged in."

Dad came into the kitchen carrying the *Union Leader*. "What's all the commotion about?"

"At Fellowship today, Father Murphy announced that two of us were getting scholarships to Camp Benedictus next summer for being great altar boys and setting a good example for the younger kids." We were all paying attention now. "And then he announced that the winners were Paul and me!" Joe pulled the certificate out of the envelope, and we passed it around.

"Jeez, Joe. I've been in Holy Name Society for years now, and all I get are free sandwiches. You are being sent to a lake for two weeks," said Dad.

Mom hugged him. "I'm proud of you, sweetheart. And don't worry about the snow. The floor needs a good wash anyway."

"Congratulations Joe," I said. "Beats cleaning toilets."

"That's super, Joe," said Moe. "Gene went to Benedictus in seventh grade and loved it."

With Moe, everything always circled back to Gene.

13

Walter Cronkite reported another series of battles being fought in Vietnam. Pictures of The Battle of Dak To flashed across the screen.

Dad sighed and shut off the television. Since my Uncle Danny was shipped out to Vietnam, Dad was less interested in watching the news. He got angry every time he saw anti-war protests, and it seemed as though the news showed at least one every night.

"Let's think positive thoughts and decorate the Christmas tree," Dad said.

The Christmas tree went up early in the Donovan house every year.

"It's a lot of work so we may as well enjoy it for as long as we can," Mom reasoned. After the tree was trimmed and dripping with tinsel, we lit the treetop angel and went outside to admire it .

"I think she's a real beauty," said Dad. "It may be our best tree ever." I smiled because Dad said that every year. We ran back into the house when we heard the phone ringing.

"Hi Kathleen. Good to hear from you. How's the baby?" Mom asked. "Sure. I'll put Tom on."

"Tom, telephone!" Mom yelled.

"Hey Kath." He looked out the window, nodded his head and said, "uh huh, uh huh." Finally, he got a chance to interrupt. "Kathleen, you talked to Danny recently? Do you know where his platoon is heading?"

Kathleen said something and Dad hung up. "He's headed to the Central Highlands. Up near Dak To." His voice was barely more than a whisper.

Over the next week we felt jittery. Every time the phone rang, we jumped and held our breath. One morning as we were running around getting ready for school, the phone rang.

"Hello," answered Dad. "Dan, DAN…we've been so worried about you. You're where? What happened? Oh my God, no…."

He hung up the phone. "Danny was hit by an explosive device during Operation MacArthur. He was airlifted to a field hospital near Saigon. They couldn't save his leg." And he began to cry.

I'd never seen Dad cry before. Mom hugged him. "Let's kneel and say a prayer for Danny."

Moe didn't say a word and Joey cried. I knelt, but I didn't think praying would do any good. Uncle Dan's leg was blown off, and prayers wouldn't change that. I hoped that my family wouldn't be next standing at Grenier Field watching Uncle Danny's flag-draped coffin being carried off a military plane.

14

Uncle Danny called Rosemarie on Christmas Eve. He said that he'd been evacuated from the field hospital north of Saigon and transferred to a hospital in Germany. "He thinks he'll be sent home sometime in late January," said Rosemarie.

I heard my parents talking quietly in the living room. "It's my fault, Helen. He'd have never joined the Army if I hadn't shamed him into it." It reminded me of the night Dad said that he felt responsible for Pamela Mason's death. He thought that everything that went wrong was somehow his fault. Mom called it Irish Guilt.

That night in our bedroom, Moe and I talked about how weird it would be to see Uncle Danny walk around with a fake leg. "Do you think it will be made out of wood or metal?" I asked Moe.

"How would I know? We'll have to see when he gets home," Moe replied.

I was glad that Uncle Danny had survived. But I fell asleep thinking that it wouldn't be a good idea to buy him slippers for Christmas.

1968

"Where's Dak To?" asked Joe. I was surprised he remembered where Uncle Danny's leg got blown off. I'd forgotten.

"I don't know. But I'll look it up in the library during study hall."

I trudged up the hill to Saint Agatha's. We'd had a warm spell, and brown puddles dotted the sidewalks. I wandered into the cafeteria to see if any of my friends were there. Patty and Linda waved me over to a table in the back.

"How was your break?" asked Patty.

"Pretty good. Except my Uncle Dan lost half his leg in Nam."

"I'm sorry," said Linda.

"Will he be alright?" asked Patty.

"My mom and aunt are nurses, and they think so. He's in a hospital in Germany and is getting sent to Boston for rehab," I said.

"I hope he'll do okay. When my cousin came home from Nam, he was kind of nuts. He fought with his wife and yelled at the neighbors," said Patty.

"How's he now?" I asked.

"OK, I guess. His wife left him, but he's working and has a girlfriend."

The bell rang, and we headed off to Biology.

As I left school that day, I looked up at the portrait of Saint Agatha. What a fool to choose torture. I would've married the jerk and stabbed him in his sleep.

For the next few days, race riots and anti-war protests filled the news.

"Negro children have every right to a decent education," said Dad. "Education helps people get ahead in society."

"I'm not sure everyone wants negroes to get ahead," I said.

"Nora's right." Mom closed the drapes in the living room. "Many white people feel that they are better than negroes."

"Sometimes I hear that kind of talk at work, and I hate it," said Dad.

I wondered if Dad said anything, or if he just hated it. Manchester had only a few negro families. I didn't know anyone who said bad things about negroes except Uncle Danny and people on TV like George Wallace.

The TV news showed guys with long hair and braless, doe-eyed-girls in gypsy skirts burning a flag. "I'll bet most of them are high on marijuana," Dad fumed. "Imagine burning our flag!"

It seemed like there were even more race riots than anti-war protests. Martin Luther King argued that racism and the Vietnam War were two parts of a whole. He said that racism made negroes poor, and the poor get sucked up in Johnson's draft to fight in an immoral war.

"King's right about negro poverty." Dad stretched his legs out. "But the military gives young negroes discipline, a paycheck, and the offer of a cheap education. Just like the military is doing for Dan."

"Not all return home, and some have terrible burdens." Mom picked up Agatha Christie's *Peril at End House*. She didn't want to talk. I didn't want to talk, either. I picked up the newspaper. The front-page photo was of a South Vietnamese cop holding a gun to the head of a Viet Cong soldier. The young soldier had round apple cheeks, and his eyes were squinted shut as if that would prevent him from hearing the gun go off. Looking at the photo gave me the sense that time had frozen. It seemed that the cop and the soldier had days and weeks and years leading up to this moment. Next to the Vietnam photo was an article about Ground Hog Day. Punxsutawney Phil had seen his shadow, so winter was staying around. How could anyone know what the groundhog saw or didn't see, I wondered. Maybe the groundhog's vision was bad. He could have been an old groundhog and going blind. Or maybe the morning sun was too bright for his little eyes, so he squinted like the Viet Cong soldier and just thought he saw his shadow.

2

It rained the day Uncle Dan flew into Logan. Rosemarie and her friend met his plane. Dad, Mom, and I crowded around the phone when she called. "The ambulance guys were wonderful. They let me ride with Dan to the VA, and Ginny followed in my car," said Rosemarie. "I was so happy I couldn't stop crying."

"How was he, Rosemarie?" asked Dad.

"He's doing okay."

"We'll visit him this weekend," said Mom. "What can we bring?"

"He'd probably like some magazines." Rosemarie paused. "It'd be better if you didn't bring the kids."

"That's okay. They're busy with school stuff, and Dan will be home before too long."

Aunt Kathleen asked me to babysit Colleen while she went with my parents to see Dan. Linda joined me because we were working on a project for religion class.

Aunt Kathleen laughed. "Please tell me that you girls aren't thinking of joining the convent?"

"No!" I was shocked. "In sophomore year we take *The Philosophy of Religion*. It's cool. Linda and I are working on something called liberation theology. You'd like it. It's a bit like Communism."

"Heavens, Nora. Where did you get the idea that I liked Communism?" Kathleen filled two baby bottles with apple juice and put a box of Goldfish crackers on the counter.

"You started a ruckus at Thanksgiving a few years ago when you said that Jesus was the first true Communist." I was disappointed that Aunt Kathleen had forgotten her position.

"Oh, that. I guess I think that Communism is a good idea in theory, but it never works. Just look at Vietnam."

I wanted to say that neither Communism nor anything else was being given a chance in Vietnam because of the fighting, but Colleen started yelling. She was sixteen months old and babbling non-stop. Linda played peek-a boo with her while I got her a bottle. I was about halfway through *Blueberries for Sal* when she conked out.

It was Linda's idea to use Martin Luther King in our paper. "His ideas tie in with liberation theology. King says that society can't advance spiritually unless it eliminates income inequality. And liberation theology demands that we help the poor."

"Eliminating poverty would cut down on racial violence," I mused.

We got a lot done before Colleen woke up fussing.

"I'm hitting the road," said Linda. "Bye, cutie!" But Colleen was too busy with her doll to notice Linda leaving.

I'd just put her down for the night when Dad pulled into the driveway. Aunt Kathleen handed me $20.00. "Take it," she said. "You were here all day, and I never worried about Colleen." Marcel, usually so friendly, just hugged me and muttered thanks after hanging his coat in the closet. I headed out to our car, my parents sitting like two silhouettes in the soft glow of the streetlight.

"How was your day?" asked Mom.

"Oh, we had fun with Colleen. How's Uncle Dan?"

"He's doing okay. But anyone with an amputation goes through a lot of physical and psychological pain."

Dad looked in the rear-view mirror. "Dan's in for a rough few months. But he's a fighter."

"Is he walking yet?" I asked.

"Oh, yes. The VA rehab is excellent," said Mom.

That made me feel a little better. "Will he have a wooden leg or one of those metal ones?"

"Hon, they don't put wooden legs on people anymore," said Dad.

"Well, I've seen them on people downtown." Ever since Dan lost his leg, I'd been on the alert for folks who hobbled around to figure out what kind of legs they had.

"You're right. But now guys who get wounded in Nam are given metal prostheses."

Prostheses. I liked how the word sounded. But the image of metal legs all lined up in a hospital corridor waiting for a doctor to come by and attach them to guys who had the bad luck to lose a leg was creepy.

"When can we visit him?" I asked.

Dad paused before he spoke. "Not for a while. Many of the patients have severe injuries. It's not a place for kids."

"Are the patients mostly negroes?" I asked.

"Ah, now we have Martin Luther King in the back seat," said Dad.

Mom turned to me as we got out of the car.

"They are mostly negroes," she whispered.

I knew it.

3

Joe dropped his books on the kitchen table. "I can't wait to graduate," he sighed. He put an English muffin in the toaster and stood tapping the counter with his knife.

"What's going on at All Saints'?" I asked.

"You know how nutty Francis is. She liked Imelda's idea about book reports and art projects. We read *Frankenstein*, and I don't know what I'll do for a project." He slathered grape jelly on his muffin.

"Anything else going on?" I asked.

"I heard Mom on the phone talking to Aunt Kathleen. Dan gets PT in a room where trapezes hang from the ceiling. Guys who've lost legs swing from trapeze to trapeze to build upper body strength." He wiped some purple drips off his chin. "She said that they look like big spider monkeys."

"That's terrible," I said. "Was Uncle Danny on one?"

"She didn't say. But when he comes home, we can see how strong his arms look."

"This war will be over by the time you're eighteen, Joe. And I bet those guys like the trapezes," I said.

"Not as much as they like having legs," said Joe.

Race riots continued all over the country. Teachers ignored them except for a new young guy who taught history.

"Mr. Rostyn is cool," said Catherine.

"What's that?" Marie peered at Catherine's tray.

"Roast beef hash."

"Yeew. Glad I brought a sandwich." Debby wrinkled her nose.

"What did Rostyn do that was cool?" I asked.

"He got tear-gassed at a war protest in Wisconsin."

"Did he say if it hurt?" asked Debby.

"No, but I'm pretty sure it burns your eyes," Catherine answered.

Dad was getting crabbier and crabbier. Coolidge's appeal, Uncle Dan losing his leg, and the anti-war protests. Everything was driving him nuts, and he was driving us nuts.

Joe and I decided to make chocolate fudge. He sat at the kitchen table, asking me every two minutes when I thought the fudge would be at the soft-ball stage. I let him lick the spoon and put the fudge on the porch to harden.

Dad came home, briefcase in one hand and the fudge in the other. "Who the hell left this out?" he asked.

"Nora," said Joe.

"Nora, what were you thinking? The Larkins' dog will be up on our porch eating the whole pan. He'll get sick and Larkin will saddle me with the vet bill." He hung up his coat and went upstairs.

What a jerk. How would the Larkins know that we left chocolate fudge out and who says Major Larkin would eat it?

Mom rolled her eyes. "Dinner will be ready in twenty," she called.

"He's so mean!" Joe said.

"Your dad's under a lot of pressure," said Mom. "You know he loves us."

I was sick of Dad's version of love but knew Mom didn't want to hear it.

4

Footage of Father Dan Berrigan and Professor Howard Zinn visiting Hanoi flashed across the screen. North Vietnam had agreed to release three American POWs to Berrigan and Zinn.

"If the Church doesn't watch its step, it will lose its tax-free status," seethed Dad.

"I'm sure these men's families are thrilled to have them home, Church tax status be damned." Mom's voice was sharp.

"Helen," Dad began.

"Don't you Helen me, Tom Donovan. You saw those poor young men in Dan's rehab place. The country's on fire. I'm glad priests are speaking up."

Dad got up and went out to the porch to have a cigarette.

"Good for you, Mom," I said.

She sighed and picked up her knitting.

Days later, Rosemarie called. "Hi Nora! Get your parents. I've got news."

"Mom's shopping, but Joe, Dad, and I are here."

The three of us gathered around the phone. Uncle Danny got on the line. "I'm happy to announce that Rosemarie is now Mrs. Donovan."

"Congratulations!" exclaimed Dad. "Rosemarie, you've no idea what you've gotten yourself into!"

"I'm the luckiest woman in the world!"

"Where are you?" asked Dad.

"At the hospital. The chaplain performed our ceremony, and Dan's physical therapist and his psychiatric social worker were our witnesses. His therapist made a cake, and Dan got me flowers from the gift shop."

"Did you take pictures?" Joe asked.

"We have pictures up the wazoo," said Dan. "And I'm being transferred to the Manchester VA in a few days."

"Great news, Dan," said Dad.

He gave Mom Dan's news as they unpacked the groceries. "Two people stood up for them. His physical therapist and his psychiatric social worker."

"Psychiatric social worker?" Mom looked at Dad. "Probably all wounded vets get one," she said.

Why did Mom think only wounded got psychiatric social workers? I thought of Patty's uncle who wasn't wounded but came home and fought with everyone. Maybe the soldiers who needed help the most were the ones whose wounds were psychological.

5

I told Joe I'd help him with his *Frankenstein* project. "Francis will love it if you tie in the seven deadly sins."

"What are they?" asked Joe.

"Pride, greed, wrath, envy, lust, gluttony, and sloth. I wrote them down on a piece of paper. "Pride" still smarted ever since that priest yelled at me in confession when I'd tried to be perfect.

"I thought sloth was an animal," said Joe.

"It means laziness."

Joe looked blank.

"Just think. Look at this list. What sins was the monster guilty of?" I asked.

"He was wrathful. And envious."

"Okay, what were the scientist's sins?"

"What's lust?"

"People who go see strippers and read dirty books are lustful," I answered. I thought of Mr. Wyman's sweaty hand.

"I guess Victor was proud because he wanted to be a great scientist. But he was wrathful, too."

Joe put together a decent project. He stuck a picture of Lurch from the *Addams Family* on one side of his poster and a picture of a wild-haired scientist on the other. He listed the seven deadly sins across the top and stuck wrath and envy under the Monster and wrath and pride under the Scientist.

"Relieved to see there are no graham cracker crumbs, Nora," Mom teased.

Joe and I finished the dishes when the news switched to Hanoi. Walter Cronkite stood in blazing sunlight in front of a bombed-out building. Palm trees swayed in the background. Dad drummed his fingers on his armrest. The connection was tinny and had an echo, but we heard Cronkite ask if anyone could win the war in Vietnam. The camera then cut back to Cronkite's news station in New York where he continued questioning America's role in Vietnam.

I thought about death. I thought about war. I thought of Uncle Danny's leg rotting away in Dak To. I thought of the Berrigan brothers, both priests protesting the war. I thought about all the negroes fighting in Nam. I wondered what sin war would be. Wrath? Pride? Greed? Lust? Envy?

"I'm going out on the back porch," Dad said.

"Tom," Mom began.

"Helen, leave me alone," Dad snapped.

He slammed the door, and I thought Mom was going say something. But she picked up her book and started reading.

That night I thought about serial killers. What sins were they guilty of? Wrath, for sure. And lust. Maybe envy as well. I'd read an article that said men who kill and torture do so because they feel inadequate. Maybe serial killers had mean mothers. Or tiny penises. Or both.

I wondered what sin I was most guilty of. I had been accused of pride, once by a priest and once by a nun. But I knew that I was more wrathful than proud. I hated perverts who raped and killed innocent women. I hated Richard Speck who raped and murdered the student nurses, I hated Juan Miranda who kidnapped and raped a young woman as she left work, and I hated Albert De Salvo who strangled women and worried my father to death. But most of all, I hated Eddie Coolidge, who haunted Manchester for years and who might be out of jail soon because of some legal loophole that I feared involved my father.

6

Rosemarie threw Dan a party a few weeks after he got discharged from the Manchester VA. Dad wondered why we hadn't been invited over sooner.

"I'm sure Rosemarie wanted to give Dan time to get used to being at home," said Mom.

"Right," said Dad.

When we crossed the river, Dad chuckled. "It's hilarious that Dan, who was furious about Kathleen marrying a Frenchie, now lives on the West Side himself."

"Tom, don't start anything." Mom looked at the cars lining Dubuque Street. "Looks like quite a party." Dad parked around the block. Mom asked Joe to carry the lasagna, Dad carried the cooler loaded with ice and soft drinks, and I brought the oatmeal cookies I'd made yesterday.

The place was rocking and rolling. When I heard *Sgt. Pepper's Lonely Heart Club Band* blasting, I knew that it would be a fun. A big WELCOME HOME, DAN sign stood in the front yard. "Maybe there'll be some cute guys here," I thought.

We didn't ring the doorbell. Between the music and the people laughing inside, no one would have heard it. Mom pushed the door open. The house was thick with cigarette smoke. Red, white, and blue crepe paper streamers dangled from the ceiling. It seemed like every table was covered with candles.

"What a fire hazard!" Mom exclaimed. She blew out some candles and pulled down the streamers that had been dangling close by.

A guy with long hair and a headband sat half-asleep on the bottom step leading upstairs. His white tee-shirt had an American flag on the front. Dark blue tattoos marched up both arms and a red plastic cup sat on the stairs next to him. His eyes flickered when he saw us come in. Definitely not boyfriend material.

"Hey man, what's your problem?" he asked Dad. At least that's what I thought he said. It was hard to tell over the noise.

Dad ignored him. "Helen, I'll leave the cooler on the porch."

"Kids, follow me." Mom pushed us past the guy in the flag tee-shirt. "Joe, put the lasagna down someplace where no one will get burned. It's still hot."

The kitchen counter was covered with food. Munchkins from Dunkin' Donuts, three-bean salad, two other lasagnas, and lots of dips. Folks had already gotten into the chocolate cake with M&Ms in the frosting, and a pan of brownies was half-gone.

Somebody poked me from behind.

"Nora! Good to see you!"

Uncle Dan hugged me so hard I thought he'd break my ribs. He turned to Joe. "Great to see you, man!" He leaned on his crutches and grinned.

I could tell that Uncle Dan had been working out on the trapeze. He looked like GI Joe, at least from the waist up.

"Do you think marriage agrees with me?" he asked.

I didn't have time to answer. He was talking like a pressure cooker. Rat-a-tat-tat.

"I'm happy that you guys got married. But your hair makes you look like you're in the Special Forces or something," I said.

"Special Forces? They're psychos. Real head-cases. No, the infantry were my guys, and look where it got me." He pointed to his folded-up pant leg.

"I'm sorry, Uncle Danny," I said.

"It's okay, honeybunch."

Mom came over. "Welcome home," she said, kissing him on the cheek.

"Helen, great to see you. Every day, walking around in the jungle, I thought of you and Tom and the kids."

He stopped, and his eyes filled with tears. Mom's did, too.

Dad shook Uncle Dan's hand.

"Who's that hippie sitting on the hall steps?" asked Dad.

"Oh, that's Spider. He's had some problems, but I owe him big time. He's going to be staying with us until he gets his feet on the ground."

My father shot my mother a look.

Uncle Dan turned to my brother. "Joe, sorry about your ankle."

"It's okay," laughed Joe. "And your skateboard was my favorite birthday present."

I was glad Dad said nothing.

Dan pointed his chin towards the dining room.

"Why don't you go see the new Mrs. Donovan? Right now, I need to take my pain medication and put my stump up. I'll be high as kite in ten minutes. Earth to Danny." He winked and hobbled to his chair.

I followed my folks over to Gene and Moe. I couldn't believe Moe's outfit. She was wearing a tight red turtleneck and a black mini skirt with tall black boots.

"How are you?" Gene asked.

"Good," smiled Mom. She still thought Gene could do no wrong.

Dad was more guarded. "Nice to see you," he said. He leaned over to kiss Moe and whispered in a nasty voice that she looked like a streetwalker.

Gene asked Joe about Youth Fellowship. Joe said it was okay. I hoped it meant that he was getting sick of it.

"I want to see that ring, Rosemarie Donovan," said Mom. Rosemarie extended her hand so we could admire what had to be the tiniest diamond in the world.

"It's beautiful," said Mom. "Welcome to the family!"

Marcel had a beer in one hand and held Colleen with the other. But she was having none of it, arching her back and rubbing brownie crumbs all over his shoulder.

"We should get home. This is too loud, and the baby needs to get to bed," said Aunt Kathleen.

Spider came over and Colleen stopped fussing. Whether it was his American flag shirt or his headband that she liked, I had no idea. But she couldn't stop smiling at him.

Aunt Kathleen grabbed Marcel by the elbow and headed for the door. Colleen waved happily at Spider from her father's arms.

"Helen, I want to say bye to Dan before we leave." Dad's voice was pressure-cookerish, just like Dan's was earlier. It was the first time I'd thought of them as being alike.

"But we just got here," I said.

Dad gave me a look. "I'll see you at the car in five minutes."

Mom kissed Rosemarie. "Thank you for bringing us together," she said.

Marvin Gaye was belting out "Ain't No Mountain High Enough." Two guys pushed the couch and coffee table to one side. People started dancing. It looked like fun. Too bad I didn't meet a cute guy. But I was happy to see a negro couple dancing. At racist Uncle Dan's of all places.

We waited for Dad in the cold for what seemed like forever.

"Helen, why didn't you bring your car keys?" Dad's voice was sharp.

"If you came back when you said you would, Mom wouldn't need her keys."

He pushed me against the car. "Don't you talk to me like that."

"What's wrong with you?" I shouted. "Why are you so mad all the time?"

He looked like he wanted to slap me. But he turned and unlocked the door.

I refused to sit with my parents in the living room and watch *Saturday Night at the Movies*. Joe said he was tired and going to bed. I didn't give them any excuse. I just went upstairs.

I left my door open and tried to read. I wondered why I didn't hear the TV. I worried about Dad; everyone and everything was driving him nuts. Moe looked trashy, but Gene was such a straight arrow I figured he'd talk some sense into her. He was in the Young Republicans at Saint Anselm's, and he seemed more like a Manchester Country Club type than someone who'd hang out in Boston's Combat Zone, which is what my sister looked like. I was sorry about Uncle Dan's leg, but I liked Rosemarie and was happy that they invited negroes to their party. And as for Dad fussing about the Coolidge case and the anti-war protests, there was nothing he, or anyone else, could do.

I tip-toed into the hall. I could hear my parents talking.

"He got mad when I told him that I saw Spider smoking marijuana in the back yard."

I couldn't hear if my mother said anything.

"The last thing Dan needs is a drug rap. And our kids were at that party. What if they went out and he encouraged them to try it?"

"Tom, I think that you are getting ahead of yourself."

"He blames me for everything," said Dad. "He said growing up it was always, Tom this, Tom that, and no one gave him the time of day. I told him it was our father, not me, who caused these problems."

"Everyone knew your father was a jerk. Everyone."

"Yeah, but Dan thinks that I should've helped him. He said that we invited Kathleen over for weekends all the time, but never him. He was stuck at home getting the crap kicked out of him."

"He's probably just saying that to make you feel bad."

"Helen, I don't know. I remember that he'd had bruises and wondered about them."

For the first time in months, I felt compassion for my father creep into my heart.

7

"Cat got your tongue?" asked Mom. She was driving me to Drivers Ed.

"No, just half asleep." I didn't realize that I'd been quiet. I'd been thinking about Dad, who wanted the world to be right, wanted Danny to shape up, wanted Joey to like sports, and wanted Moe not to dress like a hooker. I didn't know what he wanted for me.

I took my seat in the classroom, and Ray Courtemache handed out our text: *Get the Big Picture.* Ray had granny glasses like John Lennon's, but the similarity ended there. Roy was short and fat with a thin white moustache. He loved Jack Russell terriers and told us that patriotic Americans must support the Vietnam War. He'd driven ambulances in World War II, and if anyone knew danger, he told us, it was he. If anyone wanted to hear blood-curdling stories of heroism, they could ask him.

"These are the three basics every driver needs to know," he said. He wrote the following on the board:

Look Far Ahead

Get the Big Picture

Have an Escape Plan

"During the war when I was driving in France, the roads were ruined. Little kids, cows, you name it, were walking all over the place; potholes everywhere, and bridges dangling over rivers. It was in France where I learned to, and here he pointed with a flourish to the blackboard and boomed, "LOOK FAR AHEAD."

My watch read 9:20. To my annoyance, I saw Colleen Fitzpatrick sitting across the class from me. It was going to be a long morning.

"If I hadn't looked far ahead," asked Mr. Courtemarche. "What might've happened?"

Colleen raised her hand. The girl couldn't stop herself.

"You could've hit a child or a cow. Or ruined your tires."

"Hitting a child or a cow is the correct answer," said our instructor.

I slumped in my seat as Ray launched into "get the big picture." This time he brought us to 1945 Germany where he first developed his strong affection and admiration for the finest of breeds, the Jack Russell Terrier.

Mom was standing outside Courtemarche's when I got out class.

"Please tell Colleen we'll give her a ride. Joyce Fitzpatrick called this morning. We're going to carpool."

"Colleen," I yelled. "You're riding with us."

Colleen jumped in next to me. "I'm so excited about Drivers Ed," she said.

I gave her a thin smile. I didn't want her thinking that we were going to start hanging out just because our mothers made us carpool.

We pulled up in front of Colleen's house.

"Thanks, Mrs. Donovan."

I slouched in my seat. Drivers Ed stunk, especially with Colleen added to the mix.

The following Saturday, a new passenger joined our group. Bill Robbins was Colleen's cousin and a year ahead of me at Saint Benedict's. He worked Saturdays at Mickey Finn's. Bill lived down the street from Colleen, so we picked him up on our way to Courtemarche's.

"I can't believe Courtemarche is still teaching Drivers Ed," he laughed. "His stories are insane."

I looked sideways at Bill. He was cute in a nerdy sort of way. Thin with blond curly hair.

"Are you and Colleen good friends?" he whispered.

I didn't want to be rude. "We've known each other since first grade."

"She's a good person." His voice was guarded. "But do you know that she goes down to Windham Castle and decorates our great-aunt's room on holidays?"

We both laughed. I decided that I kind of liked Bill.

8

Johnson shocked my father when he pulled out of the race.

"The poor guy," Dad said. "Kennedy got us entrenched in Vietnam and Johnson's been in agony about it. And now Bobby Kennedy is the Great White Hope."

I thought the war was bullshit but would never say so to Dad. The next time I saw Uncle Dan, I'd ask him about it.

The following Saturday, Bill slid into the back seat next to me.

'What do you think about Bobby Kennedy running for president?" I asked.

"I'm a McCarthy fan, but Bobby can win. He's got the Democratic machine and the Kennedy name behind him," said Bill. "What do you think?"

I hadn't thought about who'd have a better chance of winning. "You're right," I said. "We need a winning candidate."

"*The Globe* says that black people like Kennedy."

"Why didn't you say "negroes"? I asked. I thought it was cool he read *The Globe.*

"Get with it, Nora. Calling someone a negro is rude now."

I sat back, thinking that I'd have to remember to call negroes "blacks" from now on.

Mrs. Fitzpatrick pulled over. "Girls, ace your quiz. And Bill, have a good day at work."

Colleen flew out of the car, probably wanting to study more before Ray handed out questions. Bill got out after me and asked if I could meet him at the Puritan for dinner.

A date! My heart almost stopped.

"I have to check with my folks, but I'm sure it's okay."

"Give me your number. I'll call you before I leave work," he said.

I scribbled my number on a piece of paper. He stuffed it in his pocket.

I walked into Drivers Ed, sure that I would fail the quiz because I hadn't studied and was too distracted by my budding romance with Bill, reader of *The Boston Globe*, to even think clearly.

I needn't have worried. Ray added an extra credit question at the end. What three things must every good driver keep in mind when driving?

Mom said it was fine if I met Bill for dinner if I was home by 9:00. "But make sure he walks you home. Manchester's not as safe as it used to be."

Like she needed to tell me.

I spent the afternoon reading the *Union Leader*. I wanted Bill to know that I was smart. We ordered burgers and fries. Bill told me about his enthusiasm for Eugene McCarthy, and I told him about my interest in liberation theology. He was surprised that the brothers hadn't mentioned liberation theology, and he thought it would be a good debate topic.

"Are you in debate?" I asked.

"Yeah. You should think about it. It's what thinking kids do. Most kids are only interested in the prom or football."

I didn't want to tell him that I was interested in both prom and football, so I nodded, flattered that he thought that I was a thinking kid. If I remembered correctly, the cool Mr. Rostyn was Saint Agatha's debate coach. I'd probably sign up.

9

Bill called me almost every evening. We talked about politics. I told him how I planned to join debate in September, how Linda and I got an A+ on our liberation theology project, how I worried about Joe who had been acting a bit down lately, and how I felt bad for Uncle Dan.

Bill liked that I was joining debate and thought that Joe was just going through teen-age stuff. He was interested in Uncle Dan. He scared me when he said that he'd read in *The Globe* that wounded soldiers were getting into trouble with drugs. He was excited about Bobby Kennedy being president. And then he asked me to the Saint Benedict Junior Prom.

For once, it seemed as though Moe and I had something in common. I called to tell her about my prom invite. I was lucky because she was walking by the dorm pay phone and got it on the first ring. Sometimes it took hours to track her down.

"Have you thought about your dress?" she asked. I hadn't. "Let's go to Jordan's and look at some. When you find a dress you like, you can find a similar pattern at Martin's, and I'll help you make it."

"Thanks," I said. "Better not be a halter. Mom will die if another daughter goes braless to the prom."

Moe laughed. "How's Dan doing? I worry. Lots of vets came home with psych problems and some are addicted."

"You think that Uncle Dan is addicted?"

"I don't know. But I heard a lecture that soldiers with amputations are at a high risk for depression and drug abuse."

That scared me. I told her about our parents' conversation the night of Uncle Dan's party. About Dad being mad that Spider was living with Dan and smoking pot in the backyard. And how our alcoholic grandfather beat Dan.

She sighed. "For now, don't worry about Uncle Danny. And I have some news."

"What?"

"It's a secret, but Gene and I are engaged."

I almost fell off my chair.

"I'll be graduating in two years, and Gene will have his degree. His grandfather wants Gene to run the dealership, and his brother Jake can help once he graduates." Moe sounded excited. "Gene is his grandfather's favorite because he's so smart and kind."

I'd never thought of Gene as smart or kind. "How come you don't want the family to know?" I asked.

"Dad gives Gene a bad vibe sometimes. And Gene wants to be on his good side before we announce anything."

Huh, I thought. Maybe Gene was smarter than I suspected.

10

Sister Rosita bit her lip before announcing that Martin Luther King had been assassinated in Memphis. She asked us to bow our heads in silent prayer for the repose of the soul of this great negro leader. Black, I wanted to say. As I bowed my head, I wondered why so many assholes were running around while good people got murdered. And I knew that the race riots roiling our country would escalate now that MLK wasn't preaching nonviolence.

I was right about the increased rioting. Dad now went out on the porch every evening, often skipping the news. He smoked two or three cigarettes each night. I watched him from the kitchen window. He'd lean into his cupped hands, protecting the flame from the wind until his cigarette tip glowed bright orange. Then he'd exhale and look up at the spires of All Saints' as if the sky could answer some puzzling question.

Bill started walking me home from school.

"The King assassination will set civil rights back another fifty years," he predicted.

"I thought that, too," I said. "But Johnson just signed another Civil Rights Act. Don't you think that will change things?"

He side-stepped a mud puddle. "It should, but it won't."

I hoped that he was wrong.

"I'll call you tonight," he said as he headed down Sycamore.

Joe was watching *Dark Shadows* when I came home. I got up to make sure the door was locked. I hated vampires. They reminded me of communion where we eat the body and blood of Jesus. They also reminded me of Eddie Coolidge's victims, covered in bite marks, drained of blood, and tossed in snowbanks.

When the commercial came on, Joe told me that he aced his *Frankenstein* project.

"The only thing Francis didn't like was my definition of lust. I said people who went to strip clubs and looked at dirty books suffered from lust. She wanted to know where I got my definition, but I told her that I forgot."

"Thanks," I said. I didn't want people thinking that I sat around talking about lust with him. "And you talked in front of the class? Good for you!" I said.

"I did. I guess I'm getting normal," he laughed. And when I heard him laugh, it sounded like his voice was changing.

Moe came home three days before the prom. I stood on a chair in my dress while she marked the hem. "You don't want it to be too long because you'll trip. But if it's too short you'll look like a hick."

I turned as she inspected me, a few common pins between her lips.

"That blue looks beautiful on you," she exclaimed. "Gene and I will swing by on prom night. I want to meet Bill and get a picture."

I stood in front of the mirror in my prom dress. I'd gotten my hair done at Houle's and wore Mom's rhinestone earrings. I put on mascara and pink lipstick. I looked really pretty.

Bill smiled as I walked into the living room. He pinned a corsage of red and white baby roses to my dress and Gene and Dad took pictures. Hand in hand, we walked down the sidewalk and into his car.

When we got to the Wayfarer, I waved to Catherine, my lunch table buddy, but I didn't get a chance to talk to her. Bill and I danced a bit and then pushed two tables together to sit with the Saint Agatha and Saint Benedict debate teams. The national debate topic for 1967-68 was whether the US government should guarantee a minimum yearly income for all Americans.

"It would help the poor that Bobby Kennedy is so concerned about," noted Bill.

"But some people will just lounge around and do nothing," argued Jean, a skinny senior at Saint Agatha's.

The election of the Prom King and Queen broke up our discussion about universal income. Marilyn Marchand and Steve Brady were the winners. The gym lights grew dim as the DJ played *Nights in White Satin*, and we joined Steve and Marilyn on the dance floor.

Much to my surprise, Bill gave me a quick peck on the cheek when he walked me to the door. I was expecting a bit more. I tiptoed upstairs, my feelings a bit hurt. At least he didn't suffer from lust.

11

Mom turned on the radio. Some nut job shot Bobby Kennedy in the kitchen of a Los Angles hotel. "How could they?" She exclaimed. "Bobby would've brought our nation together."

Race riots and anti-war protests continued sending shock waves through the country. Bill worried that the Democratic Party was in free-fall. I went back to the Sacred Heart full-time, washing beds and mopping floors. I was turning sixteen in a few weeks and had set up a job at Jordan Marsh right after my birthday. I was now one of Flo's favorites. She liked how quickly I cleaned my rooms. When we had coffee in the break room she told me about Phil, the no-good husband she left. "I was brought up Catholic and never believed in divorce, but believe me honey, Phil Demers was a walking advertisement for divorce." She took a drag on her cigarette. "The smartest thing I ever did was to leave that lazy shit."

I'd given the hospital my notice, but I wasn't sure Flo had gotten the news, so I told her it was my last day on her team. Her response was typical. "Don't marry someone like my ex. And don't think you can slack off just because it's your last day."

I went with my parents when they took my brother to camp. "This is going to be so cool," Joe said. As we rounded a curve, a sign welcomed us to Camp Benedictus, "A Community devoted to strengthening the Catholic faith in young men."

"What activities will you sign up for?" Mom asked.

"I'll decide after I look around," Joe said.

A priest in a blue bathing suit named Father Flynn introduced himself. I'd never seen a priest so undressed before and tried not to stare.

"You must be the Donovans." Father Flynn looked at his clipboard. "I've heard good things about Joe. Father Smith said he'd never met a boy more deserving of a Benedictus scholarship."

Joe beamed.

Dad introduced Mom and me, and Father Flynn turned to Joe. "Young man, let's take your trunk to Cabin Eight. Your mother can see where you'll be sleeping and not worry. And then it'll be time to sign up for activities," Father Flynn winked at Joe. "And if I were a betting man, I'd say you'll be a star at archery."

Joe blushed. He was thrilled by the compliment.

Mom got teary on the drive home. "Helen, this is the best thing to happen to Joe since Alan Shepherd's flight," said Dad. "This experience will help him grow up."

Benedictus would be good for Joe, I thought. It had been a while since I agreed with Dad.

12

Linda and Patty took me to Hampton Beach for my birthday. When Linda pulled into the driveway, Mom was outside hanging laundry.

"Doesn't look like much of a beach day," said Mom.

"Oh, it's going to clear," I told her. It was going to do nothing of the kind. Showers were predicted, but I was desperate to get out of Manchester. I threw my beach bag into the trunk and got in the back seat.

"How's the new job going?" Patty had started waitressing at IHOP two weeks before.

"It's okay. The tips weren't great in the morning, but now that I'm working evenings, the money is better." She rolled up her window. "And guess who I'm working with?"

"Who?" asked Linda.

"Pamela Mason's mother."

"Wow! What is she like?" I asked.

"She's nice but quiet. And very pretty. Often cops come in and sit in her section. The manager thinks they're looking after her. They leave her a good tip." Patty twisted around to look at me. "Nora, your father comes in too, but he's always alone."

I wondered why Dad was visiting Mrs. Mason and if Mom knew about it.

"Here's a space," said Linda. I looked up at the gray sky as I fed the meter. It rained a bit. But not much. The girls treated me to lunch and then to salt-water taffy at Sanborn's. On the way back to Manchester, the traffic on 101 was bumper to bumper. I felt sort of sick. I was glad that Patty said nothing else about my father going to IHOP.

When I got home, I was surprised that Mom had organized a birthday party for me.

"I thought that we weren't celebrating my birthday until Joe came home from camp," I said.

"I wanted to surprise you," said Mom. "We can do another cake when Joe comes home, but today you're sixteen. Sweet sixteen. Pretty special."

Dad turned off the kitchen lights, and Mom came in carrying my birthday cake, all sixteen candles flickering wildly. My stomach turned.

"Your favorite, Nora. Chocolate with vanilla frosting. Make a wish!"

I closed my eyes and wished that I'd pass the state driving test. And I also wished that Dad would stop swinging by IHOP. My parents cheered as I blew out the candles. I crossed my fingers that both wishes would come true.

13

"Where's Joe?" I asked.

"He's upstairs sleeping," said Dad.

"Man, archery must have been harder than he expected," I said.

"I'm sure we'll get the full scoop once he crawls out of bed," said Mom.

I saw Joe's trunk sitting outside his room. He was quiet that night and didn't have much to say about camp. I asked him about archery, but all he said was that he was no Robin Hood.

"Did you have fun?" I knew something was up with him.

"It w-w-was okay," he replied.

I didn't like his stuttering, but my parents didn't seem to notice.

Starting work at Jordan Marsh and the imminent arrival of Aunt Kathleen's new baby pushed worries about Joe out of my head. I started in Basement Coats the day after my sixteenth birthday and was in heaven. Marge, my boss, was a sweetie, probably still in her twenties, and as big as Mrs. Robichaud, my old sewing teacher. She helped me out the first few times that I had to do exchanges and said that I was doing a good job keeping the department neat. She had no idea that keeping Basement Coats neat was a piece of cake after tidying up the nurses' lounge at Sacred Heart.

On August 1, Aunt Kathleen had a baby boy. "We're naming him Michael Thomas Boucher," she announced. I got to hold Baby

Michael in the hospital. When Uncle Dan and Rosemarie came to visit, he could not take his eyes off the baby.

"Stay out of Nam, kid," he joked. We laughed politely, but no one thought his comment funny.

"How is that high-end prosthesis working out?" asked Marcel. Dan had been having trouble getting fitted, and this was the third model he tried.

"Third time's the charm," he said, lifting his pant leg to show us his new leg.

"Can you look for a job now?" asked Dad. The mood in the room darkened.

Rosemarie smiled at Dad. "We're lucky that Dan's collecting a check from the Army and my job at the phone company pays well. And guess what?"

I knew what was coming. "Dan and I are expecting a baby in February!" Rosemarie's face lit up.

"Wonderful news," said Aunt Kathleen. Uncle Danny smiled as everyone congratulated him.

That week, one of my birthday wishes was granted. I aced my written driving test and parallel parked like a champ in front of Bon Ton. Whether Dad stopped visiting Mrs. Mason remained to be seen.

I joined the Saint Agatha debate team as soon as school started. "Who likes to argue?" Mr. Rostyn asked at the first meeting. Everyone in the room raised her hand. "Debate is argument…with rules," he said. The room echoed with nervous laughter.

Bill was proud of me for joining the Debate Club. "It's a sport for people who think," he said.

When I told my parents that debate was my choice for an extracurricular activity, Dad laughed. "Nora, God help the poor soul who has to face you in a tournament."

For the first few months we debated simple resolutions like *Summer is better than Winter* and *Fairy Tales affect kids' perception of Reality*. I realized that I liked debate. And that I was good at it.

14

The Republicans nominated Richard Nixon for president. Nixon gave me the creeps. I read that he had black coffee and a broiled grapefruit for breakfast every day. No wonder he always looked so crabby.

Bill predicted that the Democratic convention was going to be wild because the party couldn't agree about Vietnam. "McCarthy wants us to stop bombing North Vietnam and get out of the war. Humphrey wants us to continue bombing because he's sure it'll bring Hanoi to its knees."

Thousands of anti-war protestors flooded Chicago for the convention. Their leaders made idle threats to bait Richard Daly, Chicago's hot-tempered mayor. "We are dirty, smelly, grimy and foul...we will piss and shit and fuck in public...we will be constantly stoned or tripping on every drug known to man." They threatened to put LSD in the city's drinking water. Enraged, Daly increased the number of cops on the street, sealed the manhole covers with tar so protesters couldn't hide in the sewers, and called out the National Guard to keep violence at bay.

Dad shared Daley's reaction. "Imagine putting LSD in the city's drinking water. Daley should lock up every one of these dirty hippies."

"Dad, protest is legal in our country. And the LSD thing is just a joke," I said.

"What do you know? You're a girl who's barely left Manchester. What'll happen if all of Chicago gets hooked on LSD?"

"You don't get hooked on LSD. I read it's not addictive," I said. "War is what our country is hooked on."

"Our guys are over in Nam trying to preserve democracy and these spoiled kids are doing everything they can to destroy democracy here!" Dad had steel in his voice. "Daley's right."

I thought Daley was full of shit.

Dad turned on the national news. I watched Daley's police beating unarmed protestors outside the hall. The same footage was played inside the convention, creating outrage among attendees. One speaker, Connecticut Senator Abraham Ribicoff, condemned Daley's handling of the protest. Ribicoff said that if we had another leader, "we wouldn't have Gestapo tactics on the streets of Chicago."

An enraged Daley screamed "Fuck you, you Jew son of bitch! You lousy motherfucker! Go home!"

"Tom, Daley's language and behavior is appalling. Whatever you think about the war, Daley's thugs shouldn't be beating peaceful protestors." Mom turned off the TV.

Dad drummed his fingers on his armrest. "I agree that Daley's language is appalling. But the hippies forced him to take action to protect the city."

"Good night," I said and went upstairs.

15

I get my mail. Lots from sob sisters who want to help me if I get out. I wonder if they are the type who like things a little rough.

"I think no one understands your needs," writes one. Well, she got that right. "I have a degree in social work, and I'm sure you were sexually traumatized in your childhood," writes another. Piss me off. I ball that one up and toss it into the wastebasket. I miss.

"Nice one, Eddie," Conway says. I ignore him. Conway sits in his cell, watching me like he always does. Conway is fat with a gray walrus moustache and short, stumpy legs, but I've seen him move like a bat out of hell when anyone crosses him. The guy is an asshole, and I don't want to piss him off. He has a radio in his cell, and I want to listen to Game One of the World Series. It would be just like Conway to turn the volume way down just so that I can't listen. "Get any more titty pictures?" he asks. He never gets mail and watches me as I read mine.

Titty pictures. That's a scream. Conway is jealous that women write me all the time, some sending pictures. The guards would have taken any titty pictures anyone sent me, but I do have a collection of women's non-titty pictures taped to my bulletin board. I'd given a couple of pictures of the ugly ones with their return addresses to Conway to stay on his good side.

Shit. I get another one of her letters.

"Eddie Coolidge, I hate you. If you ever get out, I'm going to hunt you down and kill you.. I'm going to cut off your balls, make you roll on broken glass, and burn you to death."

It was signed "Saint Agatha."

Saint Agatha writes me a couple of times a year. She says the same stuff. If I get out, she'll find me and kill me. There's no return address, but her envelopes have a Manchester postmark. She must have gone to that Catholic girls' high school. I don't know why, but her threats creep me out. Maybe it's the religious stuff. I looked up Agatha in the missal the priest left me. What she wants to do to me is what exactly what was done to Saint Agatha, Virgin Martyr, in 251.

"So, what do you say, Eddie?" Conway is frowning at me.

"Sorry, Conway. I was reading a letter from my mother and didn't hear what you said." No one knows about Agatha. She's my secret, and I think about the things I can do to her if she tries getting funny with me. Maybe I'll ask her out.

"Who do you think will win tonight? I'll bet Detroit will clobber St. Louis," says Conway.

"You're probably right," I say. I'm sure Conway is dead wrong. I'd been following St. Louis, and Gibson is on fire. But I'll say anything to listen to the game.

16

Joe and I walked to school together now that he was a freshman at Saint Benedict's. Sometimes Paul joined us.

"God, it's so nice out," I said. "It kills me to go back to school."

He kicked a stone across the street but said nothing.

"Are you nervous about starting high school?" I asked.

"N-no," he said. "W-w-why do you ask?"

"Because you're stuttering again."

"I kn-kn-kn-know," he said.

"Have fun today," I said as I headed into Saint Agatha's.

I looked for him after school but couldn't find him. When I got home, he was in his room listening to music.

"Where were you today?" I asked.

"Oh, s-s-sorry. I h-h-had study hall last period, and B-b-brother Matthew said that we could leave if we wanted."

He was acting odd. Something was wrong

Rosemarie and Dan invited us over to watch the last game of the World Series. Joe refused to come. "You kn-kn-know that I don't care about baseball, and I have school in the morning."

"Jesus, Joe. Who doesn't want to watch the final game of the World Series?" Dad was annoyed.

"Leave him alone, Tom. Joe, we'd love you to come, but if you don't want to, no one will make you."

I cornered Mom in the kitchen. "Have you noticed that Joe has gotten skinnier and is stuttering a lot?"

"Oh, Dad and I think that he's nervous about high school. We don't want to say anything about his stuttering because we don't want to make it worse. But we're pleased that he's getting taller and leaner. All that that exercise at camp was good for him."

I wasn't convinced that she was right about Joe.

Mom brought a salad, and Rosemarie fixed sloppy joes for dinner. Spider was still living with them, and he bought chips and dip. Uncle Danny mentioned that he thought Joe was feeling a bit down and noticed he was losing weight.

"It's just normal teenage stuff," said Mom. "We aren't worried. He's probably losing baby fat now that he's fourteen and gotten taller."

Uncle Danny shot Rosemarie a look, but neither of my parents noticed.

Rosemarie fell asleep at the bottom of the third, and Mom soon followed at the top of the fourth.

Spider pulled a joint out of his pocket, lit it and passed it to Dan.

Dad stood up. "Dan, what you're doing is illegal. You could cost me my job!"

Mom and Rosemarie woke up.

"Sorry, Dan," said Spider. "I didn't mean to cause problems."

"No need to apologize, man. It's my brother who's the problem," said Dan.

Rosemarie began crying.

"It's time for us to go," said Dad.

"Bye, Tom," said Dan. He didn't even get up.

My parents said nothing on the ride home. Mom broke the silence once we got inside. "Tom, tomorrow you have to call Dan and apologize." Her voice was firm.

Dad said nothing.

"Tom, promise me you'll call."

"Okay, okay, Helen. I will." Dad turned on the TV. "Do you want to stay up and watch the end of the game?" he asked.

"No," Mom responded. We both went upstairs. I listened to the end of the game on my clock radio. The Tigers won, but I didn't care. I was too upset by what had happened between my uncle and my dad.

The next morning when Joe and I got up for school, my folks were already at work. Joe didn't ask who won the World Series, so I didn't tell him. The *Union Leader* reported that two black Americans competing in the Olympic 200-meter run, raised their arms in a black-power salute after winning the gold and bronze medals. Bill thought it was terrific. "It's free speech," he said. "These are high-caliber athletes who will get a lot of attention."

"We'll see how many sponsorships they'll receive. That's where the money is," I said.

"Yeah, but these guys knew the risks that they were taking. Yet they spoke out anyway."

Bill's words rang in my ears. I felt like I should be speaking out about a lot of things, and I knew most of the things that I should be speaking out about were things happening in my family. But I had no words for what was happening to us. And even if I did, I didn't know if I was brave enough to take the risk.

17

"NA-NASA's launching Apollo 7," announced Joe through a mouthful of Cheerios.

Finally, he showed interest in something. "Tell me about it," I said.

"Th-th-there are three astronauts on board, and they're going to broadcast live from space."

I wasn't a space buff, but even I thought that was cool.

"It's sad that we can get TV shows from outer space, but we can't bring our soldiers home from Vietnam," said Mom.

"M-m-maybe it's good that Uncle Dan lost his leg," Joe said. "N-no one can make him go back."

Neither of my parents said a word.

Dad's mood went even more downhill when the New Hampshire Supreme Court started hearing the Coolidge appeal. The idea of Coolidge walking the streets of Manchester terrified me. But the kids at school didn't seem worried.

"They'd have to be nuts to let that animal out," said Marie.

"And even if they did, someone in Manchester would kill him," said Catherine. I wasn't so sure. But maybe I should stop sending him anonymous letters. I don't want him finding me if he ever gets out.

On Christmas Eve, something shifted for the good, pulling my attention away from Manchester's killer. US astronauts Frank Borman, Jim Lovell, and William Anders became the first humans to see the far side of the moon. We sat glued to our TV as the astronauts read aloud from Genesis.

"Merry Christmas, and God bless you," said Frank Borman.

Mom burst into tears. I felt a lump in my throat as the Apollo spacecraft spun through the starry night hundreds of miles above our heads.

1969

Things heated up for the Saint Agatha's debate team. Our team was joining Saint Benedict's and sending two girls and two boys to the New Hampshire State Championship in March. We could combine our teams because our schools were small.

"We're going to study together, practice together, argue together," said Mr. Rostyn. "By late February, we'll decide which students will represent our schools."

The teams met in the Saint Benedict's cafeteria. "We're looking for adaptability, fearlessness, and the ability to think on your feet," said Mrs. McGovern, the Saint Benedict's coach.

"And whatever you do, don't ever, ever let the other side see you sweat!" said Mr. Rostyn. Everyone laughed nervously.

"Nora, we both have to make the team that goes to States. Won't that be cool?" said Bill as we walked home after practice.

Mr. Rostyn told me that I was born to debate. "You've got talent, Nora," he said. "You're able to analyze an issue and attack it logically, piece by piece." I'd never heard Bill debate, so I didn't know if he had talent or not. But I hoped that he did.

That night we watched news coverage of Nixon's Inauguration. "He looks like he can't be trusted," I said. "People with beady eyes and bad posture shouldn't be allowed to be president."

"Nora Donovan, just when did you become such a cynic?" Mom asked.

"I'll tell you when," Dad piped in. "It's ever since she joined the debate team. I swear that Jewish coach encourages these girls to run their mouths and criticize everything."

"I ask you to share with me today in the majesty of this moment..." began Nixon.

"Majesty?" I exclaimed. "Does he think he's king?"

"Sit down and listen, young lady. If you can't be respectful and give the guy a chance, go to your room," warned Dad.

Nixon mopped his forehead and squinted into the camera. "Our destiny offers not the cup of despair but the chalice of opportunity."

Chalice my ass, I thought as I went upstairs. People who use figurative language don't make good debaters. Mr. Rostyn made that clear. "Stick to the facts, and you can't go wrong."

I flashed back to when Nixon and Kennedy were in the first televised presidential debate. Nixon looked tired and pale. He was sweating and kept dabbing his forehead with a handkerchief. Rostyn's rule #1: never let them see you sweat. I flipped open my Chemistry book to study for the unit test on acid, base and the calculation of pH.

2

Uncle Danny and Rosemarie came by unannounced.

"Good to see you," said Dad.

"Kids, this is a private conversation," Mom called up the stairs. "Please stay in your rooms."

I couldn't hear what they were saying. Then, I heard the front door open and their Rambler drive away.

The next morning, I asked Dad what the secret was all about.

"It's good news, Nora. Joey, get down here. I don't want to have to repeat myself." Joey made his way into the kitchen.

"Uncle Danny wants us to know that he has a problem with alcohol. And ever since he lost his leg, he's gotten dependent on pain pills." I thought that anyone who spent time with Uncle Danny would have to be dumb as a post not to know that he had an alcohol problem. "He's joined a 12-step program at the VA to get his life back on track," Dad continued.

"That's a smart thing for Dan to commit to," said Mom. "Problems with alcohol tend to run in families and your grandfather was a drinker."

"I never touched a drop of liquor because I didn't want to be like my old man. I'm relieved that it looks like neither does Dan," said Dad.

Between school, working at Jordan Marsh, and debate, time flew by. Towards the end of February, the students chosen to represent our schools in the debate tournament were announced. I was sure I'd be chosen based on Mr. Rostyn's comments. I was right. Marie Chalifour and I were selected from St. Agatha's, and Tim Higgins and Bill were chosen from St. Benedict's. I was pleased that Colleen Fitzpatrick was named designated alternate. It sort of made up for her robbing me out of crowning the Virgin Mary in eighth grade. After the announcement, the rest of the debate club members left the room disappointed.

"Be prepared to work your butts off for the next month, ladies and gentlemen," said Mr. Rostyn. "Tournament rules are different. You won't know your topic ahead of time. And you must be prepared to present both the affirmative and the negative points of each topic." He paced back and forth. "You need to read as much as you can about current events, you need to prepare for the unexpected, you need to ask questions and to challenge the status quo. Think, feel, act. Most of all, let's build a strong sense of camaraderie."

The room was silent as we considered his words. "Do you have anything to add, Mrs. McGovern?" asked Mr. Rostyn.

"You must have confidence in yourselves and in each other. Debate isn't for the weak of heart. It's a demanding sport. Go home and get a good night's sleep. We'll see you back here every day after school until the tournament is over."

Bill and I walked home, pleased that we'd been chosen but at the same time overwhelmed by the challenge. "I never realized that arguing is a sport," I laughed.

The next day, an editorial appeared in the *Union Leader* that created a furor. "Helen, get a load of this," said Dad.

"Jesus, Mary and Joseph," exclaimed Mom. "This editorial suggests that Mr. Rostyn is a Communist who's hiding behind the skirts of innocent girls at Saint Agatha's."

"What? Rostyn teaches us to think and to question. That doesn't make him a Communist. Mr. Rostyn is the best thing that ever happened to Saint Agatha's." I was mad.

"Calm down, Nora. It's an editorial, just the author's opinion. And it's written by Tim Delaney who's an ass in my book," said Dad.

"Joannie Delaney didn't make the tournament debate team. Her father's probably mad and is taking it out on Mr. Rostyn."

Everyone at school talked about the editorial. Marie suggested we write a group letter to the *Union Leader* supporting Mr. Rostyn. "Girls, it's not worth the time of day to even discuss the nonsense spewed in that letter. False accusations don't deserve the dignity of your time," advised Mr. Rostyn. He was right. The crisis faded as quickly as it appeared. I liked Mr. Rostyn. Unlike other adults, he taught us how to challenge the status quo. And how to be successful at it.

3

Aunt Rosemarie and Uncle Dan came for Sunday dinner. He talked about his commitment to kick booze and pills. "Nothing's more important to me than being a good husband and father." He patted Rosemarie's tummy.

Rosemarie blushed and said she was grateful for our family's support.

"I'm proud of you, brother." Dad's voice cracked.

The next Wednesday, Mom called from work. "I won't be home for dinner, kids. You'll have to fend for yourselves. Rosemarie's here in the Maternity Ward and I'm going to stick around until the baby is born." I could hear the hospital intercom in the background asking Dr. Hanley to call the operator. "Dad's leaving work and will keep Dan company until the baby arrives."

Joe and I raided the stockpile and split a can of beef stew. The next morning, my exhausted parents shared the news. "Kids you have a new cousin—John Martin Donovan. 8 pounds, 10 ounces," reported Mom.

"John Martin was a buddy of Dan's in Vietnam. He was injured in the raid that cost Dan his leg," said Dad. "Martin was bleeding from shrapnel to the gut. But he went back in and carried Dan to safety. What a man!"

I wondered if John Martin died saving Uncle Danny. I didn't dare ask.

4

I raced home after debate. Moe and Gene were holding hands as they walked in the door. Mom was smearing ketchup and onion soup mix on top of the meatloaf. Dad was in the living room reading the *Union Leader* and grumbling about the price of pork chops.

"Come into the living room. We have an announcement," said Moe.

"Joe, get down here," I yelled. "Big news."

Joe straddled the arm of the couch.

"We're engaged!" exclaimed Moe. She threw her arms around Gene.

"Congratulations, you two!" Mom jumped up and kissed them. Dad hugged Moe and shook Gene's hand.

"This is exciting!" I exclaimed. My parents would be annoyed that I'd known about the engagement for months.

Mom's eyes sparkled. "Any plans yet?"

Gene spoke first. "We'll be graduating next year, and I have a job lined up at the dealership. I'm sure Moe won't have a problem getting a job at the Sacred Heart."

"We'd like to get married next October if we have your blessing," said Moe. Moe's never asked for anyone's blessing her whole life. I guessed Mr. Young Republican tamed her into submission.

"Well, you've lots of decisions to make, so better start now," said Mom.

"Nora, will you be my maid of honor?" asked Moe.

"Absolutely!" I replied.

Gene turned to Joe. "My brother Jake's going to be my best man and I'd like you to be an usher."

"Yeah, sure." Joe didn't sound very excited.

Mom shot Joe The Look. "Joseph that's a great honor!"

"Let me have another peek at that beautiful ring," said Mom as we finished dinner.

"It's a family heirloom," said Gene. "It belonged to my great-grandmother Tardiff."

"Well, she certainly had beautiful taste in jewelry," Mom said.

Dinner and clean-up were done by 7:00, and Moe and Gene said their goodbyes. As I headed up the stairs to start my homework, Mom asked Dad why he was so quiet. "Damn it, Helen. Gene should've known that it's customary for the boy to ask the father for permission to marry his daughter. I felt blindsided."

"Oh, Tom. That's so old fashioned. This is 1969. People are skipping in fields and weaving chains out of daisies for weddings these days. It's high time young people do what they want. Customs be damned."

"Okay, Helen. But I've my doubts."

"Tom, you're still holding a grudge about something that happened years ago at a high school basketball game. It's time to let it go."

"I'll try," said Dad. "What do you say we watch *Hogan's Heroes* and call it an early night?"

"Sure, honey." Mom wasn't nuts about *Hogan's Heroes,* but I knew she'd been trying to take his mind off the Coolidge appeal. She curled up next to him on the couch.

Why did TV shows about the war make Dad laugh? Maybe it was because he hadn't changed. He liked being a young man in the 1940s, a time when you always knew your enemy and a time when respectable young men came to their girlfriend's father to ask for her hand in marriage. Dad was a relic.

5

The push was on with debate. The coaches challenged us by shortening the prep time before each practice round. First Affirmative, First Negative, Second Affirmative, Second Negative. Resolutions became more difficult. We started out with *Students should be able to grade teachers* and *Homework does not promote learning.* We quickly moved on to tougher challenges like *The death penalty should be abolished in the United States* and *Euthanasia should be legalized.*

The coaches kept us on our toes, and we argued until early evening. "Remember, debaters. There will only be eight minutes of prep time for each resolution, so you must be always on point. Trust yourselves. Trust each other," advised Mrs. McGovern.

The state debate was at Portsmouth High. Mr. Rostyn rented a van and met us outside Saint Agatha's early Saturday morning. "Okay, let's shake out your nerves," he said to the van full of sleepy-eyed debaters. "What are you most nervous about?"

"That we don't know the topics and might get brain freeze," I said.

"I'm nervous about having an audience," said Bill. "We've never debated in front of a lot of people."

"Do you ever argue with your parents? Stick to your guns without wavering?" asked Mrs. McGovern. She got a lot of nods. "Pretend that the only people in the room are your parents and teammates."

"You've worked your butts off for this. You're strong debaters. Now it's up to you to show everyone just how good you are," said Mr. Rostyn.

In the first round, we faced Keene. *Talent is a better predictor of success than hard work.* Bill and I had to present the negative argument.

"Talent can be, and often is, wasted. Hard work is never wasted," we argued. "Hard work isn't just measured in the investment of time but in commitment and determination."

The affirmative team launched a weaker argument. "Talent concerns the abilities, skills, and expertise that determine what a person can do. If you can achieve that without working hard, you can be successful. And then you have more time left over for fun stuff," said the girl with the curly red hair. Some in the audience chuckled, but I guessed only a few thought she was funny.

The quarter final round began with *Nuclear Weapons should be controlled by an international organization.* Our team was racking up points left and right. We won the round against Nashua and found ourselves in the finals against Concord. The word in the auditorium was that Concord had been crucifying the competition all day. "So have you," Mr. Rostyn reminded us.

The moderator tapped his gavel. "This final round will determine the championship of the 1969 New Hampshire Debate League. You've all worked hard to prepare for this day. And remember, no matter who walks away with the 1st Place trophy today, you're all winners."

We walked onto the stage with nervous excitement. I looked out into the audience and saw my family and Gene seated near the back.

"Ladies and gentlemen, this final round will assume an unusual format, which is the prerogative of this association. Before I disclose the resolution to be debated, each team will receive a copy of the 4th amendment of our Constitution."

255

Bill and I locked eyes. I hoped he knew something about the 4th amendment because I sure didn't. "And now I will share the resolution to be debated. *The constitutional rights of Edward Coolidge were violated when he was arrested and convicted of 1st degree murder.*

"The Saint Agatha/ Saint Benedict team will present the 1st affirmative case. Concord, you've been selected to present the 1st negative. Teams, you have eight minutes to prepare."

I was shaking when we sat down. "He's guilty Bill. He killed that girl and probably Valade and Paquette, too. How can we say his rights were violated?"

"Calm down, Nora. Everyone knows he's guilty. That's not the question here. We have to argue that his rights were violated. It must have something to do with the 4th amendment or they wouldn't have given us a copy. Let's read it."

"Bill, the amendment is about search and seizure. The police had more than enough evidence to get a warrant to search the scumbag's car. How could his rights have been violated?"

"Maybe this is our answer. It says here that a search warrant has to be signed by an unbiased and impartial magistrate. I know that you don't want to hear this, but Attorney General Maynard signed the warrant."

"What's wrong with that?" I asked.

"What's wrong with that? The AG can't possibly be impartial and unbiased. He's the police's boss, for God's sake!"

Bill was right. My heart sank. How could I argue that my father and his colleagues violated the Constitution?

Bill grabbed my hand and squeezed it. "Nora, whatever you do, don't let anyone see you sweat!" he whispered.

The moderator tapped the gavel. Our eight minutes were up. Bill spoke first and explained the 4th amendment in simple terms. He stated, "though there is little doubt that Edward Coolidge was guilty of 1st degree murder, a person who could be neither impartial nor unbiased signed the search warrant, which allowed the police to illegally seize evidence." Bill turned to me.

"If evidence was obtained through an illegal search, the constitutional rights of the accused were violated." I looked up and watched Dad leave the auditorium.

Concord gave a weak rebuttal. They argued that Coolidge's rights weren't violated because he gave up his rights when he killed Pamela Mason.

We were given a twenty-minute break while the judges decided which argument was more convincing. Two trophies stood on the table in the middle of the stage. The moderator, a short balding man wearing a blue vest with a pocket watch and chain, addressed the crowd. "Congratulations on your excellent presentations. There can only be one 1st place winner and today the honor goes to---Saint Agatha's and Saint Benedict's High Schools of Manchester." The audience applauded and cameras flashed. Bill and I held the big trophy high as our team, Mrs. McGovern, and Mr. Rostyn smiled in the background.

The mood on the van ride home was boisterous. I was thrilled we won but dreaded facing my father.

Mom was in the kitchen when I walked into the house. "Congratulations, darling. I'm so proud of you."

"Nice job, Nora," said Joe.

"Thanks," I said.

I went into the living room. My father stood by the window watching the rain. "Dad. I'm sorry."

"Don't be sorry. You did a great job and I'm proud of you." He kissed me and settled into his chair.

"So why did you leave?"

"I had to use the restroom," said Dad. "Then I stood in the back."

"I thought you were mad because of what we said about the 4th amendment."

"Of course not. You and Bill presented an academic argument. But academic arguments don't work in the real world." He leaned back and opened the paper. "Do you realize that we've had two inches more rain this month than in previous years?"

How could he be talking about rainfall? "Will the NH Supreme Court dismiss Coolidge's guilty verdict because the AG signed the search warrant?" I asked.

"No. Coolidge's defense team isn't interested in the 4th amendment." He looked at me over the paper. "In their appeal they're questioning the accuracy of a new scientific method called neutron activation analysis. It was used to test the evidence found in Coolidge's car."

"And what happens if the NH Supreme Court decides that the test used isn't reliable? Will he go free?"

"Oh, honey, he's as guilty as the winter is cold. We've got enough evidence to keep him in prison for the rest of his life."

I hoped Dad was right.

"But what if the defense team also decides to use the 4th amendment to dismiss the murder verdict?"

"They won't. Every lawyer in New Hampshire knows that our AGs have been signing search warrants for years. No verdict has ever been challenged because of it."

He frowned. "This article says acid rain might wipe out forests in New England."

I wondered why Dad thought federal law did not apply in New Hampshire. And why he was more concerned about the effects of acid rain than he was about Eddie Coolidge being on the loose.

I went up to my room. I knew I should be happy about winning the state debate but instead, I was afraid and angry. A psychopath might get out of jail on a technicality. Who might be the next victim if Coolidge walked?

6

I haven't heard from Saint Agatha in months and can't figure out why she stopped writing me. I'd saved all her letters. I wonder if she's dead. She probably is if she was one of the ancient nuns at that girls' school. Too bad. I really wanted to meet her. The way she described how she'd make me roll on cut glass and burn me to death made me think that we had a lot in common.

My lawyer Jack Doumas doesn't like me. When we first met, he told me up front that he has a couple of daughters, but he'd do his best to defend me. We'll see about that. The guy doesn't look at me unless he has to. Any time I ask him a question, he runs his hands through his bristly hair and looks at the floor while he answers me. And when he visits, he basically just reads stuff off his legal pad. Daughters or not, I'm betting it'd make him look good if the New Hampshire Supreme Court rules that the fucking neutron analysis the prosecution used to convict me is tossed out. Doumas would be in high demand. He could put an in-ground pool in his yard. And install a security system so his precious girls would be safe, at least while on his property. Then Fast Eddie will be out on the streets again, a free man.

7

Joey was lying on his bed with his math book on his chest, staring at the ceiling. "What are you up to, Joe?"

"N-n-not much." he grumped.

"Well. I heard something that you'll be interested in," I said. "In a few months, NASA is planning a moon landing for Apollo 11," I said.

"Th-th-that's impossible. Apollo 10 hasn't even launched yet."

"I know but 10 will only be a practice run for 11, when the astronauts actually land and walk on the moon," I explained.

Joe sat up straight. "That's awesome!"

Bill graduated second in his class from Saint Benedict's. In his salutatorian speech he called upon the audience to embrace the concept of liberation theology. He nodded in my direction. "Liberation theology asks us to practice our religion by helping the poor through political and social involvement. It's concerned with raising awareness of socioeconomic structures that cause inequality." I was flattered that Bill paid attention when I described Linda's and my research project. "To the class of 1969: we have a responsibility to move forward and make this world a better place; a world that is free from poverty and war. A world that is free from racial inequality and hate." Bill got a standing ovation when he finished speaking.

Mr. and Mrs. Robbins took us to The 88 to celebrate. I had never been to such a fancy restaurant before. Dim lighting and a red patterned carpet greeted us as we walked in the door. Ladies in floral printed dresses with aprons and caps carrying baskets of piping hot popovers circulated among the tables. The white tablecloths and flickering candles made it seem elegant.

"Bill, you won't be eating this well once you get to Boston College," Mr. Robbins said as he dabbed his mouth with his white linen napkin.

"And you'll be heading off to college in another year, is that right, Nora?" asked Mrs. Robbins.

I nodded my head and hoped they wouldn't bring up their smart and talented niece Colleen Fitzpatrick.

8

Mom and I were throwing a potato salad together on the last day of June when Dad burst through the door. "Have you heard the news, ladies?"

"What news, darling?"

"The New Hampshire Supreme Court announced its decision on the Coolidge appeal. The conviction has been upheld! Coolidge again has gotten what he deserved." Dad poured himself a glass of ginger ale.

"That's wonderful! The guys at the station must be ecstatic," Mom responded. "And I hope it provides some relief to the poor Mason family."

"The defense team vowed to bring the case to the United States Supreme Court. But I can't imagine that the highest court in the land would be willing to hear a slam dunk case like this one," said Dad.

The United States Supreme Court. Miranda. I started to worry all over again.

Then scandal hit the airwaves. President Kennedy's brother Teddy drove his car off a bridge in Chappaquiddick, off Martha's Vineyard.

"Tom, Cronkite said it took him ten hours to report the accident to the police. There was a young woman in the car that he tried to save, but she drowned."

"That sounds fishy," said Dad.

Mom said she'd heard a rumor at the hospital that the woman in the car was pregnant.

"That's the end of that man's political career, guilty or not," said Dad. "Listen to this headline: *Teddy Escapes, Woman Dies As Car Plunges into Vineyard Pond.*"

I wondered if Senator Kennedy made a conscious decision to let the young woman drown. I copied her last name onto a new page in my notebook. KOPECHNE. And I wrote the senator's name next to hers with a question mark. I didn't want to believe that any man in the Kennedy family would kill a young woman. But my notebook had to be accurate. I would go back later and either erase his name or erase the question mark.

9

Marge the Barge was waiting at the register in Basement Coats. She was about five feet tall and three feet wide so the guys in

Basement Shoes came up with the name. Marge the Large Barge and Large Marge the Barge were scrapped because they were too long, and Marge the Barge she became.

The Coat Department in the basement store was my usual post, but coats were not a big seller in the summer. "Nora, I need to float you to Housewares today. They had a call out." Marge dropped her pencil into her cleavage and headed off to Linens.

Housewares was my least favorite department. I couldn't believe how many fussy ladies came off the escalator looking for stuff that I'd never heard of.

A lady came in and asked, "Where can I find a spurtle?"

"I'm sorry, a what?" I responded.

"You know, a spurtle," she said, and she followed with a stirring motion. Her hand signals were a giveaway. I led her to the mixing spoon section, and she found the perfect spurtle. "You'll never have lumps in your oatmeal if you stir it with a spurtle." She walked away looking satisfied.

A man with a red nose wearing a green and blue plaid golf cap came in a while later and asked where he could find an olive elevator. I had to ask what an olive elevator was. "It's a small ladle that fits inside an olive jar and lifts olives out one by one, so you don't spill the juice. It's a must have if you're a martini man like me," he laughed.

I wandered over to the section with bar stuff. I pleased the customer when I found an olive elevator.

I couldn't wait for summer to end and fall to begin so people would start shopping for coats again. Coats either fit or they didn't. The color was perfect or terrible. The collar was itchy or soft. Coats made my life much easier.

10

We sat glued to the TV set. The first spacewalk on the moon was about to be televised. The footage was grainy, but I got goosebumps watching Neil Armstrong's walk. "That's one small step for man, one giant leap for mankind," said Armstrong.

"President Kennedy predicted that landing a man on the moon would happen before the end of the decade," mused Dad. "And he was right."

"Too bad he's not alive to see this," added Mom.

People in the Fellow Workers' Cafeteria were more interested in talking about some crazy murders in California than they were about Armstrong's spacewalk. "Nora, have you heard about this?" asked Monica from Basement Lingerie.

"About what?" I pulled some brown-flecked bits of lettuce out of my salad.

"The actress Sharon Tate was murdered Thursday night. She was eight and a half months pregnant," said Monica.

My stomach turned over. Who would murder a pregnant woman?

"Yeah, and the sickos wrote "Death to Pigs" and "Helter Skelter" on the refrigerator door," added another guy. The bloody messages scared me. I've been worried about women and girls getting killed for years, but now I had to worry about cops getting killed, too.

"The LAPD thinks that these recent murders were committed by a cult that lives in the area. The leader is a serial offender named Manson. They're sure that he didn't act alone."

I had a hard time falling asleep that night. I reached under my mattress and pulled out my plaid notebook. I read through Sandra Valade, the eleven Boston Strangler victims, Pamela Mason. The student nurses who were raped and murdered in Chicago. I included all their names. Mary Jo Kopechne. I picked up a pen, turned the page, and added Sharon Tate.

11

I stopped by Artie-Lou's to get a candy bar. "Traffic Uptight at Hippiefest," screamed the *Daily News*. On the shelf below, *The New York Time's* headline read "Hippies mired in a sea of mud." I'd heard about a music fest that was taking place in upstate New York, but it didn't interest me. My parents would have killed me anyway. I had to work my butt off and save money for college.

Walter Cronkite interviewed a skinny sociology professor from Northeastern about the Woodstock festival on the evening news. "Surely the parents who helped create the society against which these young people are rebelling must bear a share of the responsibility for this outrageous episode," the professor said.

"Go ahead, blame it on the parents," muttered Dad.

Cronkite said that an estimated 350,000 people descended on Woodstock. The conditions I saw on TV looked awful. People were crowded everywhere, sitting under cardboard boxes and shower curtains that they'd tied to trees, trying to stay out of the hot sun. Cars were abandoned on the road because there was nowhere to park. After the rain on the second night, the site was turned into a giant mud puddle. Cronkite reported a shortage of fresh water and toilet facilities as mud-covered teens stood in long lines outside portable toilets.

"Dirty hippies." Dad left the living room. His generation didn't get how fed up my generation was with their racism, their bullshit war, and their insistence on rules. Screw the fifties.

12

Five National Guardsmen from Manchester were killed in Vietnam when their truck struck a land mine. It was just one week before they were due to return to their families.

"Not since the First World War—a half century ago—has a single American city suffered such wholesale casualties in a foreign war zone as did Manchester this past week," reported the *New*

Hampshire Sunday News. Gary Blanchette, Richard Genest. Gaetan Beaudoin. Roger Robichaud. Richard Raymond. All Manchester boys, all killed in action together.

"Oh, those poor families," said Mom when we heard the news on WMUR. "So much heartache." News footage showed a military plane landing at Grenier Field. An honor guard started its drum roll as the flag draped caskets were taken off the plane and wheeled toward a crowd of sobbing friends and family.

Bishop Primeau and Mayor Mongan offered words of comfort to the distraught crowd. "This is the saddest day for Manchester that I can remember," said Mongan. I wondered why the Bishop and the Mayor didn't speak out against the war. I would if I had their power.

Manchester's flags were flown at half-staff until all the funerals were over. The city tried to return to normal. But in this world that we lived in, I wondered if people knew what normal was anymore. My heart broke for the grieving families.

13

I snooped around Danny and Rosemarie's house whenever I babysat baby John. I looked for signs that Uncle Danny was drinking again. But I didn't find alcohol anywhere. There were a few books in the living room like *Alcoholics Anonymous: The Big Book* by some guy named Bill W. and *Living Sober* that made me think that Danny was serious. He was a lot more pleasant to be around when he wasn't drinking, that's for sure. He called Rosemarie honeybunch, and he was always bringing home flowers and leaving her sweet notes on the refrigerator.

I went out to the porch to get the mail when Johnny was napping and found a letter in a business sized envelope addressed to John Martin. The return address was *United States Department of Defense*. I thought it was odd that a baby was getting mail from the Army. "Looks like they want little Johnny to enlist." I laughed as I handed Uncle Dan the letter when they got home.

"Oh no Nora, that's not for Johnny. It's for Spider. You remember him, don't you? He lived with us for a while."

"Wait. Spider is John Martin? The guy who rescued you?" I was amazed.

"That's right. I owe him my life. We still get his mail from time to time."

I couldn't wait to tell my parents when I walked in the door. "How was the baby?" asked Mom.

"Great. But you'll never guess what."

"What?" asked Dad.

"You know the guy who carried Uncle Danny out of the jungle and kept him alive until the helicopter arrived?"

"Yes, John Martin. What about him?"

"He's Spider. One and the same."

Dad's jaw dropped. "I feel terrible. Here I was critical of the guy for the way he looked and dressed. It never occurred to me to ask his real name. He's a true hero."

Good for Dad for admitting that he was wrong about Spider. But I doubted that his opinion of long hair and bell bottoms, mini-skirts and peaceful protests would ever change.

14

Bill and I treated ourselves to ice cream at Goldenrod.

Most East Siders thought that Goldenrod had the best ice cream in the city. The kids from the West Side argued that Glendon's on Second Street was better.

"Nora, let's debate," said Bill. We dangled our feet in Massabesic Lake as we ate our waffle cones. We debated all the time. It was the way we conducted many conversations. "There's an affirmative and negative side to every decision," he said. "And debating takes the emotion out of it."

"Okay. Debate what?" I asked.

"First, you decide if you want the Affirmative or the Negative position."

I thought about it and chose the Affirmative.

"Okay, here we go," said Bill. "Bill and Nora should break up before Bill leaves for college."

I stared at Bill. "You never mentioned anything about breaking up. Why don't you just do it if that's what you want?"

"That's just it. I don't know what I want," said Bill. "Let's debate and see where we end up."

"Okay, Bill. Yes, I think we should break up. Then I can start my senior year without any distractions or commitments. And it would be good for you to begin college with a clean slate and not feel guilty when you go to parties and meet other girls."

"I don't think it's a good idea to break up," said Bill. "It would be good for me to have someone I can depend on to make me laugh and keep me company when I come home on vacations and weekends. And it would be nice to call you and hear your voice when I get lonely." He looked at me with puppy-dog eyes. I realized his argument was all about him. "But if we break up, we can still be friends and you can call me anytime."

We looked at each other and burst out laughing. "I'll bet we're the first couple in history to discuss the pros and cons of breaking up in a debate format," said Bill. "Your argument is stronger, Nora. I'm just being selfish. You should enjoy your senior year, we'll still be friends, and see what happens."

"Okay, fine. Will you at least come over to say goodbye before you head to Boston next week?" I asked.

"Of course, I will." Bill smiled at me. I felt hurt that he looked so relieved.

The following Sunday morning the phone rang. It was Bill. "Hi Nora, I called to say goodbye. We're leaving for Boston in a few minutes, and I won't get the chance to stop by. My parents want to leave early to beat the traffic."

Good riddance to Bill Robbins, I thought as I hung up the phone. If he couldn't find the time to stop by and say goodbye, then I didn't have the time to give him a second thought.

15

I was excited to begin my senior year. I decided to quit debate since I was taking six classes and knew I'd have to work my butt off to do well. It was for the best since the news traveled quickly that Mr. Rostyn was not returning to Saint Agatha's. He was moving back to Wisconsin. I hoped that he was going there to organize more demonstrations.

Religion was bound to be interesting this year. I was assigned to Sister Bernadette, who looked ancient. She shuffled about with a cane, and her false teeth looked like they were too big for her mouth. I wondered if her dentures got switched with someone else's in her last trip to the hospital. Standards may have started slipping since Flo wasn't around to crack her whip.

The second day of class Sister Bernadette handed out copies of *A Catholic Girl Grows Up*. She read Chapter One out loud, and every girl in that class must have been on the verge of wetting her pants. "A kiss is like a sip of wine," read Sister. "One sip is harmless but too many sips can lead to disaster." Sister looked at Marie Chalifour who was frequently seen kissing her boyfriend in the parking lot behind the school. Sister flipped a few pages forward and read "if a girl is in a car with a boy and he tries to kiss her she should immediately say 'not now Ambrose, I'd like a hamburger'."

At lunch we couldn't stop laughing about Sister Bernadette. Sandra Wilson said "Okay, girls the next time we go parking at Derryfield, we tell the guys 'not now Ambrose, I'd like a hamburger'."

"I'm afraid that ship sailed a long time ago for me. Steve Dugan and I have been making out for a long time," said Marie. "But we still haven't gone past second base." She'd had Steve on her arm since she moved here from Nashua. Moe once told me that Nashua girls are much faster than Manchester girls because they live closer to the Massachusetts border.

I laughed with the rest of them, but I didn't say anything. I'd be embarrassed if they knew that Bill and I kissed just once, and it was just a peck on the cheek.

One day in early October we sat in Religion, waiting for Sister Bernadette. Sister Annunciata walked into our class. "I have some sad news to report. Sister Bernadette had a stroke and is in the hospital." None of us dared to look at each other. "Until we find a suitable substitute, I'll be teaching this class. Now who can tell me what you have been studying?"

Linda brought Sister her copy of *A Catholic Girl Grows Up*. Sister frowned as she flipped through the pages. "Please leave your books on my desk after class. Today marks the feast day of Saint Francis of Assisi. Who can tell me about the life of this great saint?"

Doris, a girl with Coke bottle glasses who sat in the back of the room, said that she knew he liked animals. No one else raised their hand. Bernadette never gave us Religion homework, but one class with Annunciata and we got stuck writing an essay on Saint Francis.

"Helen, Dan's coming over tonight to watch Game One of the World Series," said Dad. "Rosie goes to bed early with the baby and he wants some company."

"That's fine, Tom. I'm reading *Airport* and I can hardly put it down. I'll be upstairs."

I really wanted to watch Game One, but I had to write the stupid essay on Saint Francis. Tom Seaver was pitching for the Mets, and it wasn't going to be easy for him to beat the Oriole's offense with Boog Powell and the Robinson duo. What I really wanted to do was see Nolan Ryan's 108 mph fastball, but the Mets were saving him for Game Two.

I was flipping through *The Lives of the Saints* trying to get smart about Saint Francis, when Uncle Danny walked in. It wasn't long after the national anthem when Dad and Dan's voices started getting louder.

"Why was your car outside the SACA Club this afternoon, Dan?"

"What's it to you?"

"Are you drinking again?"

"It's none of your business, Tom. But if you really need to know, I saw a couple of the guys' cars outside. I popped in to say hello."

"I don't know if I believe you. You've a history of disappointing people, and I don't want to see Rosemarie and Johnny get hurt."

"You want to talk about disappointment, Tom? You were going to be a big shot lawyer back in your Saint A's days, but instead you wound up a two-bit cop. And you want to know what else?"

"What?" My father's voice had an edge.

"One of the cops in my AA group has a brother-in-law who clerked for a judge in DC last summer. He said that the defense team is going to bring Coolidge's case to the United States Supreme Court. The cop said that you were the one who had the AG sign the warrant to search Coolidge's car. So, who's the disappointment now? If Coolidge walks, it's on you, brother."

The front door slammed. I peeked through the slats of my blinds. Uncle Danny's car backed out of the driveway. I couldn't bring myself to go downstairs. I didn't want to deal with Dad. What if Dan's alcoholic friend was right? Coolidge could walk and it would be my father's fault.

16

"Helen, do we have any Pepto-Bismol?" I heard Dad rummaging around in the bathroom.

"Tom, why are you using so much of the stuff? You usually have a strong stomach."

"I don't know. I've been having a lot of indigestion lately. I don't think it's anything I'm eating. Ever since my argument with Dan, I've been thinking about Coolidge walking the streets again. It's literally making me sick."

"Maybe you should think about taking a few days off. Go do something fun to take your mind off it."

"It sounds good, but my mind goes with me wherever I go." I understood how Dad felt. My fear of Eddie Coolidge stayed with me wherever I went.

17

Nixon had promised to get us out of Nam, but instead he started a draft lottery. The lottery would determine which guys would get shipped off to Vietnam and which guys could stay home. Boys in their senior year of high school, their parents, sisters, girlfriends, and neighbors worried. On December 1, CBS cancelled *Mayberry RFD* to televise Roger Mudd at the Selective Service Headquarters.

"Good evening. Tonight, for the first time in twenty-seven years, the United States has started a draft lottery."

A big container stood on a table in the center of the stage. It held 366 blue capsules. Each capsule held a birthdate. Each capsule determined who would stay safe in the United States and who would be shipped to Vietnam. A New York congressman in an expensive-looking suit stepped up to the table. He picked a capsule and announced "September 14. September 14 is 001."

A college student from Rhode Island pulled the second capsule and read "April 24. April 24 is 002." Nixon was crafty in getting young people involved so they looked supportive of the stupid war.

"It's a good thing Gene's in college, said Mom. "At least he can't be drafted until he graduates."

I waited for Bill's number to be drawn. January 28th was 077. He was safe for now because he was in college. I wondered about Donald Morse's and Billy Sweeney's birthdates. It made me think about Martin Luther King's belief that the poor fought America's wars.

"There are other ways to beat it, Mom," I said. "I was reading *Newsweek* and an article said that you can run away to Canada, make up a health condition, or say you're a homosexual or a conscientious objector. All those things can keep you from being drafted."

"No one with an ounce of patriotism would avoid the draft, young lady," said Dad.

"Maybe people who have the courage of their convictions would do everything to avoid it." I left the room.

I wondered if Bill might be homosexual like Liberace or Andy Warhol. I kind of hoped he was because that would keep him from being drafted. It would also help me believe that the reason he never wanted to go parking at Derryfield wasn't about me at all.

18

Aunt Kathleen answered the doorbell. "Thanks so much for babysitting, Nora. I've got tons of errands to run."

I peeked into the living room and saw Colleen jumping with delight, hands clapping wildly. She was watching a giant yellow bird dancing with a bunch of puppets to a song about sunny days and clouds being swept away.

"What the heck is she watching?" I asked Kathleen.

"Oh, it's *Sesame Street*, a new show that the kids just love.

"Wow! We never had anything like that when we were growing up," I said.

"I know and it's too bad. It teaches kids valuable lessons about being kind." I wished that we had *Sesame Street* around when we were kids. Maybe Billy Sweeney wouldn't have stolen Timmy Moore's inhaler. Maybe Timmy Moore wouldn't have had the nickname Wheezy. And maybe kids wouldn't have made fun of Joey's stutter.

19

When I pulled into the driveway, the light over the sink was still on. Dad was sitting at the kitchen table in his undershirt and boxers with a glass of milk.

"What's going on?" I asked. Dad usually went to bed when Mom headed upstairs.

"I couldn't sleep. I have heartburn."

"Did you try some of that pink stuff you've been drinking?"

"Yeah, but it's not helping. I decided to try some milk."

I turned on the kitchen light and looked at him. His face was gray. He was sweaty and rubbing his chest.

"I'm getting Mom."

My mother took one look at him. "Tom, I think you're having a heart attack." She grabbed the phone. "I'm calling an ambulance."

Seconds later, I heard sirens in the distance. The neighbors spilled onto their porches as the ambulance guys hauled Dad out on a stretcher. I looked up and saw the bright spires of All Saints' against the night sky.

Mom rode with him as they raced to the Sacred Heart. I ran upstairs and shook Joe awake. "Get dressed," I yelled. Panicked, we drove to the hospital.

A nurse hustled us into a tiny waiting room. "I'll let you know how your dad is doing just as soon as I get any information." The beige walls were bare. The magazines were old and falling apart. A January issue of *Time* was sitting there with a picture of Nixon at his inauguration. I counted and re-counted the number of tiles in the ceiling and then counted the number of water stains. Joe sat there and fiddled with the zipper on his jacket.

The door opened, and Mom came in with Moe on her heels. I could tell that they'd been crying. Mom hugged us. "Dad is on his way up to Intensive Care. He's had a bad heart attack. Hopefully he'll be okay, but the next four days are critical." Her voice cracked. "He's on a breathing machine."

We went into the ICU. A nurse greeted us at the desk. "Mr. Donovan is sedated so he won't know you're here. It's best not to speak to him. He needs his rest." She led us to his room.

We stared at Dad in silence. He looked old. A tube connected to a breathing machine was shoved down his throat. Each time the machine sighed, Dad's chest would rise and then fall. Another tube came out of his nose that was draining disgusting green stuff.

I heard footsteps hurrying down the corridor. They stopped behind us. Father Smith stood there with his hat held over his chest. "Helen. I'm sorry. I came as soon as I heard the news."

He looked at Joe with his good eye, while his glass eye stared at the crucifix above Dad's bed. Joe went back to the waiting room without saying anything to Father Smith.

"Shall I give Tom Last Rites?" Father asked. Mom nodded yes, dabbing her eyes.

I almost fell over. Last Rites were only given if a person was in grave danger of dying. *"Through this holy anointing may the Lord in his love and mercy help you with the grace of the Holy Spirit. May the Lord who frees you from sin save you and raise you up."* Father Smith made the sign of the cross on Dad's forehead with holy oil.

Mom put her arms around Moe and me and held us close. Father Smith left.

The next two weeks were a blur. The nurses in the family thought that Dad was doing well. He was coming out of his coma and his breathing tube was removed. He wore an oxygen mask, which he didn't like much more than the breathing machine. The nurses had to keep reminding him not to pull it off.

His doctor stopped in one afternoon when we were visiting. "You are one lucky man, Tom Donovan. Anyone else would have died—but you're too stubborn to die, you old son-of-a-gun."

Mom smiled and ruffled Dad's hair. "He's right Tom. You dodged a bullet with this one."

Dad was discharged to the VA for rehab two weeks before Christmas. At the VA, an orderly remembered Uncle Danny from when he was a patient there. "You have a hell of a kid brother, you know that, Tom? He'd give the shirt off his back to anyone. He said he felt lucky that all he lost was the half a leg when so many of his buddies were dead."

I looked at Dad.

"I'm lucky to have him as a brother," Dad replied. I wondered if he believed what he said.

20

Moe and Gene walked into the house. Gene was dragging a Christmas tree, and Moe was carrying coffee and donuts from Dunkin Donuts. With all that had been going on with Dad, we hadn't bothered decorating for the holidays. "Everyone needs a Christmas tree," said Moe.

She held the tree straight while Gene tightened the screws on the stand. They tested the lights before stringing them around the branches. Dad always said that there was nothing worse than putting the lights on the tree then realizing one of the lights was burned out and the whole string was kaput.

I hung the stockings on the mantel, while Joe helped Mom unwrap the Nativity scene figurines. "Oh, shit!" Joe exclaimed as the Virgin slipped through his fingers and fell to the floor. Her head rolled across the rug, coming to a stop at Dad's Barcalounger.

"Nice going, Joe. Mom and Dad bought that Nativity scene the first Christmas they were married." Moe glared at Joe.

Mom picked up the Virgin and her head. "It's no problem. A little Elmer's Glue and Mary will be as good as new."

"Elmer's Glue won't work on pottery," Gene said.

"Actually Gene, it's porcelain," Mom snapped. She headed to the kitchen to rummage in the kitchen junk-drawer looking for the glue.

I shot Gene a dirty look. He wasn't even family yet, so he should just keep his big mouth shut.

Mom came back into the living room a few minutes later. "The glue on Mary won't be dry for a couple of hours. I'll stick her in with Jesus and Joseph before I go to bed tonight. She'll be as good as new." She turned to Joe. "Don't feel bad. Broken things can always be fixed one way or another."

I wasn't sure that Mom was right about always being able to fix broken things, but I said nothing.

We decorated the tree in silence. Only Mom made an occasional comment. "Maureen, here is the baby ornament from your first Christmas. Nana bought it for you the year before she passed, God rest her soul."

Gene placed the Christmas angel on the treetop. "Now let's go outside and admire the tree like we always do," said Moe. We agreed the tree was beautiful, but nobody's heart was in it.

That afternoon, we went to the VA's holiday celebration. Dad was in a good mood because his doctor told him that if all went well, he could be discharged in a few days. We sang Christmas carols, drank punch, and nibbled on cookies that the nurses baked. Santa arrived and gave each of the patients a gift-wrapped box topped with a red ribbon. I noticed that Santa walked with a limp. I looked down and saw that he wore only one black boot. At the end of his other leg was a metal foot. I realized that Santa was probably a patient here too.

We kissed Dad goodnight and when we reached the door, we turned around to look at him one last time. His Santa gift was a bell with a red bow tied to its handle. He picked it up, rang it several times and said "Ho, ho, ho...Merry Christmas, my wonderful family."

"Th-th-this has to be the worst Christmas ever," said Joe when we got in the car. He was sitting in the back seat looking with disgust at the bag of candy one of the VA elves had given him. I agreed.

As we left the VA and turned right onto Smyth Road, I thought of Sandra Valade. Just down the road from the hospital was where she stepped off the bus on a dark and snowy winter night almost ten years ago.

1970

"Rise and shine, my loves!"

Moe groaned and rolled over.

Mom stuck her head in our room. "The tree needs to come down, and I need help in the kitchen."

We tromped downstairs.

"Next New Year's I'll be married and have my own place. Mom won't be dragging me out of bed to vacuum," grumped Moe.

"If you're tired from being out last night with Gene, you've no one to blame but yourself." Mom looked over her glasses. "Joe, please sand the driveway and the steps. Moe and Nora can take down the tree."

"Don't you all wish you had heart attacks like me and got to sit on your duffs all day?" called Dad from the living room.

I grabbed my coffee and went to sit with him. "Are you excited about going back to work?" I asked. If he wasn't excited, the rest of us were plenty excited about him going anywhere.

"It'll be good to get out," he said. "It kills me to be on the desk. I'm a detective, not a secretary." Dad opened the newspaper. Okay, I tried.

I went to the hall closet and pulled out the boxes for our Christmas decorations.

"Hey, Moe," I called.

"Yeah, yeah." Moe trudged into the living room carrying a stack of newspapers to wrap up our best ornaments. I don't know what Mom thought were our "best" ones. Most of our Christmas decorations were things normal families would have thrown out years ago.

I attacked the Nativity scene first, grabbing the three-legged sheep we always leaned against the red-robed shepherd so it wouldn't fall over. I couldn't recall how the poor thing had lost its leg, but for as far back as I could remember, it had only three. I wrapped him up in newspaper. I picked up the Virgin, mindful of her recent decapitation. Mom had done a crummy job with the repair. Blobs of dried glue stuck to Mary's blue robe, and so much porcelain was missing from her neck that you could see her spinal cord if she had one. But no one would notice this next year if we turned Mary to a slight angle. I wrapped her up with extra newspaper just to keep her safe.

Moe looked at me in surprise.

"It'll give me something to laugh about in December when we're pulling this stuff out again."

"And Gene and I will be in our new place with new ornaments," mused Moe. "I think I'll get one of those silver trees with a color-wheel, so we won't have to deal with this tinsel mess."

"You'd get a silver tree with a color-wheel? They're so tacky," I exclaimed.

"When did you become an expert on holiday decorating?" sniffed Moe.

"I can't hear the TV with all your yakking," snapped Dad. He turned it off and walked slowly upstairs. Moe and I looked at each other.

"Did he expect us to take down the tree in silence?" I asked.

Moe sighed. "Men get depressed after heart attacks. Ignore him."

"Easy for you to say. You get to go back to the dorm. Joe and I are stuck here with Mr. Bad Mood." I pulled off some tinsel and draped it over the cardboard so it wouldn't get crinklier than it already was.

"I'm sorry. Maybe once he gets back to work, he'll brighten up a little. Do you think Gene should have a talk with him?"

"I don't know." I could think of nothing less likely to brighten Dad up than a talk with Gene.

"Sanding's done," said Joe.

"Thanks," said Mom. "Now help Nora with the tree. Moe, I know Gene is coming, so go get ready."

Moe hot-footed it upstairs.

"W-w-what do you want me to do?" Joe had his hands in his pockets and stared at the tree.

"Grab some cardboard and help me finish off the tinsel. The lights are easy, and then we'll drag it out to the curb."

We removed most of the tinsel and rolled up the lights. We put the tree on a blanket, and Joe dragged it out of the house, leaving a swath of pine needles, bits of tinsel, and shreds of Christmas wrap in its wake.

No sooner had I started the vacuum cleaner than I heard Dad. "How can I get any rest with all that noise?" he shouted.

"Stop complaining!" I yelled.

I hit HIGH POWER and the vacuum cleaner roared into action.

2

The Bouchers and the Donovans were doing the Irish good-bye, taking forever to leave. Aunt Kathleen came into the kitchen carrying the leftover pork pie.

"Sorry you and Joe are stuck doing clean up. I'd help, but Colleen is falling apart."

I could hear my little cousin screaming in the front hall.

"Don't worry about it, Aunt Kathleen," said Joe.

I went out to the living room to retrieve dirty glasses. When I returned to the kitchen, Joe had opened a bottle of Blue Nun. He tried to hide his glass behind the paper towel holder, but I saw it.

"Joe, what are you doing?" I asked. "That's a lot of wine for a kid."

"I've h-h-had this much before," he said.

"Where did you drink before?" I was shocked.

"At the rectory."

"You drank communion wine?"

"Oh, no. Th-that stuff's gross. The priests serve wine at dinner."

"How old were you when they started serving you wine?" I asked.

"Ab-about ten."

I couldn't believe my ears.

"Father told us that drinking wine with dinner was a way of honoring Jesus because Jesus changed water into wine."

Didn't Jesus drink water? I wondered.

"What are you going to do if anyone wants some?" I asked.

"Oh, Dad doesn't drink. Mom might if we have company, so I'll replace it. Want some?"

I paused. I'd had only two beers in my entire life. "Sure. Give me half of what you have."

I noticed that he stopped stuttering. Maybe it was the wine.

"I'm going upstairs." He downed the rest of his wine and stuck the glass in the dishwasher.

When I went up, Joe was asleep. A dog-eared copy of *The Poetry of Robert Frost* was next to him. "To Joe Donovan, with love and respect, Father James Smith" inscribed on the flyleaf. It gave me the creeps.

I shook his shoulder. "Joe, come downstairs. Mom will be up in a minute if she thinks you're sick."

"I am sick," he muttered, wiping drool off his cheek.

"Why?"

"Because of all that wine."

I looked at my brother. "Well, I guess I can understand that at parties a kid might think it's cool to get hammered."

He sat up, swinging his legs to the side of the bed. "Nora, it's not just at parties."

"Nora! Joe!" called my mother.

"Be right there," I yelled.

"Joe, you need to tell Mom and Dad. Mom will notice that the wine is gone."

"It's okay. Father Murphy can replace it. Mom won't notice for a few days."

I thought of Uncle Danny and my mean Donovan grandfather.

"Nora!! Joseph!" Mom would be coming up the stairs in two seconds if we didn't move. Joe ran into the bathroom. I could hear him throwing up. Serves him right, I thought.

3

Joe and I walked to school. Paul was home sick. I asked Joe how his classes were going, but he just shrugged. I'd no idea what he was thinking about, but I was worried about him. And Dad's bad moods were pissing me off. Was he still visiting Mrs. Mason at IHOP?

I decided I'd talk to Lin about Joe.

"Drinking at ten doesn't sound cool," said Linda. "Some priests are clueless about how to act around kids."

"If my father finds out about Joe's drinking, it'll kill him."

"Whoa," said Lin "You're getting ahead of yourself. AA has teen groups. Joe could get help there."

I'd no idea what could help. The thought of Joe spending so much time at the rectory scared me. I knew I'd have to keep an eye on him because my parents were not.

"Big day," grumbled Dad. "My one-and-one half-legged brother started sorting mail at the Post Office, the kids are back at school, and all morning I got to field phone calls from old biddies who'd lost their pets or their minds, or both."

If Dad was looking for sympathy, he got none from me. I cornered Joe in the kitchen.

"Did you replace the Blue Nun?"

"Sure." He opened the cupboard revealing a full bottle.

"That was quick."

"It's easy for priests to get booze. Parishioners buy it for them all the time."

"You know Dad and Mom would hit the roof if they knew about your drinking. Dad's death on alcoholics."

"Dad's death on a lot of things," said Joe. "He's really a 50's guy. Father Smith is like that, too."

I didn't want to hear about how Father Smith and Dad were alike. I grabbed some plates and started setting the table.

Dad came home ecstatic from Dr. Marzoni's office. "I'm back to being a detective!" he crowed. "No more secretarial duties for this guy!" He called the station to see what his assignment would be for the next week and insisted on broiling steak and making mashed potatoes and peas for dinner that night.

Joe took a small piece of steak and poked at his potatoes.

"What's going on at school?' Mom asked.

"Nothing," Joe mumbled.

"Are you thinking of joining Student Council like Moe?" asked Mom.

"I'm busy with Youth Fellowship," said Joe.

"Joe, you've done Youth Fellowship for years. Dad took a sip of milk. "What about applying for a counselor-in-training position at Camp Benedictus?"

"Leave me alone!" Joe shouted. He ran up to his room.

"I can't believe that kid." My father's voice was angry. "I'm going to the rectory to talk to Smith about this Fellowship stuff."

"Easy, Tom. Joe just doesn't know how to handle his emotions," said Mom. "But I'll go with you to the rectory."

I wanted to give Joe a heads up about Tom and Helen visiting the rectory. I knocked at his door, but he wouldn't let me in. Around 11:00, I heard him go into the bathroom and brush his teeth. Screw him, I thought. I rolled over and went to sleep.

My folks were at work when we got up for school the next morning.

"Sorry, Nora, but a friend's picking me up, so I can't walk with you."

I didn't feel like walking with him anyway. I left the house before he did and saw him going by in a black Cadillac. Father Smith was driving, and Joe pretended that he didn't see me.

I wondered if my parents had made an appointment at the rectory.

4

The lunch table was abuzz with talk of college admissions. Linda and I were both going to UNH. I planned to major in history, and Linda was thinking about Parks and Recreation. "When do you ever go to any parks except Derryfield?" I asked her.

"Never. But I like recreation, and I think it'll to be a big thing in the future."

I hoped that history would be a smart major. Majoring in history might help me get into law school. I wanted to help girls like Pamela Mason. And I wanted to lock up killers like Eddie Coolidge. Dad said that lawyers were scallywags who just wanted to make money. He insisted that the real work of serving justice was done by cops on the beat. But I thought that Dad might be wrong.

A big storm was expected to hit New England that night. Snow was already falling, and wind howled around our house. It promised to be the kind of storm that sent Eddie Coolidge into a killing frenzy. I liked knowing that he could only fantasize about torturing girls as he looked through barred windows at the swirling snow.

"Where the hell is Joe?" Dad asked. It was almost dinnertime, and we hadn't even gotten a phone call. Mom looked out the window anytime she heard a car go down the street.

"This isn't like him," she said.

The phone rang. Mom grabbed it.

"Yes." She listened for a few seconds and said, "Oh, if you think that's best. Thank you, Father." She hung up.

"Joe's at the rectory. Father Smith doesn't want to drive him home in this weather, so he'll bring him home in the morning."

"Helen, call Smith and tell him I'm coming to get Joe." Dad headed out to the garage. I looked out the living room window and watched the car fish-tail in reverse out our driveway.

Mom turned on the news. The murder of Green Beret Jeffrey McDonald's family by strung-out hippies in North Carolina was the lead story. Rumors circulated that McDonald murdered his pregnant wife and two young daughters. It was hard to believe that a decorated war vet would kill his pregnant wife and kids. But I remembered the comments surrounding Ted Kennedy and the young woman on the Chappaquiddick bridge. Maybe all kinds of men killed women. Politicians and military heroes. Not just psychos like Coolidge. The news moved on to the big snow hitting the northeast, and then returned to an interview with the distraught McDonald.

Mom clicked off the TV. "There's a lot of sadness in the world, isn't there?" she said. "I'm just glad that Joe's safe." I didn't share her gladness. I didn't think that my brother was safe from Dad, the priests, or himself.

Our car careened into the driveway a half hour later. Joe and Dad kicked the snow off their boots and came in.

"How are things?" Mom asked.

Joe looked pale and red-eyed. He grunted, "fine" before going upstairs.

"Father Smith said that Joe drank communion wine and passed out at the rectory," said Dad. "He planned on keeping him overnight. He was hoping that after a talking-to, Joe would shape up."

I was shocked.

"We're lucky that this happened at the rectory and not at a friend's house where it would've spread all over Manchester," said Mom. She opened the cupboard. "I'm putting this wine in the stockpile."

"Joe's lucky," said Dad. "Father Smith has offered to counsel him."

I had to say something. "Dad, I hear from a lot of kids that the priests at All Saints' let the altar boys drink, even the little kids. I'll bet that's how Joe ended up drinking too much today."

My father slammed his fist on the table. "Nora, you've had the worst attitude towards the Church ever since you had that Jewish debate coach. Father Smith and Father Murphy are at Holy Name Society every month. You couldn't meet finer men."

I turned to my mother. "Mom, Sandra Wilson went to Catholic grade school in Nashua. She said Father Murphy got sent to Manchester because boys' parents complained about him."

"Why are girls at Saint Agatha's spreading gossip like that?" Mom looked over her glasses.

"Enough, Nora." Dad was adamant. "Parents complain about priests and nuns all the time, usually because Johnny or Suzy didn't get into the National Honor Society or some other baloney. I won't have you ruining peoples' reputations."

I was furious. "Ask Joe."

"I did. Joe said that he and some of the other boys have occasionally snitched altar wine." Dad chuckled. "I had friends who did it, too. But this time there was more than just a few sips. He's not used to drinking, so he passed out."

Jesus, I thought. I went upstairs. I knocked at Joe's door. The light was on, but he didn't answer. I tried opening his door, but it was locked. As I closed the blinds in my bedroom, I could see the lit-up spire of fucking All Saints' Church in the distance.

I confronted him the next day.

"Joe, I don't know what's going on with you, but you're scaring the shit out of me. And you lie all the time."

"I c-can't tell anyone the truth."

"Well, lying isn't getting you anywhere. Are you an alcoholic?"

"I drink too much sometimes, but then I stop. So I'm not an alcoholic. Just leave me alone."

I was mad that everybody was blaming me for this mess. My parents thought I was picking on Father Smith, and Joe thought that I was picking on him. We walked in silence up Chastain Street. I wished I'd worn my boots instead of my penny loafers. My feet were soaked by the time I got home.

I sort of forgot about Joe until he came down for dinner. He left *The Collected Poems of Robert Frost* on the coffee table. I snuck a peek. The flyleaf with its inscription by Father Smith had been torn out. I hoped that this was a good sign.

5

"Glenlivet? Wow, Tom. That's generous of you." Mark Tardiff kissed Mom on the cheek. "Helen, good to see you and the kids."

We followed Louise into the living room. Jake and Sarah said hi, and Mark asked us what we'd like to drink.

"I'd like to try the Glenlivet," said Gene. "I've never had it. Moe, you should try it."

She, my mother, and Louise, after looking at each other, decided on Glenlivet, too.

"I've got Moxie for the kids," said Mark.

"I'll be the assistant bar tender." Dad followed Mark to the kitchen. He came back carrying a tray of soft drinks for the kids. I'd never had Moxie before. It tasted like Alka-Seltzer with pepper. I put it down on my coaster.

"Let's toast Gene and Moe," said Mark. I looked around the living room with its blue velvet drapes and sweeping view of the Merrimack. Moe was marrying into serious money. "All the best to this young couple," said Mark.

"May I kiss the bride-to-be?" asked Gene. Without waiting for an answer, he swooped Moe into his arms and kissed her for what seemed to be a bit too long.

The families discussed the wedding. By evening's end, all arrangements were in place. Financials were settled. Moe had her attendants lined up, Jake would be best man, Gene's college friends and Joe would be ushers, and Colleen would be the flower girl. The Chateau would cater the event, Mark would arrange a tent, Jacques would do the flowers, Kelly would be the photographer, and Father Smith would officiate. Smith had baptized all the Tardiff and Donovan kids, and the parents agreed that he was the obvious choice. I looked at Joe as Smith's name was mentioned, but his face was blank.

"And of course, I am still searching for my gown," said Moe. I was sick of her gown. "Searching" made it sound like she was on the prowl for the Holy Grail. But that was Moe.

The US Space Program competed with Moe's wedding plans for our family's attention. "Joe, listen to this," Mom said. "Explorer I has re-entered our atmosphere after being in orbit for twelve years."

"And Apollo 13 is heading to the moon today carrying three astronauts," said Dad.

Joe looked up from reading the back of the Wheaties box.

"Y-y-yeah. It's going to be cool." Joe's voice didn't sound like he thought it was remotely cool.

"Joe, take your time reading the Wheaties box. I've got to be at school early." I pulled on my parka and grabbed my books. I didn't have to be at school early, but anything was better than hanging around with my parents trying to jolly up Joe. Let him jolly himself up.

6

The Larkins' forsythia had just started opening and the Burkes' crocuses were already in bloom. Snow was predicted that night, and I hoped the crocuses would survive the cold. A New Hampshire spring usually has a couple of warm days followed by blasts of Arctic weather. Our English class had just finished a unit on T. S. Eliot. The man had April nailed. It was the cruelest month.

Dad turned on the evening news. Astronaut Jack Wigert's message: "Houston. I believe we've had a problem," sent shockwaves through America. An oxygen tank exploded on Apollo 13, forcing the astronauts to make a dangerous return home.

"Blessings on those poor men," murmured Mom.

"W-w-will they be okay, Dad?" Joe asked.

"I hope so." Dad sounded worried.

Americans cheered when the Apollo 13 crew dropped safely into the ocean. "I've prayed for those men ever since that tank exploded. What a blessing!" exclaimed Mom.

"Still thinking of being an astronaut, Joe?" I asked him.

"N-n-not if so much swimming is involved," he said. I noticed that he tucked *The Collected Poems of Robert Frost* under his arm when he went upstairs.

7

"Nora, this is unbelievable!" Dad pointed to the TV where hundreds of students were rioting at Columbia. Young men with ponytails carrying signs protesting the war marched across the campus. Young women with long hair carrying peace signs and flowers marched alongside.

"Dad, innocent people are dying in this stupid war. The TV is only covering this to make the protestors look bad."

"I fought in World War II, and if I were young enough, I'd go again to serve my country."

I said nothing. I wanted to serve my country, too, but I didn't see that getting my ass shot off in the jungle would do a thing to help anyone.

The cliché that violence begets violence played out before our eyes. In Ohio, Kent State students burned down the ROTC building. The National Guard was called out. They arrived and opened fire, killing four students and injuring nine.

"Why the hell did the students have to burn down the ROTC building?" asked Dad. "They were asking for trouble."

Joe and I went upstairs without saying a word. "Do you want to talk?" I asked.

Joe pushed a pile of clothes off his bed so I had room to sit.

"I don't know what's going on. But it seems like it's all bad stuff," I said.

"I know. And Dad, Mr. Law and Order, seems to think the bad stuff is okay."

I pulled some little balls of wool off my sweater. "It seems that everything is crazy. Rockets exploding in space, people getting slaughtered in Vietnam, soldiers coming home nuts, and now the National Guard is shooting college students."

I looked at his books.

"What do you have for homework tonight?" I asked.

"Oh, g-g-geometry problems which I think are kind of cool, and then I have to study for a history quiz on the Cathars." He pushed his glasses up on his nose. "W-w-why do you want to major in history? It's boring."

"I like it. You learn about the present by studying the past."

"Explain th-th-that," he said.

"Okay. Take the Cathars, for example. They lived in medieval times. The Pope hated them because they believed in two gods: one good and one bad. The good god wanted the Cathars to follow the teachings of Jesus. The bad god went around causing pain and suffering. So the Cathars thought things were either completely good or completely bad."

"I think that most things are in-between," said Joe. "How does knowing about the Cathars help you today?"

I hadn't thought of that before. "The Catholic Church and our country are behaving like Cathars. The nuns and priests think that they know best, and if you don't toe their line, you're a bad person. Ditto for our government. Those National Guardsmen shot students because they thought the students were bad."

As I spoke, it occurred to me that Dad was quite a bit like the US government, the Catholic Church, and the Cathars. But I didn't mention this to Joe.

"Y-y-you could be right about the guardsmen." Joe pushed two pillows behind his back. "But maybe the guardsmen shot the students because they thought the kids were rich spoiled brats." He paused. "Or m-m-maybe the guardsmen were just jerks."

He had a point. Maybe the guardsmen were just jerks.

8

My high school commencement was a quiet affair. No National Guardsmen showed up for a shooting spree, no ancient Cathars showed up to cast spells on the graduates.

Moe's nursing school graduation took place that same evening. Like mine, hers had no National Guardsmen nor any ancient Cathars. A sweet ceremony in the Cathedral followed by family pictures outside. "There's a lot to these traditions," mused Aunt Kathleen. "This evening's ceremony was just as I remembered mine a few years back."

"And just as I remember mine over twenty years ago," added Mom. Her eyes glistened.

Moe started working evenings the day after graduation, so it was a week before I could talk to her about Joe.

"What do you think about a fifteen-year-old guy who's still an altar boy and spends lots of time at the rectory?" I asked.

Moe was shaving her legs in the sink. "Do you think he has a vocation?" She moved the razor slowly up her calf and then turned on the water to rinse it off.

"I think what he has is a drinking problem." I told her about the Joe drinking at the rectory.

"Do Mom and Dad know?"

"I tried to tell them, but they just got mad."

Moe stuck her right leg up on the sink. "Do you want Gene to talk to him?" she asked.

I couldn't believe how Moe thought anyone with a problem would benefit from a chat with Gene. "No, he and Gene aren't close. Don't you think there's something weird about Joe and Paul hanging out at the rectory so much?"

"Well, if they get free booze, I think that explains a lot," she said. "What do you think?"

"I don't know," I said.

"Let's talk later," Moe said. "Gene's coming any minute, and I have to get dressed."

No sooner had she popped into Gene's car when the phone rang.

Dad picked it up. His voice was sharp. "Okay, okay, Dorothy. It's 5:45. I'll call the rectory now and say that I'm coming to take Paul home."

The dial whirred as he called the rectory.

"Father Smith? Tom Donovan here."

There was a pause.

"No, I'm not calling about my daughter's wedding. I'm calling because Dorothy Connors wants Paul home. I'm leaving now to pick him up."

Father said something.

"No, of course not. See you in five. Good-bye."

"What's going on?" asked Mom.

"I've no idea. But Smith is paranoid. He thinks that I want to arrest him."

"Arrest a Catholic priest?" Mom was shocked.

Dad grabbed his keys and headed out.

We ate supper. Mom put Dad's plate in the oven. The phone rang, but whoever called spoke to Joe for only a few seconds.

"Who was that?" asked Mom.

"Dad. He's stuck with some police business. He said that he and Paul are fine. But he won't be home before eight."

"I'm glad he called, or I would've worried." She turned on the local news. Cameramen from WMUR-TV stood outside All Saints' rectory. Yellow police tape surrounded the building. A reporter said that Father Smith had just been found shot dead.

My mother blessed herself. "Sweet Jesus," she exclaimed.

The TV camera zoomed in on local news guy Chad Zimmerman. He reported what the housekeeper Miss Kilgore had said. At 5:45, Father Smith received a phone call on his private line. Miss Kilgore was sure of the time because she always served dinner at 6:00. She heard a gunshot from upstairs. She ran to check on Father Smith, but his door was locked.

"It may have been a blackmailer or a mentally unstable individual who called the rectory at 5:45. Police suspect a suicide." Zimmerman's voice cracked when he said that he'd been an altar boy at All Saints'.

Mom began to cry. "Your poor father," she said. "This is the last thing he needs with his bad heart."

"I hope Dad wasn't the one who found Father's body," said Joe.

"I hope to God not. But let's say a rosary for the repose of Father Smith's soul," said Mom.

I didn't care if Father Smith's soul reposed or not. But I got down on my knees because I'd no choice.

I looked over at Joe. He was crying.

Dad came home before we went to bed. His face was ashen. We followed him into the living room. Mom pulled up the hassock so she could sit beside him. "What happened?"

"I got to the rectory. Miss Kilgore was hysterical. She said that Father Smith got a phone call just before dinner. I was the caller. But she had no way of knowing that." Dad sighed. "She heard a gunshot and called the police."

Dad took a deep breath. "I ran upstairs, hoping it wasn't the Connors boy. I kicked the door open just as Callahan and McCarthy came up the stairs behind me. Smith was on the floor. Blood was everywhere." Dad pulled out his handkerchief and mopped his forehead.

"Dear God in heaven," murmured Mom.

"Callahan sent me to the station to make a statement because I was first on the scene."

"What about Paul?" Joe's face was white.

"He's fine. He left for home before I arrived." Dad raised the footrest on his chair. "There's no way that Paul and Dorothy will be involved in the investigation."

He turned to Joe. "I know that you and Father Smith were close. He's liked you ever since you were little." Dad sighed. "Joe, priests are a bit like nurses and cops. They see a lot of hard stuff, and it takes a toll. Father Smith might have just cracked under the strain. Or maybe he had a health problem."

Joe wiped his nose on his sleeve. "I'm g-g-going to bed."

"Sorry that this has been such a terrible evening for you, Dad," I said.

"Worse evening for poor Father Smith," murmured Mom.

As I curled up in bed, I wondered what had driven Father Smith to kill himself. And now I understood why he was so fond of Frost's poem:

The woods are lovely, dark, and deep
But I have promises to keep
And miles to go before I sleep.
And miles to go before I sleep.

I remember learning that suicide was a sin of pride. A person who commits suicide believes that their ability to sin exceeds God's ability to forgive.

Father Smith's funeral was a quiet affair. Suicide was never mentioned. I wondered if he'd be buried in Saint Joseph's Cemetery because suicide victims weren't supposed to be buried in hallowed ground. I asked Linda about it. "Oh, if it were a hundred years ago, Smith would get buried at the corner of Union and South Willow," she said. "People believed that ghosts of those who committed suicide could rise up and cause trouble, so it was important to bury them at crossroads."

I didn't think that Smith's ghost would rise to torment anyone. The word was out that the Catholic Church shuffled problem priests from one parish to another. If the Bishop could shuffle living problem priests from one parish to another, shuffling a dead one into sanctified soil would be simple.

9

I worried that it'd be hard for Joe when I left for UNH. Youth Fellowship ended abruptly after Smith's death, and Father Morgan, a new young priest, was assigned to work with Father Murphy at All Saints'. Neither Joe nor I knew much about Father Morgan. I had no interest in learning about him, and Joe stopped serving Mass after Smith's suicide. And we both stopped going to church. Instead, we drove to Dunkin' Donuts on Sunday mornings where we drank coffee and talked.

I asked Joe how he was doing after Smith's suicide.

He was silent for a minute before speaking. "I l-liked him a lot. He was kind to me when I was little. But as I got older, I felt like I was the adult, and he was the needy kid. It's easier for me that he's gone, but it's terrible that he killed himself."

I could tell he didn't want to talk about it anymore. I was glad that he seemed okay. And that he was stuttering less.

"I'm going to start volunteering at the Humane Society," Joe said.

I was surprised. "What made you decide to do this?"

"I'm n-not into extra-curricular stuff at Saint Benedict's. You're a good fighter, so debate was perfect for you. And I don't like sports." Joe took a sip of his coffee. "Something good about Youth Fellowship—"

I groaned, but he continued. "S-s-something good about Youth Fellowship is that it made me understand that I had to give back to the community. I talked to Uncle Dan about helping to train dogs for the police Canine Unit."

I took a bite of my donut. "Those dogs are scary, aren't they?"

"They probably are. Uncle Dan thinks that I'd have to be on the police force to train their dogs. A retired cop in his AA group does it. He thought I should volunteer at the Humane Society to see if I like it. He said that training dogs for the blind or the disabled might be right up my alley."

Joe might be better working with dogs than with people. I suspected that Uncle Dan had the same thought.

"I told the folks, and they're fine with it. My birthday isn't until September, so I can't get a real job. I'll volunteer three days a week at the animal shelter and learn about the Big Picture in Drivers Ed."

I laughed. "I have a question, Joe. Did you ever think about being a priest?"

"I d-did when I was little. But Father Smith was lonely, and I knew that I didn't want to be like him."

He looked at his watch. "Right now, the Mass has ended. Let's go in peace." He clasped his hands and looked heavenward.

10

"We're so proud of you." Mom's eyes filled with tears as she hugged me.

"I don't want to see you in any campus protests," warned Dad.

I waved as he tooted the horn and headed back towards Manchester. Within an hour, music was blasting from a stereo, and what seemed to be half of Hitchcock Hall was dancing in the quad. Several other dorms joined in. Campus police moved around the crowd's edge, but the National Guard was nowhere in sight.

The weeks flew by with classes, football games, and partying. Dad picked me up from school two days before Moe's wedding. He filled me in on the preparations on the way home.

"Moe and Gene are well-organized. Moe loves her dress, the bridesmaids like theirs, and she's thrilled that most on the guest list can come. How's school going for you?" asked Dad.

"I like it. My classes are good, and the campus is beautiful."

"Nothing's more beautiful than a New England fall, but you may be singing a different song in February," said Dad. "And good news. Your brother is a star at the Humane Society."

I was glad for Joe.

Moe was in full bridal mode when we got home. "Nora, I'm not sure that the dye on your shoes exactly matches your dress." She pulled a pair of heels from a box on her bureau and placed my maid of honor dress on the bed. The color wasn't identical, but it was close.

"Moe, they're perfect. Now show me your gown," I said. I was sure that it was fine, but I knew that she'd like to show it to me. It had a scoop neck, fitted bodice, and a full skirt. I told her it was beautiful.

Moe's wedding day was a gift: sunny and warm for mid-October. As we crossed the Notre Dame Bridge on our way to Saint Anselm's Abby Church, we stopped at a red light. I looked out the window. I saw the sign "Coolidge Avenue." Eddie Coolidge was the last person I wanted to be thinking about. Of course, I knew that the street was named after a president, not Manchester's slime-ball killer of teen girls. I looked down at my dress and smoothed out some wrinkles.

The bridal party pulled up in front of the chapel where we sat waiting for last-minute guests to scurry up the steps. When Joe stuck his head out the door and gave us the high sign, we marched into the vestibule.

The organist began playing the "Love Theme from Romeo and Juliet," and the bridal party started down the aisle. Gene was staring at the vestibule anxious to see Moe, and his brother Jake winked at me. As the organ sounded the first strains of "Here Comes the Bride," the congregation rose to their feet.

I looked out at the crowd and thought how lucky I was. Joey seemed to be happier, and Dad seemed relaxed even though the United States Supreme Court was going to review the Coolidge case very soon. I thought about Pamela Mason as I stood on the altar. And Sandra Valade. Neither would have a wedding and raise a family of their own. I wished that I hadn't seen that stupid street sign. I pushed the dead girls out of my mind and looked at my family. Uncle Dan, who seemed to have dealt with his demons. Aunt Kathleen, who was still my favorite. And the Tardiffs seemed like good people. Louise and Mark were nice to Moe and welcoming to all of us. I was jerked out of my reverie when I heard the priest proclaim, "I now pronounce you husband and wife." Gene kissed Moe, and the church burst into applause.

I made sure not to look at any street signs until we crossed the Merrimack and headed up to Tardiff's. A huge tent filled the backyard and guests were at food stations, piling hors d'oeuvres on little plates. People walked around searching for their tables so they could dump purses and cameras. An enormous dance floor took over most of the tent, and the heaters glowed orange as the sky darkened. I put a few crab cakes on my plate.

The DJ got his screeching mic under control and called out Mr. and Mrs. Gene Tardiff. Guests cheered and tapped their wine glasses.

There were the obligatory dances. Moe and Gene danced to "Make it With You," a weird choice, but maybe I was just being prudish. The bride and groom's parents danced to "I Love How You Love Me," which was thoughtful of Moe as it was Mom's favorite song. Gene danced with Mom, Moe danced with Mark, and everybody danced with whomever they were supposed to. It was like Farmer in the Dell.

From the corner of my eye, I spotted Dad, Mark Tardiff, and some other guy involved in conversation. I looked around the room and saw Mom sitting with Uncle Dan and Rosemarie. Baby John was wearing a navy-blue suit and chewing on his tie. Rosemarie tried to distract him by offering him a cracker, but he would have none of it. She tried to remove his soggy tie, and he screamed. When the DJ started playing "Momma Told Me Not to Come," Rosemarie scooped John up and headed out on the dance floor, singing as she spun him around.

I made my way to Auntie, who sat at a table with a younger nun, probably her attendant. "Auntie, it's me. Nora."

"Of course, I know you, dear."

I suspected that she had no idea who I was. The other nun introduced herself as Sister Angelus.

"Nice to meet you, Sister."

I kissed Auntie on the cheek. Although she was in her eighties, her skin was as soft as a baby's.

Moe and Gene came out in their going-away outfits. Moe looked terrific in a yellow dress, but Gene looked like a lounge lizard in his powder blue leisure suit and white shoes. Whatever prompted him to pick out that outfit was beyond me. Cameras flashed as they jumped into their new Chevy Nova and headed off to Cape Cod.

Joe worked the next day at the Humane Society, but Dad, Mom, and I sat around all morning reading the Sunday paper and eating blueberry coffee cake.

Mom turned to Dad. "Tom, you spent a lot of time talking to Mark and some other guy."

Dad put down the paper. "That was Jack Doumas, the lawyer who defended Coolidge before the New Hampshire Supreme Court. Nice guy."

"What did he say about Coolidge?" I asked.

"Well, he probably shouldn't have said anything, nor should I. But I will anyway because I've hated the son of a bitch ever since the Mason girl's murder." Dad reached for another piece of coffeecake. "Doumas said Coolidge was the most self-important, cowardly, and angry guy that he'd ever met."

"But was that all he had to say? You talked for a while."

"No. He said that former Solicitor General Archibald Cox, who graduated Harvard Law, was just appointed to defend Coolidge in front of the US Supreme Court. Jack thinks that Coolidge's verdict will be overturned, based on the 4th amendment." Dad turned to me. "Your argument at the State Debate Tournament nailed it, Nora."

My heart stopped.

Mom gasped. "Does that mean Coolidge will get out?"

Dad sighed and poured himself another cup of coffee. "I hope not. Jack assured me that Attorney General Wyman promised to either re-try the case or go after Coolidge for the Valade murder."

"I won't sleep if that animal is out on the street," said Mom. "But why did Doumas tell you this? At your daughter's wedding, of all places?"

"Doumas said that the legal team was impressed by the work done by the Manchester Police. But they acknowledged that the search and seizure protocol used for over a hundred years in the Granite State violated federal law." Dad sighed. "We made an innocent mistake with a terrible outcome. Doumas just wanted to let me know that no matter what tricks Cox has up his sleeve, the state of New Hampshire will not rest until justice is obtained for Pamela Mason."

I felt like I'd been kicked in the stomach. I was relieved that New Hampshire would go after Coolidge if the Supreme Court ruled that the search of his car was illegal. Yet it didn't change the fact that Dad was the one who bungled the investigation, and that Coolidge might walk. I didn't want my father to have another heart attack. And I couldn't deal with any more teenage girls getting murdered in Manchester. I had too many names in my plaid notebook.

The drive back to UNH was beautiful. It was mid-October, and the fiery foliage was at its peak. Reddish-orange leaves tumbled from trees all the way up Route 155.

"Dad, are you okay with all this Coolidge stuff?" I asked.

"Nora, I guess I have to be," he said, turning on the radio. His way of saying that the conversation was over.

I watched the falling leaves and thought about search and seizure. I thought about the Supreme Court. After hearing about Mr. Doumas's conversation with Dad, I had a sinking feeling that the Court would decide in Coolidge's favor.

11

I can't stand sitting in the rec room and watching the game anymore. The Celtics depend too much on Havlicek. Red Auerbach must be choking on his soggy cigar. I walk over to the barred windows and watch the snow fall. I remember driving around Manchester delivering Coca-Cola and meeting so many pretty girls. Pretty girls with beautiful dark curls.

The US Supreme Court is going to hear my case. And Archibald somebody, a DC hotshot, will defend me. He'd better be better than that loser Doumas. But at least Doumas came to see me. Archibald has never met me, and I wonder if he's ever even set foot in the state. I wanted to go to DC to testify and thought maybe whoever took me there would drive me by the Capitol and the Lincoln Memorial. But I was told that the hotshot had all the information he needed. So, no DC tour for this guy.

The wind howls, bringing me back to the present. I stand by the window, watching the storm. I wonder what Saint Agatha is doing.

I haven't heard from her in ages. If I were free, tonight would be a perfect night to hunt her down.

12

I couldn't wait for Christmas break. I had a big sociology paper due, and I was writing on childhood sexual abuse. It was making me crazy. I did my research and it seemed like abuse was happening all over, but no one was talking about it. I pulled an all-nighter and pushed it under my professor's door the morning it was due. Dad picked me up, and I slept in the car all the way home.

Uncle Dan and Rosemarie were hosting Christmas Eve for the assorted Donovans, Bouchers, and Tardiffs. It was snowing when we arrived at Uncle Dan's and the Christmas lights on the hedge twinkled in the dusk. The women stood in the kitchen yakking and sampling the appetizers, and the men drank beer in the living room.

A guy with short brown hair wearing a blue blazer and tie was talking to Uncle Dan. "Merry Christmas, Nora."

I had no idea who he was.

"Nora, you remember my friend from Nam," said Uncle Dan. "You knew him as Spider."

"I don't go by Spider anymore. I go by my real name, John Martin." John stuck out his hand.

I gasped. "You're the guy who saved Uncle Dan's life." Spider was the last person I'd imagine showing up at Uncle Dan's wearing a tie and a blue blazer.

John burst out laughing. "No one recognizes me anymore," he said. "And by all reports, that's a good thing."

"So, what are you up to these days, John?" I asked.

"I work full-time at Radio Shack and I'm going to Hesser at night working on a computer science degree."

I never heard of anyone majoring in computer science. "What got you interested in computers?" I asked.

"Gene talked to me about it. Said it was going to be an up-and-coming field."

Finally, someone taking Gene's advice, I thought.

I looked at John Martin and thought he was kind of cute. I watched him follow Uncle Dan over to Dad and Gene. I wondered how old he was.

A baby fussed behind me. The young black couple I saw dancing at Uncle Dan's welcome home party a few years back stood by the chips and dip, trying to calm their little girl, who would not stop crying. I went over to the baby and stuck out my tongue. She broke into peals of laughter and grabbed my necklace.

"Hi," said the mom. "I'm Natalie, this is my husband Jack, and little Miss Fussy-Pants here is Pearl."

"I'm Nora, Dan's niece," I said. "I remember seeing you dancing at Dan's welcome home party a couple of years ago."

"That's the night we got pregnant with Pearl," said Jack.

"Yeah, on Boone's Farm Apple Wine," laughed Natalie.

Moe put her arm around me. I turned to introduce her to Pearl's parents, but they were tangled up in another conversation, so Moe got my full attention. Marriage agreed with her. Her hair was lustrous and her skin soft and clear. Across the room I saw Gene and Joe yakking about something.

"Moe, I have a special present for you," I said.

"For Gene, too?" she asked.

Was she turning into a fifties wife or what, I thought. "You can share it with him, but I think that you'll appreciate it more." I handed her a shoebox tied with a red bow.

She pulled off the bow and opened the box. Inside, wrapped in newspaper from January of 1970, were the figurines from our family Nativity scene. The poor three-legged sheep, Joseph with eyes heavenward, the little ceramic Infant Jesus fastened to his manger, and to my horror, a headless Virgin. Mom's glue job hadn't lasted a year. I rummaged around the crumpled newspaper and pulled out the Virgin's head.

"I found it!" I said.

Moe looked at me. I couldn't tell if she thought it was a terrible gift, or if she was charmed.

"Thanks. But who wants a broken nativity scene with a headless virgin?"

Apparently, she wasn't charmed.

"I thought you'd like it to remind you of our childhood. Joe and I bought Mom and Dad a new Nativity set."

"You're sweet, Aunt Nora." Moe kissed me on the cheek.

"Aunt Nora?" I asked.

"Shhh," she said. "Yeah, don't tell anyone. I'm due in late May."

She could tell that I was doing the math. "I got pregnant on Joe's birthday."

"So, when are you telling Mom and Dad?"

"Not yet, but I will." Maybe Moe was not as fifties as I thought.

"How do you feel?"

"Fabulous," she replied.

Aunt Kathleen came by with champagne, but Moe just walked away. "Moe's not drinking?" Aunt Kathleen raised her eyebrows.

"Aunt Kathleen, I am not saying a word." Kathleen sashayed away but stopped to whisper in Marcel's ear. Burl Ives replaced Bing Crosby as "A Holly, Jolly, Christmas" filled the room.

I looked around the room. Dad and Gene were laughing about something. The babies played on a blanket under Colleen's supervision. The men were talking about the Celtics. "Not looking good for us this year, boys," said Marcel. "Havlicek and Cowens can't carry the team alone."

"You're probably right, Marcel," said Uncle Danny. "But keep your eye on that kid from UCLA that went to Milwaukie. Lew Alcindor. He's a winning machine with that skyhook shot of his."

Everyone looked happy, but I couldn't shake the worry that I'd been carrying around for the past six years. Coolidge might go free. In just eighteen days, his hot-shot Washington lawyer was going to argue the case in front of the US Supreme Court. The court didn't care if he was guilty of torture, rape, and murder. They only cared if his rights were violated.

My father waved at me from across the room. As I headed to the closet to grab my coat, I saw our old Nativity scene lying in its box on the end table. I guessed that Moe thought that the set was too broken for her silver-Christmas-tree-taste. Or maybe she didn't believe that broken things could be fixed.

I picked up the box holding the headless Virgin and the three-legged sheep. It occurred to me that, like them, many of us were broken. Dad, broken by the stress of two murders—one that he was powerless to solve, and the other solved but justice threatened because of a legal technicality. Uncle Danny, emotionally broken by his abusive father and physically broken by a senseless war. Joey, broken by a speech impediment that defined him as a not-too-bright weirdo and resulted in him developing a friendship with an equally needy priest. But Dad continues to go to work and move on with his life, Uncle Danny's now a happy and sober family man, and Joe is a stalwart at the Manchester Humane Society where he is recognized for his skill in communicating with abused and neglected animals.

Of course, there were those who could not be fixed: the murder victims. Personable Sandra Valade smiling into the camera at age eighteen, sweet honor student Pamela Mason wanting to earn a little money babysitting, and well-meaning Rena Paquette, the middle-aged wife and mom who went to the police with information about Pam's murderer.

The three, probably all murdered by the same guy who left a swath of fear and sorrow in his wake. The victims' families and friends, the detectives like my dad who worked long hours on the case, the people of Manchester who now locked their doors every night. And little kids like me afraid to take the bus because the killer might be on it. And worried every time a winter snowstorm hit the state that the psychopath would be driving around Manchester prowling for a new victim.

I got in the car with Mom, Dad, and Joe.

"Nice party," said Dad.

"I thought Moe looked beautiful," said Mom. "Marriage must agree with her."

I kept Moe's secret to myself.

"What do you say we drive up Elm Street to see the Christmas decorations on our way home?" asked Dad.

The light turned red at the corner of Hanover and Elm. We craned our necks to admire the lit-up star suspended above our heads.

Dad turned to Mom. "Aren't you going to say it, Helen?"

She laughed. "This is the most beautiful Christmas display ever."

Epilogue

I sat on the stage as people filled the seats. The audience was mostly parents and grandparents with an occasional young couple holding a baby. A few folks brought bouquets; I wondered what the flowers would look like after sitting in the sun for a few hours.

I thought about the gossip Linda and I shared over too many glasses of wine last night. I told her that former prom queen Marilyn Marchand remained cancer-free. Marilyn wrote me that she and her husband took Jake out of Catholic school and sent him to the therapist in Concord that I'd recommended. He'd graduated from Worcester Polytech and worked for Raytheon. News like that made all the shit I had to deal with worthwhile.

Then I told her about my family. Linda was pleased to hear that Joe's business *Winning Dogs* was an enormous success. We laughed at the irony of Gene, now father of three, receiving the Coach of the Year award for instilling good sportsmanship in his players. I told her that Moe was busy with tennis and running the PTO. Somehow Lin hadn't heard that she and Gene moved into the Tardiff family home on Vista Drive and the Tardiff seniors retired to The Villages in Florida where Mark played golf, and Louise raised orchids.

But what I knew was nothing compared to what Linda knew. She'd purchased the health club that she used to manage and now got all the Manchester scoops from the members of *Fitness Plus*.

Sister of Mercy Colleen Fitzpatrick taught art at All Saints'. It seemed that the Holy Ghost, who once ignited tongues of fire in Colleen's head continued to kindle her love of art.

Donald Morse had moved to Maine, married a social worker, and was an electrician at Bath Iron Works. I thought of how he'd lied years ago about getting a fishing rod from Mickey Finn's and hoped that BIW paid him well enough to buy himself good fishing equipment. Mrs. Robichaud's house had burned to the ground while she and her husband were bowling at *Lakeside Lanes*. One of her cats knocked over a burning candle Mrs. R had left in the bathroom. The Robichaud house, crammed with bolts of polyester, was destroyed. Minnie was relieved that the property was insured and grateful that Lawrence, the guilty cat, was found alive huddled in a neighbor's garage. Marge the Barge was now Marge Duval and looked fabulous. She lost over 100 pounds and appeared regularly on WMUR TV as New Hampshire's *Weight Loss for Women* spokesperson. Ray Courtemarche, after instructing generations of Manchester teens in the importance of Seeing the Big Picture, managed to miss the Big Picture himself. He died after running a yellow light on the corner of Maple and Webster. And Linda, the oldest Benson girl that Mom had always warned us about, was doing well. She'd left the dope, graduated from Shirley's School of Cosmetology, and now owned a popular spa by the Mall of New Hampshire. Hillary Clinton went there to get her make-up done while campaigning with Bill in New Hampshire.

The Chancellor interrupted my on-stage musings when she introduced Marie Chalifour, now Dr. Marie Rousseau. Marie lowered the mic, thanked the Board of Trustees, thanked the audience for coming, congratulated the grads, and then turned to thank me for accepting the invitation to speak at the University of New Hampshire's commencement.

"Nora and I have a special connection going back to high school and continuing here as students at UNH," she said. "Nora is passionate about seeking justice for victimized women and children. She believes that policemen working the streets are the strongest advocates for victims who are too often silenced." I saw my father break into a grin when Marie mentioned the importance of working the streets. "Nora became a police detective and for three years worked in New York City's Special Victims Unit. There she proved to be not only an outstanding police detective but an outspoken advocate for the implementation of Special Victims' Units across the country. She has authored two books, and her writings have appeared in countless journals informing policy on the state and national level. Please join me in welcoming my friend and our keynote speaker Detective and Special Victims' activist Nora Donovan!" She turned to me and clapped as I made my way to the podium.

I waited for the applause to die down. I looked at my family seated in the front row. Dad looking a little gray and every bit his age, Mom in her new black and white checked suit smiling broadly, the Donovans and Bouchers, all clapping wildly. And Linda, blowing me a kiss. Only Joe was missing. He was in Dublin giving a *Winning Dogs* seminar for disability activists, but he sent flowers and a sweet note to my apartment in DC.

I placed my notes on the lectern, raised the mic, and began. "Good morning and thank you, Marie for your kind introduction. And thanks to the University of New Hampshire for honoring me today. And congratulations to the graduates.

"My interest in seeking justice for victims of violent crime goes back decades. In the 1960s, two teen-age girls were brutally murdered in my hometown of Manchester, New Hampshire..."

Afterword

On the snowy evening of January 13, 1964, fourteen-year-old Pamela Mason was picked up outside her home by a man who responded to her bulletin board advertisement for baby-sitting services. Eight days later, her lifeless body was found on a roadside. She'd been beaten, raped, and shot.

In 1965, Edward Coolidge was arrested, convicted, and sentenced to life in prison for Mason's murder. He appealed his conviction, and in June, 1969, the New Hampshire Supreme Court upheld the decision of the lower court.

Coolidge's defense team vowed to bring the case to United States Supreme Court, and the case was presented in January, 1971. This time, the defense argued that the search warrant used to gather evidence from Coolidge's car was illegal because it was signed by Attorney General Maynard. According to the Fourth Amendment of the United States Constitution, a search warrant must be signed by an impartial and unbiased magistrate. The court ruled in favor of the plaintiff, stating that the Attorney General could not fairly determine probable cause because of his political interest in apprehending the killer. The search warrant was deemed illegal by the court, and all evidence seized in the search of Coolidge's car was considered inadmissible. It should be noted that it was common practice for the Attorney General to sign search warrants in New Hampshire at that time.

The State of New Hampshire could have retried Coolidge for the crime without the evidence found in his car, but instead reached a plea agreement with the defense team. Coolidge pleaded guilty to second-degree murder and was given a maximum sentence of 19-25 years.

In 1984, after 16 years in prison, Coolidge applied for parole and partial parole was granted.

Acknowledgements

Just as it takes a village to raise a child, the same is true in writing a novel. We are grateful to the many people who read excerpts of *Flashbulb Memories* and gave us helpful feedback. Big thanks to Walter Chop, Joni Cole, Kathleen Corbett, Kathy Liptak, Marcie Lister, Deb Merrill, Rose Mulligan, Marty Riehle, Lisa Walsh, Michael Walsh, Ben Wiley, Chris Wiley, Michael Wiley, and Monica Wood.

We had helpful conversations and email discussions with writers, legal experts, and people who lived in Manchester. Thank you to Michael Ames, Patrick Anderson, Jaed Coffin, Edward Cross, John Harding, Michael Jauchen, Joanne Palys, Ronda Randall, Michael Roy, and Richard Shine who shared personal memories of Manchester during the sixties, information regarding research material, or advice about navigating the world of publishing.

Many thanks to Tess Kimsey, Reference Librarian at the Carpenter Memorial Library, who helped us become adept at using the library's balky microfilm machines to access back issues of the *Manchester Union Leader*. The "Things I Remember growing up in Manchester, NH" Facebook site triggered memories of sixties' events and popular businesses. We are grateful to the Manchester Historical Association for the use of their resources. Thanks also to Stacy Ziegler in the NH Department of Justice who provided us with transcripts of Coolidge's first murder trial.

Any errors in this novel must lay at our feet and is not the fault of anyone listed above.